TRIPLE
DUTY
BODYGUARDS

LILY GOLD

AUTHOR'S NOTE

This reverse harem romance features graphic steamy scenes between multiple partners (don't be fooled by the cute cartoon cover — it's very spicy!)

While this is overall a sweet, steam-filled romance, it does touch on several sensitive topics, including military PTSD, harassment, anxiety disorders, and violence. You can find a much fuller list on my website at: www.lilygoldauthor.com. Happy reading!

CHAPTER 1
BRIAR

"Now, don't be dramatic, darling," my PR manager drawls, examining her nail beds. "It's not like the man was trying to *kill* you."

I close my eyes, rubbing my temples. It's just turned four AM, and my head is still spinning from last night's rosé. Red and blue lights flash through the window of my little pink-tiled kitchen, shining in from the police car parked in my drive. Over my head, I can hear the heavy footsteps and low voices of the police officers investigating upstairs.

I am tired.

"A stranger climbed the side of my house, broke my bedroom window, and jerked off in my bed," I say slowly. "I'm not being dramatic."

Julie shrugs from her position at the marble breakfast bar, fishing her compact out of her designer purse. "He didn't even touch you, babe," she mumbles, patting powder over her pert nose. "This hardly seems like a reason to fire poor Rodriguez."

My eyes slide to Rodriguez, my home security guard. He refuses to look at me, shifting uncomfortably in his spot next to Julie. His hair is ruffled, his fly is undone, and his shirt is unbuttoned. Julie's red lipstick is all over his neck.

It's not too difficult to work out how the intruder managed to get past my gate.

"Yes," I say flatly. "It is. Rodriguez, do up your trousers and go."

His eyes widen. "But, ma'am—"

"Don't *ma'am* me. You don't work for me anymore." I wave at the front door. "Go."

He stands, puffing his chest out. "Ma'am, really, that's not fair—"

"Of course it's *fair*," I snap. "You were too busy shagging my staff to notice the strange man *breaking into my bedroom*. I pay you six figures, and you still can't get through an eight-hour shift without getting your rocks off. You're fired. Now get out of my house, before I call your wife and tell her why you no longer have a job."

I turn on my heel and leave the kitchen, ignoring the muttered *'bitch'* behind my back.

Right. That's me. I'm not the one who screwed around on the job and cheated on my pregnant wife. But as per usual, *I'm* the bitch.

Of course, most people would agree with him. I'm a well-renowned cow. I even have titles: you are talking to the proud three-time winner of *Goss* magazine's 'Biggest Celebrity Diva' award. A major UK newspaper crowned me 'Britain's Biggest Bitch' just a couple of weeks ago. I don't think they're actually *supposed* to be awards, but I'll take them all the same.

I suppose it is kind of my fault. As I step into the corridor, I catch a glimpse of myself in the diamond-studded hallway mirror. Highlighted blonde hair. Veneers. Fake nails. I'm the kind of woman people *love* to call a bitch.

There's footsteps on the stairs, and I look up to see a policeman stepping onto the landing, holding a clear evidence bag.

"You got a sample?" I ask, leaning heavily against the wall.

He nods. "Doesn't guarantee we'll find the guy, though. If he's not a repeat UK offender, we won't have his DNA to match with."

"Don't you have databases? Hospital records, or something?"

He rolls his eyes. "We might do that for a more high-profile case, ma'am. Nothin' as minor as a break-in." He pulls his phone out of the back pocket of his pants and wiggles his thick black eyebrows. "By the way, my daughter was a massive fan of that TV show you were in, back in the day. You don't mind snapping me a quick pic, do you?"

I look down at myself. I'm wearing a stained Minnie Mouse pyjama set. Last night's makeup is smeared around my eyes, which are red, because I've been crying. Because I was just the victim of a home invasion.

"Yes," I tell him, trying to keep my anger under control. "I do mind, actually."

His face hardens. He turns towards the door, then pauses like he's remembered something. "Oh. I think this is yours." He hands me the clear plastic baggie.

I frown, taking it. There's a Polaroid inside. "What is it?"

"It was under your pillow. Very dramatic." He presses his lips together. "I have to wonder exactly *how* someone would manage to lift up your pillow and put something under it whilst you were sleeping. Unless the intruder was the tooth fairy, it doesn't seem very likely, does it?"

I don't respond, taking out the photograph.

It's a picture of me asleep. I'm sprawled over my sheets, my mouth open, my arms both flung out. Tight bands suddenly squeeze around my chest.

"The note was a nice touch," the man adds, grabbing his jacket from my coat rack.

"Note?" I say numbly. He makes a spinning motion with his finger, and I flip over the picture. Scrawled on the back in florid cursive are the words:

You look beautiful when you're asleep, my angel. And soon, we'll be sleeping next to each other forever. X

"Oh my God," I whisper, staggering back into the wall. I can't breathe. "Oh my *God*. Please, just—" I try to pass the photograph back to the policeman, but he steps away, putting his hands up.

"That's for you."

I frown. "You don't need to take it?"

He shrugs. "Don't know how much good it would do us, ma'am."

"What do you mean?" I demand. "It's evidence!"

He huffs a laugh under his breath. "Right. Do you know what the penalty is for wasting police time, Miss Saint?"

"What? I didn't waste your time, this is your damn job!"

He gives me a nasty look. "And I'm sure the paparazzi who photographed our cars coming onto your property just *happened* to be hanging outside your house at four AM on a Tuesday morning?"

I'm gobsmacked. "Probably! It's not *my* fault they make their living by invading my privacy! If I set all of this up, how exactly did I get a pile of come in my bed?!"

He shrugs. "You got your boyfriend to do it? I don't know, ma'am, but I *do* know that my officers don't appreciate being used in your publicity stunts."

I gape at him.

There's a scuffle behind me. Rodriguez and Julie both step out of the kitchen, whispering to each other. I snap my mouth shut and wave them to the door. "You. Both. Out. I'll send you your severances. Enjoy unemployment."

Julie runs a hand through her platinum curls. "C'mon, Briar," she wheedles. "It was just a mistake. How was I supposed to know one of your creepy fans would try and break in tonight?"

I stare her down. Julie has been my PR manager for the last eight years. She's a typical rich Chelsea girl: blonde, always made up, and constantly draped in a fur coat. During her time working for me, I've almost fired her about fifty times, but she somehow always manages to worm her way back into my life.

She apparently finds my silence encouraging, grabbing my hand. "Listen, will you forgive me if I get you a new security team?" Rodriguez looks hurt.

"No," I tell her.

"But—"

"You got me *this* security team," I point out. "And then you *slept with* my security team. So, no, I'm not letting you pick out my new guards." I shake her off me. "You're fired. Get out."

She pouts. "But—"

My last fibre of control snaps. "For God's sake, will everyone just get the Hell out of my house!" I shout. I'm shaking. The Polaroid drops out of my hand and flutters to the carpet.

There's a few seconds of silence, then the front door opens, and everyone starts to file out. I swallow hard, feeling tears roll down my cheeks. I lift a hand to swipe them away.

There's a sudden flash of light. I look up, and see the policeman facing me in the doorway, holding his phone up and snapping a nice little shot of my breakdown. He flashes me a smarmy grin. "'Preciate it, Briar Saint."

I step forward to grab the phone out of his hand, but he slams the door shut behind him.

I stare at the door for a second, breathing hard. Then all of the energy drains out of me, and I sink to the ground, wrapping my arms around my knees. The Polaroid lies on the floor by my elbow. The note on the back stares up at me.

Soon, we'll be sleeping next to each other forever.

I bury my face in my hands. I'm so screwed.

CHAPTER 2
MATT

I sit back in my chair, glaring at the file in front of me. "No. No way in Hell. Absolutely not. I'm never doing another celebrity case again."

Our boss, a petite blonde woman named Colette, glares at me. "You haven't even met the girl," she points out.

"Don't need to," I say simply. "I'm not doing it."

My partner Kenta pushes his cup of coffee across the desk. "Drink that and stop complaining," he mutters, reaching for the cafetière to pour a new mug. He looks half-asleep, his white shirt crumpled and his long, dark hair falling around his face. As I watch, he scoops the loose strands back, tying them into a neat ponytail. I bite back a rude comment and pick up the coffee.

To be honest, I really need the caffeine. It's five in the morning, and the rest of London's *Angel Security* headquarters is silent and empty. I should still be in bed, but instead, our deranged boss called us all in for an emergency meeting.

A massive hand stretches over my shoulder and nabs the coffee cup right before it touches my lips. My other partner, Glen, heaves his huge body down into the chair on my other side. At six foot six, he can barely fit his legs under the table.

Colette glares at him. "You're late."

"Aye," he agrees, taking a leisurely sip and smacking his lips. "That I am." He runs a large-knuckled hand through his thick hair and stretches. The pink dawn light filtering through the large windows catches on his face, lighting up the mangled scar cutting down the side of his cheek.

Colette sighs and pulls out a company-issue briefing file: a black folder with the Angel Security logo embossed in gold. She flips it open, showing us an A4-sized photograph. It's a paparazzi shot of a woman getting out of a car. Glen stiffens next to me.

"This is Briar Saint," she says. "Twenty-eight years old. Former child star, rose to fame when she was thirteen and starred in the TV sitcom *Hollywood House*. Now she does blockbuster movies."

Kenta leans forward, examining the picture. "She looks familiar."

I nod. She does. I could swear I've seen her before, but I can't put my finger on where.

I certainly doubt I'd forget her face. She's stunning. Honey-coloured hair, soft, tight body, tanned skin. In the picture, she's dressed in an icy white fur dress like Cruella De Ville, and her lips are painted shocking red. She's pouting at the camera like a fashion model.

"You've probably seen her before," Colette says. "She's got a very impressive IMDb page. She's been in ads, music videos, TV shows. Plus, the posters for her new movie are plastered all over the tube." She flips the page, showing us a close-up headshot. I take in her high cheekbones and perfectly sculpted lips. She has the most striking eyes I've ever seen, a bright turquoise colour, framed with long, fluttery lashes.

The picture has probably been edited in post, I remind myself. I doubt she actually looks this good in real life. No human could.

Glen tugs the photograph closer. "What's wrong wi' the lass?" He asks, his Scottish accent thickened by tiredness. "Someone hasslin' her?"

Colette shrugs, reaching into her purse for her compact. "I got a call from her PR manager an hour ago, begging for us to come and protect her client. She said it was an emergency." She flips the mirror open and checks her lipstick.

Even though it's the crack-ass of dawn, our boss is still perfectly turned out, in a full face of makeup and a pale pink dress that matches her nails. Just looking at her, you'd never guess this pretty, doll-sized woman has spent half of her life defusing land-mines in Mozambique.

"What kind of emergency?" Kenta prods, when she doesn't expand.

Colette sighs, snapping the mirror shut again. "She wouldn't say. Said that it's 'confidential information'. She wants to meet so she can have you sign an NDA and tell you in person."

I groan. I *hate celebrities*. What, does she think we're going to sell her private details to the press? We're a *security* company, for God's sake.

Colette purses her lips. "If I had to guess, I'd say Miss Saint has found herself an enemy. Her behaviour is… controversial."

I frown. "What does that mean?"

Colette flips to a new tab full of media cuttings. My eyes widen as I take in the headlines.

> *Briar Saint Leaves 'Emma' Cast Mid-Way Through Shooting, Calls Director an 'Absolute C*nt'.*

Star Actress Briar Saint Told This Enthusiastic Fan to 'F*ck Himself.'

Mean Girl: Ex-Friend Describes Briar Saint as a 'Reincarnated Regina George'

Bratty Diva Briar Saint Called 'Ungrateful, Rude, and Condescending' By Ex-Manager.

I look up at Colette, incredulous. "You want us to work with *her?* She looks like a nightmare."

"Who's Regina George?" Glen asks. "Is she famous?"

Colette rolls her eyes.

I flip through some more press clippings, scanning over the photographs of Briar scowling at the camera. Yes, she might be beautiful, but in most of these photos, she's sneering at the camera like she's just smelled something bad. I don't think I've ever seen someone look so openly snobby.

I glance over another article. "Hey, there's one about her previous security guard. Apparently, she fired him a few days ago for using the bathroom whilst he was on shift," I read. "Wow. She sounds delightful."

Colette gives me a flat look and pulls the file back. "Matt, this is tabloid trash. There's a good chance it's all just made up so magazines can make money off the girl."

"And if her security guard *sold a story to a gossip rag*, he was clearly shit at his job anyway," Kenta points out.

I shake my head. "I don't care. I told you. I'm not working for another celebrity. Especially not one with a reputation of acting like a spoiled child."

Our last celebrity gig was a total nightmare. The girl was a seventeen-year-old social media influencer who spent all day snorting drugs and trying to stick her hands down my pants. When we finally dumped her in rehab, I swore I'd never touch another celebrity case again.

I don't know why Colette is wasting our time with this. Glen, Kenta and I are the best-trained guys in the company. We've been working here for five years, ever since we got discharged from the SAS. Last month, we recovered the daughter of a British billionaire who'd been taken for ransom. The month before that, we were protecting an American presidential candidate after she got shot at a rally. We don't work for young, spoiled celebrities, shoving back overzealous paparazzi and carrying their shopping bags through the mall.

"I think we should at least check it out," Kenta says. "It's only fair."

"Me too," Glen chips in. "It's shitty to refuse to protect someone who's in danger, just because of their reputation."

I frown. "But—"

"C'mon," Glen rumbles. "Just a preliminary meeting. Face it, you owe me." He shoots me a crooked grin. The thick scar slashing down his cheek stretches, and guilt slams into me like a freight truck. Without meaning to, my eyes drop to his arms, taking in the matching scars around his wrists. They're a few inches thick, raised and red. Even though we retired half a decade ago, they never really healed right. Spending months in shackles will do that.

Kenta shifts on my other side, and I can't help but envision the scars that I know are slashed into his back. My fingernails grip hard into the wooden table as memories flood through me.

"Matt. *Matt.*" Glen claps a hand on my shoulder, and I blink, snapping out of it. I don't even realise how hard I'm breathing until Colette passes me a bottle of water with a sympathetic look. I stare at it in my hands.

"I didn't mean it like that, mate," Glen says roughly. "I just meant, you've put me on the night shift for the last three jobs in a row. Not..." He pauses, redness climbing up his neck. "You *know* I don't blame you for what happened." He gestures vaguely at his face. "Neither of us do."

I shrug him off and rub my eyes. He's right. I owe him and Kenta. I owe them both a Hell of a lot more than this. If they want to meet the girl, we'll meet with her.

"Fine," I mutter. "But she better have a real damn problem."

CHAPTER 3
BRIAR

I'm in the middle of a design meeting about my upcoming nail polish line when Julie comes whirling into the room, panting.

"Textured lids on the bottles can really help with accessibility," my product designer is explaining. "If we use a glossy plastic lid for the regular polishes, and a matte finish for the mattes, visually impaired users will be able to identify the products they want a lot more easily."

"Great. Let's do that, then," I murmur, turning my fingernails under the light. The shade I'm wearing right now is *British Bitch;* a blood-red colour, full of flecks of crimson glitter. We're currently in the product testing phase, and I have a slightly different formula of the shade on every one of my fingers.

"What's the point in that?" Julie asks loudly. "Why would blind people paint their nails?"

"Aren't PR people supposed to be politically correct?" I wonder, as she saunters into the room.

She snorts. "I'm supposed to keep you in the headlines, babe. That's it." She drapes her fur coat on the back of a chair and sits down opposite me.

I glare at her. "Didn't you hear? You're fired."

"Oh, you don't mean that." She reaches across the table, picking up a bottle of *Stiletto*. It's a black varnish, glossy like patent leather. "Babe, are you going through a goth phase? You *know* pink is your signature colour."

I *am* a big fan of pink. What can I say? I take my style inspiration from fashion's three biggest icons: Paris Hilton, Sharpay Evans, and Elle Woods. I glance around my office, taking in the pots of pink fluffy pens, the pink marble floor, the pink crystal chandelier hanging over my head. Hell, my house is like Barbie's Dreamhouse.

But no one wants to be cute and girly all the time. I'm sure even Barbie sometimes wanted to dress like an assassin about to kill a man.

"What do you *want*, Julie?"

She rummages through her Gucci purse and slams a thin file on the table. I recognise it immediately. It's the folder of information I've collected about the break-in. I don't have much: some photographs of my broken window, the police report, and the terrifying Polaroid. My heart starts to beat faster. "Why do you have that?" I'm sure I left it in my bedroom.

"I've solved your security problem," she announces triumphantly.

I grit my teeth. "I told you. I'll find new security myself. I—"

A man's voice suddenly rumbles through the office wall, and I freeze, listening. Footsteps move across the living room next door, and there's the sound of someone tapping on the wall.

Fear washes over me in a wave. The walls of the room seem to close in on me, squeezing all of the air out. "Who the Hell is in my house?" I whisper.

"I swear that these guys are good," Julie promises. "They're ex-SAS soldiers. You don't get better training than that. I heard Kylie Jenner used them for her last trip to Paris." She leans in, lowering her voice. "People in the business call them The Angels."

I stare at her. "Are they a boy band?"

"Like guardian angels, I guess." She shrugs. "They're in the living room. Waiting for you. *Three of them!*"

I close my eyes. "You invited three soldiers to my house," I say slowly. "Without asking me. After a strange man broke into my bedroom. And you didn't think that might upset me in any way."

She stands up, smiling brightly. "Yep. Come on, then. They're already getting fussy. I don't think they like being kept waiting." She waves away my product designer. "You can go now. Briar has an appointment she needs to attend."

The woman blinks at me, surprised to be so suddenly dismissed. I sigh, getting out of my seat. As much as I feel bad about cutting our meeting short, I *really* don't like the thought of leaving those men alone in my house. "We're pretty much done here, right, Sarah?"

"Well, yes, I suppose." She frowns. "We still haven't talked about the embossed lid names—"

I wince, guilt plucking at me. Sarah's one of the best in the business; she flew in from Paris to be here. "I'm sorry. I trust your judgement. Pick whatever you think is best, I'll approve it by email. Thank you *so* much for coming all the way out here, I really appreciate it." An idea crosses my mind. "Oh! Do you want to come to the premiere of my new movie? It's a murder mystery called *Players*, it releases in a couple weeks." I pull out my phone, already tapping out an email to my agent. "I'll be flying to America for the LA premiere, but there's going to be a big event here in London, too. I can get you a couple tickets?"

Her eyes widen. "I would love that," she says slowly. "I've seen the posters everywhere."

"Great. My agent will send them right over. Thanks again."

I toss her one last smile, then Julie grabs my hand and pulls me out of the room. "Come *on*," she mutters. "I don't want them to get fed up and leave."

I yank my hand free, turning on her. "Julie, what the Hell? Why would you do this? You put my life in danger. I don't want you working for me anymore." She barely batted an eyelid when my house got broken into, for God's sake.

Her brown eyes shimmer with tears. "Briar, please. Another chance. I really want to make this up to you." She takes my hand again, squeezing. "Think of everything we've been through together, babe."

I sigh. The truth is, I don't have many people in my life. My reputation means most people hate me on sight. Julie's been with me the longest out of any of my team. We go to the gym together. She gives me terrible boy advice and brings over low-calorie wine when I'm upset. She's not a *friend;* I know, if I weren't paying her, I'd never see her again. But right now, she's the closest thing I've got.

"Screw this up, and you're fucking fired. I mean it."

She nods, brightening back up like a lightbulb, and pushes open the door to the living room. "Just *wait* until you see them. You're going to *die.*"

"What does that mean?"

She just beams, waving me into the lounge. I step inside, and my mouth falls open. "Are you *kidding me?*"

Sitting hunched on my crushed velvet sofa, their giant knees knocking against the edge of my crystal coffee table, are three of the most handsome men I've ever seen in my life.

I see handsome men every day. Models. Movie stars. In my upcoming film, my co-star was named 'the hottest actor of 2020'.

These three men knock him out of the park. Dressed in matching dark suits, they're like a smörgåsbord of broad chests, cheekbones and jawlines. It's pretty clear why Julie *hand-picked* them.

"For God's sake," I snap at her. "I want actual security guards. Not more eye candy for you to drool over!"

"I swear," she insists. "These guys come really well recommended! The looks are just an added bonus. They'll look *so* hot in paparazzi shots." Her eyes twinkle. "Did I kill it or *what*, babe?"

"No!" I snap. "You didn't kill it! Get out of my house!"

The man sitting on the far left stands, glaring at me. He's probably the most classically handsome of the three; bright blue eyes, strong jaw, black hair. He looks like Clark Kent crossed with an Abercrombie model.

And he looks like he wants to murder me. "Alright," he barks, turning to his teammates. "This is bullshit. Let's go."

"But!" Julie starts.

I nod at him. "Please do. I don't know what kind of job you were expecting, but I'm looking for actual security. My *PR manager*," I toss Julie a black look, "must have made a mistake. I'm really sorry for the inconvenience. We'll reimburse you for time and petrol."

He snorts, disgust curling his lip. "I'm sorry, you think *we're* not good enough for *you*? We're ex-SAS, princess. Including our time in the force, we've each been working security for nineteen, twenty years."

I raise an eyebrow. "Seriously? That's the actual army, right? You're not just strippers people hire to come to their hen dos wearing camo?"

Yes, okay. That *was* bitchy. But this man is looking at me like a piece of dog shit that got stuck to his shoe. And I don't like being called *princess*.

His scowl deepens, blue eyes smouldering. "Yes, *seriously*. And we sure as Hell did not go through all that training to be your damn *eye candy*."

The man sitting next to him rolls his eyes and tugs at his wrist. "Sit *down*," he mutters. "Give her a chance." He turns to me with a calm smile. "I think we're getting off on the wrong foot, Miss Saint. We're from the London-based private protection service, Angel Security. We're a fully-qualified close protection detail with a lot of experience dealing with high-profile cases like your own." He holds out his hand for me to shake. "I'm Kenta Li."

Oh, thank God. A polite person. I sit down opposite him, taking his hand. Kenta is East Asian, with strong shoulders, angular features, and long, dark hair pulled back in a bun. He has a tattoo on his hand, curling up from his wrist, and his dark eyes are cool and friendly. As my fingers close around his, I could swear a spark of electricity jumps between our skin. I pull back like I've been burned.

Kenta blinks and clears his throat, slapping Clark Kent on the back. "This is Matthew Carter. You can call him Matt. As you can probably tell, he's not very good at making new friends."

Matt's face flickers with annoyance. Neither of us offers a handshake.

Kenta tips his head to the man on his left. "And this is Glen Smith."

My eyes skip to Glen. He's bigger than the other guys: several inches taller, and so broad that he barely fits on the sofa. His thick hair is full of salt-and-pepper streaks, and his grey eyes are so pale they look almost silvery. An impressive scar runs down the side of his face, stretching all the way from his temple, through his eyebrow, and slashing into his cheek. The skin is puckered and raised, like the wound healed badly. As I watch, he tilts his head slightly, like he wants to hide the scar from view.

I reach across the table to shake his hand. He grips my hand gingerly, his huge fingers dwarfing mine. "Nice to meet you," I tell him, and I could swear I see his face tint pink with a blush. Something warm thrums deep inside me. I *like* this one.

I lean back, my mouth suddenly dry. "Sorry to keep you all waiting. I was in a meeting." Clark Kent—Matt—snorts. I turn to him. "Something funny?"

He shrugs a shoulder. "We've been in this business for a long time, Miss Saint. We're trained to observe our surroundings. And we're not *idiots*."

I quirk an eyebrow. "I'm glad to hear that. And?"

He nods at my hands. "Your fingernails are freshly painted. I can smell the nail polish. You weren't in a meeting, you were getting a manicure."

I take a long breath through my nose. "I'm collaborating with a major beauty company to create my own line of nail polishes. I was in a product design meeting. Do you have any other non-idiotic *observations* that you'd like to make, or can we get started?"

CHAPTER 4
BRIAR

Matt sits back, his eyes flat and cold, but doesn't say anything else. I nod. "Right. First of all, I'd like you all to switch off your phones. I don't want any of you recording this conversation."

Glen and Kenta both do as I say. Matt snorts. "Princess, if we wanted to do that, we wouldn't be using our *phones*. We have slightly more advanced equipment at our disposal."

I stare at him. "Just turn off your phone," I enunciate the words slowly. "And don't call me *princess*."

"Briar…" Julie starts. "Please. You're being rude."

"I'm not being rude," I say evenly. "This is the protocol for anyone new entering the house."

She rolls her eyes and turns to the men. "Don't mind her," she murmurs, her voice dropping to a sexy purr. "She's been moody the last few days." She bats her eyelashes at Kenta. "You know, I was honestly only expecting one guard to show up. Getting to meet *three* of you is a *lovely* surprise."

"We work as a team, ma'am," Kenta replies, apparently unaffected by her flirting. "I'm afraid we're a package deal."

"Oh." She looks taken aback. "Ah, what are your rates, then?"

"That's impossible to calculate until we know what we're dealing with, what level of security we would need to provide, whether you require overnight or international coverage—"

"Ballpark figure," Julie demands. "What are you charging celebs with similar public profiles?"

Kenta shrugs. "Our company recently had a celebrity singer hire close protection for about 1.2 mil a year."

Julie blanches. If I weren't so annoyed, I'd probably laugh. Apparently, she's bitten off more than she can chew with her bribe. The agency isn't going to be happy that she's hired me a seven-figure security team that they now have to cough up for. "Um, she probably doesn't need all three of you," she starts. "I'm sure we can come to some kind of arrangement—"

I cut her off. "Calm down. I'll pay out of pocket."

She frowns. "But it's written in your contract that the agency is supposed to provide you with security."

"I know. And you did. And it was shit. So I'll be paying for my own security, from now on. That way, I know no one's cutting corners to save some cash."

"But—"

Matt sighs heavily. "Will you please just tell us why the Hell we're here? Because there's a *very* good chance you won't even need to hire us in the first place. We only take on serious cases. Where the client's life is endangered."

"My—" I look down at my hands, digging my glittery red nails into my palms, and take a deep breath. "My house was broken into a few days ago. A guy in a ski mask climbed over my fence, scaled the side of the house, broke my window and climbed into my bedroom while I was asleep."

A ripple goes over the three men. Their faces stay completely stoic, but they stiffen slightly in their seats. Whatever they thought they were called out here for, it wasn't that.

"Were you assaulted?" Kenta asks softly.

I shake my head. "No. And he didn't steal anything valuable. He took a couple of my t-shirts, left me a little *present* in my bed, and put this under my pillow."

Julie pulls open her purse and pulls out the file of evidence. "Here you go, babe."

"Thank you." I open the file, taking out the Polaroid of me sleeping and pushing it across the table.

Kenta looks at the picture, but doesn't touch it. "Shouldn't you have turned this in to the police?"

I press my lips together. "I tried to. Paparazzi caught their cars driving through my gates and started shooting them, so they assumed the whole break-in was some kind of publicity stunt. They barely listened to anything I said."

Kenta frowns. "Even if they thought your allegations were false, they should have collected the evidence. This is extreme negligence. You could take it to court."

"I don't want to take it to court, I want someone to take me seriously. Check the back."

He delicately flips the photograph. His eyebrows raise as he reads the message scrawled across the back.

"I've gotten threatening letters before," I continue. "I've always disregarded them before now."

"Threatening how?" Matt demands.

"Crazy declarations of love. People telling me they'll stab me in the street. People saying I deserve to be killed. I'm not a popular person."

"It really is normal in the industry," Julie cuts in, back-pedalling frantically. "Really, I'm not sure how necessary all of this is."

Kenta frowns. "Ma'am, it's very necessary. Your security system is clearly faulty, and if this is some kind of obsessed fan, I would be *very* surprised if their success didn't encourage them to strike again."

Julie looks desperate. "I know plenty of other stars who have had break-ins. They didn't need 24-7 bodyguards! Just an updated alarm system, maybe some on-site guards. I'm sure just one of you would be fine."

"This wasn't a break-in," Kenta counters. "It was a home invasion. Had Miss Saint woken up whilst the fan was in the room, the likelihood of a violent altercation would have been incredibly high."

Matt speaks up suddenly. "What did the police say?"

"Not much. They didn't dust for prints, because he was wearing gloves on the CCTV footage."

He nods. "Not surprising, if he thought forward enough to mask up. Nothing useful on the video?"

I shake my head. "You can look at it if you want. All they could tell was he looked about five-ten, medium build. They also took a DNA sample from my sheets, but apparently they didn't find a match."

Matt raises an eyebrow. "Your sheets? What did he do, spit on them?"

I set my jaw. "He... ejaculated on them."

Kenta's eyes widen. "Wait. *While* you were in the bed?"

"Yes," I say stiffly.

All three men share a dark look. I notice Glen's hand twitch slightly on the table, like he wants to clench his fist. Matt visibly flinches.

"I see." Kenta's warm voice is suddenly icy. He looks back down at the photograph. "I see."

"Again, it's pretty common," Julie chips in. "You know, I heard just last week, some creep broke into Tye Kavanagh's hotel room —you know, the rock singer? The guy masturbated in Tye's guitar case. All Kavanagh did was call security to escort him out, he didn't *hire three ex-SAS soldiers* to tail him around—"

"Could you please leave?" Kenta asks suddenly. "We'd like to speak with the client alone."

She scoffs. "If we're paying for your services, surely we are the clien—"

Matt glances up from the Polaroid. "Out," he orders.

I wonder if he was some kind of commander in the army. I think Julie's halfway out the door before she even realises what's happening. The door clicks softly shut behind her.

"You need 24-7 protection," Matt says. "Your current system is completely unacceptable."

My mouth drops open. "24-7? Are you serious?"

"Someone has broken into your house, violated you, and threatened further assault. You need 24-7 protection. That means at least one of us staying in your house with you, at all times." He ticks off a finger. "You need updates to your home security system. More CCTV. Motion-detecting floodlights. A more advanced alarm system. Reinforced windows."

I shake my head. "I don't think you understand. I'm not looking for 24-7 bodyguards. Just someone to fix up my security system and protect me when I'm out in public."

"I don't care what you're *looking* for," Matt bites out. "I'm telling you what you *need*. If we take on a job, we do it properly. We're not half-assing it and putting a client in danger, just because she doesn't want the hassle of having us around."

"I'm sorry," Kenta says, softly. "But this really is necessary for your safety." He taps the Polaroid. "He mentions that he'll try to meet with you again *'soon'*, and frankly, I don't like the wording *'we'll be sleeping next to each other foreve*r'. It sounds like a kidnapping threat. Potentially murder-suicide."

My heart freezes in my chest.

"You said you wanted someone to take you seriously," Matt says brusquely. "We're taking you seriously. Stop complaining."

"Don't talk to me like that," I snap, rubbing my temples. I'm scared and tired, and he's already doing my head in. "They don't teach you manners in the military?"

He snorts. "Like you know anything about manners. I've seen you in the tabloids, princess. And I've heard first-hand the shitty way you talk to your staff. What was it?" He pretends to think. *"Screw this up, and you're fucking fired?* Was that what you said to your PR woman before you came in here?"

My mouth falls open. He leans in. "If we do take this job, I want to make some things clear." He raises a finger. "We are not servants. We are not butlers. You might be paying us, but you will have to follow *our* orders. No tantrums. No arguing. No stamping your little kitten heel in the middle of the mall, because we tell you that you have to go home. We need you to trust us completely with your safety."

"I see," I drawl. "And this is how you inspire trust? By insulting me? Because right now, I wouldn't trust you to hold my handbag, let alone save my life."

He opens his mouth to answer—and then an odd expression flickers over his face. He stiffens, his free hand gripping the table. I watch as his jaw clenches so hard his teeth click. For a few very long seconds, he sits there in silence, completely unmoving, every muscle in his body tensed.

I blink, confused. "Are you okay?"

He relaxes, his shoulders slumping the tiniest amount, and reaches for the glass of water in front of him, not meeting my gaze.

"Let's see the house," Kenta says, standing abruptly. "We'd like to scope the place out before looking at any contracts."

CHAPTER 5
GLEN

"This is the guest room," Briar waves around a large room papered in pale grey. "Will you guys be staying here or going home at night?"

"That's up to you," Kenta says. "Our commute is around an hour, which obviously isn't ideal in an emergency. We'll go home sometimes, but probably not every night. You can either let us stay here, or have your people book us into a nearby hotel."

She nods. "The pool house has two bedrooms and a bathroom, if you're okay staying out there. Feel free to use the pool and the gym. And you can take whatever you want from the kitchen, but I'm vegan, so you might want to buy your own food."

"You got it, princess," Matt drawls from the doorway.

Briar whirls on him, her eyes flashing. *"Princess?"*

Matt shrugs a shoulder. "Your code name. Fitting, don't you think?"

She gives him a cold look, crossing her arms. "How exactly is this going to work? Will you just... follow me around?" She glances at me. "All the time?"

"We'll split the day into three eight-hour shifts," Kenta explains. "12AM to 8AM, 8AM to 4PM, 4PM to 12AM. Whoever's on shift will stay with you, the others will do their own thing. If it's necessary, we'll increase protection when you go out."

Her nose wrinkles. "When is it necessary?"

"Just one of us would be fine if you wanted to pop to the corner shop. All three of us will attend formal events with you."

"So you *do* have to follow me around all the time," she says flatly.

Matt lopes over to the window and starts examining the view outside. "That's what 24-7 means, yes."

"I'll never get to be alone?"

"We'll leave you alone, if that's what you want," Kenta says soothingly. "But there will always be someone within earshot of you. They'll check in on you once or twice an hour, make sure you're okay."

"Great," she mutters. "Absolutely fantastic. When did this become my life?"

I'm surprised. A celebrity who likes her alone time is pretty unusual. In my experience, most of them are desperate to be around people.

We leave the guest bedroom and she starts showing us down the hall. I look around, kind of gobsmacked. I'll never get over celebrity houses. Briar's is actually relatively small—just a standard three-bedroom—but the whole place is dripping with luxury. She has two walk-in closets full of clothes, a professional chef's kitchen, and a 'glam room' which I think is dedicated to doing her makeup. There's an in-home gym, a weight room, and a huge, rippling swimming pool behind the house. Most of her walls are papered in shimmery pink, hung with oil paintings and giant gilt mirrors. Like all celebrity clients I've ever met, she has ridiculously large bowls of fruit placed decoratively on all the counters.

As she leads us back into the kitchen, she trips, her heel catching on the doorframe. I reach for her automatically, grabbing her waist to steady her. My fingers splay over the soft leather of her skirt.

Heat touches my face. I clear my throat, pulling my hands away. "Okay, lass?"

She blinks. "You're Scottish?"

I give her a small smile. "Aye."

She doesn't smile back, but her face is curious as she looks me over.

"That's why he never speaks," Matt drawls, kneeling to examine the window pane. "He's embarrassed about it."

I fight the urge to flip him off.

Truth is, I've not said much since I got here because I've been slowly dying from the inside. Matt might not remember why Briar looks so familiar, but I sure as Hell do.

While we were on one of our first tours, years back, I had a photo of her pinned up in my barracks; a modelling shot, cut out of a magazine one of the guys got sent. Every goddamn day, I woke up to Briar Saint's pretty face smiling down at me.

And now I'm here, in her house.

She's nothing like I imagined. In my photograph, she was smiling brightly on a beach, eating an ice cream. I always pictured her to be bubbly. Sweet.

The woman standing in front of me is certainly not *bubbly*. She's pure ice. She's wearing a white leather miniskirt and stilettos in her own house, and her eyes are cold and sharp as she assesses us. She looks like a woman who doesn't take any shit.

I only realise I'm staring when she takes the opportunity to do the same. I can feel her eyes trailing the side of my face. It's probably the first time she's seen a scar so bad. In the industry, celebrities call their plastic surgeon every time they get a paper cut. When my face got sliced open, all I had to fix me up was Matt, crouched in the bottom of a dripping, damp cave, sewing up my face without anaesthetic while I bit my tongue to pieces to stop myself from yelling. I know he feels bad about how shitty it looks, but honestly, I'm lucky the damn thing healed at all.

I glance out of a window as an excuse to turn my head away. "Your house has too many windows," I blurt out.

She raises an eyebrow. "Okay," she says slowly.

I feel my face reddening. I nod awkwardly and step past her, scanning the ceiling for good CCTV spots.

She follows me. "What did you do in the army?"

"We were SAS. Special forces."

"And that's how you met? You were in the same... squadron? Troop?"

"Patrol," I grunt. "We worked in a four-person patrol."

"You three?" She looks between Matt and Kenta. "Who was the last person?"

"Damon didn't make it."

She freezes. "He died?"

I nod, trying not to think about it.

She's quiet for a minute. We walk into the next room. Kenta and Matt start arguing about blackout blinds. I can feel her cold blue eyes on me, like lasers melting through my skin.

"What does the SAS do?" She asks suddenly.

"Lots of things. We mostly focussed on counter-terrorism."

She opens her mouth to ask another question, but I cut her off. "How come your agency didn't give you better security? You had, what, one guard?"

Her lips press together. "Money. They like to cut corners."

I frown. "Security isn't something you can skimp on. Your life is always more important than money."

She tilts her head. "That's the nicest thing anyone's said about me in weeks."

Something about her voice makes me think she's not joking.

Kenta steps forward, scanning his notebook. "Okay, I think we have everything. I'll put in an order for the new equipment." He smiles at Briar. "So, what do you think? You want to sign the contract?"

She hesitates, pursing her red lips. I'm suddenly nervous. I don't know what I'm going to do if she says no. I don't know how I'm going to be able to sleep at night, knowing that she's in here all alone with perverts climbing in through her bedroom windows.

To my surprise, she looks up at me, her ponytail flicking over her shoulder. "What do you think, Glen?" She asks quietly. "Do *you* think I need all this?"

"Yes," I say immediately. "I do. I'm sorry."

She nods firmly. "Then, yes. Let's sign the paperwork."

"Great," Kenta says brightly. "Don't worry. We can be very discreet. You won't even know that we're here."

CHAPTER 6
BRIAR

stab a button to slow down the treadmill and bend my body across the machine, panting as the track comes to a stop. Sweat drips down my skin, sticking in my hair. My lungs ache. My whole body feels like it's on fire.

I'm going out of my damn mind.

It's been four days since the Angels arrived in my house, and I'm officially losing it. They're everywhere. Everywhere I turn. They're currently working on fitting my new security system; installing cameras, lights, blinds, gates, locks, alarms. The whole nine yards. They arrive every morning, dressed in jeans and t-shirts, and spend all day screwing and wiring and hammering. I can't walk through my own damn house without getting a front-row seat to my own personal Magic Mike show. Yeah, there's no dancing, but there's plenty of flexing abs and bulging biceps. The air feels thick with their pheromones. I can barely breathe.

Groaning, I grab my phone and leave the basement gym, climbing the stairs shakily. The *Players* premiere is coming up in just a couple of weeks, and my PT has put me on a strict exercise regime. Normally, I'm not a fan of working out, but recently, I've been embracing the exercise. It's the only way I can work off all of the sexual frustration that's constantly buzzing through my veins.

I reach the top of the stairs and turn towards the kitchen, running slap into Glen. His hands shoot out and grab my sweat-slicked waist, keeping me upright. I'm only wearing leggings and a sports bra, and the feeling of his fingers on my bare skin sends heat thrumming through me. I pull away quickly.

"Morning," he says roughly.

I nod tightly and head to the fridge, yanking it open and grabbing a bottle of juice. Heat fizzes under my skin. I take a swig and fight the urge to fan myself.

Glen sits silently at the counter and pulls out a book. Without meaning to, my eyes trail back to his face, taking in the curl of hair falling into his eyes as he reads.

He's my favourite. I'm not sure why. He doesn't talk much. After our one conversation the day we met, I don't think he's ever said more than a few words at a time to me. But there's something about his silence which feels secure and comforting. Whenever I'm in the room with him, I can feel his eyes on me, watching me steadily.

As I watch, he flips a page, biting his full bottom lip. Heat pangs through me.

Shit.

There's movement from outside the glass patio doors. I look up to see Kenta by the pool. He's standing on a ladder, a screwdriver clamped between his teeth, fixing a CCTV camera to my garden wall. His hair is pulled back into a bun, and he's taken off his shirt. I gape at his back. He's tattooed—a full backpiece that goes from his shoulders to his waist, done in swirling black and red and gold ink. I can't see much from here, but I think it's some kind of dragon, or maybe a phoenix. The sweaty, tattooed muscles flex as he pulls a screw out of his pocket and starts twisting it into the wood.

Something in me breaks.

It's too much. I can't do this anymore.

"I'm going to lay down," I say to no-one in particular, and Glen nods, not looking up.

Matt is installing a camera in the hallway outside my room. Which is terrifying. As I watch, he bends down to pick something out of his toolbox. His faded denim jeans stretch against his thick thighs as he rummages, giving me a stellar view of his perfect butt.

Jesus.

I clear my throat, but he ignores me, sorting through tools. "Excuse me," I say, raising my voice.

With a heavy sigh, he straightens, icy eyes meeting mine. The first time we met, he'd been in a suit, and he looked incredible in it; but now, in a thin, worn t-shirt that practically melts over his broad shoulders and chest, and his black, wavy hair falling over his forehead, he looks damn *edible.*

"Princess," he says faux-politely, pushing my door open for me.

"Thank you."

I step into my room, carefully shutting the door behind me. My skin is hot and crawling. My chest feels tight. There's a tickling feeling deep in my belly, and a throbbing pulse between my legs.

I'm suddenly feeling a lot less judgemental about Julie shagging Rodriguez.

I sigh, looking around my room. It's pretty standard: big and white, with fluttery gauze curtains and a big pink bed. I have a black-and-white Dior rug covering the floor, a shelf full of crystals, and expensive scented candles melting on every flat surface. When I first decorated, I wanted the room to feel like a calm, safe space. And it did. I used to spend most of my time here, but ever since the break-in, everything about the room just makes me uncomfortable. Before the Angels came and stationed themselves in my house, I was actually falling asleep on the living room couch most nights. But now one of them is always sitting at my breakfast bar, drinking coffee or doing paperwork. So I have to sleep in here.

Try to sleep, anyway. I've been getting about an hour a night. I'm starting awake at every tiny noise and slight disturbance. I'm too scared to get any real rest.

I head to my bed and flop down on top of the quilt. Yanking open my bedside table drawer, I fumble around inside, pulling out a vibrator still in its packaging.

I'm a big fan of toys. They're much more stimulating than men, and I don't have to worry about them trying to use me for clout. This one was sent to me a few days ago by a company looking to form a partnership. I pull open the packet, shaking out a small bullet, pink and glossy. I flick it on. It buzzes quietly, not loud enough to attract attention. Perfect.

Settling back on the pillows, I close my eyes, kick off my leggings, and picture Glen kneeling over me. I can still feel his handprints burning into my hips. I trace the vibe lightly down my stomach, imagining those big, strong hands stroking me, smoothing over my body. My skin heats and warms.

I don't love the idea of wanking over my employee. But I'm losing my mind, here. I need some kind of relief before I go mad.

When I finally touch the bullet between my legs, I imagine it's Glen's tongue swiping through my folds. Swirling around my entrance. Dipping inside me. The vibration is gentle and pleasant, just a little thrum that makes my belly flip, and I arch slightly, picturing Glen's dark head trapped between my thighs.

Matt clears his throat outside the door, and I bite my lip. Something about lying here, getting myself off while he's just feet away, feels ridiculously naughty. It's turning me on even more. I grit my teeth, my face flushing.

Somehow, my mind drifts to Kenta. I remember his sweat-slick golden muscles out in the garden, and imagine running my tongue down his curling tattoo. I swallow down a soft moan and flick the vibe up a notch.

Right at that second, Matt mutters something under his breath, and I gasp as the image of him pops into my head. I picture him standing over me, pulling my legs apart and sliding into me. The rush of arousal is so hot I swear I almost come right there. My eyes fly open.

I don't think I've ever fantasised about sleeping with multiple men before, but now I can't stop. I'm not even picturing a real scene anymore; just sensations. The feeling of hands and mouths and muscle all over me, tugging at my breasts, massaging my ass, filling me deep inside. It's overwhelming. My body burns and aches, and I fumble my grip on the bullet, accidentally brushing the button with my thumb. I cry out as it speeds up, buzzing furiously against my core.

My bedroom door slams open. I shriek, grabbing the quilt and tugging it up to cover me. Matt stands in the doorway, square jaw clenched, his eyes alert as he takes in the scene. His gaze runs over me, the windows, the wardrobe—then flicks back to me.

"Oh," he says.

I clumsily try to turn off the bullet, but it's slick and wet and falls right through my hands, clattering onto the floor. We both stare at it as it lies, glistening and buzzing, on my pale pink carpet.

"Oh," Matt says again. "You screamed. I thought... shit." His throat bobs. He looks down. "Shit."

"Get *out!*" I gasp.

"Right. I..." He takes a step back, then his eyes fall on the little toy again. "Shit," he says, then finally turns and leaves, shutting the door behind him.

I sink back onto my pillow, silently dying of embarrassment. I can hear footsteps down the corridor. "Is everything okay?" Kenta asks, his voice muffled.

There's a *thunk* sound. I imagine Matt banging his head against the wall. "Shit." He says.

"What?"

"*Shit*," Matt repeats. "Motherfucking-god-shitting-*damn-it.*"

"Alright, then."

I slide off the bed and pick up the shiny pink bullet, switching it off with a shudder. This is it. It's time. I'm going to shred all my credit cards, fake my death, and go live in a hut in the woods. I slink off to the shower, and I'm too humiliated to even finish myself off with the shower-head.

When I step back into my bedroom, drying my hair, I hear chairs scraping in the kitchen and low voices. It sounds like all the men are discussing something. Probably me. God, is Matt telling them what just happened? All I want to do is curl up in bed and never leave, but I know the longer I hide, the more embarrassed I'll become. I change into a pair of clean pyjamas, then straighten my spine and force myself to step out of my room.

I mean, it's not like it's anyone's *fault*, I tell myself, as I walk down the hall. He was just doing his job. And there's no shame in masturbating.

My little pep talk doesn't work. As I step into the kitchen and see the three men bent over a pile of papers, I can feel my cheeks set on fire. Matt stands as soon as I come in, staring at me with wide eyes.

"What did you do to him?" Kenta asks, sounding amused. "He's broken."

Matt flips him off, then takes my elbow and tugs me into the corner of the kitchen. "Look," he says, his voice low, "I'm so sorry about—"

"It's not your fault," I say stiffly. He nods, looking a bit dazed. "I'm still getting used to having you guys here."

"That's so incredibly understandable," he says hoarsely. "I'm still sorry."

"Well. Unnecessary apology accepted. Can we please never talk about it again?"

"I would love that." He clears his throat. "You're still planning on going to that homeless charity event tomorrow, aren't you?"

"Yep." I've been organising the Help for Homeless Gala for the past five months. I can't exactly back out now.

He nods. "We're just discussing the logistics of the event."

"Right."

"Feel free to take a seat." He waves at the table.

"Thanks. I actually own them all, but I appreciate the offer."

"Jesus," he mutters, running a hand through his hair. It's the first time I've seen him anything less than composed, and it sends a flutter through my stomach. I kind of *like* watching him squirm.

I grab a knife and a teaspoon from the cutlery drawer, then head to the kitchen table, picking a fat grapefruit out of the fruit bowl.

Matt sits down awkwardly opposite me as I slice the grapefruit in half. "What's the plan, then?"

Kenta stacks up a handful of papers. "That depends. How would you feel about an undercover angle?"

I frown. "I think most people know who I am. That's the bit that makes me famous."

"Not for you. For us. You've been single for a long time, right?"

"About five years, probably."

Kenta nods. "It's possible that finally seeing you with another man will discourage your stalker from pursuing you."

I take a bite of grapefruit. "You want me to take one of you as my date?"

"It's a good idea. That way you'd have a visible protection detail, but someone close to you, as well."

I run my eyes over the men. Even though they're all incredibly attractive, they'd stick out like sore thumbs on a red carpet. "You'd need to dress up. Tux, designer gear, all of it. You'll need to blend in with the other stars."

Glen snorts. "Guess I'm out of the running, then," he says, waving at his face. I wince, because he's right. God knows what the magazines would say about him. I imagine the words *Beauty and the Beast* would be tossed around a little. I study the other two men. Kenta's an option, and he's definitely less annoying, but his striking features and long hair would still grab attention.

No. If I want someone to melt into a red carpet, I'm going to have to go with the chiselled white guy.

Great.

I turn to Matt and smile at him as sweetly as I can. "Makeover time."

Hopefully, the look of horror in his eyes will make up for the rest of my shitty day.

CHAPTER 7
MATT

Briar ignores me completely on the drive to her dress fitting. We sit in silence as her driver navigates the London streets. The memory of me walking in on her this morning hangs awkwardly between us.

I'm honestly surprised at how well she handled the situation. If she wanted, she could easily have reported me and sued the shit out of Angel Security. But she apologised to me. It's confusing, considering her reputation.

In fact, for the past few days, she's not really been living up to her reputation at all. She's cold, but she's polite enough. For the most part, she just ignores us, which suits me fine. Maybe Colette's right, and her catty public persona really was just made up by the tabloids.

As we turn a street corner, Briar leans her face against the car window like she's tired. I glance across at her, and a memory niggles at the back of my mind. Sometimes, when I look at her from a certain angle, I get this feeling that I've seen her before. I can't put my finger on where, but I'm pretty sure it was during our time in the military. Which doesn't make any sense. How the

Hell would I have seen her face while I was serving? We didn't exactly have regular movie nights. Without meaning to, my eyes track the soft curve of her cheek.

"Jesus," the driver says suddenly. I blink back to reality and lean forward to look through the windshield. I see the problem immediately.

We're just pulling up to the curb outside the designer's address, and the street is packed with paparazzi, clutching their cameras as they see the car approach.

I turn to Briar, fuming. "Did you tweet where we were going?" I demand.

She checks her lipstick in her phone camera. "I have a stalker," she drones. "No, I didn't *tweet my location.*"

I jab my finger out of the window. "How did they all know that you're here?"

She shrugs. "They always know where I am," she says quietly. "I don't know how."

I sigh, looking out at the heaving crowd. Shit. I really should have brought one of the others as backup. We weren't expecting this. It looks like there's about fifty men out there, all jostling each other to get a better position. "We're going to have to be fast," I say. "Don't stop to take pictures. Don't answer questions. Stick close to me."

She slips her phone back into her bag and squares her shoulders. "We'll see."

I frown. "Not *we'll see.* You say *yes, Matt,* and do as I say."

"Talking to the press is part of my job," she says flatly. "I'll give them a few shots."

"No—"

Without warning, she tugs open the car door. A wall of sound hits us as the paps immediately start screaming. Camera flashes light up the inside of the car.

I swear, scrambling over Briar and half-falling onto the pavement. The photographers jabber around me, and I turn and block their view, offering Briar my hand and helping her out of the car.

"What the Hell do you think you're playing at?" I hiss as she steps onto the pavement, fluffing up her hair.

She shrugs. "Just testing your reflexes." She raises her voice. "You get one shot each," she calls. "Make it count, boys."

"Very funny," I growl, wrapping my arm around her shoulders and ploughing us through the crowd.

The noise is incredible. Bodies crowd all around us, shoving, elbowing, grabbing. Flashes burst in our faces, half-blinding us. The men start screaming questions as we push through them.

"BRIAR! TELL US ABOUT YOUR NEW MOVIE!"

"HAVE YOU GAINED WEIGHT, BRIAR? BRIAR, ARE YOU PREGNANT?"

"IS IT TRUE YOU SLEPT WITH HARRY STYLES?"

Briar poses as she walks, pouting at the lenses and blowing kisses. Gritting my teeth, I tighten my grip on her shoulders and push her forwards. A bald guy in his twenties throws himself in our path.

"BRIAR!" He shouts, right in our faces. We both wince as spittle flecks our skin. "WHAT'S YOUR RESPONSE TO ELLIOT WHITE CALLING YOU A STUCK-UP COW?"

Briar pauses, right in the middle of the street. I try to shove her along, but she's surprisingly strong. She considers, biting her lip. "I suppose I'd tell him to shut his mouth, brush his teeth, and pay the taxes he's been evading for the last five years," she says thoughtfully.

"Stop," I say in her ear, pushing her forward again. More people are joining the crowd now; passersby attracted by the commotion. I start getting worried. Briar suddenly seems very small and delicate, surrounded by this heaving group of men.

"Get the fuck back!" I call, warding them off. "Step away. You'll crush her, for God's sake!"

They ignore me. One guy lunges forwards, grabbing her arm. I reach for him, but Briar moves faster, shoving him away. He staggers back a few steps, staring at her.

"You can't fucking push me!" He sputters.

"Grab me, I'll grab you back," Briar says, sounding bored.

"I'll report you!"

"Whatever." She flips him off. "Get a real job, loser."

I grit my teeth. "Briar," I growl in her ear. "Stop provoking them."

She looks up at me innocently. "What? It was self-defence."

Sighing, I manage to crowd Briar across the pavement and up to the entrance of the building. Just as we're about to step inside, one last pap, a dark haired-guy in a baseball cap, hops up onto the steps next to us, shoving his camera in Briar's face.

"BRIAR! WHY DID YOU CHEAT ON THOMAS PETTY?" He shouts.

Briar freezes, the blood draining from her face.

I frown. I know this story. I stumbled across it when I was reviewing her case files this morning. Apparently, when Briar was a teenager, she dated a co-star on her show, Thomas Petty. The two went out for a few months, then she broke his heart when she cheated on him with another teenage boy.

Why the Hell is this middle-aged guy asking a woman about her sixteen-year-old sex life? That's just plain creepy.

I put my hand on Briar's back, preparing to shoulder her through the doorway, but she digs in her heels and gives the pap a bright smile. "Honestly?" She raises her eyebrows, leaning in. "I'll give you the scoop." She pauses for effect. "Because he was shit in bed. I've never met a man so utterly incompetent. Getting eaten out by him was like getting licked by a Saint Bernard. He kissed like an iguana catching flies. And his prick was about an inch long, and always stank. I think he had some sort of fungal issue, or something." She tosses her hair back. "Quote me on that."

With that, she breezes right past him into the building.

"Bit harsh," I mutter, stepping in behind her and closing the door. The thick glass immediately shuts out the noise, although flashes still flicker behind us.

She rolls her eyes. "Whatever."

We step into a ridiculously luxurious reception area. The walls are papered in pale gold, and the floor is tiled with marble. A massive crystal chandelier hangs down from the middle of the ceiling.

"Hey, Anna," Briar flounces up to the front desk. "I have an appointment with Michel?"

The receptionist smiles and checks her computer. "Good afternoon, Miss Saint. I'm afraid he's currently meeting with another client, they've run a bit overtime. If you'd just take a seat in the waiting area, I can get you some bubbly—"

A nearby door flies open. I whirl around to face it, automatically moving in front of Briar as a man dressed all in white bursts into the room. He's tanned and dark-haired, with a peroxide-white smile and a tape measure dangling around his neck. "Briar!" he exclaims. "God, you look *stunning* today, babe."

"Hello, Michel. He's fine, Matt."

"You the designer?" I ask, ignoring her.

The guy nods. "Michel Blanc, at your service."

I wave him over. "I need to pat you down."

"*Excuse* me?"

"If you're going to be touching my client, I need to confirm that you're unarmed."

"You know he'll be using needles and scissors, right?" Briar drawls. "If he wanted to stab me, he wouldn't need a concealed weapon."

"It's fine, love," Michel assures her. I give him a quick pat down, then slap him on the back.

"You're good to go."

He winces, rubbing his back, then flits over to Briar, kissing her on both cheeks. "Come in, come in!" He starts to shepherd her to the studio. "I've been looking forward to this all week!"

"B-but what about your current appointment?" Anna squeaks from behind the desk.

Michel waves a hand dismissively. "He can come back some other time. ALAN!" He calls over his shoulder. "YOU NEED TO LEAVE NOW."

A red-faced man scuttles out of the room, shirt unbuttoned. "But I still need a pocket square!" He complains, trying to fix his cufflinks.

"You can make your orders on my website," Michel says, not taking his eyes off Briar. "I always have room for my favourite client. We're fitting your dress for the gala, right? You are going to *love* what we came up with for you!"

Briar nods. "And my bodyguard needs a suit."

The designer flicks his eyes over me dismissively. "Big boy, huh? I'm not sure we'll have any pants that fit you. Spin for me."

"No."

He sighs. "Well, judging by your thigh size, I guess you probably have a pretty big ass, too. We'll get to you later." He turns on his heel and heads for the open door. "Come on, then."

I rub my forehead, following Michel and Briar into the fitting studio. This is why I like working for politicians. Don't get me wrong, most of them are unbearable, but at least no one ever comments on my ass.

The inside of the studio is big, with overhead lighting, plush sofas, and huge floral arrangements on every flat surface. The walls are lined with racks stuffed with dresses and shirts and suits. I eye a flamingo-pink tuxedo decorated with sequin pineapples.

"Like it?" Briar asks. "It'd look cute on you."

"Try it. See how fast I quit."

"Right," Michel sings, leading Briar to the centre of the room and setting her in front of a wall-to-ceiling mirror. "Let's get you sorted. How many lives have you ruined today, babe?"

Briar examines her nail beds. "Depends. Matt, is your life ruined?"

"It'll take more than you could ever give me, princess."

She sighs. "Then I guess I haven't ruined any. But it's only early." She tilts her head. "What have you got for me?"

"*So* much gossip," Michel chirps. "I swear, people tell me *everything* when I'm getting them done up. It's like they think I have some kind of confidentiality policy."

They both laugh. I grimace, crossing to the window. It's facing away from the street, and looks out over a large square courtyard filled to bursting with bushes and flowers. I scan the foliage. I can't see anybody down there, but the plants are too dense to be sure. I grab the white curtain and drag it over the windowpane.

There's a gasp from behind me. "What are you *doing*?" Michel cries.

"She's going to be changing. I'm closing the curtains."

"We need the natural light! How else am I going to correctly match the shade of her nude pump?!"

My head is starting to ache. "I'm sure you'll work something out," I mutter.

"Leave them open," Briar orders. "He needs light to work. I'm not coming back here and doing all of this again."

I can't hide my irritation. "And what if paps get down there?"

She shrugs. "I'll beat them up."

I snort. "Yeah? You know how to fight?"

"I do all of my own stunts. I've been trained in four different martial arts." She pauses. "I'm also great at kicking men in the nuts. That's my speciality."

"Somehow, I don't doubt that," I mutter, watching as Michel heads to one of the racks, pulling out a dress. It's a silver flapper dress, with long, glittery tassels sewn into the fabric.

"Here you go, love." He hangs it up next to the mirror.

"Thanks." Briar reaches behind her neck and unties the back of her shirt. It's a tiny thing; it looks more like a silk handkerchief tied over her chest than an actual piece of clothing. As it falls away, I catch a glimpse of her pale pink bra reflected in the mirror, before I spin on the spot, turning to face the wall. Blood thumps through me. I can feel myself getting hard.

Fuck.

CHAPTER 8
MATT

take a deep breath. "Is that a flapper dress?" I say, to cover up the heat rising in my face.

I hear a zip being pulled. "It's a nod to my new film."

"Is it a reboot of *Chicago*?"

I can practically hear her glare. "It's a murder mystery film set in a 20s speakeasy. One of the patrons is mysteriously killed in a backroom, and we have to find the murderer before they strike again."

"Hm. Is it you?"

"What do you think?" There are sounds of fabric crumpling. "So, what happens now?" She asks, her voice muffled. I picture her with the dress over her head, and try to blink the image out of my mind. "You just follow me around until, what, exactly? The police aren't going to help, so I don't think the threat will just go away."

"We've got people back at Angel HQ tracking X down. Since you have CCTV footage and a DNA sample, when we find the right guy, we can get him locked up. Then you're free to go."

"X?"

"Since it's the name he's apparently given himself, that's what we'll call him until we can prove his identity."

She hums. "And how exactly are you going to find *X*?"

I examine the wallpaper. "We've got the Stalkers on the case. They'll come back to us in a few days with a list of potential suspects. We'll work from there."

I hear her freeze. "Excuse me?"

"That's probably a bad choice of words," I admit. "The Stalkers are our cyber-analyst team. They'll be trawling through all of your social media messages and comments, selecting profiles that seem suspicious, and then finding out as much as they can about the person behind the account. You'd be amazed at the information they can get. Address. National Insurance number. Bank details."

"Huh. All legal?"

I don't deign to answer that. There's movement in the courtyard outside. I frown, leaning forward for a closer look. I can't see anything out of the ordinary, but there's a sick, uneasy feeling in my stomach. I scan the bushes, trying to work out what's wrong with the picture.

"Matt," Briar calls. "Can you give Michel his pin cushion?"

"Not a butler," I remind her.

"No, but you have two free hands, which is more than both of us."

Sighing, I straighten, turning to face her. When I catch sight of Briar in the silver dress, I freeze. It looks incredible on her, hugging her chest and hips. The sparkly tassels flow down her slight figure like she's dripping in water, and the zipper is open, showing off her smooth, white back. Both she and Michel are holding it up, pinching the fabric where it needs to be pinned. I scan the workstation for the pincushion, handing it to the man.

"Ta," he says. "Hold the sleeve here, please."

"Seriously?"

"Unless you want your poor girl having a serious nip-slip, yes, I'm serious. My assistant called in sick today."

Cursing internally, I hold the fabric where he directs me to, pinching it in place. Briar's breath hitches slightly as the pad of my finger brushes her collarbone. Her skin is impossibly soft, like warm silk. Michel hums. "Here on the waist too, please."

Wordlessly, I pinch another few inches of fabric. Briar's trim, but I can still feel the soft curve between her waist and her hip. My hand itches to spread out and fit that curve in my palm.

Great.

Michel steps back and slides the pin cushion onto his wrist. "Excellent. Let's get started, love."

The next hour feels like some perverted form of torture. I hold scraps of silk to Briar's hot skin as she breathes softly against me, her chest rising and falling very visibly under the low neckline. Michel has me touch her all over. Waist. Hip. Back. Shoulder. Every time she changes position, I get a whiff of her candy-scented perfume.

I can't stop thinking about how I found her this morning; lying in bed, a toy inside of her, her cheeks flushed with pleasure. It was like stepping straight into a sex dream. I swallow, shifting my hips away from her as my pants tighten.

As he works, Michel natters on about celebrity gossip. "Let's see. Oh, you know that influencer, Lola Snow? She landed a deal with Sosex Fashion."

"Gross." Briar wrinkles her nose. "Sorry, how come I get called a stuck-up whore when I wear a pair of designer sunglasses, but no one has any issue when she promotes a brand everyone knows uses sweatshops? This is like, the third time she's done this." She hisses as Michel's finger slips, and he pricks her with a pin.

"Sorry," he apologises when I glare at him. "Call her out, babe."

She pulls out her phone and starts tapping at the screen. I look over her shoulder. She's drafting a tweet to the other actress.

> @LolaSnowOfficial do u really think it's okay to encourage people to buy clothes made by Bengali kids getting paid five pence a day? You make fifty million a year, do u really need such a gross brand deal? xo

My jaw tenses. I'm starting to get a sense of where her reputation comes from. "Is this what you do?" I ask. "Ruin other celebrities' careers?"

She shrugs. "Everyone needs a hobby."

"That's shitty," I say flatly.

She wheels on me. "Is it *shitty*, Matt? Is it more shitty than hundreds of eight-year-olds being shoved into dirty, damp rooms, sewing two-dollar t-shirts until their fingers bleed and they inevitably die from inhaling fabric fibres? Is my *tweet* the shitty part of this equation? Is—*ow!*"

Her whole body flinches as Michel pricks her with another pin. I look down and see blood spotting her pale skin.

"Watch what you're doing!" I snap. "Stop fucking hurting her!"

"It was an accident!"

"Once is an accident. Twice means you're being careless. If you *can* do your job without turning my client into a human pin-cushion, I suggest you start now."

There's an awkward silence. Michel gives a small nod, turning back to his work.

"Mattie. I didn't know you cared," Briar murmurs.

"It's my job to stop you getting hurt," I mutter.

She doesn't respond, looking down. Her dark lashes stroke her cheek. A few more minutes pass, and then Michel finally pulls back with a flourish.

"There. Done!" He beams at Briar. "You just wriggle out of that, sweetheart, and we'll start on your friend's suit." He runs his eyes over me assessingly. "I'm thinking blue. You'll give me a hand with the pinning, won't you, Briar? I think we'll need to tailor something from scratch to get around that ass."

"I'll help," she says, refusing to look at me. I swallow thickly. I need this girl's hands all over my body like I need a hole in the damn head.

"Great," I grit out. "Thanks so much."

CHAPTER 9
X

I don't like Briar's new dress.

It's too glitzy for my taste. Some girls need sparkle and glitter to look good. They hide behind makeup and fancy clothes. But Briar is so naturally beautiful, she doesn't need any distractions. I prefer her in plain colours. White is my favourite; it makes her blonde hair glow and her skin look all smooth and creamy.

I kneel in the bushes, watching through the window as she twists and turns in front of the mirror. A fly buzzes around my ear, but I don't dare reach up to bat it away. Any sudden movement might draw attention to me.

I've gotten very brave since my first visit to Briar's house. The night I climbed over her fence and into her bedroom, I didn't even feel real. It was like I was dreaming, or playing a computer game. I couldn't believe that I got away with it, but I did, and now, it doesn't feel like a game anymore. Now I know that I can get close to her.

It was easy enough to follow the paparazzi to the designer's house. Someone had left the gate to the courtyard open, so I sneaked in and hid in the bushes. I have an excellent view from down here, although I wish I had thought to buy some binoculars to watch closer.

As I watch the window, a big man suddenly steps forward, looking outside. His eyes scan the courtyard, and I curl back into the bush, scowling.

He's the kind of man I hate. Naturally handsome. He has a perfect jaw and tanned skin and floppy black hair. A man that looks like that can have any girl he wants.

A horrible thought occurs to me. Is he Briar's new boyfriend? The idea makes me feel sick. And angry. Very, very angry. For a moment, I'm so angry I think about doing something drastic.

Then I realise *how* he's looking out the window. He's scanning the courtyard, left-right-left-right. I notice the earpiece in his ear and the insignia on his collar. He's not a boyfriend; he's a security guard. That makes me relax a bit, although I'm still nervous that my Briar is spending so much time with such an attractive man.

Briar says something to him, and he steps away from the window. She starts to undress, and he quickly turns around to face the wall.

Definitely not a boyfriend.

I watch, entranced, as Briar strips down. When I see her pale pink bra reflected in the mirror, I start to ache.

She shimmies the dress onto her body, showing off her little waist and pretty hips. My mouth goes dry. My hands start to shake. I get lightheaded. No one should look this beautiful.

I lift up my camera and take a picture.

CHAPTER 10
BRIAR

O n the day of the charity gala, I wake up feeling gross. I sit up slowly, rubbing my thudding head. My sheets are soaked and twisted around me, and my blood is fizzing with adrenaline.

I had another nightmare. It's already fading from my mind, but they're always the same: a tall, faceless, bone-white figure chasing me down a maze of endless corridors. No matter how fast I run or which direction I take, he's always right on my heels. Breathing down my neck.

I sigh, forcing myself out of bed and opening the curtains. Bright sunlight streams into my bedroom, hurting my eyes. I put my cheek against the cool windowpane, looking down at the street outside. It's an ordinary summer day in London. The sky is cloudless and blue. Trees ruffle in the breeze. I watch a bird hop onto a nearby streetlight, warbling.

I'm too exhausted to enjoy any of it.

I know I should go for a jog, but I can't stand the thought of it. Just like I can't stand the thought of eating breakfast, or working, or showering. My mental health has been steadily nose-diving since the break-in, and it's getting harder and harder to cope with. I feel like I'm losing my mind.

I sigh, dragging myself to the wardrobe to shimmy into a bikini and grab a cover-up. Some fresh air and sunshine is better than hibernating in my bed feeling sorry for myself. As I step out into the hallway, I silently pray that I won't bump into any of the men on my way to the pool.

I can barely look at them anymore. On top of my weird foursome fantasy, ever since Matt walked in on me jacking off, my brain has developed an incredibly stupid, ill-advised, nonsensical crush on the man. When he was helping Michel at my fitting, gently touching me all over, it was all I could do not to moan out loud. I spent the entire car ride home in damp underwear.

Then, when I did arrive back home, I was greeted by Glen and Kenta. Who I swear get more attractive every day.

I don't know if the stress of my potential stalker has driven me to the brink, but I've decided it's probably safer that I just stay out of the guys' ways as much as possible. Which is difficult, when they're literally hired to watch me 24-7.

Luckily, when I step into the kitchen, it's blissfully empty. I stumble over to the coffeemaker and start brewing up a cup. Just as the machine starts to steam, I spot movement outside the glass patio doors. I look up to see Matt swimming lengths in my pool.

The pool is my pride and joy: almost full-sized, lined with turquoise tiles inlaid with little blue glass gems. It's set in a mosaic patio surrounded with lush greenery, overlooked by a couple of sun loungers. I watch Matt's muscled body effortlessly cutting through the water, barely making a splash, then decide to pour another cup of coffee. Using my tablet as a tray, I carry them both out onto the patio.

Matt notices me and swims over, straightening. His whole body shines slick and wet under the sun. I do not look at the water dripping through his hair and down the hard, rigid lines of his abs.

"Problem?" He asks as I approach.

I shake my head. "I saw you out here and thought you might want a coffee. I don't know how you take it." I put the mug on the edge of the pool.

He looks at it warily. "Black, without cyanide, if possible."

"Are you accusing me of poisoning you?"

"Wouldn't put it past you, princess."

"Well, why don't you use your incredible observational skills to find out?"

Narrowing his eyes, Matt picks up the mug and takes a tentative sip. I watch his throat move as he swallows. "It's good," he says, his voice deeper than usual. "Thank you."

I nod and head to a nearby sun lounger, setting down my drink and tablet.

"You're not swimming?" He asks behind me. "I can get out if you want to do some lengths."

I give the pool a longing look. The water ripples, reflecting shimmers of light onto the high garden walls. "Can't. Not before events. Chlorine might damage my hair."

"God forbid," he drawls.

I stretch out on the lounger. "You can keep going. I don't mind."

He nods, taking a couple more gulps of hot coffee, then dives back into the cold water. I settle back and turn on my tablet, flicking through some emails. It's surprisingly hard to concentrate when a man with about ten abs is wet and half-naked in front of you. More than once, I find my eyes flicking up to track Matt as he swims. The sun beats down over me, soaking into my skin as I watch the blue water roll off his tanned, muscled body. Every five lengths, he stops and turns to check in on me.

All of the guys do this. Check on me. When I'm in the gym, Kenta will pop his head in every half an hour. The other night, I fell asleep in the bath and woke up to a worried-sounding Glen tapping at the bathroom door. When I hired the Angels, I really wasn't prepared for just how protective they were going to be. It's definitely contributing to my impending breakdown.

As I watch, Matt finishes his lap. His eyes flick back to me, and our gazes meet. His full lips part. He gives me a little nod and dips below the water again.

I turn back to my tablet, my heart thudding uncomfortably, and stare blankly at my emails. I can't remember what I was doing. On a whim, I type *SAS military* into Google, clicking the first result that comes up.

I skim the information. It's impressive stuff. Apparently, the SAS is one of the most elite units in the UK military. A lot of their actions are classified, but they seem pretty high up in the food chain. As I scroll down the page, one particular word stands out to me.

Torture.

I back up, rereading the paragraph.

> *One facet of the gruelling SAS recruitment process is said to be Resistance to Interrogation training, during which applicants are subjected to torture methods commonly used upon British prisoners of war.*

My mouth falls open. Horror floods through me as I start to connect the dots.

There's a splash, and I look up to see Matt jumping right out of the pool and jogging over. "What is it? What's wrong?" He demands. "Did X contact you?"

"What? No, I'm looking up the SAS." I stare up at him. "You did *torture training?*"

He blinks, shaking droplets of water out of his hair. "Torture… resistance to interrogation, yeah."

"They…" I look back at the website. "They did these things to you? Just so you could qualify for a *job?*" My eyes skip over the words. *Humiliation. Starvation. Sleep deprivation. Hooding.*

He glances at the paragraph I have highlighted, then lets his eyes flick away again. "Among others."

"But that's barbaric!"

"It's necessary," he snaps. "Soldiers need to be trained to face what they're actually fighting. That's the only way they'll survive."

"And was it?" I ask. "Necessary?"

A horrible, bitter feeling is building in my stomach. I've wondered about Glen's face for a while now. There's something strange about his scar. He doesn't look like he was stabbed or burned or shot; he looks like he's been purposefully carved up.

"Glen's scars," I say. "Is that how he got them? Why did you guys get discharged from the army, anyway?"

I know immediately that I've crossed a line. Emotions flicker across Matt's face, too fast for me to read. He snatches up my tablet, powering it down.

"Don't ask any more," he barks, a vein throbbing in his forehead. "Don't look this shit up. These are men's *lives,* not entertainment for you to flick through while you're getting a fucking suntan." He dumps the tablet back on my lounger, scowling. I wince internally. Shit.

I start to apologise, but I'm interrupted by a buzzing noise from the poolside. Kenta's staticky voice rings out through the patio. *"Carter."*

Eyes not leaving mine, Matt stoops and picks up the two-way radio he left by the pool's edge, holding it to his mouth. "What."

"A courier just delivered a package. Jack Ellis. He's got a brown unmarked box, about 750 by 750. The service is called Jameson's Delivery."

"Courier still there?"

"Yes. He says the package is from the designer."

"Hold him until I clear it."

"Roger."

Matt turns to me. "Are you expecting a delivery?"

I nod, pulling out my phone. "That will be my dress for this evening. Yeah, the tracker says it's just arrived." I show him my screen.

He nods. "Let the guy go, Kenta. When's Glen coming in?"

"I'll text him to come check it out."

"Copy." He puts down the radio. I stand, and he grabs my wrist. "Where are you going?"

"To check out the dress. I still need to pick out my makeup."

He shakes his head. "You're not touching an unmarked, couriered package until Glen comes in to clear it."

"Why Glen?" I protest. "Why can't you do it?"

"He was our dems specialist. Demolitions. He knows the most about things that explode."

Nerves clutch at my stomach. "You think it will *explode*?"

"It's not impossible." He sits down on the lounger next to mine, picking up his towel. "Better safe than sorry."

I nod numbly. We're silent for a while, staring up at the still blue sky. Even though we're not touching, I can feel his presence twenty centimetres away, like electricity prickling down one side of my body. I don't know if it's the sun or a blush warming my cheeks.

"You know," he says, "from a security standpoint, going out tonight is a really bad idea. If you care that much about homeless kids, make a donation. A party won't help them."

"I have to go. I organised it."

He blinks. "Wait. What?"

"I organised the event. It's my charity." He stares at me. I snort. "Sorry, isn't that diva-ish enough? I can call you a pathetic asshole or something, if that would help. Wouldn't want to get in the way of your terrible assumptions about me." I stretch out my neck, rolling it from side to side. "What's that about, anyway? Do you have a vendetta against all celebrities? Or have you just been keeping up with me in the tabloids?"

"All celebrities," he grunts. I wait, but he doesn't expand.

"… Why?"

"Bad experience."

Ah, shit. I can only imagine what self-important idiots he's had to work with before. I've met plenty of stars who let the fame get to their heads. "Fair." I wiggle my toes, examining my pedicure. "I don't trust famous people, either."

"No?"

I nod. "So many people want to be in the industry. The ones who actually make it to the top are usually the most ruthless. They've had to step on a lot of people to get their spot."

"You didn't," he counters. "You didn't have to do anything to get famous. It landed in your lap."

I narrow my eyes at him, and he shrugs. "I looked you up. You were scouted at a school talent show. Two months later, you were in LA, shooting what would become the most popular daytime television show since *Friends*. You didn't have to fight for your fame, you just got lucky."

"Yes," I say softly, my lips twisting into a smile. "Of course. I was very, very *lucky*."

Matt looks like he wants to say something else, but before he can, his radio crackles again.

"Glen's here," Kenta says. *"Come to the kitchen, please."*

"News?"

"The Stalkers got back." Even through the tinny speaker, his voice sounds grim.

"And?" Matt prompts, standing.

"It's not good."

My insides curl. Oh, God. What the Hell did they find?

Matt picks up his coffee and turns to me. "I'm gonna speak to Kenta. Do me a favour and stay out here until Glen clears the package. He'll leave it outside your bedroom when it's done."

I nod numbly, laying back in the lounger as his footsteps disappear over the patio. My heart is pounding in my throat.

CHAPTER 11
KENTA

Matt comes in from outside and crosses into the kitchen, sitting on the stool opposite mine. I pass him the hoodie I left on the back of my seat.

"Thanks," he says, pulling it on and shaking his damp hair back into place. "Give it to me."

I push a pile of papers across the counter. I stopped by Angel HQ this morning to speak to Colette and collect all the info the stalkers found. It turns out they found a lot. Which is never good.

"The guys picked up on hundreds of social media accounts who have made consistent sexual threats against Briar in the last year," I explain. "Given what we know about X, they've nixed any women off the list, anyone who seemed like a troll, and anybody who seemed to actively *hate* her, rather than love her. There are forty major suspects left."

Matt nods sharply. "We'd better get to work, then."

We go through the profiles together. It's nasty shit. On pretty much every post Briar makes, she gets people threatening to kill her, rape her, or beat her up.

"This is bullshit," Matt mutters, flipping through the list of men who have sent her nude photos. "How the Hell does she put up with all this?"

"I suppose you grow a thick skin," I murmur.

To my left, the glass patio door shunts open. I look up as Briar steps in from outside. She's dressed in a tiny black bikini, with a translucent pink robe made of some kind of fine mesh thrown over top. Her thick blonde hair is piled on top of her head, and her skin is flushed from the sun.

I clear my throat, focussing on her face. "Good morning, Miss Saint. Glen cleared your package."

"Hey, Kenta. Please, call me Briar." She steps forward, looking over my shoulder. I'm suddenly hyper aware of her almost-naked body next to me. "Ah. I see you've found my fan mail."

"Do people always talk about you like this?" Matt demands.

"Since I was thirteen years old. As I said. I was a very *lucky* child." She drops her mug off in the dishwasher, then sashays back to her room. I watch her go, fiddling with the edge of another dossier.

So far, Briar's been a bit of a mystery to me. I have to admit, when we first got here and heard her swearing at her PR person, I was worried that she'd just be another spoiled celebrity. But I think she's actually pretty sweet. She always makes extra food for us when she cooks. She's allowing us free rein of her gym equipment and pool. She's even giving us a place to sleep, for God's sake.

I have a theory: I don't think she's rude or bitchy at all. I think she's just a very private, intelligent woman who is playing the media like a fucking violin.

The past few nights, after my shift has ended, I've gone back to my room in the pool house and researched Briar. I've read everything from magazine articles to twitter threads. From what I can gather, Briar's 'mean girl' persona mostly comes from her starting 'drama' with other celebrities, but I've looked through her state-ments, and it's not like she's starting petty arguments. In just the past week, she's criticised a supermodel for advertising dangerous weight loss drugs; a director for underpaying his female actors; a rapper for getting handsy with his staff. Unless she's just making the stories up—which is possible—she's not stir-ring drama. She's using her reputation to expose powerful people who think that they can get away with doing shitty things.

It's an interesting PR model. Instead of trying to avoid public feuds, she actively calls out misbehaving celebrities, picks fights with them, and stays trending. It's not like she has to worry about making enemies, since her whole schtick is being bitchy and unlikeable. And the more stars that hate her, the more relevant she becomes. It's genius, really.

Of course, I don't know that's what she's doing for sure. I still need more data.

Matt nods at the folder under my hand. "Saving the best for last?"

I blink. "Ah. Yes. This is the one Colette was most concerned about." I pass him the file, and he shakes out a few pages of printer paper.

"Daniel F," he reads.

I nod. "A few years ago, he ran a fan account where he uploaded pictures of Briar out and about. Nothing that the paparazzi weren't doing; but instead of selling them, he uploaded them all onto his page with terribly written poetry calling her his 'wife'. I spoke to Julie, and apparently, he used to send her flowers every year on her birthday." I tap the page. "These are just some of the thousands of DMs from that account."

Matt flicks through the list of messages. *"Happy Birthday, Angel,"* he reads aloud. *"I watched you at your pool party. Do you shave all over? X."* He grimaces, glancing at the next one. *"Angel, don't wear such revealing clothing around other men. You should be saving your body for me. X.* Christ."

"Keep going."

"Every time I think of you, I smile. Don't you think I have a nice smile? X."

"The photo he attached is on the other side."

Matt flips the page. His face darkens when he sees the picture. It's not of X's smile.

"Daniel stopped posting under that name in 2017," I explain, "but a bunch of anonymous accounts have written creepy messages on her page from the same IP address. One of those accounts messaged just last night. *'I spent all day ordering furniture for our house. I can't wait for us to finally live together, my beautiful wife. X'*"

"Daniel always ended his messages with an X?"

I nod. "It might just be a kiss. But I don't believe in coincidences."

"No," he says flatly. "Me neither. We need to look further into him."

Behind us, Briar's door opens. "Matt," she calls.

"Hm?"

"Come here."

Matt doesn't move. My gut twists. Something's wrong, I can hear it in her voice. Dropping the papers, I make my way to her bedroom. The cardboard box is sitting open on her rug, and a sparkly silver dress is laid out on her bed. Briar is standing next to it, holding an envelope. I'd assume it was a note from the designer, if it weren't for the frozen look on her face. She hands it to me wordlessly.

I shake out a photograph. It's a blurry picture of Briar standing in just her underwear. It's been shot through a window.

Shit.

"This is from the fitting?" I ask, trying to keep calm.

She nods. "There's a message on the other side." Her voice is hoarse. I flip the photograph.

The silver is pretty, but I like you best in white. X

I swear under my breath. "Carter," I shout. "Get in here."

"What's going on?" Matt asks, coming in behind me.

I show him the photo. He takes one look and pulls out his phone. "Briar. Give me the designer's number."

"I'll call the courier," I say. "Find out who got it put in the package."

We split. I dial the courier service. A female voice answers.

"Jameson's delivery, how can I help you?"

"Hello," I say politely. "I'd like to speak with one of your couriers, Jack Ellis, please. It's urgent."

"Of course, sir." There's a click and a fuzz of static. A teenager's voice sounds down the line.

"Um. Hello?"

"Who tampered with the package you brought to Briar Saint's house?" I ask. "Did someone give you something to put inside it?"

"Wh-what?" The boy stammers. *"I don't know what you're talking about."*

"I'm not going to report you," I say calmly. "I just need to know who gave the letter to you. Miss Saint's security is at risk if we don't find out."

There's a pause. *"I don't know anything,"* his voice is muffled.

"If you tell me now, you won't get into trouble. If you don't tell me, and Briar ends up getting hurt, your name will be splashed on every magazine and newspaper in the damn country. I'll see to it personally."

There's an even longer pause. *"He was standing on the street by her security gate,"* he says eventually. *"Offered me five hundred quid to cut the box open and put the envelope inside."*

I lean forward. "What did he look like?"

"I didn't see his face. He was wearing a hoodie and sunglasses. He had a scarf tied over his mouth."

I take a deep breath through my nose. "And the fact that he was dressed like a ninja didn't tip you off that maybe you shouldn't be smuggling for him?" I ask, keeping my voice as even as possible.

"Look, man, I'm sorry. I figured it was just a fan letter, or something. I wouldn't have done it if it was like, a bomb." He hesitates. *"Shit, is she okay? Is she gonna sue me? I—"*

"Thank you for your cooperation," I interrupt. "Please call this number back if you remember anything useful." I end the call just as Matt walks back into the kitchen. "Well?"

He scowls. "There was a blip in the alarm system a few minutes after we left. They thought it was an error."

I bite back a curse, running a hand through my hair. What the fuck is the point of having a security system, if you ignore it whenever it goes off? I give Matt the rundown of my conversation with the courier, and his face just gets more thunderous.

"We should report the kid," he growls. "He put her in danger."

"He was just young and poor and dumb. What I don't understand is how X found her in the first place. Did you notice anyone following the car when you drove to the appointment?"

Matt shakes his head. "There were paps outside, she wouldn't have been hard to track down. I think—" He jumps as Briar comes up behind him, tapping his shoulder.

"I have a nail appointment," she says quietly. "I need to go to the salon."

"No," Matt says immediately. "There's no way. You're not going anywhere until we figure this out."

She rubs her eyes, looking tired. "I can't go out with my nails like this. They have mani cams at these things."

"Mani cams?"

She glares. "I don't really want the headlines tomorrow to be about my cuticles, instead of disadvantaged kids."

Jesus. She lives in such a strange world.

An idea pops into my head. "We have a neighbour who works as a beauty therapist. I can call her and ask if she's available to do a house call."

Matt nods. "Good idea."

Nin is a very sweet sixty-year-old woman who lives in our building. Glen helped unblock her sink once, and ever since, she's been calling us upstairs to feed us homemade meals once a week. She works as a beauty therapist, but from what I can tell, work is pretty light for her at the moment. We've been discretely loading up her electricity meter for months.

I expect Briar to protest, but she looks almost bored, waving her hand vaguely. "Sure. Whatever. Make the call." She looks around the room. "I'm gonna take a bath. Exfoliate, and... whatever."

She flounces out of the room. At least she doesn't seem bothered by this mess.

CHAPTER 12
BRIAR

I can feel myself starting to crack.

I'm so tired. So, so tired. I can't handle the insomnia and the nightmares anymore. I'm holding myself together with stubbornness and under-eye concealer, but I can feel myself fraying.

Nin, the sweet beauty therapist that Kenta and Matt called in, natters cheerfully as she carefully applies a top coat to my nails. I try to respond, but I just can't bring myself to focus on what she's saying.

He found me. Again. He's following me. He's watching me. Even now, he could be peeking in through a window, ready to snap a picture. I glance to my bedroom window, then my bathroom, like he might just pop up out of nowhere.

Luckily, Nin is happily chatting, keeping up the conversation for both of us.

"When I was a teenager, I didn't like beauty at all," she chuckles, using a Q-Tip to clean off the edges of my nails. "I was such a tomboy. I just wanted to study."

"How did you get into manicures, then?" I ask, forcing myself back into the conversation.

"I'm trained in Public Relations. When I was in Thailand, I worked for the CEO of a big phone company. But the company went bust, so I moved here with my husband." She sighs. "He left pretty soon after we moved. I tried to get a job in PR, but employers here don't trust foreign degrees. That's why I do beauty. My ex-husband, he didn't pay anything for the children when they were growing up. I want them to be able to go to good colleges."

I frown. "That's illegal. If he refuses to pay child maintenance, you can sue him for it."

She laughs like it's the funniest joke in the world. "Oh, I can't afford a lawyer. Your nails are all done, sweetie, we're just gonna moisturise, and then you're good to go."

"Thank you," I rasp. As she reaches for a bottle of lotion and warms some between her hands, I think of the letter again. I hate the idea that something X has touched is in my house. I'm not even safe from him here.

I like you better in white.

"Oh, oops!" I jump as Nin turns too suddenly, knocking over the bottle of lotion. For a moment, I just sit there, frozen, staring at the lotion spilling over my bare thigh. Onto my carpet. Some even splatters on my bedsheets.

And then I just completely lose it.

"WHAT ARE YOU DOING?" I shout, my voice spiralling up. Fear is bolting through me, and I stagger upright. "LOOK WHAT YOU DID!"

I rub at the lotion on my leg, trying to wipe it off, but it just buffs into my skin. Nin grabs for the bottle, babbling apologies, but she just knocks it over. I watch as it spills onto my floor, shining stickily on my carpet. I'm going to be sick.

My mouth opens. "GET OUT!" I shout. "IT'S *EVERYWHERE*! WH-WHAT HAVE YOU *DONE?* I—"

Hands clamp down on my shoulders, and I gasp as Matt appears and unceremoniously shoves me out of the room, into my walk-in closet. He pulls the door shut behind us, but I can still hear Nin starting to cry in the next room. Slamming his hand on the light switch, he stares me down. He looks furious, his jaw clenched, nostrils flared.

"WHAT THE *FUCK* IS WRONG WITH YOU?" He roars. I open my mouth, but he interrupts me. "For God's sake, I don't know why I expected any different. You're just like all the others! A little spoiled rich girl who thinks just because she has money, she can treat other people like *shit*."

I don't know what to say. My mind is running at fifty miles an hour. I don't know what just happened. I don't understand it. I don't know why I got so scared—

I shove Matt off me. "Go away."

He takes a step back, fuming. "What? What could she *possibly* have done, to make you go off at her like that?"

"She… she spilt the lotion—"

"She's barely making enough money to eat!" He bellows. "She works three jobs to support her kids, who she never even gets to see! You earn five times her yearly salary just by making a bloody sponsored social media post, so don't you *dare* shout at her like she's worth less than you!"

His blue eyes burn into mine with such raw, utter hatred that I can't breathe right. "Get *out!*" I suddenly scream, grabbing the closest object to hand—a fluffy pink pom pom bag—and throwing it at his head. He ducks it easily, scowling at me, then turns and leaves, slamming the closet door behind him. I can hear Nin's muffled sobs through the door, and his low, soothing tone as he speaks to her.

I drop to the floor. Tears prick my eyes. I'm shaking all over. I'm *scared*, more scared than I've been since I was sixteen years old. I feel like I'm going mad.

Don't break down, I tell myself firmly. *Don't break down. You can't.*

I take a few deep breaths, then get up and force myself to keep getting ready. I wipe the sticky lotion off my skin, touch up my makeup, slip into my silver flapper dress. When I first tried it on, I thought it was glitzy and sexy, but now, I don't *want* to be sexy. I feel naked as a slug. I wish I could just wrap myself up in a coat and sunglasses and fade into the background.

There's a gentle tap on the door. I open it to see Kenta, dressed in a neat black suit. Instead of his usual gentle smile, his face is frozen and hard. Of course it is. I just reduced his sweet sixty-year-old neighbour to tears. He probably hates me. "Are you ready to leave?" He asks coldly.

Swallowing hard, I nod, smoothing down the skirt of my dress and picking up my clutch.

I don't know how I'm going to make it through tonight.

CHAPTER 13
BRIAR

Cameras flash around us as the car stops outside the gala. Matt steps out into the road first and stiffly offers me his hand. I swing my legs around, careful not to flash my underwear, and let him help me out onto the street. Photographers crowd around me, jabbering questions. Behind them is a press pit; a long row of reporters from various news outlets, standing next to their cameramen. I invited as many stations as possible to get word of the charity out. Right now, though, I'm starting to regret that.

I still feel shaky and odd. I spent the whole car ride trying to calm down my whirling thoughts. My freakout in the bedroom is playing over and over and over in my head.

Matt goes to push through the crowd, and I grab his sleeve, tugging him back. "Give me your arm," I mutter.

He looks at me like I'm a lunatic. "What?"

"Your arm. Did you pass kindergarten? It's this thing." I poke his bicep through the thick fabric of his suit jacket.

I have to admit, he looks incredible in his new outfit. Michel fitted him out in a navy tuxedo with black lapels and a matching tie.

The clothes mould perfectly to his body, and the colour makes his eyes look inky-blue. Before I screamed at her, Nin did something to his hair, styling it with gel so it flops fashionably over his forehead. He'd look like the picture-perfect Hollywood boyfriend, if he wasn't glaring daggers at me. Slowly, he offers me his elbow, and I wrap my hand around it, giving him a subtle tug towards the rose-covered archway that leads to the garden party. As we step forward, the closest journalist steps forward, pushing her microphone into my face.

"Not now," I say through gritted teeth.

Matt frowns as we walk past her towards the entrance. Glen and Kenta follow us at a distance, melting away into the shadows. Neither of them said a word to me on the ride here. Even Glen wouldn't meet my eyes. "Isn't the whole point of tonight that you talk to the press?" His voice is dripping with disdain.

"Later," I say. I need a drink before I can face that. "Let's talk to guests, first. I need to thank them for coming."

"I don't have anything to say to any of these people."

"Then scowl and ignore them all," I mutter. "People will think we're a match made in heaven."

He gives me an annoyed look. I ignore it, pulling him through the archway and into the garden. I look around, admiring my work.

The event took months to perfect. I booked out a sprawling private garden on an old Tudor estate, full of plum trees and big, carved bushes. Fairy lights and streams of soft, translucent fabric are strung through the trees, giving the whole place a whimsical, dream-like effect. On a small raised stage, a string quartet is playing a classical version of Taylor Swift's *Wildest Dreams*. Behind them is the only evidence that tonight is a charity event: a single, tasteful poster announcing the name *Help for the Homeless*. There are a handful of influencers taking selfies next to it. I sigh.

Yes, I understand the irony of rich people coming together to drink thousand-dollar bottles of champagne to raise money for homeless children. Unfortunately, this is just how celebrities work. They want to be *seen* donating. If I just sent all the invitees a link to the GoFundMe page, it would go straight into their spam folders. This event is a spectacle. It's a place to *be*. It cost over ten grand to set up, but the tickets are fifteen hundred quid a pop, and we have hundreds of guests. Add in the donations we've already received, and we're looking at over a million pounds earned in one night. Plus an immense amount of media coverage. The profit is worth it, but *God,* it feels tasteless to be splashing out on caviar and ice sculptures when the kids we're trying to help are dying on the streets.

Matt is silent as we trail through the clusters of people chattering quietly, glittering in their fancy dresses and expensive earrings. Most of them step up to speak with me, politely thanking me for the invitation and unashamedly looking Matt up and down. I nod and answer all of their questions, but I feel like I'm in a haze. My mind is back in my bedroom. I reach out to shake someone's hand, and my silver nails sparkle under the fairy lights. Embarrassment scrunches my insides.

God. I was *awful* to that poor woman. I made her *cry.*

A man in a white suit passes by, holding a silver tray of canapés. He offers one to both of us, and Matt waves him away, looking irritated.

"Caviar?" He asks me. "Wouldn't Tesco Value baked beans be more appropriate?"

"Shut up."

"Where are all the homeless kids, exactly?" He asks loudly, looking around. "The party is supposedly for them; don't you think they'd enjoy the canapés and the live music?"

"You think it would be better to invite some?" I mutter. "They'd be used as props for everybody's social media posts. It would be dehumanising. They're better off just getting the money."

His mouth twists.

Irritation flicks through me. "Look, can you please just tell me what your problem with famous people is? I get that you think we're all spoiled idiots, but we're actually trying to do something good, here." He doesn't respond. I scowl. *"Tell me.* What was your 'bad experience' with a celeb? Because right now, you're just acting like an asshole for no reason."

He shoots me a glare. *"I'm* acting like an asshole? That's funny; I don't think I've made any poor people cry today."

Heat flushes to my cheeks. I ignore it. *"Tell me."*

"Fine." We float past a crowd of drunk footballers. One of them staggers towards me, and Matt puts a hand on my back, glaring at him until he walks off again. "On our last celebrity job, the girl was obsessed with seducing me. It was like her own personal challenge. She was always grabbing me, trying to sit in my lap. Do you have any idea how hard it is to escort someone through a crowd of paparazzi when they keep trying to stick their hands down your pants?"

"I've not personally had the pleasure. I'm usually the escortee." Although I get the attempted hands down my pants pretty much every time I leave the house. A lot of people think that touching celebrity genitals is a massive achievement, consensual or not.

He nods, scanning a nearby group of actors. "She didn't care that I didn't actually want to sleep with her. She was used to getting whatever she wanted, and she wanted me, so she figured she could just take me. She thought, since she was paying me, she owned me. My opinion didn't matter." He glares at a guest shoving her phone into a waiter's hand, knocking over a full tray of drinks as she asks him to take a picture of her. "That's what I don't like. The entitlement."

I smile blandly at a passing acquaintance. "What happened?" I ask through gritted teeth.

He's quiet for a second. "One night, she kissed me in the back of the limo. I'd had enough. I quit on the spot, and she was so mad I'd rejected her that she called her parents, whining and crying, saying I'd forced myself on her."

My heart drops. "Oh my God, Matt."

He nods. "Luckily, she forgot there was CCTV in the car. If there hadn't been, I wouldn't be here today." He glances across at me. "You can see the tape, if you don't believe me."

I stop walking, gripping his arm. "I'm sorry that happened to you," I tell him honestly. "No one should be sexually harassed at work."

He pushes my hand off him. "No one should be verbally abused at work," he says quietly. I feel like I've swallowed a stone.

Before I can respond, a photographer steps into our path, brandishing a huge camera. I'm jumpier than usual tonight, and his sudden appearance startles me.

"Aren't you supposed to be in the press pit?" I ask sharply.

The photographer blinks, taken aback. "I'm the event photographer. You hired me to take pictures for social media?"

Oh. Right. "Sorry," I mumble. "Sorry, I didn't mean to snap. I'm just... nervous."

He grins. "No problem, Miss Saint. You look beautiful this evening." He wiggles his camera. "Can I get a shot of you with your new man?"

I glance up at Matt. He shuts his eyes briefly, then bends, brushing his lips against my cheek. The camera flashes, and Matt's mouth is gone before I can even really register what's happening. All I'm left with is a warm face and the lingering scent of lemony aftershave.

"Gorgeous." The man says, checking his camera. "You two make a lovely couple." He floats away to snap some shots of the band.

"So, is there a reason you think it's okay to treat your employees like shit?" Matt asks conversationally.

I close my eyes briefly, then pull away from the crowd and make a beeline for the buffet table lining one side of the garden. It's laid out with delicate crystal plates stacked with finger foods. An ice sculpture of a swan is melting and glittering in the middle of the table, surrounded by flutes of sparkling champagne.

"What's he going to do with that photo?" Matt asks, coming up behind me. "I'm not going to be plastered over some teenage girl's bedroom wall, am I?"

"You really think you're that attractive?" I mutter, nabbing a glass of champagne and tossing it back. God. I really don't feel good. My skin is numb, and my head feels swimmy. I wonder what would happen if I passed out. Would Matt catch me, or just let me fall and walk right over my unconscious body? I put the empty glass down with a shaky hand, and reach for another. "D-do you want a drink?"

Matt doesn't reply. I glance up at him. He's frowning, staring into the middle distance. "Matt?"

"That's it," he mutters. My stomach twists. Oh my God. Has he just seen X? I turn to follow his gaze, but all I see is trees.

"That's what?"

"I remember why you look so familiar." He huffs a sudden laugh. "Glen had a picture of you, years ago. He carried it in his pack for a whole tour."

My blood pressure spikes. "Are you serious?"

He closes his mouth so quickly his jaw clicks. "I shouldn't have told you that."

"*Okay*, then." I honestly don't have the emotional bandwidth to process that information right now. I'll get to it later. I take a deep breath and lift my glass to my lips.

"B!" Someone exclaims behind me. "Is that you?!"

I freeze, a wave of cold flowing through my body. No. There's no way. There's only one person in the world who's ever called me *B*, and he is the last man I want to see right now.

Maybe this is my karma for being such an asshole.

Slowly, I force myself to turn around and look into the face of my ex-costar, Thomas Petty.

CHAPTER 14
BRIAR

He looks so different from the gawky teenage boy I remember. He's filled out a lot, and his brown curly hair has been cut short, slicked back with gel. Either puberty has been exceptionally kind to him, or he's invested in some jaw filler.

The fairy lights twinkle in his eyes and set a soft glow over his skin as he smiles at me tentatively. I feel a pang in my chest. The last time I had a proper conversation with him, I was sixteen years old, sobbing on his doorstep, begging him to make a statement to the press.

It's odd. I always thought if I ever had to speak to him again, I'd be mad. But instead, a wave of longing washes over me. He used to be my best friend, before he utterly ruined my life. I've never had a friend since. Not one friend in the thirteen years since I lost him.

How depressing.

A ruffle goes around the crowd. I can already hear the whispers starting as people see the two of us together. As I stand there stupidly, a nearby model turns to her friend and loudly hisses, "Isn't he the guy she cheated on? Think they still have beef?"

"Thom," I croak. "What are you doing here? I thought you lived in LA, now."

He shrugs easily. "I'll be heading back tomorrow. I'm on a business trip, and I didn't have anything better to do tonight. Hope you don't mind me dropping by."

Yes, I want to say. *I do mind. Get the fuck out.*

"Just make sure to donate," I mutter.

He laughs, his shoulders easing slightly, and grabs a flute of champagne off the table. "Sure thing. And who's this?" He turns to Matt with a broad smile. "You're dating, now?"

Matt practically transforms next to me. One minute, he's silent and stoic, and the next, he's the picture of friendliness. He clasps Thom's hand between both of his, grinning.

"The name's Matt Carter. It's great to meet you, man. Briar's told me all about you."

I stare at him.

Thom snorts. "I doubt you'll have a very good impression of me, then. What was it you said to *Goss* magazine?" He shoots me an amused look. "That I ate you out like a Saint Bernard?"

Matt waves him off before I can respond. "She told me you two used to be friends on the *Hollywood House* set."

Thom blinks. "Yeah," he says slowly. "We were. B and I were really good friends." He shakes his head slightly. "What do you do, again?"

Matt's smile gets wider. "I work in weapons manufacture, mate."

Thom sputters on his champagne. "Excuse me?"

"Military stuff, mostly. Guns, bombs, rocket launchers—you name it, we make it. Huh, princess?" Matt takes my hand and looks down at me, his blue eyes twinkling. I don't say anything, weirded out by his odd behaviour. He just laughs. "Sorry, sorry. I know you hate when I talk about work. Tonight is about you, baby."

Then he puts a hand on my jaw, tilts my chin up gently, and bends to give me a kiss.

He doesn't actually kiss me; he just traces his lips over my cheek, nuzzling into me. But with his hand blocking Thom's view, it should look to him like he's just grabbed me and snogged me, right on the lips.

Electricity forks through me like lightning as his slightly stubbled cheek rasps against mine, and I breathe in a huge lungful of his warm, lemony cologne. My mouth falls open, my lips accidentally brushing the side of his throat. I can feel his pulse battering like a jack-hammer under the sensitive skin. He freezes for a moment, then slowly pulls back. As I blink stars out of my eyes, he grabs Thom's hand and gives it another firm shake. "Listen, we've got to go, but it's good meeting you, man. We should hang out sometime."

"Um. Yeah." Thom gives me one more glance, and then takes the hint and leaves, disappearing around the corner. Matt keeps holding my hand until he's out of sight. I notice several people in the crowd around us lowering their phone cameras disappointedly. They were clearly hoping for some kind of bust-up.

For a second, I feel absurdly grateful. It would've been so easy for Matt to drop the act, or just stand there silently as I fumbled through an awkward interaction. Instead, he maintained his cover perfectly, just so I would look good. It was uncharacteristically nice of him.

Kenta steps forward behind me, and I jump. I hadn't realised he was so close. Matt drops my hand like it's a bit of nuclear waste, wiping it on his jacket. "Petty seems benign."

"Agreed," Kenta says. "He didn't show any strong emotional reaction when you kissed her."

"Well, that's one down, I suppose," Matt mutters.

I look between the two men. "Wait, what? What just happened?

"Petty was on the list of potential subjects," Matt grinds out, sounding bored. "Your scorned, cheated-on first love. I needed to speak with him face-to-face to assess the risk he posed."

"That..." My head rushes, trying to keep up.

He turns cold eyes on me. "What, you thought I was just trying to make you look good?"

I open my mouth, then close it again. My brain is throbbing. "I didn't cheat on him."

"So? The whole world thinks you did. And that's all that matters, right?" He waves a hand around the garden. "It's like this whole event. Everything is just for show. A bunch of obscenely rich people coming together once a year to have a damn *party* to help the homeless. For God's sake—" He points at the melting ice sculpture. "How much did all of this *cost*? These drinks you're serving could be paying for those kids to have a roof over their heads!"

I can't even argue, because he's right. He's right, and I hate it too. "It's not about the event, it's about the money it brings in—"

I trail off as something catches my eye. Standing in the corner of the garden, illuminated by a paper lantern hanging from one of the trees, is a man in a grey hoodie. He's facing away from me, talking to another guest, but immediately, my mind flashes back to the CCTV footage of X outside my house. He was wearing a hoodie. Black or grey, the police said. I can feel my heartbeat in my ears as a wave of anxiety rushes over me.

Oh God.

It's been a long time since I've had a panic attack. Years. I'd hoped that I was over them. I close my eyes, trying to keep my breathing steady, but I can't stop my chest tightening painfully. Crap.

I really don't know why people call it 'anxiety'. It doesn't feel like being anxious, it feels like I'm about to have a fucking stroke. My vision swims. All of the colours around me seem too bright. I rub my fingers together, but they're so numb I can't feel anything at all.

Forcing myself to ignore the rising sensations, I look around, scanning the crowds for the man in the hoodie. He's gone. Oh, God. I spin, but I can't see him anywhere. The shadows behind the trees seem unnaturally dark and deep.

Matt grabs my arm, and I flinch. "Shouldn't we go talk to the press, then?" He asks loudly. "I want to get out of here as soon as possible."

I don't answer. Kenta frowns, looking at me closely. "Are you okay, Briar?"

"I—" I rub my face. A little boy I don't recognise runs past, slamming into my hip. He smiles up at me apologetically, holding up a napkin and a sharpie. I can't pick out what he's saying from the noise around me. I'm gasping for air. I'm going to faint. Oh, God, I can't faint *here*, with all of the cameras and the press and other celebrities, I can't. It's too much. I can't do it anymore. I can't *breathe*. Forcing back tears, I slip away from the kid and stagger through the crowd, making a beeline for the nearest bathroom.

CHAPTER 15
MATT

"**W**hat the Hell is wrong with her?" I ask, staring after Briar as she shoves the kid away and storms towards the main building, heading for the gold bathroom sign.

Kenta bends and says a few calm words to the child, who looks like he's about to start crying, then gently hands him off to the nearest server.

Anger rips through me, heating my veins. I hate all of this. I look around the whimsical, pretty party. The sky is darkening, and the band is starting to fire up. Everywhere around me, billionaires are getting drunk and dancing.

This isn't what I wanted to do with my life. Never. The reason I joined the army was to protect innocents from people in power. People who hurt others, just because they can. Whether it's my neighbour getting bullied to the point of breakdown by Briar, or a corrupt police force beating citizens for the fun of it, it all stems from the same place. Evil. It's *evil*. And I'm sick of it. I don't want to protect someone thoughtless and selfish and cruel.

I've been on the wrong end of that cruelty for far, far too long to sympathise.

Kenta straightens, and we head towards the bathroom to stand guard by the doors. "Is she… okay?" He asks, lowering his voice. "She's behaving oddly."

"No, she's behaving completely normally. Every single magazine and tabloid and news outlet will tell you so."

He shoots me a look. "She's under a lot of stress."

Typical Kenta. Always the diplomat. "Do *you* reduce minimum wage workers to tears when you're stressed?"

He presses his lips together unhappily. "Will Nin be okay?"

I sigh. "She's dealt with worse in her life. She's mostly just worried that Briar will tweet about her, or leave a bad review, and she'll never work again." Kenta's jaw clenches. "We negotiated an open-ended contract," I remind him. "Maybe we should just terminate."

I expect him to protest, but he says nothing, watching the bathroom door with steel in his eyes. He's just as pissed off as me.

Glen comes to join us from his perimeter check, and we all stand stupidly outside the bathrooms. Five minutes pass, then ten. A tipsy-looking woman in incredibly high heels tries to squeeze past us, and I politely inform her that the toilets are out of order.

She snorts. "I'm sure. What, is she doing lines in there, or something?"

She totters off, and Kenta checks his watch. "Someone should check on her. She's been a while."

"Maybe she's taking mirror selfies," I offer. "Or texting her girl-friends about the manicurist who dared to knock a lotion bottle over her twenty-grand designer bedsheets."

Glen pushes himself off the wall. "I'll check," he mutters, heading inside the bathroom. My thoughts go back to Nin. Maybe I should get her a gift basket, or something. A *sorry my awful boss made you cry* sympathy gift basket. I pull out my phone to make a note.

"CARTER," Glen roars. My stomach drops. Kenta's already pushing past me into the bathroom. When I step in behind him, I pull up short.

"Oh my fucking God."

Briar is sprawled on the floor of a cubicle, her cheek against the tile. Her blonde hair is spilling over the dirty floor, and she's gasping for breath, every exhale coming out as a moan. Her fingers are clawed and spasming, and there's makeup running down her face. Glen's kneeling by her side, a hand on her heaving back. He looks up at us. "I don't know what's wrong with her."

I drop to my knees next to her, sliding my fingers over her throat to find her pulse. It's thrumming unhealthily fast.

"Glen, get the door. Briar, look at me." She focuses on me. There's raw *terror* in her eyes, and for a moment, it sends me reeling back to another place.

A knife catching the light. Glen's horrified eyes staring at me.

I shake off the feeling. "Speak."

She closes her eyes again, curling into herself, panting.

"She has allergies, right?" I ask Kenta, who's picked up her bag and started rooting through it. "Could it be anaphylaxis?"

"To mould. It shouldn't be this severe, she's not prescribed an epi pen."

"Overdose?" I squeeze her shoulder. "Briar. Open your eyes. Did you take something?"

She shakes her head, still gasping.

"Do you hurt anywhere? Are you hurting, princess?"

Another head shake. I'm starting to panic.

"Did she drink anything?" Kenta asks, still rummaging in her clutch. "Could she have been drugged?"

"A glass of champagne. I didn't watch it getting poured, she picked it up off a buffet table. I—"

"Wait," he interrupts me, pulling a tiny pink pill box out of her purse. He flips the lid, examining the contents. "Benzo."

"Are you having a *panic attack*?" I ask her, incredulous.

I've seen a lot of clients have panic attacks; generally, when someone is in enough danger to require a 24/7 security team, their lives are pretty anxiety-inducing. It would normally be my first guess in a situation like this. But Briar has done absolutely nothing to suggest she's even capable of feeling *nervous*, let alone panicky.

She nods jerkily.

"Okay. Okay. Kenta, get her some water. Briar, you're hyperventilating. Slow down your breathing."

She rolls her eyes, like *yeah, duh*.

"Sit." I help her sit up, propping her up with my shoulder, then take her sweaty hand and put it on my chest, breathing exaggeratedly. "Inhale. Hold it. Then exhale. That's it. Good girl."

"I'm…" she chokes, twisting her fingers weakly in the front of my shirt, "Not… a dog."

"It would probably be easier for you to breathe if you stopped talking back," I advise. "Come on. Inhale. Hold it. Exhale."

She glares at me, but tries to do as I say. I breathe with her for the next couple of minutes, and her breaths slowly get smoother and deeper. Eventually, she pushes her hand off me, sitting upright.

"There we are." I stroke back some hair sticking to her sweaty forehead. "There you are. Can you talk, princess?"

"Yeah," she rasps, taking the water bottle Kenta offers her. "Thanks." She tries to open it, but her hands are still shaking. I take it off her and remove the cap.

"This happen a lot?"

"Since I was sixteen. N-not much, anymore." She closes her eyes. "God. I'm so dizzy."

My stomach twists. "Let's get you your meds." I reach for her pill box, shaking out a tablet, but she shakes her head. "You don't want it?"

"Makes me feel gross." She wipes her eyes, smudging mascara onto her cheeks. "S'only for emergencies."

"You collapsed in a public bathroom. What exactly do you think qualifies as an emergency?"

"Worse than this." She takes a sip of water, her hand shaking so much she spills droplets onto her silver dress. "I can handle this."

"Princess, it's okay. You don't have to fight through everything. You're allowed to have some help." For some reason, I find myself reaching out and taking her hand. Yes, I'm mad at the girl; but I can't stand to see her like this, shaky and struggling to breathe. Her fingers are cramped up and frozen solid, and I start to slowly massage them, like I can encourage the blood back into her extremities.

She hesitates for a while, her chest heaving, staring at the pill— then gives a tiny nod. Kenta holds it up to her mouth for her, and she swallows it down with a shaky gulp of water, sagging against the wall and closing her eyes. I soon feel the muscles in her hands unclasp and loosen as her breath evens out some more.

"Good girl," I say, my voice low. "Let's go home."

"Don't call me *good girl.*" She shakes her head. "Still have interviews."

Kenta kneels down in front of her. "Sweetheart, you're sick."

"I'm not *sick.*"

"You can barely stand."

"Th-then I'll do them sitting down. Find me a lawn chair, or something." She pushes me off her and forces herself upright. Kenta and I watch, gobsmacked, as she totters over to the mirror, pouts at her smeared makeup, and pulls a mascara wand out of her bag. "God. I look like a fucking raccoon. I didn't even cry," she mutters, rubbing under her eyes.

I sit back on my haunches. "Briar, you really should go home and rest. You're not in any state to go out there and perform."

"I didn't hire you to give me health advice," she bites out. "I hired you to make me feel safe."

Kenta and I both go still. The reprimand is pretty clear. We found her lying with her head next to a toilet, so scared she couldn't breathe. We didn't make her feel safe tonight.

"Briar," Kenta says softly. "You know that your behaviour will never affect how we do our work. Just because we're having a disagreement—"

"I don't want to talk." She orders. "These meds always knock me out. I have fifteen minutes b-before I'm a zombie, and I have twenty stations left to talk to. C-come on." She marches out of the bathroom, wobbling slightly in her heels. I go to put an arm around her shoulder, to steady her, and she flinches violently away. "Please don't touch me."

I step back. She half-staggers over to the press line, where the camera crews are all set up, and waves to the closest journalist. "I'm ready. Come interview me," she calls.

For a moment, the guy stares at her in shock; but he recovers smoothly, sticking his microphone in his face. "Miss Briar Saint. You organised this event tonight. Tell me, what does the subject of child homelessness mean to you?"

"I don't think children should be homeless," she mutters.

He blinks at her directness. "And yet you're one of the highest-earning actresses of the year. How do you reconcile your values with your income?"

"I donate my income."

Irritation crosses the man's face. "You know, many people are accusing you of using charity events like these as a PR move to boost public opinion. What's your response to such accusations?"

"Does it matter?" She asks flatly. "Money is money." A shiver wracks through her body, and Glen puts his jacket over her slim shoulders. She pauses for a second, then turns her face into it, like she's smelling his cologne. "Thanks," she says to him, and he just nods, concern tightening his face.

She talks with the guy for a few minutes, then moves on to the next. And the next.

They're not good interviews. In fact, they're completely disastrous. Her anxiety picks back up as more and more people surround her. I see her eyes darting through the crowd, like she thinks someone is going to jump out at her. Her breathing gets choppy again—she keeps having to pause in the middle of words to gasp, and her eyes are huge and glazing over with the meds. More than once, she has to ask an interviewer to repeat a question five or six times, because she can't focus on what they're saying. It's torture, watching her fall apart, over and over again, as she struggles to keep her composure.

"Jesus," I hear a cameraman mutter behind me, as she moves on to the next crew. "This is a charity event. She's out of her head."

"I mean, it'll make good headlines," the reporter points out. "You get the bit she almost fell?"

I grit my teeth and stride up to Kenta, who's hovering a step behind Briar, watching her intently. "They think she's high."

He winces, putting a hand on her arm. "Briar, I really think we should go."

"Three more," she mumbles.

"They think you're on something," I tell her flatly.

"I *am* on something."

"The headlines tomorrow aren't going to be pretty."

She snorts. "They never are, when they're about me."

"But—"

She looks up at me. "Don't you get it? This isn't about my reputation, it's about bringing attention to the cause. If I have to look like an idiot in the process, so be it. I've looked like an idiot ever since I got into this industry at thirteen. I may as well raise some money while I do it."

I snap my mouth shut. She makes it through two more interviews before she starts wavering on her feet. Glen grabs at her before she trips and falls, pulling her into his body.

"Okay," he says softly. "We need to go, lass. You're barely making sense."

This time she doesn't argue, letting us bundle her out of the event and towards the car. Paparazzi spread across the road, shouting at her, snapping pictures. I scowl at them, but she ignores them all, keeping her head high until Kenta pushes her gently into the backseat. The driver starts the car, and she slumps back against the leather upholstery as we pull away from the street.

Before we even hit the road, Glen's phone rings. He picks it up, then winces. "Hi, Mrs Chen," he says. I close my eyes. Nin. "Yes, I did hear what happened. I'm very sorry. She's... having a bad day." He glances at Briar, who seems to shrink into herself. "Oh, no, I'm sure she wouldn't do that. Please don't cry. Yes, I'll speak to her, if that's what you want. But really, I don't think there's anything to worry about."

He spends the rest of the ride soothing Nin while we all sit in awkward silence. When he finally hangs up, Briar rubs a hand over her face. Her cheeks are bright red.

"Jesus. Look. Can you bring her to the house?"

I startle. "What?"

"The house. I want to talk to her."

"I don't think that's a good idea," Kenta starts.

She shrugs. "Fine. I'll go drop in on her, then."

"You will not," I growl. "You're going *home*."

She wilts a bit, like she's too tired to argue the point. "We can Skype, I guess. I need to apologise to her. I'd rather do it face to face."

The car pulls up in her driveway, and we flank her as she stumbles back inside her house. She kicks off her high heels, slips out of Glen's jacket, then holds out her hand to me. "Her number, please."

I frown. "If you're just calling her to take it out on her some more—"

Her eyes flash. "Give. Me. Her. Number."

I sigh, texting the contact details to her. She thanks me quietly, then heads into her bedroom and shuts the door.

CHAPTER 16
BRIAR

After I hang up the phone, I just sit in my bed, stewing.

I feel awful. Absolutely awful. Matt was right: I acted like a spoiled little rich bitch, today. I hurt someone.

I sigh, leaning back against the headboard. The medication I took feels thick and clunky in my veins, fogging up my thoughts. I've got a throbbing headache, and I just want to go to sleep. But I *can't* sleep, because I can't handle being in this room anymore. I rub the back of my neck, my skin prickling, and let my eyes jump between the shadows, checking the wardrobe, and the bathroom door, and the bookshelves.

There's a light tap on the door. Glen sticks his head in, running his eyes around the room. "Just on my rounds." He turns to me, noting my red eyes. "Oh, sweetheart."

"I'm not a sweetheart," I mutter, guilt choking me. "I'm a total bitch."

I did what I could to apologise to Nin. I even asked one of my lawyers to help chase up her child maintenance arrears. But I can't really properly apologise, because I still don't know *what the Hell happened.*

I think back to the moment when she knocked over the bottle. It was a split-second reaction—one minute I was fine, and the next, I was possessed. The sudden lightning bolt of fear that flooded through me scared the shit out of me. Even thinking about it makes my breathing pick up. I close my eyes and take a few steadying breaths. I don't know what's wrong with me.

When I open my eyes, Glen is still in the doorway, studying me with serious grey eyes. "Do you want to talk about it, lass?" He asks, his voice so gentle, I want to cry. "It could help to get it off your chest."

I sigh. I don't want to talk about it. I want to curl up in a ball and die of embarrassment. But I know that I owe the guys an explanation.

Pulling myself together, I nod, sliding out of bed and following Glen back into the lounge. Both Kenta and Matt are sitting on the sofa, talking quietly over a laptop. Kenta smiles when he sees me, but Matt's eyes are cold.

I take a deep breath and cross my arms. "Matt," I say firmly. "I'm so sorry about your friend. You brought her here to help, and I was awful to her."

His lips press together. "Well. She called and said you'd offered to pay for her lawyer. So, thanks for that, I guess."

I nod, sitting on the end of the sofa, away from the guys.

"It did seem a little out of character for you," Kenta says tentatively.

I snort. "Did it? I thought it was perfectly in-character. You're talking to Britain's Biggest Bitch, remember?"

"That's not how you've come across to us the last few days," Kenta replies. "Did something happen that upset you?"

I'm quiet for a long time, my heartbeat pounding in my ears. Because the truth is, deep down, I *do* know what freaked me out so much. I just don't want to admit it. "It was the lotion," I force out eventually.

"You got upset because she spilled lotion," Matt's voice is flat.

Anger flares up in me. "Can you not judge me for *ten seconds?*" I snap. "You made your mind up about me before you even met me. I'm just a villain to you. A superficial bitch. That's all you ever want to see me as." I rub my eyes. "For God's sake, a strange man *wanked in my bed.* I rolled into it. Got it all up my legs. I woke up in a puddle of a stranger's semen." My throat tightens. "I've never felt so terrified in my life. I thought I'd been drugged and raped. And now, even though it's done, I can't stop thinking about it. It's always in my head. So when she spilt that lotion, all over my legs, and my sheets, and it looked exactly the same, I just—panicked." I swallow thickly. "And then I was so embarrassed, I lashed out. Made it her fault, instead of mine. It was a defence response, I guess. But it was an awful thing to do. And I hate that I upset her so much."

There's a few moments of silence. I can't make myself look at any of them. "As for what happened at the event…" I wince. "I'm sorry. It's been a long time since I had a panic attack, so I didn't think to warn you. My anxiety gets a lot worse when I don't sleep."

"Why haven't you been sleeping?" Matt asks, his voice strained. "Have we been making too much noise at night?"

For some reason, I start to laugh. And then I just keep laughing. I laugh and laugh, until there are tears rolling down my cheeks. "No," I gasp. "It's not you. It's not you at all." I suck in a deep breath, trying to stop the hiccuping in my chest, but I can't. It gets stronger and stronger, until I'm not laughing, I'm outright crying. The built-up terror of the last week finally rushes up and washes over me, and I cover my face as I start to shake with sobs.

"Briar—" Kenta starts, his voice soft.

"I can't do this anymore," I whisper. "I'm falling apart. I see people, everywhere. Shadows in the mirror, in the bushes, behind all of my furniture. My bedroom feels unsafe. No matter how much I wash my sheets, my bed feels dirty. Whenever I go out, there's people watching me, shouting my name, taking pictures, following me, and I have *no idea* if he's there. If he's one of them. I can't sleep, I can't eat. It's like the walls are just closing in on me."

"Christ," someone mutters. I feel the sofa cushions sink, and inhale the warm scent of spice as Kenta sits next to me. He puts a cautious hand on my back. When I lean into it, he starts rubbing smooth circles between my shoulders. "Briar," he says quietly. "I am so sorry."

"W-why?" I spit. "You haven't done anything wrong."

"We have. Briar, look at me." He crooks a firm finger under my chin, directing my face up until our eyes meet. His expression is serious. "I'm *sorry*," he repeats. "We should've noticed that you were feeling this way. The psychological effects of being stalked can be very severe, and they're incredibly normal. I've got a background in psychology, for Christ's sake. I should have realised that you were struggling." I gulp. He sighs, patting my back. "Up until now, you acted so strong, I thought you weren't bothered by the threats."

I stare at him like he's speaking another language. "How could I *possibly* not be bothered by them?" I whisper. "What human being wouldn't be?"

He shakes his head, looking at his lap. "I'm sorry. It was incredibly negligent. You're right. We have been making assumptions about you based on what we've seen in the media. Which is disgusting."

I sniff, reaching for the tissue box on the coffee table. "It's not your job to be my therapist."

"It's our job to keep you safe," he impresses. "If you feel so unsafe that you're getting physically ill, then yes, we're not doing our jobs right." He pauses, thinking. "I have some literature which might be able to help."

"She doesn't need books, she needs a therapist," Matt says bluntly. He looks like he wants to hit something.

I wipe my cheeks off. "I know I do. I've already booked an appointment."

"That's great," Kenta soothes. "And what about right now? Is there anything we can do to make you feel safer, short term?"

I sigh. I know the answer straight away, but God, it's embarrassing. "Just... look, could one of you sleep with me?"

They all stare at me, speechless.

My cheeks stain, but I didn't get this far in my life by not asking when I wanted something. I cross my arms. "I mean, two of you are going to go sleep in the pool house, right? If one of you could just... come sleep in my bedroom with me. I keep feeling like someone's going to come in, and I won't wake up, and—"

"Who?" Kenta asks firmly. "Who do you want with you?"

My eyes flick to Glen. "You don't have to," I say. "This is pretty above your pay grade."

He stands. "You pay us to make you feel safe, lass," he rumbles, picking his way across the carpet. "C'mon. Get in."

He holds open my bedroom door, and I head back inside. The room is dark, cut through by moonlight, but the shadows don't seem as deep with Glen standing behind me like a guard dog. We're still for a moment, then I nod to the bed.

"You can undress," I tell him. "You don't have to sleep in your trousers."

He hesitates, then slowly unbuttons his shirt. As he shucks it off, I see more scars striping up the skin of his upper arms. I turn to the bed just as he reaches for his belt, flipping up the covers and sliding under the quilt. There's a zipping sound behind me, then the rumple of cloth as Glen's pants fall to the ground. I feel the mattress dip as he climbs into bed next to me. I lie there for a few seconds, my heart beating in my throat.

I don't remember the last time I slept with a man. I'm not a massive fan of sex, and when I do have it, the last thing I want is the guy sticking around afterwards. But right now, here in the dark, the feeling of having him so close is better than I could ever have imagined.

"Is this okay?" Glen asks quietly.

I nod, rolling a bit closer. I'm so close that I can smell him. His deep foresty scent curls through my veins, softening my thoughts far better than the Xanax did. For the first time in a week, my brain finally gives in to the heavy, pressing exhaustion, slowing down and whirring to a stop. I curl up, putting my head by his pillow, and let the steady sound of his breathing lull me to sleep.

CHAPTER 17
GLEN

I lie as still as possible, watching a thin beam of sunlight slide through the room. As the minutes go by, the strip of yellow light moves slowly across the carpet, then the bed, until it's finally cutting a line over Briar's cheek, lighting up her hair in bright strands of gold.

I've barely slept all night. I couldn't. I felt too bad.

We screwed up yesterday.

I remember the raw fear in Briar's face when I found her sprawled on the bathroom floor, and suppress a shudder. We've been doing this far too long to not notice when a client is in distress. It was a real shock to see her so fragile last night; an even bigger shock when she asked me to stay with her. I assumed she'd pick one of the other two. Kenta would be the obvious option, and even though she and Matt fight, it's obvious that they're attracted to each other. I don't know why any woman would invite some giant, scarred Hulk into her bed. But she picked me. She didn't even hesitate.

I don't understand it.

She stirs. Her plump lips part, and a soft breath flutters a strand of hair off her cheek. Slowly, her big eyes blink open, batting a few times before they focus on me.

"Morning," I mumble.

She stretches slowly, a soft noise escaping her lips as she rolls out her tight muscles. Great. I thought one advantage of staying up all night would be the lack of morning wood, but apparently, that's not going to happen.

"Morning," she murmurs, then slumps back onto the pillow, looking at me. Her eyes run over my face, and I'm suddenly aware of how close we are. Just a few inches apart. I can see every detail of her face: the soft, smooth skin, the long lashes, the tiny sprinkle of gold freckles across the bridge of her nose. I'm so enchanted it takes me a second to realise that she can see every detail of my face, too.

Shit.

I turn to look at the ceiling, but her hand suddenly flies out, catching my jaw. Everything in me goes still as the pads of her soft fingers rub into my stubble. "Why do you do that?" She whispers, her voice husky and low from sleep.

"Do what?"

She twists her head, showing me her cheek. "Turn away. You always hide your scar from me."

I frown. "I didn't know I was doing that."

"Sometimes, I think you don't. But you did, just then. I saw it on your face."

I shrug. "I assumed you wouldn't want to look at it, I suppose."

Her eyes narrow. "Well, I *do* want to look at it," she snips, tugging my jaw towards her. Her fingertips trace over my cheek, just a millimetre from touching me. "Can I touch?"

I can't speak. I give a tiny nod. Her fingers smooth over the scar, feeling the bumpy, ragged texture.

"Does it hurt?" She murmurs.

"No. Itches, sometimes."

"What happened?" I tense, and she shakes her head. "Sorry. I shouldn't have asked—"

"It's fine. On our last job, we were working counter-terrorism in…" I bite my lip. "A, uh, foreign country."

Her mouth twitches. "Confidential, is it?"

"Kind of. We were supposed to be doing recon, but our patrol got captured. The guys locked us up and tortured us for information."

She sucks in a breath and pushes closer, brushing her thumbs over my face. "They *cut* you?"

"Among other things." A shiver rolls up my spine as memories press into the back of my head. Dark, and black, and full of pain.

She must see it in my face, because she switches subjects. "Matt said that you used to carry a picture of me."

Shock rocks me. That *son of a bitch*. Why the Hell would he tell her that? I'd honestly prefer to discuss the torture. "One picture," I admit. "I'm sorry. With everything going on right now, that probably seems creepy."

"No," she whispers. "Things like that aren't creepy when you're a celeb. I had, like, twenty posters of Justin Timberlake in my bedroom when I was a teenager. I didn't apologise when I met him." She tucks some hair behind my ear. It's too short to stay there, so it falls out again. She tucks it back, over and over, until she's essentially just stroking my hair. I don't understand what's happening. "How did you get it?"

I rub my face. "A guy in our patrol, Damon, had a sister who worked as an editor for a magazine. She sent all of her issues to him. You were on the cover of one. I thought you were—beautiful, I guess. I couldn't stop looking at you. He noticed, thought it was hilarious, and ripped it out, stuck it over my bunk. At first it was a joke, but then, when we moved on, I just… couldn't bring myself to toss it. So I folded it up and kept it with me. It was like having a lucky charm."

"Huh." Her face is thoughtful. "So did you, like, jerk off over me, or what?"

My mouth falls open. "I…"

She laughs. "It's okay. It's sort of a given when you do lingerie shoots that people are gonna wank over the shots. And I'd much rather it be a lonely soldier in his barracks than some creepy stalker."

"I didn't, though," I say honestly.

"Hm?"

"I didn't—do that. Which probably makes it weirder." I run a hand through my hair. I'm shit with words, and there's really no way to put this without sounding completely deranged. "It wasn't a lingerie shot. It was a picture of you on the beach, wearing a white t-shirt and this ridiculous, huge floppy hat. You were holding an ice cream and smiling at the camera, and… I don't know. You were so beautiful. And it was so *ugly* down there. Some guys had girlfriends, or kids, or families that they were fighting for, but I didn't have any of that shit. But I could look at that picture of you and remember that beautiful things still existed in the world. Sunshine, and ice cream, and happy girls on beaches wearing floppy hats. It reminded me that that's what I was putting myself through Hell for. So that stuff could still exist."

She sits up slowly, her eyes wide. I grimace, heat rising to my face. I sound like a total creep. "I'm sorry. That must be—"

She cuts me off. "I think you're the most beautiful man I've ever seen."

I stare at her. It's a completely preposterous thing to say. "I'm not *beautiful*," I sputter.

"No?"

"No! I'm… people turn around and stare at me in the street. I make *babies* cry, I'm not *beautiful*—"

She cuts me off with a kiss.

For a second, I'm taken aback. She presses closer, running her tongue against my bottom lip, and I feel almost clumsy, like I'm on the back foot. But then she softens, her body melting against my front, and my hindbrain takes over. I wrap my hands around her hips and drag her into me, yanking her onto my lap. She keens as her pelvis hits mine, winding her thighs around my waist like a vice.

God. I've wanted this ever since I set eyes on Briar. Kissing her feels exactly how I imagined. Like sunshine, and beach days, and summer afternoons. Happiness glows through me, lighting me up inside. The kiss gets harder and rougher. Electricity sparks everywhere our skin brushes; I feel the rub of her cotton shirt against my skin, and the soft press of her tits through the fabric.

Her little hands slide up my bare chest, twisting into my chest hair, then wrapping around my neck. Her nails scrape up against the skin, and I can't stop the growl that falls out of my mouth. With every little shift of her hips against mine, I feel a throb of blood between my legs. I grind back up on her, and she gasps, reaching for the waistband of my boxers.

Shit. We're going way, way too fast.

"Briar." I shake my head, forcing myself to pull away. "Briar, stop."

She sits back and looks up at me with pink cheeks, then rolls her eyes. "Let me guess." She drops her voice. *"We canny do thes. It's against company policy, lassie. A'm sorry, it's just no' ethical."*

My lips curve. "I think it would only be considered unethical if we took advantage of the asset's vulnerability."

She snorts. "Good luck taking advantage of me, mate. I'd kick you in the nuts so hard your balls fell out of your mouth." She dips her head and starts nibbling on my throat, making my whole body jerk under her. *"So dinna fash yersel."*

"No, I just—" I reach up and wrap a hand in her hair. "Don't have protection."

She swears. "Me, neither. It's been a while." She purses her lips, thinking, then just shrugs. "Well, we'll just have to get creative," she breathes in my ear. "They must teach you how to improvise in the SAS, right? I'm sure you can work something out."

My heart skips a beat. I nod, putting a hand on her waist and flipping her onto her back, landing on top of her. My pulse is pounding in my ears. I can barely believe this is happening. Briar squeaks as her head thumps against the pillow—and then moans as I drag myself down her body, nudging my face under the hem of her sleep shirt.

CHAPTER 18
BRIAR

"Tell me you want this," Glen rasps, looking up at me from between my legs. His ruffled hair brushes against my thighs. I close my eyes, trying to tamp down the painful throbbing deep inside me. *Yes,* I want this. I want this so much, I'm kind of amazed.

I don't usually like sex. I've never had a serious boyfriend. I've tried one-night-stands a couple of times, but I always ended up feeling empty and sad. Having sex with a stranger doesn't make me feel good, it just makes me feel vulnerable. And I don't like feeling vulnerable. Ever.

But now, Glen is looking up at me, his grey eyes soft, his cheeks flushing with desire. His thumb strokes my hip tenderly, and my belly flips.

I'm used to people making up stories about me in their head. They see me act in a movie, or they see a story about me in a magazine, and they decide that they know me, despite never meeting me. But this man just told me I was essentially a symbol of happiness for him for years.

It's without a doubt the weirdest, sweetest way anybody has ever objectified me.

"Gather some context clues," I whisper, bucking my hips closer to his face. His eyes drop shut, and he pushes forward, nuzzling the bottom of my stomach through my t-shirt. The pang of desire that lashes through me almost makes me cry out. I can't believe this is finally happening.

"Tell me," he growls into the cotton, and I swear I can feel his low rumble vibrate through my skin, touching deep inside of me. "Please."

"I want *you*, Glen. Please. Please, please."

He grins to himself and dives in, licking a hot line over the thin fabric of my underwear. It's all I can do not to howl. I instinctively shove my thighs together, but he wraps a strong hand around each of my knees and firmly pulls them apart, pushing his face closer between my legs. I can feel his hot breath steaming against me as he takes another long, leisurely lick, running his tongue down the line of my thong.

"Take it off," I gasp, trembling. He looks up at me, his eyes burning with intensity, then hooks a thick finger under the wispy fabric. He tugs so hard that the fabric tightens against me, creating a delicious pressure. I rock my hips, starting to grind against the thin lace. He tugs harder, and harder, and I cry out as the thong finally snaps clean off me. Glen pushes it away, then scoots down the bed and very carefully parts my labia with his rough thumbs, studying me so intently that I squirm. He glances up at me one more time, silver lashes flickering—then burrows his face in my pussy.

I half levitate off the bed. Oh my God. Oh my *God*.

I've never had someone eat me out like this. Like they're starving for it. Glen licks me roughly, his tongue sliding up and down my lips like he's mapping me out, working out what I like. Then he does it all again, harder, licking and nibbling and breathing hot air all over me until I'm a total mess.

"Oh." Is all I can say. My voice is so breathless I can barely recognise it. "Oh, oh, God—" My eyes close. My hips start to jerk and jump, and he tightens his grip on me, panting, groaning, trying desperately to burrow closer.

It barely takes a minute before I feel my stomach tightening. I gasp for breath, reaching down to wrap my hands in his hair and tug him further into me. He groans, sliding his tongue inside me. I feel my clit jump against his mouth and grind down, trying desperately to rub at the ache. He shudders, then gets his lips around the little nub and sucks, *hard*.

I fist my hand in his hair and just fall apart, tightening my thighs around his neck. My orgasm arcs through me like a rainbow, and through it all, he keeps licking me, steady and strong.

Eventually, the shockwaves die away, and I'm left gasping at the ceiling as it comes back into focus. I nudge at Glen's head, trying to push it away, but Glen just doesn't stop. He's still sucking at me, drinking up my arousal like a man dying of thirst. I start to tremble as I feel another wave of pleasure rise slowly up in me. Holy shit. I've never come twice in a row before. It doesn't seem possible, but the pressure of another release is there, deep in my belly, taunting me. I squirm against Glen's chin. "Glen, I can't—"

He rumbles disapprovingly between my legs, and the vibration of his mouth against me sends sparks flying through my veins. I let my head drop backwards as I start to gasp hard, my lungs too tight to take in enough air. More. I need more. I grab at his head, grinding against his face. I'm not even thinking. My brain has slipped into some sort of haze. I rub myself desperately into him, helplessly trying to get the friction I need. I'm so close, I can practically taste it.

"Don't stop," I beg. "Please, oh, oh God, Glen—"

Glen slides his hand up and grips my thigh hard, his trimmed fingernails biting into my skin. I close my eyes, bite my lip, grind down on his face one last time—

And suddenly, I'm flying. My hands fly out, clawing at my wooden headboard as my climax roars through me, practically obliterating me. My mind goes black and empty, wave after wave of pleasure rolling over me, so hard and fast I can't even breathe right. I practically gargle, my eyes widening as the feelings rush through me, sending every muscle in my body trembling.

Glen licks me gently through it, not stopping until my hips start to buck from oversensitivity. I grab his head and push it away, panting. "What the—"

He laughs, low and happy-sounding. "It's been a while since I've done that. Glad I didn't screw it up."

"Screw it up?!" I gasp. "You've ruined me for life!"

His laugh gets even louder. I pull him up next to me and slide my hand greedily down his muscled chest, brushing over the scars on his biceps. Down, down, following the heavy lines of his abs, combing through the brown curls of chest hair to the waistband of his boxers. He grits his teeth, a muscle jumping in his jaw.

"You don't have to—"

"I want to. Please."

He groans, relaxing and letting me slip off his underwear. The sight of his cock makes my head spin. It's thick and swollen. I let my fingers trail down his belly towards it, tickling into his pubic hair, and he hisses, running a hand over his face. Fighting the urge to laugh, I slip my hand under his heavy balls, cupping them firmly. The shudder that runs through him wracks his whole body. I feel an answering shudder deep in my stomach. Slowly, I wrap my hand around his length and start to stroke, so lightly it probably feels ticklish. His eyes fall closed.

"Too much?" I ask innocently.

"Not enough," he grits out, flinching. I watch in fascination as the muscles in his chest and shoulders flex. "Please, Briar, just *do* something, lass, you're killing me here—"

"Mm." Keeping my touch very, very light, I twist my hand around his base, my fingers barely snagging the skin. He chokes, his Adam's apple bobbing.

"Briar—"

"How do you like it?" I ask, speeding up my hand. "Faster?"

"No. Just... tighter, for God's sake—"

I bend and press a kiss to his tip, and he shouts, fisting a hand in my hair. "Mother of—!" He spasms hard against my mouth, and I smile, pulling back.

"Jesus." He mutters, "You're terrible."

"Did you expect anything different? I *am* Britain's Biggest Bitch."

"No," he grinds out. I take him in hand again, a little firmer this time, and rub my thumb just under his base. He likes that, jumping between my fingers as his thighs clench.

This is something else I've never really enjoyed. Getting a guy off. But now, seeing the colour rise in Glen's cheeks, the sudden, uncontrolled jerks of his muscles as I touch him, I finally get the appeal. Watching him get more and more turned on as I explore him is so hot I can feel myself getting wet again. I squirm on the sheets. His eyes flash as he notices, and he grabs me by the hips, dragging me onto his thigh. I wrap my legs around his waist, and he groans as I start rocking on him, riding his leg in rhythm with my strokes. He dips his head, his soft hair tickling my cheek, and nips the side of my throat. Electricity wires through me. I tighten my fist, moving faster and harder. For a few minutes, we're quiet, the only sound in the room the softly shifting sheets, and the low rumble starting up in Glen's chest. It feels like a spring is pulling tighter and tighter inside of me.

"God." I close my eyes. "God, I'm so close, I—"

"I know," he rasps. Of course he knows. He can feel me twitching and throbbing against his bare skin. He wraps his arms around me and pulls me closer, my wetness streaking stickily over his thigh. I moan, rubbing against him as I tighten my grip, twisting my hand in a corkscrew motion that makes him start to groan over and over. I feel his heart hammering in his chest as he pants for air.

"I'm almost—" he roughs out, and I nod frantically, reaching down to cup his balls.

He shakes his head. "Wait." He reaches over me to the nightstand, yanking out a handful of tissues.

I give his balls one last soft squeeze, and he loses it. He drops his head to my shoulder and lets out a strangled shout, every muscle in his body tensing and shaking as he explodes into his hand.

I'm not far behind. When it hits me, my climax streams through me like a sunbeam breaking through a cloud. My eyes flutter closed. I shiver and cling to Glen's shoulders, muffling my tiny moans and soft sighs into the curve of his neck. If my first two releases were explosive, this one is slow and delicious, almost dreamy, slipping through my veins like hot syrup.

I eventually quieten, slowly opening my eyes. My whole body is humming and warm and marshmallow soft.

"That was the most beautiful thing I've ever seen," Glen pants. I can see his pulse jumping in his neck.

"I try." I flop against his front, patting the handful of tissues in his hand. "Good thinking," I mumble. "Depressing, but probably a good idea." I mean, if I can't handle *lotion*, I guess having a man come on my leg might freak me out.

That thought pisses me off. Fuck X for getting in the way of my sex life. I will be taking this up with my therapist immediately.

I can imagine the conversation already. *Please fix me so my sexy Scottish bodyguard can come on my tits.* The thought is so ridiculous that I laugh, giddy from endorphins.

Glen disposes of the tissues and smiles against my mouth. "Well?" He asks.

"Well, what?"

"Did me staying in your bed work? Do you feel better?"

I snort, kissing his bottom lip. "Very effective. I may have to move you in here permanently."

He nuzzles my cheek. "This is not at all how I imagined this morning would go."

"Me neither. But I'm pretty happy about it." I pet his chest. I really do feel so much better. Maybe all I needed was a good night's sleep. Maybe finally opening up to the guys helped ease up my anxiety. Or maybe Glen's dick has magic healing properties. Whatever the reason, I'm pleased.

"Thank you," I mumble, twisting a curl around my finger. "For staying with me."

"Any time, lass."

There's a sudden footstep in the corridor outside, and I hear Matt's voice, calm and clear, as he argues with someone on the phone.

I cringe. "Jesus. Did he hear all of that?"

Glen just chuckles, pulling me into his chest. "Don't worry," he mutters, pressing a kiss to my hair. "He's got much more important things on his mind."

"Like what?"

"We got the premiere details from your studio last night. Matt's having kittens, trying to work out how to get you in and out of America without getting shot."

I groan. "He's going to lock me in my hotel room, isn't he? Booby-trap the corridor and interrogate all the maids?"

Glen smirks. "You think he's overprotective now? You've seen nothing yet."

CHAPTER 19
KENTA

The preparations for getting Briar to America take almost the full week to perfect. The studio has already booked hotel rooms and plane tickets for the cast, but they're obviously insecure. Instead, we pick out a new hotel close to the premiere spot. We book a whole floor of rooms, and manage to convince hotel security to place a block on the elevator system, so none of the lifts can stop there. They give us permission to install cameras in the hallway, and agree not to send up any cleaners or maintenance staff during our stay.

We also have to change the flight arrangements. We don't want Briar flying commercial, so we call in a favour with an old employer and wrangle a flight on his personal jet.

To my surprise, Briar is very unhappy about having to fly privately. I've never seen a celebrity get so worked up about carbon emissions.

"One hundred people could be taking this flight, for the amount of damage we're doing to the environment," she says to Julie as we step inside the cabin. I've been in plenty of private jets before, usually on political jobs, but this one is particularly impressive. The aisle is wide, and the seats are essentially plush leather armchairs, set in clusters around small tables. Everything is taste-fully decorated in buttercream leather with dark wood accents. A handful of flight attendants in short red skirts and jackets greet us, handing us all drink menus.

"*One hundred.*" Briar continues. "Right now, every single one of us has the same carbon footprint as *one hundred and fifty train passengers*. Each!" She gesticulates too widely and accidentally drops her phone. "Crap." She bends to pick it up, and I try not to look at the miles of soft, white thigh revealed as the hem of her plaid skirt rides up. She's paired the skirt with a matching pink blazer, knee-high socks, and impossibly high heels. I overheard Julie calling the outfit 'Clueless-chic', whatever the Hell that means. All I know is those heels make her legs look unbelievable.

"Pity." Julie frowns at the stewardess. "Please tell me this thing has Wi-Fi."

The stewardess blinks. "Of course, ma'am."

Briar straightens and glowers at her friend. "Don't you get how hypocritical this is of me? I did all that work with ecological organisations, and now I'm putting a whole goddamn plane up in the sky?"

"Stop complaining," Matt orders, as he assesses the seating arrangement with narrowed eyes. "You need this."

Briar looks up at him, irritation flashing across her face, but doesn't respond.

We all find our seats; Julie parks herself near the front of the plane with her laptop. Matt, Glen and I all seat ourselves in the middle section, huddling around one of the tables. Matt immediately pulls out some paperwork and spreads it out in front of us, but Glen ignores it, jamming his cap down over his face and settling in for a nap. Briar disappears towards the back, pulling the blue privacy curtains across the aisle to partition herself away from us.

"Leave that open," Matt calls over his shoulder. "We need a clear line of sight on you."

"Don't worry," she calls back through the curtain. "If one of the flight crew tries to stab me, I'll scream really loud."

The flight attendant pouring my soda water straightens, alarmed, and I wave her off. "Ignore them," I advise, and she smiles uncertainly, sashaying away.

I wait until she's out of earshot before turning to Matt. His jaw is clenched tightly as he flips through blueprints of the hotel.

"You're being rude," I tell him.

His scowl just deepens. "We're not here to baby her. We're here to keep her safe."

"I'm sure you can manage to do that without being a total ass."

He thumbs at the corner of a paper. "The girl has a deranged stalker, and we're going to a country where any lunatic could be carrying a firearm. Forgive me if I'm being a bit blunt."

I snort. "You don't need *me* to forgive you. I'm used to taking orders from you. But you're not in the force anymore, and she's a civilian. Stop barking at her like a drill sergeant."

"I think you're starting to hurt her feelings," Glen mutters from under his cap.

"Since when did you care about a client's *feelings?*" Matt asks, aggravated. "Oh. Right. When you started sleeping with her. Great job, by the way. I'm sure that will really give us the protective edge, having you stare at her arse when you're supposed to be monitoring for danger."

I raise an eyebrow. Glen has been staying in Briar's bed most nights for the past week, although to my knowledge, they've only slept together once. He's clearly fond of her, though. He blushes whenever she smiles at him.

Glen opens one eye lazily, studies Matt for a second, then closes it again. "Stop being an arse," he mumbles succinctly.

I have to agree. Matt's behaviour is getting out of line. It's out of character for him to be so broody; he's usually a pretty charming guy. Something's going on with him.

As the sky darkens outside, Matt gives up on working and reclines his seat to sleep. I'd rather beat the jet lag, so I force myself to stay awake, loading up YouTube on my laptop. I want to look through some old crowd footage of Briar out in public, to see if any common faces pop up.

I sift through a few videos, then end up falling into a spiral of old clips from *Hollywood House*, the show Briar was in as a kid. It's easy to see why she got cast. Even at thirteen, she's so bright and full of sparkle that she practically lights up the set. She plays the tween daughter of two wannabe actors, and even though they both have twenty years on her, she's so funny and charming that they both fade into the background when she's on screen.

When the clip rolls to an end, I click on the next recommended video. It's of Briar, probably around fourteen or fifteen, speaking on a late-night talk show. My eyebrows raise as she walks on set, smiling nervously at the camera.

I don't recognise this girl at all. She has none of Briar's fire. None of her sharpness. She looks shy and scared and sweet, which are not words I ever thought I'd ascribe to Briar. I watch as she waves at the audience, then sits carefully in the interview chair. The host, a blonde woman with a bright smile, shakes her hand.

"Well, hello, Miss Briar Saint," the woman says, beaming. *"It's so lovely to have you on the show today. Tell me, what do you think of being nominated for the TV Excellence Awards? Do you think you're going to win?"*

Briar plucks at the skirt of her dress. *"Oh, I don't know,"* she says, her voice higher than I'm used to. *"I'm just so glad to be nominated. All of the other nominees did so well."*

"What a sweet answer," the host gushes. *"Isn't she sweet?"* She leans in conspiratorially. *"Let me tell you though, Briar, whether or not you win the official award, you certainly win the award for best body of the evening. I mean, really. Look at that tight stomach. What's your workout plan, darling?"*

My mouth falls open. Little Briar's cheeks turn bright red. She shifts, probably uncomfortable with the whole audience staring at her body instead of her face. *"Oh, um, I don't work out much. I like to go swimming, and I just try and eat healthy."*

"Oh, to be young. And this dress really shows off your petite figure. An excellent choice." The host chuckles. *"Alright, come on, get up and give us a twirl."*

Alarm crosses Briar's face. *"Oh, um… I don't know. It's shorter than I usually wear…"*

"C'mon, just twirl for us. You guys want to see the full outfit, right?" The host looks up at the audience. Everyone starts whooping and clapping. Briar's face gets redder. She shakes her head, trying to smile and laugh it off, but the host starts up a chant. Soon, the whole studio is shouting *Show us the dress! Show us the dress!*

Briar looks terrified. When she doesn't move, the host grabs her arm and tugs her, and she obediently twirls, spinning in place while the audience cheers.

I hit the spacebar, pausing the video, and sit back in my seat, trying to digest what I just watched.

She was a kid. A child. And people were already treating her like a piece of meat. No wonder she's so aloof and distant now; she grew up in a world where grown *adults* were openly manipulating her. The thought of it makes me sick.

I'm about to click onto the next video when Matt twitches next to me. I look down at him. There's sweat on his forehead, and his face is twisted. He flinches again, harder this time.

"Matt." I put a hand lightly on his shoulder. "Hey." I wouldn't normally wake him up from a nightmare, but if he starts thrashing around, he's probably going to smack his leg into the table. "*Matt.*"

He suddenly surges upright, gasping like a drowning man. I wait as he stares with wide eyes around the plane, taking in the soft leather seats and dim lighting. When his eyes land on me, he lunges at me, grabbing my face. "Ken—"

"I'm fine," I tell him, keeping still. "Look at me. I'm completely fine, man. I'm safe." I nod to Glen, snoring happily in his chair. "We're both safe."

Matt's eyes finally focus. His face closes off. He drops his arms and slumps back into his chair.

"You're getting worse," I tell him, as he heaves for breath. It's been years since he grabbed me like that.

"Yeah, no shit," he snarls, slamming his hand on the *call service* button built into the arm of his seat. An attendant scurries over, and he forces himself to smile at her. "Whiskey on the rocks, please."

She nods and disappears, and he straightens his chair so it's upright again, wiping a hand through his hair.

"Is this happening every night?" I ask, shutting down my laptop.

"And half the Goddamn day, too," he mutters.

I nod. That explains why he's being so snappy. "Do you know why?"

He shakes his head jerkily, rubbing the back of his neck.

"When did it start?"

"A week ago."

"Let me guess: after the charity gala?"

He shrugs. "I guess." He sounds exhausted.

"I know a trauma therapist in LA. If you want, I could—"

He squeezes his eyes shut. "Don't," he bites out. It's probably meant to sound like a warning, but he just sounds empty. The flight attendant bustles up with his drink, and he smiles tightly at her, taking the glass and swigging deeply.

"What an excellent coping mechanism," I say drily. "I'm sure this could never go wrong."

He flips me off, and I stand, stretching out my back. He could probably use some space, and it's been a few hours since anyone checked on Briar.

I'm expecting her to be asleep, but when I pull aside the privacy curtain, I see that she's still awake, sitting curled up in her seat. There's a box of Greek salad on her lap, and she's picking at it dispiritedly, pulling out the olives and ignoring everything else.

She looks very beautiful, and very, very tired.

"Briar?" She glances up, and I gesture to the seat opposite hers. "Can I sit?" She nods, and I sit down. "I just wanted to check in. See how you're doing."

Her lips twist. "I'm not going to break down and scream at the pilot. I promise."

"Wow. The therapy must be working."

She smiles slightly, but it doesn't touch her eyes.

"Are you okay?" I ask her. "You look—subdued."

"Have you ever eaten vegan feta?"

"No."

"It's pretty subduing."

I lean forward. "Go on, then." I open my mouth. Her smile gets a bit wider as she stabs a beige cube and pops it between my lips. I grimace, swallowing the lump of soggy tofu. "Christ."

"How do you feel?"

"Marginally depressed."

She rolls aside some cucumber and unearths another olive. "I'm still waiting for vegan scientists to work out cheese," she says glumly. "They've got meat and milk in the bag. But cheese needs some work."

I watch as she eats another olive. I'm pretty sure it's not her dinner that has her looking so upset. I try a new tack. "I was thinking: do you have any family in America? Matt won't like it, but we can find a way for you to arrange visits, if you like. Maybe on your birthday?" According to our files, Briar turns twenty-nine the day before the premiere. "It's important to have a strong support network."

She snorts. "That's a pity, then. I don't have any family."

I frown. "What, no one at all?"

She shakes her head. "I never knew my dad, and I cut my mum off when I was sixteen."

"*You* cut *her* off?"

She nods. "I'd just got fired from *Hollywood House*. When I got home, I found out that most of the stuff in my bedroom had gone. Clothes, photographs, toys. Turns out she'd been selling it online." Her face twists. "She'd also sold most of my baby pictures to the press, and she was halfway through writing a tell-all book about my childhood."

"*Jesus.*"

She shrugs. "It wasn't a big deal. I moved to LA when I was thirteen, and I barely saw her after that. We have an arrangement now; I send her enough money to retire in a mansion, and she refrains from making up stories in the tabloids."

My throat aches. I can't imagine being betrayed like that, especially by your own family. My mum still demands that me and all of my siblings Skype her once a week so we can all eat dinner together.

And Briar's all alone.

She fidgets in her seat. The silence stretches out. I sigh. "Look, is something bothering you? Honestly?"

Her eyes trail to the blue privacy curtain. Her face hardens. "*He's* avoiding me."

"Matt?" That's not what I expected. "He does that, sometimes. He's horrendous with emotions."

Her jaw clenches. "He never forgave me. For what I did to Nin."

I frown. "He did." I study her. "Did he tell you what happened on our last celebrity job?"

"He said that the girl sexually harassed him."

I nod. "It bothered him more than he'd ever admit. Even to himself." I remember that assignment. Watching him get tireder and jumpier every day. Of course, he'd never accept that a seventeen-year-old girl could faze an elite soldier.

"Well, yeah. I figured. If I went to set, and the director kept shoving his hands down my pants and dragging me onto his lap, it'd fucking affect me, too. Just because he's a big strong man, doesn't mean that wouldn't screw with his brain."

"It definitely jaded him when it comes to celebrities. He's wary, now. Of rich, entitled people throwing their power around. Using people."

"Hm." She considers that. "If it's not Nin, why is he being weird? Was it the panic attack? Is he that freaked out by mental health episodes?"

"It's definitely not that." I think of how to word this. "It's very difficult for him to watch people suffering," I say carefully. "When you told him how you've been feeling… it upset him, a lot."

"That's dumb." She stabs a tomato violently. "It's not *his* fault."

"Matt has a tendency to blame himself for other people's pain. But trust me. He cares about you a lot. More than he'd like to admit."

Her mouth twists unhappily. She puts the salad down and runs a hand over her face. "I just feel so stupid," she mutters.

"Stupid? Why?"

"For freaking out like that. Collapsing on the bathroom floor, and then crying all over you. You guys have been through Hell and back. When you were a soldier, I bet you used to live like this every single day. Always looking over your shoulder. Always on guard."

"It's not really the same thing," I say gently. "We were at work. It was what we signed up for. We were unsafe, but we were holding guns, too. We got to shoot back."

She just frowns, looking down at her lap.

Without thinking, I reach across and take her hand, pressing it between mine. Her fingers are soft and warm. She raises an eyebrow, but doesn't try to move away. "I know you're scared. But I also know you can handle whatever this bastard has to throw at you. You're more than strong enough to deal with this."

She studies me for a few seconds. "You really think that, don't you?" She says softly.

"I think you can handle anything," I say honestly. She looks at me, an expression I can't read crossing her face; then she leans forward and presses her mouth to mine. I go still. She smells sweet, like candy, and the blonde hair falling loose from her ponytail tickles around my face. It's a quick, firm kiss, and she's pulling away before I can really register what's happened. She leans her head back against the headrest and contemplates me, her blue eyes daring me to say something. I just hold her gaze, trying to ignore my heart pounding painfully in my chest.

"Thank you," she says quietly. "You can go now. I'm going to sleep."

CHAPTER 20
BRIAR

'm already in a bad mood when we land in LA. Jet lag is
kicking my ass, my head is hurting, and I'm covered in plane
grime. On top of that, the journey to the hotel is taking
forever.

First, our plane gets stuck in the air for half an hour because some
idiotic billionaire is parked in our spot. Then we have to stand in
the burning heat for fifty minutes as Matt checks the car the
studio sent for me, interviews the driver, sends the poor guy away
because he 'has a bad feeling about him', and orders a new car to
come pick us up. LA traffic is even worse than I remember, and
Julie spends the entire drive 'catching me up with the locals',
which essentially means scrolling through other women's Picture-
Gram accounts and telling me who's gotten a nose job, like I give
a shit. When we finally arrive at the hotel, all I want to do is
collapse into bed, order some room service, and sleep for twelve
hours, but of course, I can't. Instead, we have to wait around for
another forty minutes while the guys sweep the corridor, the
suite, the fire escape, and probably the inside of the toilet's U-
bend. Eventually, when I watch Kenta and Glen painstakingly
checking the *wainscoting* of the hallway, I snap.

"For God's sake, can I please just go inside? I'll take my chances with dying, at this point. X could sneak in through the window and slit my throat in my sleep, and it would be the highlight of my fucking month."

Kenta blinks, but holds open the door for me. I stomp into the suite. It's big; three bedrooms, a lounge space, a kitchenette, and a balcony with a stunning view over Hollywood Hills.

I ignore it all, heading for the master bedroom.

"Yours is the room with the fire escape," Kenta calls after me, and I have to fight the urge to growl at him. Or maybe run back, grab his face, and snog him until I run out of air. My head has been all over the place since I kissed him. I don't know why I did it, other than he's really nice and hot and he kept staring at my mouth. Which is a dumb reason. I step into my room and slam the door, leaning heavily against it.

I feel terrible.

I know I'm being a bitch. And I'm not angry at the boys, really. They're just doing their jobs, and they're doing them well.

I'm angry at X. I'm angry that my life has become this stifling. I'm angry that one anonymous man can have such a massive impact on my safety that I need private planes and a special suite. I'm angry that I can't stop myself from checking my socials every few minutes, to see if he's posted anything about following me to LA. I'm just angry.

There's a knock at the door, and I fight the urge to scream. "Briar," Matt says. "Unlock the door. You need to keep it open at all times."

"Piss *off*," I hiss. I don't want to talk to him. He hasn't said one word to me in the last week that wasn't an order. It's getting on my nerves.

He pauses for a moment, then I hear him mutter something that sounds an awful lot like *fucking celebrities*. I rub my eyes, looking around the room, then walk over to the bed and flop my aching body onto the mattress. I'd like to take a nap, but I don't think I can sleep alone anymore.

I've spent the last week sleeping with Glen. We've had a few cuddles, but we haven't fucked again. He usually gets into bed after me, and he's always gone by the time I wake up.

I hope that he's just an early riser. Although I certainly can't blame him if he's lost interest. I wouldn't shag someone as annoying as me.

Fumbling in the pockets of my skirt, I pull out my phone to check twitter. I go to the 'Search' function, typing in my name and the word 'angel'.

> *Actress Briar Saint looks ANGELIC in this white Valentino evening gown!*

> *Is it just me or does Briar look preggo from this angel?*

> *Does briar really think this charity stuff will help her career? We all know she's no angel.*

Outside my room, I hear footsteps and raised voices. I ignore them, clicking on a new tweet. It's a response to a promo picture for the movie; I'm standing in red lipstick and a flapper dress, pouting at the camera, my elbow-length gloves spattered in blood. Someone has responded:

> *Briar you look so beautiful, my angel. X*

I stare at the words, my chest getting tight.

There's another light rap on the door, and I jump, dropping my phone. "Briar," Julie calls. "The studio director is here to talk to you about your schedule."

"In a minute," I mumble.

"Now," she orders. "Before your Angels murder him."

"What?"

"Come see."

When I open my bedroom door, I'm confronted by the sight of my security team in a heated debate with Derek, the studio director. Everyone is crowded around the large dining table, red-faced and scowling. They all look up as I step into the lounge.

"Briar." Derek stands up and takes my hand in both of his sweaty ones. "Thank God you're here. Will you please inform your damn guard dogs of your *contractual obligations?*" He gives me a nasty look.

I pull away and wipe my hand on my skirt, looking between everybody. "What's happening?"

"This *idiot,*" Matt declares, "is insisting that you attend some bloody party tomorrow night."

"You mean the press party?" I nod. "Yeah. It's in my contract."

"You never told us that!" He snaps. "We'd get in, do the premiere, get out. That's what we agreed on."

"The press party is part of the premiere. It's where we do most of the interviews."

Matt shakes his head. "You're not going."

"She has to!" Derek cries. "If she doesn't promote her own movie, people are going to assume it's a flop, and she's cutting her losses before it's even out!"

I swallow back a sigh and sit down next to Kenta. This will probably take a while.

The conversation rages over my head. Other executives call or Skype to chime in. The studio's PR manager, the movie's director, my agent. I sit in my chair, watching all of these extremely well-paid people argue about what to do with me.

It's weird, being a product. Sometimes I feel like my mum signed my life away when she brought me to LA and handed me over to the *Hollywood House* producers. Ever since then, I've belonged to other people. You think that celebrities are powerful, but my opinion matters the least at this table.

After a while, I just tune out. I check my phone again and again, scrolling through my Facebook DMs. Every time I see a message with a kiss at the end, my stomach lurches.

An hour passes. The bright LA sun is shining through the window and slanting over my face. I can feel beads of sweat popping up on my forehead. Kenta reaches over and passes me a bottle of water. I force myself to smile at him, cracking the lid and gulping it down. He doesn't smile back. His eyes are concerned.

I try to focus on the conversation. "We have to use the limos," Derek is telling Matt. "We don't have a choice. We have a brand deal with the company."

Matt leans back, running a hand through his hair. "Jesus, do you people never just *buy* things?"

"Why don't you ask Briar if she has a preference?" Kenta asks.

I open my mouth, but Matt waves me off. "What Briar wants doesn't matter."

I rub my eyes. Across the table, Julie waves to get my attention. She points to my bedroom door. *I need to tell you something,* she mouths.

"Excuse me," I mutter, standing. "I'll be back in a sec."

I head back to my room, Julie hot on my heels. The argument continues behind me, like no one even realises I'm gone.

I shut the door behind us. "Yes?"

She purses her lips unhappily. "I've got some bad news," she says.

"What is it?"

She offers me her phone. "It looks like someone leaked the story about X breaking into your house. I'm doing what I can to crush the rumours, but—"

"Give me that." I grab the phone and look at the news article on the screen, horror curling in my gut.

STALKER BREAKS INTO ACTRESS BRIAR SAINT'S HOME, PLEASURES HIMSELF IN HER BED!

My mouth goes dry. *No.*

This is the last thing I ever wanted. Now no one will give a damn about the movie. Instead, I'm going to get followed down the street by grown men yelling at me about the time a guy wanked over my sleeping body. The worst night of my life will be sold as front page news.

"Do you have any idea who could have leaked it?" She asks quietly, studying my face with uncharacteristic softness.

"It must have been either the policeman or Rodriguez."

She nods. "I'll track them down. Get them to retract the statements."

I take a deep breath through my nose. My hands are shaking. I hate this. I *hate* that reporters and magazines can make money off my pain. I hate that there's a table of men outside arguing about how to control my life. I clench my fists, feeling my nails biting into my palms. I'm done. I'm so done.

Handing Julie back her phone, I stomp back into the living room. The argument is still going strong.

"I don't think you're getting it," Matt is saying. *"She can't leave this hotel room.* She will not be attending any dinners or drinks. She will not be going to fittings. She will not be going shopping to get candid paparazzi shots. *Nothing."*

Derek looks like he's about to explode. "You're being ridiculous," he spits. "Briar's not just a person, she's a *brand.* Hundreds of people make money off her image!"

"She's not a brand," Matt snarls back, "she's my *client.* I'm not backing down on an assignment just so you can take photographs of her!"

I clear my throat. "Can you all please shut up?" I call.

The conversation immediately dies down. I turn to Matt. "We're doing the event tomorrow."

He stares at me. *"What?"*

I keep my voice level. "I didn't hire you to stop me from doing my job. I hired you to keep me safe while I do it. I always honour my contracts." I turn to Derek. "I'll make the appearance. Please leave. We can discuss my timetable over email or Skype later tonight."

Derek opens his mouth.

"Now." I order. He makes a hasty exit.

Matt watches him leave, then jumps to his feet. "Briar, when you hired us, you agreed to let us make decisions about your safety—"

"I'm doing the event," I snap at him. "I don't want to talk about this anymore."

"This might be hard for you to understand, *princess,* but not everything is about what you want."

I laugh hollowly, throwing up my hands. "Of course it isn't. Why would it be? It's *my* career. It's *my* professional reputation. It's *my* life. But I'm not a person, am I? I'm a *brand,* or a *client,* or a *job.* You act like I'm this spoiled diva, but all anyone cares about is what they can take from *me.* Magazine articles, or brand deals, or autographs. Pictures of me half-naked." I look down at the papers scattered over the table. "I'm not trying to make your job difficult. And I appreciate your work. I'll let you pick out my cars. I'll do all my other interviews remotely. I *promise.* But I will fulfil my contracts. That's my final decision."

Matt looks down at me. A muscle twitches in his jaw. I hold his stare. Seconds pass.

He turns on his heel and leaves, slamming into the hallway.

CHAPTER 21
BRIAR

"I'm, ah, going to see if I can stamp down those stories," Julie says, breaking the awkward silence. I nod listlessly, and she creeps out of the door of the suite, shutting it softly behind her.

I sag in place, the anger draining out of me.

Maybe all the magazines are right. Maybe I *am* the Biggest Bitch in Britain. And LA too, apparently.

"Briar," Kenta says softly from the table.

I shake my head. "I'm sorry," I whisper, rubbing my face. "That was rude. I didn't mean to snap at you all."

Glen opens his arms. "Come here, lass."

I take a step back. "Don't. Don't coddle me and cuddle me and say it's okay. It's not. I'm being horrific." I rub my face. "I'm sorry for ending the meeting. I just—I'm *sick* of feeling so out of control."

I drop down onto the sofa, pulling out my phone. "I mean, look at this." I tap on my latest PictureGram post. It's a picture of me laying by my pool in a bikini. As per usual, whenever I show more than five centimetres of skin online, a ton of guys instantly blow their loads. "'*I don't care if she's a bitch,*'" I read aloud, "'*I'd still do her.*' '*Thanks for the addition to the spank bank, love.*' '*Can you tell I'm typing this with one hand?*'" I drop the phone onto the sofa, disgusted. "It just never stops. Never, ever, ever. I've got stalkers taking photos of me naked through windows. I've got whole teams of people telling me what I can and can't do. And now, apparently the press has found out about the break-in. So I have magazines making money off me getting sexually assaulted. I just want a *modicum* of control over my own fucking life and body, you know?"

"No," Kenta says softly. "We don't. I can't even imagine how it feels."

I sigh, turning to Glen as he sits on the sofa next to me. "Look, I know we only slept together once, but do you want to do it again? I think topping you will make me feel loads better."

Glen chokes on air. "I—ah…" I stare at him. "I'm on duty."

"*Shit.*" He opens his arms again, and I slump down into them. He starts rubbing my shoulders. It feels nice, but it just makes me feel worse. He's being so sweet, and I'm acting like a spoiled child.

"I'm sorry," he mumbles in my ear.

I snort. "Don't be sorry. You're not required to shag me every time I throw a tantrum." God, it would be nice, though. To take my own body back from all of the people who are constantly objectifying and degrading me.

He bites my ear. "If you're that desperate, lass, I'm sure Kenta would happily take care of you. He loves being bossed around in bed."

I frown. "What? What does that mean?"

He tenses under me. "Sorry. I didn't mean to imply that you—"

I turn to Kenta. "What does that mean?" I repeat, slowly.

Kenta relaxes into the sofa, rolling his eyes slightly. "He's referring to the fact that I appreciate—a woman in charge."

"What? *You?*" Kenta's hardly dominating, but he's got a quiet air of authority that's even more effective than Glen's physical size, or Matt's testosterone-filled barking. Even though he usually speaks softly, everyone always hears and does what he says.

He shrugs. "I don't mind being ordered around by a beautiful woman. Gives me a break from shoving poor girls into cars and locking them inside hotel rooms all day."

I lick my lips. "Do *you* want to have sex with me?" I demand. I can feel Glen's laugh rumbling in his chest.

"What?" I scowl at him.

"You're so direct, lass. We've never been propositioned like this."

"I'm a demanding diva, remember? I'm good at asking for what I want." I turn back to Kenta. "Well?"

Kenta's eyes sparkle. "I certainly wouldn't say no."

"Right now?"

He looks amused and tilts up his head, offering me his lips. Desire blows through me, so strong I'm almost bowled over.

I've never really thought too much about power dynamics in sex. I know I like being on top, but that's just a logistical thing; it's easier to get off that way. But now my big strong bodyguard is looking up at me through his lashes, and it's hot as Hell.

Still on Glen's lap, I lean forward, cupping a hand under Kenta's jaw and pressing my mouth to his. His lips part on a sigh. He lifts a big hand, splaying it gently on the small of my back. I pull away.

"No touching," I order. His pupils blow. "Put your hands on the sofa."

He does as I say. Arousal shivers through me.

It's probably messed up that someone listening to me when I tell them not to touch me turns me on. But people touch me without my consent all the time. I can't leave my house without fans grabbing at me, begging for hugs and selfies, or paps crowding around me, hemming me in with their bodies. Kenta's not going to do anything until I tell him to, and the thought is making heat burn through me.

I glance back at Glen. "Do you mind?"

"Why would I mind?" He murmurs, an expression I can't read on his face. "None of my business."

"I don't want to cause issues between you by sleeping with you both."

Kenta laughs. "We're used to it."

"Not a lot of girls in the SAS?"

"None. They only started letting women join after we left. But that's not what I meant." His eyes drop to my lips. "Glen, Matt and I often share women."

He says it so casually, like it's not the most mind-boggling sentence that could have possibly come out of his mouth. I stare at him. "You *what?*"

He shrugs. "It's a long story."

"You have foursomes. With women. Regularly."

"I don't know about *regularly* —"

I twist back to look at Glen. His cheeks are flushed as he stares at me. "When do you get off-duty?"

Glen checks his watch. "Twenty minutes."

"Do you want to join in?"

His lips part. "*Yes*."

Holy crap. I'm about to have a threesome. My day is really turning around.

"Great," I grab Kenta's collar, pulling him upright. "I'll just keep him on edge until you're ready." Kenta groans, a low, deep sound in his chest, as I pretty much drag him into my bedroom. Kicking aside my suitcase, I lead him to the bed, put my hands on his shoulders, and push him down onto the mattress. He looks up at me, his eyes dark.

Glen steps forward to close the door. "Can I give you a tip?" He calls from the doorway.

I straddle Kenta's waist, plucking at the buttons on my shirt. "I know what hole it goes in, thanks."

Glen chuckles. "Leave the shoes on. They drive him crazy."

I turn to look down at Kenta, who's watching me intently.

"Do they, now?" I practically purr. He strokes a hand down my leg, not breaking my gaze.

"You're incredible," he says, his voice dropping lower. "You always look incredible."

His eyes are almost painfully sincere, and I feel my heart flutter in my chest. Shaking myself, I reach up to pull my hair loose from its ponytail.

Kenta goes to shuck off his shirt, but I grab his hands, stopping him. "No," I order. "I'm undressing you."

He goes still, letting me unbutton his crisp white shirt, pushing it off his shoulders. I run my eyes over his thickly muscled chest. He's a little leaner than Glen, but just as toned, and his skin is tanned golden. I run my fingertips over his abs, watching the muscles clench under my touch, then tug at his shoulder. I want a closer look at his backpiece. "Turn around."

He hesitates, a brief wince crossing his face.

I pause. "Kenta?"

He twists, putting his back towards me. My mouth falls open.

Yes, his tattoo is gorgeous. It's an intricately drawn phoenix rising from a plume of smoke. The linework is incredible. I can see every individual feather on the bird's wings.

But that's not what grabs my attention. I lean forward to get a closer look. Underneath the heavy ink, his back is covered with vicious-looking scars, criss-crossing over his skin. Some of them are thick and raised, and others are knife-thin. There's barely a millimetre of his skin left unscathed.

For a second, I'm frozen, anger rising in my stomach. Whoever hurt Glen got to Kenta, too. They cut him up. They *shredded* his back. Fuming, I lean down and kiss the bloom of fire burning from the phoenix's mouth. Kenta relaxes under me. "Anything I shouldn't do?" I say lightly.

I can practically hear his smile. "I'm fine, Briar. Really."

"Good." I drop my hands to his belt and tug. "Then take off your pants."

He laughs, sliding off the bed and kicking off his trousers. My mouth practically waters as I ogle his muscled thighs and tight black underwear. He goes to move back to the bed, but I splay a hand across his abs, pushing him up against the wall.

"Stand there," I command, my voice suddenly hoarse. "Take off your underwear."

Silently, he kicks off his boxers, tossing them onto the ground. He's big. Not as big as Glen, probably, but still so large that nerves pinch my stomach.

"Don't move," I whisper, cupping my fingers under his shaft. I run my fingertips across the delicate, velvety skin. Kenta flinches, but stays still. I can feel him throbbing in my hand.

Glancing up at him, I drop to my knees. He sucks in a harsh breath. I lean forward and kiss the bead of arousal glistening on his tip. Heat shoots through me as I roll the heady male taste around my mouth. I didn't expect him to taste so good.

"You'll have to tell me if I do something you don't like," I say softly, flicking my tongue to lick off the next bead of moisture that pools. "I've never done this before." He stiffens, surprised, and I laugh. "I know, I know. Everyone thinks I'm the next Whore of Babylon. But honestly—" I press a kiss under his shaft. "I never felt like getting on my knees for a man before."

"I don't think that," he says throatily.

I glance up at him. His eyes are dark and hazing, hyper focused on me. "I know you don't," I whisper, then wrap my lips around him, swallowing him down as deep as I can.

The reaction is instantaneous. Kenta gasps, twitching desperately against my tongue. He feels surprisingly good in my mouth; deliciously hard and soft at the same time, like a hot iron rod wrapped in velvet. I hum happily and start to move, working my mouth up and down his length. Kenta's whole body trembles under me. More pre-come pools on his head, and instead of licking, I suck *hard.*

His hands fly down to my head, fingers wrapping in my hair as his knees buckle.

"Briar—"

"Shh," I tell him. "Stay still." He makes a pained sound in the back of his throat. I suckle at him for the next few minutes, keeping the pressure of my lips firm. The steady, constant twitching in my mouth gets more and more desperate, and his hips start jerking under my hands.

"Briar, please, sweetheart—" Kenta's hands trail through my hair. I glance up at him. His handsome face is tight, twisted in pleasure and agony. "Please, just… *please* let me touch you," he begs. A hot feeling of power floods through me, and I smile. Right now, *I'm* the one in control. And it feels amazing.

I pull back slightly, so I can talk. "Tell me," I whisper. "When you're about to come."

He nods slowly, his chest heaving. I keep on blowing him, swirling up and down his length as I slip one hand between my own thighs.

Kenta glances down and notices me touching myself. Apparently, that's his breaking point. His hips buck, and he shudders all over, tugging hard at my hair. *"Briar—"* he cries out. "Stop! Jesus, sweetheart, I can't—"

I pull gently back until he pops out of my mouth. His dick is glistening wet and weeping. Kenta wraps his fist tightly around the base, panting. I look up at him.

He's *wrecked*. His cheeks and lips are red, his loose ponytail is dishevelled, and there's a faint sheen of sweat misting his golden chest.

"Please," he says again, his voice low and pleading. "Let me touch you."

I consider him for a moment, then stand up, wrap my arms around his neck, and yank his mouth to mine. He groans, kissing me back hard, his tongue plundering my mouth. I tremble against him. My whole body feels like it's on fire. Kenta's hand slides up my back, curling into a fist at the neck of my shirt.

"Can I take it off?"

I lift my arms, letting him wrench the shirt over my head. It crumples to the ground, and he stares silently at my exposed bra. Luckily, I'm wearing a nice one today: pink, covered with little flowers. He reaches to touch me, then stops, pulling his hand back. I can see his pulse beating in his throat. His dark eyes flick to mine, waiting.

God, I love that. Kenta is so much bigger than me, but that doesn't matter. I have the power here. He's only going to do what I tell him to.

"Touch them," I say. Relief floods his face. He reaches for me again, but I catch his wrist right before his fingertips brush my skin.

"Only with your mouth," I say quietly.

He groans, pushing his face between my breasts. I sigh as he trails his mouth all over my skin, breathing hot air against me. "Anything *I* shouldn't do?" He murmurs, nibbling at the lace on one of the cups.

"Don't come on me. On my skin."

"Jesus." He presses a hot kiss between the cups, making me jolt in his arms. "I know how to read a room."

I laugh, throwing my head back, and his smile gets even bigger. He tugs me back in for another kiss. His erection presses into my stomach, and I reach down to stroke him. Every muscle in his body tenses.

"Briar—" he starts. "Please, God, I can't handle any more."

There's a creak, and then the bedroom door opens behind us. I turn and see Glen's silhouette cutting through the light in the hallway. He clears his throat, his eyes running over the two of us.

"Thanks for joining us," I say politely. "Your turn."

CHAPTER 22
KENTA

've never been so glad to see my teammate in my life. Glen stands in the doorway, studying us both. "Is he still hanging on?" He asks conversationally.

Briar runs her fingers lightly under my swollen shaft, laughing when my hips involuntarily buck. "I told you," she whispers, her breath tickling the side of my face. "I'm playing with him."

Glen steps closer, studying my face. "Alright, Li?"

I squeeze my eyes shut, gasping as Briar twists her hand. A bead of sweat trickles down the back of my neck. I can barely speak. "Piss off," I manage.

Briar smiles, pulling my face to hers for a long, licking kiss, then steps away from me, pointing at a spot on the mattress.

"Sit," she tells me. I gratefully slump down onto the sheets, hot and shivering all over. She turns to Glen. "Strip."

Glen tosses me an amused look. "I don't think so, lass."

"Strip, *please*?" She tries. "Trust me, you're going to enjoy this bit more if you're naked."

He just laughs, grabbing the hem of his t-shirt and yanking it over his head. "You're a piece of work," he mutters, advancing on her. "But I'm afraid I'm not like Kenta, love. I don't much like being ordered around."

She opens her mouth, but before she can say a word, Glen wraps an arm around her and pulls her up against his chest, one hand easily unclipping the back of her bra. She squeaks in surprise— actually *squeaks*, which is completely adorable—then melts against him with a soft sigh as he starts fondling her breasts, squeezing and rolling them in his hands. She's so distracted, I don't think she even notices as he quickly unzips her pink mini skirt. It falls to the floor, puddling around her ankles and revealing a miniature pair of white panties. I run my eyes up from her stilettos to her bubble-shaped ass. The heels make her taut, smooth legs look unbelievably sexy.

Glen gives one of her cheeks a little pat. "On the bed," he says in her ear, gently pushing her onto the mattress. She wraps her arms around his neck and tugs him down with her, so they both collapse in a heap on the sheets.

I roll off the bed and stagger to Glen's suitcase, rooting around for the box of Trojans I stuffed in there while we were packing for the trip. I certainly didn't think that I'd be the one using them, but I'm very happy about this development.

There are soft moans and gasps behind me, and I turn to see Briar on Glen's lap, her arms around his neck as she grinds against his crotch. They're kissing so hard they're practically consuming each other, their hands clutching at each other's bodies. "I've missed you," she gasps against his mouth, winding her fingers in his hair. "I thought you didn't want me anymore."

"I've wanted you plenty, lass. I just—" he shudders as she licks a line down his throat. "I assumed it was a one-time thing."

"Why?"

He shrugs. "I'm not the kind of man women fuck twice."

She pulls away with a frown. "What's that supposed to mean?"

He doesn't answer, pulling her in for another kiss. She shifts, and I see a streak of shiny wetness gleaming on the inside of her thigh. It feels like all the blood in my body sinks to my balls. I can't hold out any longer. If I don't come soon, I might actually explode.

I rip open the condom wrapper and roll it on, climbing back onto the bed. Glen nods at me over Briar's shoulder.

"Ride him," he rasps. "I want to see what you look like."

She narrows her eyes at the command, but she can't hide the heat climbing up her neck.

"You're lucky you're so damn pretty," she mutters, making Glen flush bright red. She shuffles into my lap and takes my face in her hands. Her turquoise eyes melt into mine, the colour of sunlight shining through the sea. She strokes my cheeks with her thumbs, not breaking my gaze as she lifts her hips and slides onto me. I'm filled with an overwhelming wash of relief as I sink into her blazing heat. She clenches around me, and my eyes squeeze shut.

"Jesus," I croak out. She tightens her grip on my shoulders and slowly starts to roll her hips, grinding down. I tip my head back against the headboard as a wave of weakness crashes over me. *"Christ."*

She feels incredible. Silky and smooth and hot around me. Every muscle in my body shakes as I start to thrust up into her, matching her rhythm. The perfect friction sends sparks flying through me.

For a minute or so, we don't speak, our skin slapping together as we rut more and more frantically. I've been on the edge for so long, I'm struggling to hold myself back. My jaw is clenched so tight my teeth are grinding together, and I feel a bead of sweat pool at the base of my neck.

Briar leans forward and tugs at the tie holding back my hair, letting it fall around my face. I shake it out of my vision, and she winds her hands into the long strands.

"I *love* your hair," she breathes.

"R-really? It divides opinion."

"I always fancied Legolas when I was younger," she confides, tightening her fingers and giving my hair a firm tug.

I hiss as electricity sparkles through my scalp. My hips buck helplessly up into her, our pelvises slamming together. "Jesus, it's not *that* long. I was aiming for Aragorn."

She snorts, twisting to look over her shoulder. "You okay back there?" She asks Glen. "You're awfully quiet."

I glance up at my teammate. Glen is kneeling on the mattress behind Briar, his eyes fixed firmly on her behind.

"You've got a gorgeous arse," he rumbles. "Like a little heart."

"I will pass on the review to my personal trainer," Briar says. There's a smacking sound, and she yelps, leaning into me. I lift my hips, changing the angle slightly, and her pink mouth falls open into a gorgeous little O-shape. She moans, rubbing her soft tits up against my chest.

"Kenta," she murmurs, over and over. "*Kenta. God.*"

"That's it, sweetheart," I rasp as her thighs start to quiver. "Take what you need."

She makes a little agonised whimper and leans forward, pressing her forehead to mine as we rock together. I wrap my hand around the back of her neck, catching her mouth with mine. I can already feel my balls tightening.

"Glen," I warn. "Hurry up." If this is the girl's first threesome, there's no way in Hell I'm coming yet. I hear the rumple of clothes and the snap of a belt as he undresses, then Briar sighs as he wraps his hands around her waist, squeezing her breasts.

"God," she gets out through gritted teeth, arching between our bodies. "Why does anyone ever have sex with one man at a time? This is great."

Glen laughs. "You good, Kenny?"

"Not for much longer," I force out.

He nods. "Flip her over."

I give Briar one last kiss, then take a hold of her hips and gently lift her off me. She whines, and I groan as I feel her entrance clutch greedily around me, like she wants to keep me inside of her.

"But—"

"Shh." I put my hands on her shoulders and roll her over so she's on her hands and knees.

"Well?" Glen asks expectantly.

"You're right," I agree. "Absolutely gorgeous." I stroke one of her trembling ass cheeks, then give it a little squeeze. "I'd say more of a peach than a heart, though."

Briar growls. "I never realised you guys were such bloody poets," she spits, grinding back into me.

I lean forward, running a hand between her legs. She shudders over me. I lick my lips as I feel her wetness coat my fingers.

"Oh, sweetness, you're *soaked*."

Glen's eyes darken. He immediately reaches forward, his hand joining mine. We both stroke through her hot folds, rubbing and fondling and pinching in tandem, and she drips over us, writhing and mewling.

"Oh God. *Please*." She rubs down on both of our hands, desperate to get some real pressure. When that doesn't work, she groans, lunging forward and grabbing Glen's dick. His mouth drops open as she starts pressing sloppy, hungry kisses down his length.

"Christ. Lass. You don't have to—"

"Don't *have* to," she snorts, opening her mouth and swallowing him down. He groans deeply, his head rolling back and his eyes falling closed as she takes him in deep.

As she goes down on Glen, her head bobbing enthusiastically, I twist my hand and plunge two fingers deep inside her wet, pulsing core. Her thighs immediately tighten around my wrist like a vice, holding me in place.

"More," she mumbles.

"Coming right up." Instead of adding another finger, I line up by her throbbing entrance and plunge back inside her. She's tight and hot, stretching to accommodate me. She gasps, her hand flying backwards to grab aimlessly at me.

I freeze, half-buried inside her. "Too much?" I ask, fighting to keep still.

She shakes her head, shivering all over. "I…. You're so deep," she mutters. "*God.* No. You can keep going."

I bend to press a kiss to her hip and push forward, more slowly this time. She moans as I finally bottom out, my balls crushing against her ass. Heat floods my face.

"This won't take long, sweetheart," I grit out, and she nods, grasping for Glen again and guiding him back into her mouth, sucking him in sloppily. I start thrusting into her. "You look so hot," I mumble. "Jesus. You look incredible with your mouth on him, honey."

She doesn't say anything, just bucks back into me, twisting her fingers around Glen's base.

Glen makes a strangled noise. "Stop. Stop, lass, I need to—"

"My mouth is fine," she mumbles. "I'll just swallow it."

He groans as she tightens her fist around him. I grit my teeth, still pounding into her. Sweat pours down my back, sticking my skin to hers. I'm so close my vision is starting to black out. I can't breathe through the tightness wrapped around my chest. I jerk my hand forward, thrusting it between her legs and pinching at her swollen nub, rolling it between my fingers.

Briar just falls apart.

It starts slowly; first I feel her legs tensing, then her arse, then her arms. Still sucking on Glen, she starts to sputter and choke as she comes. It's like a chain reaction. As she cries out, gasping and moaning, Glen groans one last time, tightening his hand in her hair and spilling into her mouth. The feeling of her channel rippling and clutching at my throbbing dick sends me over the edge. I slam my hand into the wall and shout as I finally explode, adrenaline and pleasure surging through me in a wild, hot tide.

God knows how long I come for. It's practically an out-of-body experience, as I rut and rut and rut into her, feeling her tremble and writhe underneath me, draining me dry.

Eventually, the glow filling my brain fades away, and I come back to Earth. Glen is leaning heavily against the wall, panting. Briar kneels between us on her hands and knees, still shaking slightly. I tip my head forward, pressing a long line of slow, sucking kisses down her spine. She gasps, and I smooth a hand soothingly over her skin, trying to gentle her.

Glen moves first, pulling out of her mouth. He bends and cups her cheek. "You're okay?" He checks, his voice low.

She nods. He carefully wipes a smudge of his come off her swollen bottom lip, then straightens and heads to the bathroom to clean up. With one last kiss on her hip, I draw out of her slowly, and she flops down boneless onto the sheets. I tie off the rubber, tossing it into a nearby trash can, then wrap an arm around her shoulders, rolling her into my body. "Come here, sweetheart."

She cuddles up close to me, nestling under my arm. Her whole body is still flinching and twitching. When I skate my hand over her breast, pulling her closer, she moans as loudly as if I'm still inside her.

"How do you feel?" I ask quietly.

"So much better," she gasps. "Thank you."

"Trust me. The pleasure was all ours."

She hums happily, pressing closer. "Glen," she calls. "Get in here. My back is getting cold."

There's a muffled curse from the ensuite.

"Problem?" I ask, nuzzling into Briar's hair.

Glen steps back into the bedroom, holding his phone. "Matt's fussing about tomorrow. He wants to screen the press before we get there."

I snort. "Good luck. Best you'll get is an ID check."

He scowls. "He wants to send them all through a metal detector."

"I'm sure that will go down well."

Glen taps at his phone. It buzzes a few seconds later, and he sighs, grabbing his boxers from the floor and tugging them back on. "I've got to sort this out with him."

"Feel free to join the post-coital cuddle when you get back," Briar mumbles. "We'll be right here."

Glen kisses her cheek, pulls on his clothes, then leaves, shutting the door behind him.

Briar squirms against my front. "Mmm," she mutters. "Roll over. *I wanna hold you*." I don't move, breathing in the blossomy, sweet scent of her hair. She frowns, then shoves at my shoulders. I just clasp her tighter to my chest.

"*Kenta*."

Sighing, I relinquish my hold on her and let her roll me over, curving up against my back. Her little arms wrap around my waist.

"I don't think I've ever been the little spoon before," I muse.

"I like to hold, too." She scoots back to get a better position, and then stills. A shiver rolls through me as her hand traces over my shoulder, just brushing my skin. "Can I touch?"

"Sure." She runs her fingers over my back, tracing the curves of ink, then stroking down the jagged lines of scar tissue. I let my eyes fall shut. "I'm assuming you have some questions," I say lightly.

"Glen told me what happened on your last tour."

I'm surprised. I didn't think Glen talked to anybody about our time in captivity. Not even me, and I was *there*.

"Matt doesn't have any scars," Briar continues. Her silky hair trails across my skin, raising goosebumps. "Unless they're like, on his ass. I saw him in the pool."

I hum. "No. Our captors barely touched him."

Her fingers pause. "What? Why?"

"They figured, since he was the patrol commander, he'd have the most info, so they used hurting us as leverage to get him to talk.

They made him sit and watch as they cut us and burned us and whatever else."

"Oh my God."

I nod. "I wouldn't trade places with Matt for anything. It's one thing to resist your own torture; but it's completely different to watch people you love get punished for your actions. Our captors made him feel like he was responsible for everything that happened to us. He was already so guilty for letting us get caught, and they preyed on that guilt. It tore him apart."

Briar doesn't say anything, drawing patterns on my arms. I wince. "Sorry. This isn't very sexy pillow talk."

She's silent for a second; then she sighs heavily. *"Fine."*

"Fine, what?"

Her lips tickle my ear. "You can hold me."

I can't hold back my smile. I roll over, wrapping her in my arms. She curls up against my chest and closes her eyes.

"Thank you," I mumble.

"Shut up." She pinches my thigh. Outside, I hear raised voices as Matt starts to argue with Glen.

Briar groans. "Tomorrow is going to be Hell, isn't it?"

"He won't make it easy," I admit. "Not by a long shot."

CHAPTER 23
BRIAR

I wake up slowly, in a warm cosy nest. It takes me a few seconds to remember where I am.

I'm in a sexy bodyguard sandwich. Kenta is steadfastly cuddling me from the front, and Glen is curled up at my back, his breath hot against the nape of my neck. For a moment, I just lie there, enjoying the feeling of two men draped over me.

Eventually, though, the ache in my bladder is too sharp to ignore. I carefully slide out from under the heavy limbs, rubbing my thighs together as I register the soreness between my legs. I think I need to buy some lube. It's been so long since I had regular sex; my poor vagina is woefully unprepared.

I go to the bathroom and slip into a pair of pyjamas, then head into the main suite. Matt is sitting at the kitchen counter, taking apart a pistol. I pad across the lounge to the kitchenette, pulling a mug out of one of the cupboards. "Morning."

He grunts, fiddling with the mechanism. I watch him carefully. I've never seen any of the guys with weapons before. It feels surreal, like we've dropped onto a movie set.

"It's so weird to see you holding a gun."

He doesn't raise his gaze. "Does it scare you?"

"No. It would be bad for your business if you shot your client. You want a coffee?"

He nods, a quick jerk of his chin, and I grab a couple of complimentary coffee pods from a big glass bowl, setting the coffee maker going. As it churns and steams, I watch Matt methodically checking all of the gun parts. Behind him, there's a case full of different firearms; mostly smaller pistols, but some much bigger ones, as well.

"Where did you even get all of those?"

"Our LA office."

"You have multiple locations?"

"Hollywood is a very common destination for our celebrity assets, so we keep a base here." He reaches into the pocket of his jeans and pulls out a slim aerosol tube. "Picked you up some pepper spray. Wish I could offer you something better, but half the men in Hollywood would be dead tomorrow if you were allowed to carry."

"Hey, you're getting to know me." I weigh the bottle in my hand. I've never seen pepper spray before. "This is just point-and-click, right?"

He nods. "Aim for the eyes."

"I always do." That finally makes his mouth twist into a grim smile. The coffee machine gurgles to a stop, and I pass him his mug. "Do you prefer working in England or America?"

"Usually America. The weapons make the jobs more interesting. But I'd prefer this job be as boring as possible."

I watch in silence as he takes apart another pistol, checks inside it, and reassembles it. This might be the first civilised conversation we've had since our chat by the pool last week. Now that we're not snapping at each other, I can examine him more closely. He doesn't look good. His skin is pale underneath his tan, and there are dark circles under his eyes. As he sets the gun aside and reaches for another one, I notice that his hand is shaking.

"Matt, are you okay?"

He flinches like I've swung at him, then smiles bitterly. "Been talking to Kenta, have you?"

"No. Well, yes, obviously, but that's not why I'm asking. You look half-dead."

"Jet lag," he grunts, "I'll be fine."

"Are you sure? If you're not feeling well, I'm sure I can find someone to take your place—"

He stands suddenly, slamming the gun on the table. "I'm *fine*," he growls, then turns on his heel and heads back into the guys' room. I stand there, staring blankly at his untouched coffee steaming on the countertop.

Well, that was rude.

There's a footstep behind me, and I feel my whole body relax as warm arms band around my waist. Kenta's soft, spicy scent floods my senses as he nabs Matt's coffee.

"Hey, sweetheart." He kisses my neck. "How are you feeling?"

"Is Matt getting sick?" I ask bluntly.

He pauses for way too long. "He's got a lot on his plate right now," he says diplomatically.

I turn to look at him. He looks divine, his long hair tied back in a low ponytail, his sharp jaw shaded with stubble. I fight the urge to run my fingers along it. "He looks like he's about to collapse."

Kenta hums, noncommittal. "Are you ready for the press event tonight?"

I sigh and nod. "Any sign of X?"

"Not a peep. We've had people trawling through your socials, and nothing has popped up that matches his usual pattern of speech." He squeezes my shoulder. "It could mean that he's losing interest."

"Or it could mean he's travelling here," I point out. "Maybe he's on a plane right now."

"Hey." Kenta touches under my chin. "You pay us to worry for you. There's no point in you doing it as well." He takes a swig of coffee, and my eyes catch on the glossy red smudge on his neck.

I reach up to thumb it off. "You've still got my lipstick on you."

He rolls his neck to give me better access, his lips brushing the top of my head. For a second, my insides clutch. A memory from last night flashes in front of my eyes: me, riding him hard while he buries his face in my cleavage, sucking hungrily at my tits. I feel heat shimmering over my skin.

I hesitate for a moment, then cup his jaw and kiss him. He draws me into his firm body, kissing me back hard and slow. He tastes like coffee and mint, and as his hand slides down the curve of my back, I feel myself slowly melting against his chest.

"Are you sure this isn't breaking a company policy?" I whisper against his mouth. I don't know why, but necking with my bodyguard the morning after just feels *wrong*. In a delicious, illicit way. "I don't wanna get you in trouble."

He laughs. "Our boss met her wife on a close protection job. I think she realised pretty quick that when two people are attracted to each other, it can be more distracting to repress it." He slips a hand up the back of my shirt, and I shiver as his fingertips tickle up my spine. "I can sleep with you off-shift, and focus on my work on-shift just fine."

The hotel phone rings, and I jump as Glen practically falls out of the bedroom, yanking on a pair of boxers. He brushes past us both, pressing a quick kiss to my cheek, then stumbles to the door and out into the corridor.

"Emergency?" I ask, watching his retreating back.

"Breakfast," Kenta laughs. "He's a bottomless pit." He dips down and touches his mouth to my ear. "I think you wore him out."

"I think I should've worn you out, if anything. I edged you for like, half an hour." I look up at him through my lashes. "Very rude. Sorry about that."

He chuckles. "Do it whenever you like, sweetheart. I enjoyed it plenty."

Glen bursts back into the room, pushing a gold room service trolley loaded with jugs and cutlery and big metal cloches. The guys lift up the covers, revealing plates upon plates of breakfast food. Hash browns. Pastries. Scrambled eggs. Pancakes. There's a plate of french toast sticks with chocolate dipping sauce, and a whole jug filled with some kind of berry smoothie.

And I can barely eat any of it.

Sighing, I ladle some fruit salad into a little bowl and pour myself a glass of the smoothie. A couple of days. Just a couple of days, and when the premiere is done, I'll stuff my face.

The guys fill their plates, and I slump between them on the sofa, picking at my fruit. "I was wondering. How did you guys get started, with this foursome stuff?"

Kenta pours a cup of juice. "It was back when we were serving, and we were all pitched in the same tent. Glen met a girl he liked in a local bar, but she lived with her dad, who was openly against our presence. Matt and I both said, as long as she was fine with it, we didn't mind them just coming back to the tent."

"You dog," I nudge Glen. His cheeks redden.

Kenta laughs. "Then it just became a habit. If one of us wanted to bring a girl back, we would, and the other two would ignore it. It was—" He frowns at his bacon. "Honestly, at that point, it was less about sex, and more about comfort. Just having someone to hold, for a bit, when you spent all day thinking about death."

"You don't have to explain yourself." I bite into a grape. "I can imagine."

He nods. "One night, a girl Matt brought back asked if we wanted to join. She was pretty, we were lonely. We tried it, and it was so mind blowing that we kept doing it." He frowns down at my bowl. "Sweetheart, is that all you're having? We got lots of vegan stuff. The oatmeal, and the french toast, and I think the pancakes are good."

"You haven't seen my dress for tonight. It's essentially a gastric band. I'm on liquids for the rest of the day." He looks alarmed. "Don't worry, I get to eat like a normal person as soon as the premiere is over."

"Okay," he says slowly. "What if you get dizzy, or something?"

I shrug. "I eat some glucose tabs, drink some water, and suck it up."

"I don't like that," Glen mutters behind me.

I snort. "Yeah, well, neither do I. But I'd rather spend an evening feeling a bit hungry than have to deal with pregnancy rumours. And trust me, so would you." I spear a piece of melon. "Every time that happens, I get like, three times as much attention from the paps. I'm making your job much easier."

Kenta still doesn't look satisfied. Glen reaches down and nabs a strawberry from my bowl, rolling it generously in the french toast dipping chocolate, then holding it to my lips. "Here. It's fruit."

I roll my eyes and bite into the strawberry, humming as the sweet juice bursts on my tongue, mixing with the rich, heavy chocolate. When I'm done, I suck a smudge of chocolate right off Glen's thumb, scraping my teeth lightly across the pad. His grey eyes flare and darken, and I feel Kenta setting his own plate aside, reaching up to pull my hair back from my neck. My eyes fall closed as his hot lips touch the side of my throat. Glen pulls his thumb from my mouth, trailing his hand down to cup my cheek.

I startle as a door suddenly slams, looking up to see Matt stride into the room. His gaze goes straight to us, and colour touches his cheeks. "Seriously?" He barks. "*Again*?"

I twinkle my fingers at him. "You know, if you stop being such a sad little bitch, you can join in," I inform him, with my characteristic warmth and charm.

His disgusted look speaks volumes. He storms back into the guys' bedroom.

"Alright, then," I mutter.

Glen chuckles next to me. "He's jealous."

Somehow I doubt that. "Whatever." I stretch, then check my watch. "I've got twenty minutes before I need to hit the gym. Do you reckon all three of us can get off before I need to leave?"

CHAPTER 24

X

I pop the cork off a bottle of red wine and smile around the living room. Today, I am celebrating. Today, the house is finally done.

When mother died, she left me this old barn in the middle of the woods. It was small and falling apart, so I forgot about it for a long time; but a few years ago, I got the idea that it could be a perfect place to bring a girl.

Pouring myself a glass of wine, I wander around the cabin, admiring all of my hard work. I've been very clever with it all, I think. Very, very clever.

First of all, I boarded up all of the windows and exits. Next, I had electricians and plumbers come in. The men asked a lot of questions, but of course I didn't answer any. I paid them in cash.

After that, I focussed on decorating. I bought all sorts from the local furniture shop: cupboards, a fridge, a couch. A nice big bed. The store wanted to deliver to my address, but obviously that wasn't possible, so I spent all day driving back and forth, ferrying the furniture home. I had to take the long way around, circling through the city and then back again through the woods. I didn't want anyone watching my car and getting a sense of where I might live. You can never be too careful. People are very nosy these days.

My best buy was the front door. The front door is very special. Reinforced steel, like the kind bank doors are made of. That's what the dodgy man who installed it promised, anyway. Which hopefully means that even if Briar took a drill to it, she wouldn't be able to get out. Even if she threw her whole body weight against it, over and over, it wouldn't budge one tiny bit.

I suppose some people would be horrified if they saw this place. They would think it was wrong to try and bring a girl here. But I don't think it's wrong. Here's my reasoning:

Women are shallow. They only care about appearances. They want men who are muscular and tall and good-looking and rich. But it's all superficial. They don't actually care about what the man is like as a person. That's why guys like me can never find women, no matter how nice we are. Girls don't even give us a chance to get to know them.

But if I bring Briar here, and keep her with me for just a little while, she'll *have* to get to know me. And then, she'll realise how perfect we are for one another. My actions aren't *wrong,* since everything will turn out right in the end.

I reach again for the wine bottle, slumping in front of my computer. The *Players* press event will start soon. It's being live-streamed online, and I want to be able to relax and enjoy watching Briar stealing the limelight on the carpet. I wonder if she'll bring that blue-eyed guard as her date again. I'm not stupid, I know he's just pretending to be her boyfriend so people don't know he's her bodyguard. But it still made me mad when I saw the pictures of them kissing at Briar's charity gala.

No matter. In a few days, he'll be dead. And she'll be mine. The thought makes me giggle. The wine is getting to my head, but I don't care. I feel great. In fact, I'm in such a good mood, I think I'll send Briar a little surprise, just so she knows that it's almost time. She must be tired after her flight to LA, so I'd like to cheer her up.

I pull down the waistband of my jeans and grab my phone to take a picture.

CHAPTER 25
MATT

The air is filled with screaming. Camera flashes strobe through the night like lightning. Fans press against the metal barriers, clawing and shouting and climbing over each other to get closer to Briar.

We've been at the *Players* press event for forty minutes already, and we haven't even gotten inside yet; we're still stuck in the little fan holding area, so Briar can get her 'allotted fan interaction time'. I trail after her as she moves down the line, taking selfies and scribbling autographs. Glen and Kenta shadow us on either side, hanging around in the background, but once again, I am playing the part of her arm candy. Which is pretty ironic, since I'm the only one of us she hasn't slept with.

I rub my forehead. I feel like shit.

I'm exhausted. I spent half the night waking up from nightmares covered in sweat, and the other half listening to Briar moaning through the walls. God knows what the guys were doing to her, but it sounded like she came about fifty times. It's weird to have a flashback and a boner at the same time, but I am glad to report it is possible.

I run my eyes over the crowd pressed against the barrier, looking for the usuals; people avoiding eye contact, people shouting obscenities, people with their hands shoved in their pockets. I hate working carpets. They're death traps. Everyone is acting like a bloody lunatic, screeching and hollering at the celebs like they want to murder them. How the Hell am I supposed to pick out the ones who actually do?

As I watch, a guy with frizzy red hair leans right over the barrier, practically taking Briar's eye out with the pen he's waving in her face.

"Behind the barrier," I bark at him.

He ignores me, leaning so far over I'm tempted to give him a good yank and watch him topple to the floor. My eyes catch on the picture he's brought for her to sign. It's a cartoon drawing of her naked. Jesus Christ. I grab it out of his hand before Briar sees it, crumpling it into a ball.

His eyes widen. "Dude! That's my *art*, you've ruined it!"

I ignore him, turning to Julie. "That's enough. We're out of here."

She gives me a stern look, but waves us forward out of the fan meet area. There's a big white holding tent set up for all of the stars, where orderlies are noting their names down and staggering their entrances on the red carpet. I keep my hand on Briar's back as we step between the hot tent flaps.

It's busy inside. Hordes of celebrities huddle together in their evening wear, sipping champagne and examining their faces in compact mirrors. Each star is flanked by at least one security guard, so the pavilion is thick with huge, hulking guys in dark suits and earpieces.

Briar grabs a drink of water and touches up her lipstick, then Julie directs us out onto the carpet.

The photographers go nuts as soon as we appear, immediately starting to screech.

"YOU LOOK STUNNING BRIAR, WORK THAT DRESS!"

"GIVE US AN OVER-THE-SHOULDER, BRIAR!"

"WHO'S THE LUCKY MAN!?!"

"TO YOUR LEFT, BRIAR! LEFT! TO YOUR LEFT!"

"GIVES US A SMILE, HONEY!"

Cameras flash all around us as we pose against the logo-studded backdrop. I glance down at Briar, checking for any signs of anxiety, but she seems relaxed enough. She looks stunning tonight. She's wearing this glimmery rose-gold gown that dips low in the back. Her hair is loose, falling in soft, pale-blonde waves, and her makeup is light and shimmery. There's a deep flush on her cheekbones, and her lips look wet and pink.

Overall, she looks unbelievable.

Briar notices me studying her and tugs my elbow. I dip so she can put her lips by my ear, gritting my teeth as her sweet scent washes over me. She smells like sugar and vanilla. It's not the kind of perfume I'd expect a grown woman to pick out, and for some reason, that just makes it sweeter. She's wandering around these events, glaring at people like a cold-hearted bitch, but her hair smells like cupcakes.

"Are you okay?" She murmurs, her lips brushing my skin.

I blink. "Yes. You?"

She nods.

"COME ON LOVEBIRDS!" One of the photographers roars. "GIVE US A KISS!"

"KISS HER! OVER HERE, FACE THIS WAY!"

"GIVE US A NICE SHOT OF YOU TOGETHER!"

Briar sighs against my neck. "That okay?"

"Sure," I mutter, and she tilts her head, brushing her lips over mine. I hold still as the photographers whoop and cheer and snap away, trying to ignore the softness of her breasts and stomach against my body as she presses closer.

Far too soon, she pulls away, turning back to the crowd without a word. I close my eyes for a second, readjusting my pants to try and hide the growing issue between my legs.

My earpiece suddenly fizzes. *"We have a problem,"* Kenta mutters in my ear.

I frown, automatically coming to stand closer to Briar. She glances up at me as our bodies press together, licking her lips slightly. "You seen him?"

"No. But Colette just dinged me. X has posted on Princess's social media pages."

"That's good. It'll give the cyber team something to go off."

"No," Kenta says slowly. *"He posted* on *her pages. He hacked into two of her accounts and posted* as *her."*

Shit.

Briar drifts a few feet away to get some solo shots, and I hook my phone out of my pocket, quickly navigating to one of her socials. My heart drops into my stomach. "The goddamn *pervert,*" I growl, staring at the stumpy, swollen penis on my phone screen. Underneath is a message:

> *Good evening, my darling. I love the lipstick you're wearing tonight. I can't wait until I finally get inside that pretty mouth. X*

I glance around the carpet. Half of the reporters have their phones out. I see one journalist turn to her cameraman and point right at Briar. I'm not surprised. Every news station here will have alerts set up for when the stars post tonight.

There's another roar from the photography pit as the next celeb walks out, and Julie hurries me and Briar off the carpet. Briar takes one look at my face and sighs. "It's X, isn't it?" She says flatly.

I nod.

She pushes forward, leaning over my arm to see my phone. When I pull it out of her view, she frowns, glaring at me. "Tell me. This is my safety we're talking about. My *body*. I have a right to know if I'm in danger."

I clear my throat. "X has hacked into your social media. He's posted…" I grimace, "well, I suppose it's a picture of his dick. It looks more like some kind of rare, diseased fungus."

Underneath the layer of makeup, her face drains of colour. "What?" She whispers, grabbing at my phone. "How is that possible?"

"I really don't think you want to look at that—"

She waves me off. "I get hundreds of dick pics every day," she snaps. "I doubt it's that impressive." She snatches the phone off me and reads the message. Her jaw clenches. Red flushes up her neck, staining her cheeks.

"Briar," I say softly, putting a hand on her back.

"He wants me to *suck his dick?!*" She screeches. "I won't fucking suck it! I'll bite it off and spit in the hole! I'll flatten it out with a rolling pin and tie it into a fucking *bow* around his nuts!"

A couple of reporters turn around and stare at her.

"Shh," I mutter, looking around. "Princess, people can hear."

"I will not *shh!*" She shouts back at me. "If he wants to publicly humiliate me, I'm not going to keep my mouth shut and bloody *smile!* Get it off my page! Children follow me, for God's sake!"

Julie puts a firm hand on her arm. "Calm down," she orders, keeping her voice low. "Ignore it. It's time for you to do the press line. We have thirty-five stations waiting for you."

Briar squeezes her eyes shut and takes a deep breath. I can literally see her body trembling as she tries to swallow her emotions back down. The image of her crying on her sofa flashes in front of my eyes. I remember what she said that night.

No matter how much I wash my sheets, my bed feels dirty... I can't sleep, I can't eat. It's like the walls are just closing in on me.

Shit.

Briar exhales slowly and opens her eyes. "Right," she says softly. "Right. Okay."

"Can you do it?" I murmur in her ear.

She shoots me an irritated look. "Of course I can do it," she snaps. "You think some *creep* is going to stop me doing my job?"

And with that, she marches off after Julie towards the press line.

CHAPTER 26
BRIAR

I walk on shaky legs to the press pit, barely feeling Matt's steady hand on my back. My head is swimming. I feel sick.

The first journalist, a man with fake teeth and fake hair and a fake tan, leans over the barrier, shoving his microphone in my face. I stare at the blank, shiny lens that his cameraman points my way.

"Miss Saint," he purrs. "You look *ravishing* tonight."

I nod slightly, waiting for him to move on. I don't really want to hear any comments on how sexy I am, right now. The interviewer clears his throat.

"So, Briar. You're about to turn twenty-nine, aren't you?"

"Tomorrow."

"Well, Happy Birthday in advance. You've had a busy year, haven't you? What with filming *Players*, the upcoming release of your new beauty line, and now a new boyfriend?" He glances back at Matt, who remains stony.

I nod, smiling through gritted teeth. "It's been an interesting year."

"Full of highs and lows, would you say?" The interviewer leans in further. "Of course, we've all been following you in the news. It looks like you've attracted a bit of unwanted attention, eh?"

"I didn't *attract* anything," I snap. "This wasn't my fault, it had nothing to do with me, or the way I look, or the way I dress." Matt's hand slides to my arm. He grips me firmly.

The interviewer looks taken aback. "I'm sure," he says. "We've been trawling your social media, and it seemed just a few minutes ago, your unnamed stalker struck again. Would you like to explain what happened there?"

"The issue with her stalker is an ongoing case," Matt interrupts from behind me. "She will not be discussing it until it has been resolved. *If* she ever wants to."

Julie frowns, looking between him and me. "Well, I really don't think that's necessar—"

"No," Matt orders, and she shuts up. I look over his shoulder, and see a couple of reporters giggling over their phones, glancing up at me and whispering.

Embarrassment burns in my stomach. Everything starts to blur. I feel that old wash of panic roll over me. My eyes dart from one face to the next. I have no idea what X looks like. For all I know, he's right here, ready to jump out at me.

I grit my teeth and push through the fear. No more. No more. I spent my whole life as a child actor getting pushed around by adult men who were bigger than me and more powerful than me. I'm not doing it again. I'm not. If this guy thinks he can stalk me, intimidate me, *ruin* my life, and run me into the ground hiding from him, he's the thickest man alive. I don't let men treat me like that. Ever.

I open my mouth. "Actually," I say loudly, "I would like to give a statement about the man who has been stalking and harassing me."

Matt frowns and shakes his head, but the man looks delighted.

"Oh!" He shuffles the notecards he was holding, then just dumps them on the ground. "Okay, then. What are your thoughts on the man?"

"I think," I pause to consider my wording. "That he is the most repugnant man on the planet."

Matt flinches behind me. The interviewer whistles. "Coming in strong, there."

"Well, I've already seen his genitalia, so I would say that *he* came in strong, actually. I don't see why I have to be polite, when he's completely incapable of not sexually harassing me."

"Are you referring to the picture which was posted to your social media accounts? That was his, uh… him, right?"

"You mean the one-inch flesh-coloured slug?" I shrug. "It certainly wasn't mine."

"Briar." Matt says behind me. "Stop."

I ignore him. "Yes, that is the man I'm talking about. He's been sending me creepy love letters for years now. I'm sure you all saw that he recently climbed in through my bedroom window and jerked off over my unconscious body. Thanks to whoever leaked that story, by the way. Really fucking charming of you. I love when the worst night of my life becomes tabloid entertainment for the masses."

The interviewer glances off to someone on his right. "That sounds terrible, Briar. Just a reminder, this is live TV, so if you could keep your language PG—"

"And now I've just been told that he's followed me all the way to LA, to—" I frown. "Let's see, what was it?" I pull the message up on my phone. "Get inside my pretty mouth." I look up into the camera. "If I was ever unfortunate enough to have your prick in my mouth, X, you'd never regain the ability to have children. I bite. Hard enough to hear the bones crunch. You might think you want me, but if you had me, you wouldn't have a clue what to do with me. I would eat you alive and spit you out. So I suggest you back the fuck off, and stop living in this deranged fantasy world where any woman would want a disgusting creep like you."

Matt's voice is urgent. "Briar. *Stop.*"

"No!" I spin on him, my voice climbing higher. "I'm not going to lie down and take this! This isn't okay! It doesn't matter how big a *fan* you are, if you take it upon yourself to break into my *house,* you can fuck right off!" He grabs my wrist, and I shake him off, turning back to the camera. "But, hey, maybe I'm being too harsh. I get it. It must be hard, living life, when your very presence makes women want to staple their pussies shut. I'm sure it's *unbelievably* lonely, watching other men get dates, while you have to stalk your imaginary girlfriends from afar, hoping they won't see your face and call the police. Hell, it must be really frustrating, how every girl you talk to at a party instinctively covers her drink, because you're so goddamn *gross* — "

"Right. That's it." Arms wrap around my waist, and I shriek as I'm lifted bodily into the air and away from the microphone. The interviewer gapes, and I see the cameraman tracking the movement.

I thrash, trying to shove out of Matt's iron grip. "Get off me! I'm talking!"

"No, you're not," he growls in my ear. "You're done. You're done." He settles me over his shoulder and starts carrying me away from the press line, towards the road.

I kick him in the shin, digging in my stiletto, and he doesn't even flinch. "Get. Off. Me." I hiss.

He ignores me, pushing through the crowd roughly. Everyone turns and stares at us. I see camera flashes go off and people pulling out their phones to record me getting dragged away.

"Are you okay?" Someone calls after us.

"Is this man bothering you?"

"Would you like us to call the cops?"

"Try it," Matt barks.

I kick him again. "Put me down!"

"Will you just go back to the cameras?"

"Obviously! I was in the middle of speaking!"

"Then no. Jesus, how could you be so stupid?!" I can feel him shaking under me.

"I was defending myself, you goddamn gorilla! Put me down!"

We reach the curb. Kenta and Glen are both standing by the car, looking grim. Matt sets me back on the ground and yanks open the back door. "Get in."

"No!" I shout.

His face is a frozen mask. He looks completely blank, but I can see all the anger under the surface. His grip tightens on my elbow. "Get in before I put you in."

"I'm not done!"

Matt sighs, wraps his arms around my waist, and picks me up, shovelling me into the backseat and climbing in after me. Kenta and Glen get in as well, slamming the doors shut behind them.

"Take route E," Matt tells the driver.

The driver frowns. "Sir—"

"*Drive!*" Matt barks.

"But the freeway would—"

"Her security has been compromised. Now drive us around the long way, before the pervert following her sees all the *idiotic shit* she just spouted on live television."

Anger burns through me. "It wasn't *idiotic shit,*" I snap, "I was defending myself. How *dare* you pick me up like that?!"

"The contract you signed granted us permission to use appropriate force to remove you from dangerous situations. You were being a danger to yourself."

"I was answering an interview question!"

"You ignored me!" He bellows, his blue eyes flashing. "I told you to stop talking to that reporter, and you didn't!"

"Is that what this is about? You're mad I didn't roll over to follow your orders?"

He takes a shaky breath. "You promised, when you signed the contract, that you were going to defer to us on matters of safety. You put it into goddamn writing, but of course, you don't give a shit about that, do you? All you care about is getting in the press, and always having the last word."

I gape. "You think I did this because I wanted *attention?* I did it because I'm sick of getting harassed!"

He ignores me, turning to Kenta. "Call the PR woman. Have her order a car to the hotel and write an apology. A *thorough* apology."

"On it." Kenta pulls out his phone and starts tapping away.

I look between the men, incredulous. I can't believe this is happening. "What the Hell is wrong with you people? I'm not apologising, I didn't *do anything wrong*. He broke into my house, followed me across the world, hacked into my social media and *posted a bloody picture of his genitals—*"

"*It doesn't matter what he did!*" Matt shouts. "This isn't about your fucking *ego!*"

"No," I agree, "it's about the fact that he's *violating me.* How can you not see that I need to stand up for myself? Matt—" I reach over to grab his arm, and he turns to me, rage contorting his handsome face—and then suddenly freezes. Every muscle in his body goes rigid. His eyes slip out of focus, as if he's thinking hard about something else. I can feel him shaking slightly under me. My heart starts beating in my throat as the car falls silent.

"Briar," Kenta says quietly. "Let him go. Slowly."

CHAPTER 27
BRIAR

frown. "Is he—"

"Just let him go," Kenta instructs, "and slowly lean back. It'll kill him if he accidentally hurts you."

"He won't *hurt* me."

"It's very unlikely, yes. But he's having a flashback, so you can never be certain."

A *flashback*. The word shocks through my gut, and guilt seeps into me. Did I cause this? I try to pull my hand back, but Matt catches my wrist, squeezing me tightly. He's still not looking at me, staring hard at something over my head.

"Matt," Kenta sounds cautious. "Let her go."

Matt's fingers loosen around my wrist. Slowly, I turn my hand in his grip, twisting my fingers through his until our palms press together. I don't remember the last time I held hands with someone, but it feels surprisingly natural as I rub my thumb over the back of his hand. He closes his eyes, trembling slightly. Even though all of his muscles are locked, I can feel the energy roaring inside of him. It's taking a lot out of him to stay still like this.

"It's okay," I tell him quietly. "You're okay."

Slowly, he opens his eyes again, glancing around the car. His broad shoulders slump.

Kenta bends and pulls a bottle of water out of the mini-fridge, handing it to him. He stares at it like he doesn't know what to do with it.

"It's cold," Kenta says.

"Right," Matt mutters. "Thanks." He takes the bottle, pressing it to the side of his throat, then his cheek. "Let go of me, Briar."

I do, tugging my sweat-slick fingers out of his just as we pull up outside the hotel. There's a group of paparazzi waiting outside.

"Shit," Kenta swears. "How the Hell did they find out where you're staying?!"

"I guess it was only a matter of time," Glen says glumly.

Kenta turns to Matt. "Should we move out?"

"I don't know," Matt says, staring at the men blankly.

"Should I—"

Matt runs a hand through his hair, tugging agitatedly. "I don't know! I don't fucking know what to do!"

Kenta nods. "We'll go in," he decides.

He and Glen flank me as we cross the pavement, stepping through the flashing lights and the obnoxious shouting.

"YOU LOOK BEAUTIFUL TONIGHT, BRIAR!"

"BRIAR, ANY MORE WORDS FOR YOUR STALKER?"

"BRIAR, WHY DID YOU LEAVE THE PRESS EVENT SO SUDDENLY?"

I keep my mouth firmly shut as we step inside the hotel's glass doors and head towards the lift. Kenta uses our special keycard to unlock the block on our floor, and then we all stand in awkward silence as the lift shoots upward. I huddle into myself. The elevator car seems too small for all of us, as if there's not enough air in here for everyone. Matt stands in his own corner, his face a tight, blank mask. His posture is ramrod straight, like a soldier's.

The doors open, and we pad down the thickly carpeted corridor and into our suite. When we're finally safe inside, I take a deep breath, turning to look at Matt. He's leaning heavily against the wall, unloading his gun. There's sweat on his forehead.

"I'm—" I trail off. I don't know how to end that sentence. I'm not *sorry*, exactly. I won't apologise for standing up for myself when I'm being harassed. But I'm sorry about whatever happened to him that gave him that awful haunted look in his eyes. I'm sorry if I triggered those memories back up, somehow.

"It wasn't your fault," he grates out, his voice rough. "I never should have told you about the picture." His face twists. "Should've known you'd blow up."

Any sympathy I might have been feeling for him melts away. I narrow my eyes. "Cute, Matt."

"Go get some sleep," Kenta advises him. "I'll explain what's happening to her." Matt hesitates, and he sighs. "You're jetlagged. Go to bed. We've got everything handled. She'll make the apology."

No, I bloody well will not, but I think now probably isn't the right time to mention it. Matt nods jerkily and heads into the guys' shared bedroom.

With him gone, it feels like all of the fight seeps out of me. I run a hand over my face. "I don't understand why everyone's so mad," I mumble.

Kenta nods. "I know you don't. It's our fault. We assumed you'd just… let us take care of your statements. But of course, you'll want to speak your own mind, too." He looks exhausted.

"Well, yeah. I am a real human person. I speak sometimes."

There's a knock on the door. Glen grabs his pistol and checks through the judas, then opens the door a few inches to let Julie inside the room.

My shoulders slump. Great. This day is just getting better and better.

I turn and head to the fridge, yanking it open and studying the beverage selection the hotel left for us. I should probably have a vodka water, or something equally diet-friendly and depressing, but right now, I just can't be bothered. I grab a bottle of beer.

Julie comes up behind me and slams the fridge shut. "What the Hell were you doing out there?" She hisses.

I shrug, popping the bottle cap off with my teeth and ignoring Julie's horrified look. I'm not sure if she's more worried about the carbs or my veneers. "He deserved it. If he wants to send me pictures of his Twinkie, he should be prepared for me to review it. Not my fault it's a one-star." I take a deep swig of beer and slump down onto the end of the sofa.

"You told your fans to eff off!" She screeches, practically hysterical.

I roll my eyes. So that's what she's annoyed about. I've broken the number-one rule for female celebrities: always, *always* act grateful. It doesn't matter if your fans are assaulting you in the street, or climbing into your property, or *wanking in your bed*—you're expected to grit your teeth and tell them how much you love and appreciate them. I'm sick of it. I don't love my fans; I don't *know* any of them. I *like* them fine, I'm glad that they enjoy my movies, and I'm happy to sign autographs or whatever, but that doesn't make me a piece of public property. I still get to have boundaries. I'm still a human being, who should be allowed to tell sexual harassers to piss off.

Julie huffs, coming to stand directly in front of me. She shoves her phone in my face.

"I've written your apology. Approve it."

I stare at the screen. "You want me to tweet out a *notes app apology?* You know that everyone makes fun of these, right?"

She scowls. "I'm not screwing around, Briar. The studio isn't happy, the dress designer isn't happy, and neither is your security team. Just approve it, so I can post it, and we can move on with our lives."

I feel a stab of guilt at the *studio* remark. I don't give a shit about what the guys think, but people have worked so hard on the film. I don't want to make the opening weekend all about me. I scan through the apology.

> *I know many of you saw my outburst at the* Players *press event earlier this evening. I apologise for my choice of words; I was jetlagged and over-tired. I love all my supporters, and believe that everybody deserves kindness, empathy, and a second chance. I would like to politely ask that fans respect my privacy, and hope that you will all come out to see* Players *on opening weekend. Thank you for your understanding. Love you all.*

"This is bullshit," I say flatly. "Everyone who sees it will know that it's bullshit."

"It doesn't matter." She thrusts the phone in my face again. "Approve it."

"Approve it, sweetheart," Kenta says. "You really do need to apologise."

I shake my head, anger rising up in me. "No! No! I meant everything that I said! If I apologise, it'll just encourage him!"

Julie sniffs. "I understand that you're angry, but really. You're almost thirty. Would it kill you to act with a little class?"

I close my eyes, taking another deep drag of beer. I'm *seething*.

I've been in this industry since I was a kid. I learned that if you don't want to be taken advantage of, you have to advocate for yourself. Your PR team won't help. Your security won't help. Your director, or manager, or agent won't help. They all have their own agendas. They're all looking at you like a product they want to sell. The only person who can ever really look after me is myself. So yes, I kick up a fuss when someone screws me over. I think every girl should.

"I'm getting really pissed off," I warn her. "I'm not. Making. The statement. Don't ask again."

"Please, lass," Glen says quietly.

I whirl on him. "Don't *lass* me. You let your teammate *pick me up* and *manhandle* me away from an interview I was giving, just because he didn't like what I was saying. Do you have any idea how disrespectful that is? I was trying to stand up for myself, and GI Joe thought I was, what, being too *hard* on the guy who's been ruining my life for the past few weeks? Who's been terrifying me and threatening me, who *broke into my house?* Everyone always wants me to shut up and smile. That's all anyone has ever wanted from me, since I was thirteen years old. And *none* of you have any idea how it feels to, to always—" I trail off, my throat tightening with tears. Shit. I shake my head. "Forget it," I mutter, slumping back against the sofa cushions. "The answer's no."

There's a brief silence.

Kenta steps forward and sits on the couch next to me, running a hand through his hair. He's pulled it loose from its usual bun, and it's falling around his face. It looks really hot. Which just makes me madder.

"I think we're approaching this wrong," he says gently. "Briar, why do you think Matt pulled you from that interview?"

"Because he thought I was making a scene," I mutter. "I wasn't being *classy.*"

"No. That's not it at all." He studies me for a moment. "I think we need to talk a bit about the psychology of stalking."

I swig down some more beer. "Told you. I'm already seeing a therapist."

"Not of being stalked. Of *stalking*. Stalkers like X tend to exhibit very specific psychological traits."

I close my eyes. I hate this shit. I *hate it*. "Look, I don't care if he's a tortured soul, or depressed, or whatever, okay? I don't care if he's socially anxious, or an orphan, or his parents divorced when he was a kid. All of that stuff is shitty, but none of that justifies his behaviour." I pick at the label on my beer bottle. "I'm sure he is mentally ill. But I'm not his psychologist, or his mum, I'm his *victim*. And asking a victim to empathise with someone who is hurting them is fucked up. I'm *allowed* to be pissed at him."

He lets out a low groan. "Christ, Briar. That's not what I'm saying at all." He reaches out and puts a hand on mine. I blink at the unexpected contact. His palm is cool and smooth. "I know you're angry," he says. "And you have a right to be. And if you want to go to the gym, work off some steam, and then come back and have this conversation, that's fine, too. But trust me, I am not about to *blame* you for anything that X is doing to you." His brown eyes hold mine, completely sincere.

I believe him, I realise. I really do. Ever since I was sixteen years old, I've had people blaming me for shit I had no control over.

But I don't think this man will. Not at all.

I take a deep breath through my nose. "No gym. Let's eat. Then you can tell me how bad I screwed up."

CHAPTER 28
BRIAR

H alf an hour later, Kenta and I are sprawled on the sofa in comfy clothes, bent over a pile of papers. The coffee table in front of us is laden with plates of vegan sushi and steaming cups of miso. Glen left to sort out new security details with the hotel manager, and Julie's gone back to her suite down the hall. I haven't heard anything out of Matt, so I assume he's still asleep.

It's just me and Kenta.

This hotel has a balcony, and even though I'm not allowed to sit on it—sniper risk, apparently—the view through the glass doors is amazing. A storm is rolling in, and the sky is deepening to an intense purple as dark clouds tense over Hollywood Hills. The strange light is stroking down the side of Kenta's angular face, kissing his skin a lilac-silver colour.

I study him as he bends over his notes, his dark hair falling loose around his face. I like the way he moves. All of his movements and gestures are fluid and firm. Graceful. Even his handwriting is neat and pretty. I watch his strong fingers on the pen, and a pang of leftover want echoes through me. I remember pressing him against the wall last night. I remember his hot mouth under mine. I imagine those strong fingers inside of me.

"Briar?" He asks, and I jolt back to reality. He smiles gently, like he knows exactly what I was thinking about. "I'm sure you're tired. I'll try to be quick."

"Sorry." I clear my throat, shifting position. Our arms press together, and I can tell by the slow stiffening of his muscles that he notices, although he doesn't say anything.

He points to the diagram he's drawn on his notepad. "Stalkers like X, who engage in these obsessive romantic fantasies with strangers, are usually pretty powerless by society's standards," he explains, jotting a note. "They're usually not rich, not particularly attractive, not physically strong. They have poor social skills, and little to no family or friends. They're often unemployed, or working low-paid jobs."

I don't see why that means I should let them harass me, but I keep my mouth shut and let him speak.

"To combat this feeling of powerlessness," he continues, "they build a fantasy in their heads. It gives them a sense of control and importance, in a world that generally considers them unimportant. X has clearly imagined a world in which the two of you are in love."

"But he's wrong. So I should set him straight."

Kenta shakes his head. "If he were an average person, I would fully support your right to reject him. But stalkers of his type are usually unstable. They don't handle rejection well." He reaches under the pile of papers and pulls out a book, handing it to me. I read the title. *When Love Becomes Obsession: a Clinical and Behavioural Study of Celebrity Stalking.* The cover image shows the silhouette of a man hiding in the shadows, holding a gun. "Matt didn't want me to give you this," Kenta says. "Said it would just make you paranoid. But I think you'd appreciate knowing what you're dealing with."

"Definitely."

He nods. "Check chapter thirteen. There's a phenomenon that psychologists call the 'devaluation of the object of obsession.' Essentially, X is obsessed with you. Because he centres his entire fake reality on the idea that you are going to love him, when you reject him, you tear his whole world apart. You destroy any feeling of control or power that he imagines he has. On the carpet tonight, you announced to the whole world that he's been wrong this entire time; he's not strong, or lovable, or important."

"He's not," I mutter, flipping through the pages.

Kenta nods. "When a romantically obsessed stalker gets rejected, their obsession doesn't just go away. It often flips. In his mind, you swing from being an idealised angel to the opposite. A demon."

"I become devalued?" I guess.

"Exactly. The problem is, you're still in the magazines. You're still making money. You're still on carpets. That could be infuriating to him, if he decides that you don't deserve any of that praise. You've been devalued in his head, so he might want to devalue you in the eyes of everybody else, as well. Potentially by hurting you. Or destroying you entirely."

I look up at him. "You think he might kill me."

His face is calm. "We have to consider the possibility. John Lennon, Selena, Christina Grimmie—it happens, a lot more often than people really appreciate. For every celebrity that does get killed, there are thousands of failed attempts. *Thousands.*"

I nod. I know. Half of the A-listers I know have their assistants carry military-grade bandages with them wherever they go. I swallow, turning back to the book's front cover. The dark male silhouette seems to stare out at me.

Kenta puts a hand on mine. "I'm not trying to scare you," he says gently.

"I should be scared though, right? That's what he wants." Setting the book down, I pull out my phone and shoot off a text to Julie.

B: *Post the apology.*

She responds immediately.

J: *Done*

I sigh and drop my phone, picking up my chopsticks. "Apology sent. Do you really think it'll change anything?"

Kenta shrugs. "It certainly can't hurt. The more damage control we can do, the better."

"It's so bullshit," I mutter. "I have to write an entire fake apology just to spare one creep's feelings. I *hate* this." I try to pick up a piece of avocado sushi, but my chopsticks fumble, and half the rice falls out. I shove the remaining scrap of avocado in my mouth before I can drop that, too. "How did you get into this psychology stuff? Did you learn it in the army?"

He shakes his head. "University. I got my undergrad degree in psychology at twenty, but I hated studying behind a desk all day. As soon as I finished my last exam, I went and enrolled." He takes a sip of his drink, watching me. "I got some psychological training in the force, and when I left, I got my MSc. Knowing how people's minds work helps a lot in our field of work."

"You'd be a good therapist. I'd pay to tell you my problems." I reach for the clump of fallen rice on my plate, but it just slips back between my chopsticks again. I scowl, stabbing at it. Kenta doesn't respond. I notice him smiling down at my hands. "What?"

"Nothing." He ducks his head. "You have absolutely no idea how to use those, do you?"

"I've been trying at least twice a week for about fifteen years," I say mournfully.

His smile gets wider. "Here." He leans over me, taking my hand and carefully repositioning my fingers. As his loose hair brushes the side of my face, I get a deep breathful of his cologne, and warmth fills me. I lean into him, pressing into his side, and his dark eyes flick up to mine. Neither of us says anything for a few seconds. Slowly, he lets go of my fingers and leans back.

"Thank you," I say.

"For what?"

"For letting me be angry. And explaining this to me like I'm a regular person, and not an idiot. And…" I look down at the chop-sticks. "I don't know. Acting like I'm just as capable as you are."

Confusion touches his face. "What do you mean? Of course you are."

I shake my head. "Matt thinks I'm stupid. And Glen… I know he's just doing his job, but you'd think I was made of glass, the way he watches over me."

He grimaces. "Yes, well. They both tend to take a bit of a caveman approach to close protection jobs. They like to take control of the client to protect them."

"But not you?"

His eyes meet mine, suddenly serious. "You're smart, Briar. You know this industry better than any of us, and you're very good at navigating it. You're not a damsel in distress, and you're clearly capable of defending yourself. At least verbally." His mouth twists wryly.

"You think I'm smart?"

His brow furrows. "Of course. You're an immensely successful actress, a product designer, you own multiple businesses, you've founded charities, and you're what, twenty-eight?"

"Most people think I'm a bimbo because I dye my hair blonde and like to get my nails done."

His eyebrow quirks. "I've never really noticed a correlation between someone's intelligence, and how often they get a manicure. Hell, I'm not even sure how much you need us. You've been protecting yourself for years, haven't you?"

My mouth goes dry. I suddenly feel completely naked. Like for the first time in a very long time, someone is finally seeing through my bullshit. "What do you mean?"

He shrugs a shoulder. "The outfits, and the attitude. Flipping off paparazzi and refusing to smile in pictures. Picking fights. The 'celebrity diva' branding is really clever. Instead of worrying about public favour, you can just look out for yourself, right? You made a bad reputation part of your appeal. Everyone loves a villain."

I swallow thickly. My heart is beating in my ears. "When you're trying to make hundreds of millions of people like you," I say eventually, "they control you. They control the way you speak, and act, and think. I couldn't do it anymore. It almost killed me."

His eyes trail across my face, like he's searching for something.

There's a sudden clap of thunder, and I jump as fat raindrops start to spatter against the window pane. I guess the storm finally reached us. "Jesus." I press a hand over my thudding heart. "That scared the shit out of me."

Kenta doesn't look away from me. "You're okay," he says quietly, touching a hand under my cheek. Everything in my body stills. Slowly, he leans forward and touches his lips to mine, just as white lightning flickers through the room.

It's the softest kiss I've ever had. Barely a brush of skin on skin. For some reason, that just makes it hotter. I want more. I sway into him gently, but he pulls back, staying just out of my reach. "Stay still," he says quietly.

I don't move. I just sit there, my pulse hammering, waiting. Last night, I got to be in charge, and I liked that a lot... but now, I want to see what *he* wants.

What he wants is to be gentle.

He reaches up and gently touches his finger to my collarbone. Tingles flow through my skin, and my eyes flutter shut. I can feel him everywhere; his warm arm brushing against mine, the soft cotton of his t-shirt rubbing my chest through my clothes. His mouth touches mine again, and I taste the hot sweetness of the whiskey he's been drinking. He presses a little kiss to my cupid's bow, then another just under my bottom lip, tracing my mouth with his. I sigh as lust slowly rolls through me.

"I like this," I murmur, as he carefully nudges my lips apart with his. I feel his smile against my mouth.

"Thought you liked it hard," he murmurs, stroking a hand down my arm. I feel electricity prickle through me as all the fine hairs on my skin stand on end. "You seemed quite insistent about it last night."

"I like you," I say. "More than I expected." He makes a soft noise, his mouth becoming more demanding. I feel urgency building in my belly, but I ignore it, letting him keep the kiss slow and heavy. He touches the side of my face, tilting my cheek slightly, and then softly bites my bottom lip, sucking it into his mouth. I gasp, leaning into him.

A scream shatters through the room. My eyes widen. I pull away, staring at the guys' bedroom door. It sounds like someone's being murdered inside.

Matt.

CHAPTER 29
BRIAR

Kenta swears and jumps to his feet, jogging out of the room. For a few seconds, I sit frozen on the couch. I'm not sure what to do. Has someone come inside the suite? Do I need to hide?

The screaming suddenly stops, and I hear Kenta murmuring something. He doesn't sound scared at all. Just kind of... soothing. I slip off the couch and follow him to the bedroom. When I push open the door, the room is dark. The curtains are pushed open, and I can see the LA sky storming outside. Lightning flickers again, illuminating Kenta standing over the bed, talking softly.

"You're okay, man. You're good." There's a broken sobbing noise, and ice slips down the back of my throat.

"What's wrong with him?" I demand. "Is he hurt?"

Kenta glances over his shoulder. "Briar, he's fine, you don't have to see this."

I ignore him, pushing into the room. Matt is sitting hunched on the bed, breathing hard. He has a hand twisted in the hem of Kenta's shirt, like he's trying to hold the man in place.

"What's wrong?" I ask again.

Kenta sighs. "Nothing. He just had a night terror. They've been getting worse recently." His lips twist into a wry smile. "Nice little leftover from our time in the force."

Matt lets go of Kenta and runs a heavy hand through his thick hair. He's still dressed in dress pants and a crumpled shirt, and his skin is flushed and sweaty. "Briar…" he rasps. "I'm sorry."

I stare at him. "For what? Did you wet the bed, or something? It's fine, I don't mind having an incontinent bodyguard."

He looks up at me, panting. Heat is climbing up his neck and cheeks. He looks completely humiliated, and I don't know why. Kenta glances at me awkwardly, like he's embarrassed that I'm here.

"What?" I demand. "Why are you looking at me like that?"

Matt gulps in another breath and hangs his head. "Sorry you had to see that."

My mouth drops. "Sorry I had to *see* it? What the fuck does that mean? It wasn't particularly hard to *see*. I'm sorry *you* had to experience it."

He shakes his head, shame written all over his face.

Anger snaps through me. "Oh, for God's *sake*," I mutter, stomping forward. "Can I have a hug?"

He blinks, freezing. "What?"

"A hug. I doubt you've been given many in your life, but I'm sure you've heard of the concept. I want one."

He bristles. "I don't need—"

"This isn't about you, it's about me. You're right. *Seeing* you have a nightmare was so traumatic I need comforting. So do it."

He's still for a moment, then tentatively opens his arms. I climb onto his lap and curl up against his chest. Out of the corner of my eye, I see Kenta smile, shutting the door behind him. I bury my face in Matt's sweaty neck. "Don't apologise, you utter fucking *dipshit.*"

"I thought you were supposed to be a bitch," he murmurs, lightly laying a hand on my back.

"I am." I put my cheek on his chest and frown up at him. "A nice person wouldn't have called you a *dipshit,* would they?" He smiles tightly, but he still looks embarrassed. I'm frustrated. "Why are you acting so ashamed? I had a panic attack and, like, *dissolved* on a public bathroom floor in front of you. From what I can gather about your old job, it would be weirder if you *weren't* traumatised." I grab his hand and put it on my head. "You hug like a mannequin. Stroke my hair."

He snorts and starts running his fingers through my hair. "There's kind of a *don't ask, don't tell* policy in the military, when it comes to this stuff. People don't really trust you to carry a gun if they find out you're screwed in the head."

"Well, you're not in the military anymore, you work for me. So stop being so awkward, it's annoying me."

He muffles another laugh. "How are you making this about *you?*"

"I'm a self-obsessed diva, remember?" I shove at him until we're both lying down. We're still for a bit. I feel his battering heartbeat slowly ease up through his damp shirt.

I don't know exactly what I'm doing. I'm still mad at Matt. But I can be mad at him and also care that he's hurting.

"I'm sorry I shouted at you," he mutters into my hair. "I'm really, *really* sorry."

"Kenta explained what I did wrong. I still think you could've, you know, spoken to me like a human being instead of dragging me away like a naughty toddler."

He nods slowly. "It wasn't your fault. You didn't know. I'm sorry. I…" He licks his lips. "It has been brought to my attention that I do this, around a flashback. I can't stand being close to people, so I snap at them to make them go away. I don't mean to, I just get overwhelmed, I guess."

"Wait." I peel back to look at him. "Are you telling me that you're not always such a massive prick?"

"I'm always a prick," he concedes. "But you've definitely seen the worst of me since we met. I'm sorry." He traces a circle on my back.

"Don't apologise. I think it's kind of cute." I tuck into him. "We have matching unhealthy coping mechanisms. How adorable is that?"

He huffs a laugh. We listen to the storm rumble outside. The rain is getting heavier, hammering against the room's floor-to-ceiling windows. I look out at the grey skyline. "No fair. Your room has a better view. Can I please remind you that *I* am the Very Important Person? You're just regular, unimportant people."

He grunts. "Yours faces the back of the hotel. Less threat."

"Oh." Thunder suddenly claps outside, and he startles, his whole body stiffening. I flatten my hand on his chest, stroking over his heartbeat as he relaxes again. "What are your triggers?"

He glares at me.

I roll my eyes. "What? It kind of seems like pertinent information. I don't want to accidentally hurt you."

He shakes his head, a small jerk. "It's not really anything you could do. I…" He trails off, his jaw working. "Damp places. Some scents. Glen's voice, sometimes, especially when he yells. Which I guess is why he keeps so damn quiet, nowadays. Sometimes, just letting my mind wander is enough. But it's not like a button you press. I can be fine for months, and then—" he raises an eyebrow.

I try to process all of that. "Scents. Any of mine bother you?"

He snorts. "Yeah, Chanel Number Three takes me to a really dark place. No, princess. It's blood, mostly."

"Blood? What are you, a shark?"

"If there's enough of it, you can smell it pretty clear. Sometimes I feel like I can never get the smell of it out of my nose." He dips his face into my hair. "You always smell like cake," he says hoarsely. I curve around him, feeling his breath flutter against my neck.

"Any more?"

"The strongest..." he pulls a face, like he hates the word, "*trigger,* it's a feeling. An emotion. Feeling like I made a mistake, and someone else is going to get hurt because of it."

I don't say anything.

He heaves a breath. "On our last tour, I was the patrol leader. The others followed my orders, and I screwed up, I made a mistake. We got captured. We were imprisoned and tortured until a hostage recovery team showed up. But our captors only tortured the others, not me. They—they starved them, then gave me food in front of them, and beat them if I refused to eat. They choked them. Cut them. They killed my teammate Damon in front of me. Dragged it out for weeks. Never thought I'd be *relieved* to see a friend die."

Horror wells up inside me. I don't even want to think of what it must have been like for him. There are things too dark to let yourself imagine. "How long were you there?" I whisper.

It's too much. He opens his mouth, then snaps it shut again, his whole body freezing. I stay still in his arms, breathing softly until he relaxes again. There are tears in his eyes. He's shaking. "Sorry," he mutters, wiping his face. "*Shit*. Few months."

"Do you want me to call you a dipshit again?" I offer.

He closes his eyes. "*Please*."

"Okay. You little dipshit." The word comes out far too gentle. I roll over and reach up to stroke the blush touching his cheeks. "Kenta said you're getting worse."

"Kenta talks too much."

"He's worried about you."

He's silent for a bit. "It's not been this bad in about four years," he says eventually. "I used to have flashbacks maybe once or twice a month. The last week or so, it's been every damn day. Multiple times a day." His voice breaks a bit, and he clears his throat. "I... don't know what's happening."

Lightning flashes outside, illuminating him. For a moment, he doesn't look like my big, strong bodyguard. He doesn't look like an ex-soldier. He just looks like a scared little boy. My heart hurts. I run my fingers through his hair. "You don't want to go to therapy?"

He sucks in a sigh between his teeth. "Jesus *Christ*, not you, too. Kenta gets on my back about this every bloody time. *No*."

"Why? Therapy's great. I use it all the time."

"Do I need a reason?" He snaps. "It's my goddamn brain, if I don't want some bloody shrink poking around in there, that's my business."

His words are angry, but he doesn't pull away from me. We just lie there in silence for a while. My eyelids get heavy. I feel his breathing deepen against my neck, as if he's about to fall back to sleep.

"What if it's me?" I whisper.

He flinches. "What?"

"I think I'm the reason your PTSD symptoms are getting worse."

He snorts. "How the Hell would that work? You don't exactly look like any of the guys that caught us, princess." He reaches out to touch my hair. "The face, maybe. But none of them were blonde."

"Ha, ha. The timelines match up though, right?" I rub my fingers into the hem of his shirt. "You got worse after meeting me."

"It's probably just the stress of being around someone so terrible," he says flatly. "You're Hell on my nerves, woman."

I roll over to look him in the face. "I am, though, aren't I? That's what I mean. I think when you worry about my safety, it triggers that feeling. That feeling that if you make a mistake, I'll get hurt."

He shakes his head. "That doesn't make sense. I've never had this issue with a client before. Not in *years*."

I smile against his skin. "Well then," I say casually. "I guess you must just care about me."

He scoffs. "I do not."

"No? What other explanation do you have?" I nuzzle into his collar. "I think you do. I think you *care* about me."

"No."

I nudge his throat with my nose. "I think you *like me*."

I feel his jaw flex as he grits his teeth. "You're a job. That's it."

"Yeah? You got very angry, earlier." I thread my fingers through his hair. "Almost like you're emotionally invested."

"It would look bad if you got murdered by your stalker. You're very high profile; I'd never live it down."

I run my hand down to his collar, fiddling with the buttons. "I think the thought of me getting hurt *kills* you," I mutter. He doesn't say anything, watching as I slowly pop the button on his collar. "Because, no matter how much you call me *bossy*," I undo the next button, exposing a triangle of hard, tanned skin, "or *spoiled*," the next button goes, "or a *diva*," I slide my hand slowly under the thin fabric of his shirt, and watch a shudder roll through him. "I think you actually really like me," I whisper.

He reaches out suddenly, grabbing my hand. I look down at our linked fingers, my heart starting to pound.

"It does," he says, his voice rasping. His eyes burn into mine. "It kills me to think of you getting hurt, Briar."

Something in me softens. I flatten my hand across his bare chest. "I'll try to stay out of trouble. Promise."

He snorts. "You couldn't stay out of trouble if your life depended on it."

"I said I'd *try*."

He turns my hand over, running his thumb over the delicate skin of my wrist. "Did I scare you?" He asks quietly.

"At the event? No. I wanted to stab your eye out with my stiletto."

"Yeah, I'm pretty sure you tried, the way you were kicking me." He shakes his head. "When I screamed."

I frown. "I wasn't scared *of* you. I was just scared someone was hurting you."

His mouth twitches. "Sounds like you care about me too, then."

I shake my head. "I don't think so."

"Are you sure? Because you're in my bed. In my arms. Cuddling me after a nightmare." I try to pull away, and he squeezes me closer. "Doesn't seem like something you would do for someone you hated."

"I despise you," I inform him primly.

He leans closer until his lips brush against my ear, and I'm overwhelmed by the soft, sweet smell of his laundry detergent. "I'm sure."

"I do. You're an asshole—"

"You're a diva," he counters easily.

"You're high-handed," I continue. "Bossy."

"So are you."

I scowl. "I'm not *bossy*, I *am* your boss, you utter knob."

"Spoiled," he lists. "Demanding…"

"I'm *assertive*, not *demanding*, that's so bloody sexist—" I break off as he suddenly rolls us both over, pressing me to the mattress. His weight is hot and heavy over my body. I can't breathe. His gaze drops to my mouth, and I unconsciously lick my lips.

"Rude," he adds, his voice soft.

"Only to people who deserve it," I whisper. "I can be nice."

He reaches out to touch my hair, his blue eyes gleaming dark, then curves his hand behind my head. Heat thrums through my body as he strokes my cheekbone with his thumb. "I don't think I'd like you nice," he mutters.

Then he sinks his hands in my hair and kisses me like I've never been kissed before.

CHAPTER 30
BRIAR

Matt kisses me like he wants to eat me alive. Thunder crashes outside the windows as he drags me into his lap, sucking, nipping, biting. I can barely keep up, my heart hammering in my chest as he sucks on my tongue.

"I kissed Kenta like," I tip my head back as he presses his mouth to my throat, "literally ten minutes ago."

"Lucky bastard," he mutters, licking a line down the side of my neck. "Don't worry; he's used to sharing."

"I'm quite partial to it, too."

"Not tonight, you aren't." He slips a hand under the waistband of my joggers, and I shiver in anticipation as his rough fingertips trace over my abdomen. "Take these off."

I do, shucking off the grey material, revealing my pink lace underwear. He smooths his hands down my thighs, following the curves all the way to my calves. "You're so *soft*," he says, his voice grating. "How are you this *soft?*"

"You want my skincare routine?"

He drops to his knees and trails his nose up the inside of my thigh. I fight the urge to clamp my legs shut as he buries his face into my damp lace panties, inhaling deeply. His low groan vibrates right through my core.

"Are you sure we shouldn't call the others?" I tease, forcing myself to keep my breathing even. "I'm sure Kenta would *love* to join us, right now—"

His eyes flash. "No. Tonight, you're mine."

"Yours?"

He stares at me for a moment, jaw working as he runs his eyes over my face. Then he grabs me by the hips and lifts me off the bed, spinning me up against the wall. I gasp as his hot body brackets mine, a wall of muscle pressing me in place as he rubs his thumb down the seam of my underwear.

"By the time I'm done with you," he whispers in my ear, watching me squirm as I try to get some friction from the lace, "You're going to *wish* you were."

I open my mouth, but before I can say anything, he hooks an arm under each thigh and lifts me right off the soft carpet, pinning me to the wall with his hips. I choke, automatically winding my legs around his waist as he thrusts forward, grinding me up against the pretty gold wallpaper. My mouth falls open. I don't think I've been dry-humped since I was a teenager. I don't remember it feeling this good. My shoulders twitch and my toes curl as tingles prick through me.

"Kiss me," I demand. He does, in time with his steady rolling thrusts, and I moan, wrapping my fingers in his hair, pulling his face hard into mine. His mouth feels perfect. I could kiss him until I ran out of air completely. I would die happy in his arms.

Eventually, he pulls away panting, freeing one of his arms and sliding his hand back up between my thighs. He starts to play with the little bow on the front of my pants. I shudder as blood thunders between my legs.

"So soft," he says again, his voice low.

"Glad you like them. I'll tweet the company your review. Now take them *off*," I order.

"Take what off?" He rolls his hips again, and I moan as the bulge in his pants rubs right between my legs.

I could scream. "Are you thick? Don't they have IQ tests for the army?"

"I got 145," he informs me. "I could join a high IQ society. If I was a twat."

"Take off my *underwear, idiot.*" I shunt my hips against his, trying to wriggle out of them myself.

"What, these?" He ghosts his fingers over my pants. I jerk my hips, but I can't get enough friction. "I don't think so."

"Why not?"

"They're pretty." He slicks his fingers over the sodden fabric, making me squirm.

I snort, shivering all over. "You can have them."

"Well, in that case, princess—" He hooks his finger under the panties and tugs them right off me, bundling them in his palm and rubbing his thumb into the creamy wetness soaking the lace. "I'll treasure them forever," he says drily, tossing them onto his nightstand. I start to complain, but he reaches up and finally runs his fingers between my slick folds.

I arch, my vision going black. *"Matt,"* I choke, heaving for air.

I can feel him getting breathless, too. "Christ," he mutters. "You've been driving me mad."

"Yeah?"

"Ever since I walked in on you with that toy inside yourself. Jesus." He touches his forehead to mine, panting. The muscles in his arms quiver, veins popping out as he holds me upright and keeps stroking between my legs. "I thought," he dips his head and sucks a kiss on my neck, "I thought it would get better with time, but it's just getting worse. Every day, it's getting worse. I can barely think when I'm near you." He puts his mouth by my ear, tickling my oversensitive skin, and slides a finger into me. I cry out and dig my fingernails into his scalp, making him growl. "My body doesn't even feel right without yours anymore."

I don't know what to say, so I just kiss him again, sloppily, my chest hitching every other breath. He curls his finger inside me. I'm getting desperate now. I keep rubbing against him, slamming my pelvis against the heel of his hand. Sweat wets the back of my hair. The insides of my thighs are hot and sticky. Oh, God, I need to come so bad. I can feel it starting to happen as I begin to shake around him.

He kisses me back, groaning into my open mouth. "Gonna come?"

I nod, and he groans again, hiking me up higher against the wall, pressing his hot, muscled body completely against me. He crooks his finger as he thrusts it inside me, and I tip over the edge. All my nerves electrify, and I jolt in his arms, crying out. It washes over me, this burning wave of heat that swallows me up and crashes over my head. I gasp like I'm drowning. He holds me up against him, strong arms around me. His thumb keeps rubbing roughly against my hood, and I shudder from the overstimulation as I gasp back to reality. He apparently likes that a lot; he adds a second finger and just keeps going, ignoring me when I grab at his arm. "Matt!"

"Briar!" He mocks.

I fight the urge to kick him. "Enough. Put me down."

He presses his hot cheek to mine. "We're not done."

I take a shuddery breath as he keeps massaging my G-spot. Tingles fizzle deep inside me. "B-but I came."

"One more," he breathes, hot air touching my ear. "I need one more."

"I..." I don't think I can do it. He flutters his fingers inside of me, sending stars bursting behind my eyes. I arch, rubbing against his chest. *"I'm going to kill you."*

"Many have tried. *Come,* Briar."

Before I even know what's happening, my body spasms again, clenching around him, and I just keep coming, gasping, shaking against him all over again. I hide my face in his shoulder, tears shocking into my eyes as he adds a third finger and plunges in deep, wringing the pleasure right out of me.

Eventually, the contractions subside, and all my muscles go soft and weak. I turn my face to meet his, still panting, and he kisses the side of my open mouth.

"Good girl," he roughs out.

Rage suddenly flares up in me. "What the *Hell did you just call me—"*

He grasps my shoulders and shoves me onto the bed. I fall back onto the soft quilt, and he climbs on top of me, unbuckling his belt and shucking off his dress pants. I can feel the heavy weight of his erection pressing into my belly as he grabs the hem of my shirt and tugs it off over my head. He sits back on his haunches for a second, devouring the sight of my naked breasts spilling across my chest.

"I called you a good girl," he says quietly, then dips his head and licks a line down my cleavage.

"I'm not," I gasp, running my hand over the hard bulge in his boxers, "a damn," I grab the waistband, slipping my fingertips under the elastic, "*dog*."

I yank his underwear down. He's hard and thick and flushed, even bigger than I imagined. I reach forward and run my fingers down his length, feeling the velvety texture of his skin. When I rub my thumb under the head, he twitches, jumping in my hand. Matt growls, pushing my hand away and pinning it to the bed. When I reach for him with my other hand, he pins that one down too, leaning forward so his naked chest is pressed up against mine.

"No, princess," he rasps, nudging his nose against mine. "You're a very sweet, *good* girl."

I bite his cheek, and he throws his head back and laughs, his white teeth gleaming. It might be the first time I've seen him genuinely laugh. It's mesmerising. His whole face lights up, like he's full of neon. I can barely look away.

"Do you have something," I choke out.

He drops to his knees and pulls his black suitcase out from under the bed, rooting around inside. I melt in relief as he pulls out a little foil square. Thank *God*.

"You carry that around with you?" I try to look unimpressed and not relieved. "Pretty desperate."

He rolls the condom on. "I'm big on protection."

I snort, then yelp as he picks me up again and carries me across the room.

"What do you have against beds, you madman?"

He presses a kiss to my lips, then slams me up against the floor-to-ceiling window. I gasp as the freezing cold glass presses against my overheated skin.

"You said you preferred the view," he points out, sucking the side of my throat.

"I'm going to get arrested for indecent exposure," I mumble, tipping my head back to give him better access. "The glass—"

"It's one-way. No one can see." I whimper as he grinds down on me.

"Who has sex against a window? Is this a kink?" I cast around my brain. "Or is it the storm? I bet th-that's a thing, *stormophilia*."

"Fulgarophilia," he mutters against my neck. "No, I do not have it."

"Then how do you know what it's called?!"

"IQ of 145," he reminds me, his hands clutching at my waist as he pushes me harder against the glass.

I scoff, "Admit it. Thunder gets you hard. It's okay, I won't kink shame you. God, I bet the *Thor* movies really got you going, huh—"

"Stop talking," he mutters, guiding the swollen head of his cock to my entrance. I bite my lips as he teases it between my legs.

"Please. If you want a silent, compliant shag, you should've picked someone else."

He growls, presses his lips to my forehead, and pushes into me.

I didn't have to be worried about his size. I'm so desperate for him that he slides into me easily, filling me deeply. I lean my head back against the glass, closing my eyes. *"Oh."*

He rests his forehead against mine for a second, breathing hard. Thunder rattles the windows.

"Are you turned on," I whisper, as the sound fades away. "That was a big one."

He snorts and thrusts, hissing through his teeth. "I need this."

"Me too," I breathe, pulling his mouth back to mine. The room is splashed full of light as we start to rock together. I'm making noises like I'm crying into his broad shoulder. He nips at my neck and changes the angle. A tugging, tingling ache starts to build, deep in my belly. I grind against him faster, but it's not enough. Matt keeps rolling his hips, deep and slick and perfect, and with every thrust, the hot tingling gets more and more unbearable. I grind up harder, rubbing myself against him, but I can't reach it. My arms strain by my sides, pinned against the cold window-pane. I need to touch myself.

"Matt… I can't."

"Can't what?" He pants, his breath hot against my cheek.

"Can't come from just p-*ah*." He bites my bottom lip savagely, and I arch under him. "Penetration," I finish on a gasp, kicking his leg. "I need you to touch me, asshole. What, you never shagged a girl before?"

"No," he says flatly. "I'm a virgin. Couldn't you tell?"

I squirm, rutting up into him. The feeling in my belly gets bigger and bigger. Matt frees one hand and slides his palm teasingly down my stomach, tickling his fingers through my damp curls. I buck, but he doesn't go lower.

"G-go on, then," I prompt. "Touch me."

The room splashes with white light again. Matt's face illuminates, and my mouth falls open. He looks *stunning* like this, with the sharp contours of his face drawn starkly in light and shadow.

He looks me dead in the eye. "No. I don't think I will."

CHAPTER 31
MATT

Shock flashes over her face. "Wh-what?" She stammers. "Why not?!"

I keep hammering into her in solid, rhythmic thrusts. "I think," I say slowly, "that you need to learn a lesson."

Anger clouds her pretty features. "Piss off. I wanted a shag, not a sermon."

"*No.*" I cover her body completely with mine, pressing our foreheads together. "*I'm* in charge. You understand me?"

She bucks her hips. "Piss *off.*"

"Princess," I growl.

"Dipshit," she scowls back, bucking again. The movement pushes me deeper inside her, and I grit my teeth as my dick jerks. I'm not going to back down. She *needs* to get this through her head. I'm too scared of what will happen if she doesn't.

I almost had a heart attack when she started mouthing off in front of the cameras this evening. For a second, I actually wondered if what was happening was real, or some sort of sick nightmare conjured up by my twisted mind. Unknowingly, she was increasing the risk X posed a hundredfold. In a country where he could very easily purchase any number of weapons to kill her. And there wasn't anything I could do about it. I haven't felt so utterly helpless since our time in captivity. Yes, I feel bad about manhandling Briar, but that wouldn't have been necessary if she'd just *listened to me*.

I press even closer to her, thrusting in so deep that my aching balls crush painfully against her pelvis. "When I tell you to trust me, you *do it*. Do you understand me?"

She rolls her eyes. "Oh, shut up. I do trust you."

"You *obviously* don't—"

"Not with my public image, no. But I trust you with my body. Hey, I've been practising my kegels. Wanna see?"

She clenches, and I can't help but shout as her muscles clamp down, squeezing me.

"Touch me," she whispers, brushing her lips against my cheek. "Just touch me, Matt. Make me come."

I shake my head, turning to glance out of the window. LA unfurls under us, lit up like a circuit board.

Briar sighs. "If I didn't trust you, you wouldn't be inside me right now." At my next thrust, she bears down again. My dick feels like it's about to explode.

I groan. "It's not enough."

She rubs up against me, animal-like, and I feel her thighs shaking. She's right on the edge.

I stop moving, suddenly going still inside her. I can feel sweat dripping down the back of my neck. My cheeks are hot, my heart is beating out of my chest, my balls are heavy and straining for relief.

I reach up and cup her cheek. Her hips twitch desperately against me.

"Say it." I command. The hand falls from her cheek down to her chest. I stroke her breast, my fingers dancing along the heavy curve.

She narrows her eyes. "Fuck off."

I dip my head and start sucking down her tits. Briar sobs, her body squirming and bucking, desperate to end this, to let herself go. But I won't let her. I lick her nipple slowly, looking up at her as she grits her teeth and quivers in my arms. She looks like she's fighting the urge to scream.

"Say it, Briar." My voice is low and unsteady. "Say you trust me to take care of you. Say that the next time I tell you to do something, you'll do it. Without question."

"Two. Different. Things," she pants.

I flick my tongue over her little pink bud, and she winces like it hurts. "Not in this business. Say it."

"God, Matt. I *can't*." Her breathing is ragged now, her chest heaving against my face. I can feel her channel fluttering and contracting uselessly around me as her body strains for stimulation that is *just* out of reach. She lets one hand fall from my shoulder, cupping my full balls. I let out a strangled noise and press my face into her soft cleavage.

"Oh, shit, Briar," I mutter, breathlessly. "What the Hell are you doing to me?"

"Let me come," she orders, her voice weak, and I shake my head, pressing her harder into the glass. We're like two wolves wrestling for dominance, snapping at each other's necks, fighting to be alpha. Thunder rumbles through the window, and Briar closes her eyes.

"I promised myself," she confesses. "I promised that I'd n-never l-let someone else control me again."

"Why?" I demand.

"People," she has to heave in a gasp as I shift slightly, a look of tortured pleasure crossing her face. "People manipulate me every day. They have done since I was thirteen. The director. The studio. Fans, managers, agents, brands. When I was a kid, I let myself get talked into things I never, ever wanted to do."

I stare at her. *"You?"*

She laughs. "I wasn't always like this, Matt. When I was younger, I was a people-pleaser. A doormat. You've never met a kid m-more desperate to be liked. I did whatever they asked."

My stomach twists. "What did they ask?" She doesn't answer immediately, so I rock my hips slightly. Her eyes scrunch closed.

"Everything. They wanted everything. Too many examples."

"Pick one."

She swallows. "My first kiss was on-camera. I didn't want to do it. I couldn't stop crying. But the producers made me do it over and over, in a room full of men watching me, until I got the shot right. It took all day. I was just a kid, and I had no adults who wanted to protect me." I can feel her heartbeat pounding against my chest. "So I learned to protect myself. I *promised* that I wouldn't be that kid anymore. I'd never let myself be manipulated again."

I feel my face softening. "I'm not trying to manipulate you, Briar," I whisper. "I'm trying to keep you *safe*. I just want you to be okay."

She stares at me, breathing hard. Another bolt of lightning shatters through the room, lighting up her face bright white. Her eyes glow this pale, unreal blue, and they're filled with raw, naked *fear*.

"I won't hurt you," I promise. "Just trust me."

"I'll try," she whispers. "I'll try. It's all I can do."

The lightning fades and her face falls back into shadow. Slowly, far too slowly, I straighten, bringing my lips back to hers.

And then I move. My fingers tighten on her arse as I slam into her roughly. She screams, and I feel the building groan as thunder roils and smashes in the sky above us. Blood roars in my ears, deafening me. It only takes a few more thrusts before I feel her beginning to fall apart.

I press my open mouth to her sweaty neck and groan, low and desperate, as she starts to come. My hips shudder and thrust as I finally explode and unload inside her. The feeling is intoxicating. I practically black out. I can't think. I can't see. It's all I can do to keep holding Briar up as she wraps herself around me, choking and shaking. It's like I'm draining my soul into her.

Eventually, eventually, the glow starts to fade. When I open my eyes, Briar is shivering hard against me, her head buried in my chest.

"Down," she gasps. "Before you drop me."

Still inside her, I carry her to the bed. We flop down onto the sheets. For a minute or so, we both just lay there, panting, slick with sweat. Briar cuddles into my side, breathing me in like she's huffing my scent.

I curve a hand against her cheek, tilting her face to mine. My thumb strokes her cheekbones as I assess her expression. "Alright?" I ask quietly.

She nods sleepily. I press my lips to her forehead, then gently pull out, sliding out of bed and walking awkwardly to the bathroom. I clean up and wash my hands, then turn to see Briar still sprawled over the pillows, staring unabashedly at my ass. I lean in the bathroom doorway, staring right back. "What now?" I ask.

She lifts the corner of the duvet. "Come back."

"Yeah?" I can't hold back my smile. I climb back under the sheets and wrap my arms around her again. "I never would have expected you to be so cuddly," I murmur.

"I've literally been using Glen as a human teddy bear for the last week."

"Does it help?"

She nods into my shoulder, and I pull her closer, my chest swelling. The sounds of LA filter through the window, filling the room with the muted sounds of car honks, sirens, and shouts.

She curls a bit of my hair around her finger. "What does it feel like? A flashback?"

Not this again. I give her a flat look.

She shrugs. "Sorry. I'm nosy. You don't have to say."

I press my lips together. I don't really want to tell her, especially not *now*. But she's promised to trust me. It's only fair that I trust her, as well. "They're not all the same," I say quietly. "Occasionally, I see things. Most of the time, I just feel the emotions I was feeling when it happened."

She frowns. "What, like, you're just having a conversation with someone, and then you suddenly feel like…" she trails off.

My stomach lurches. "Like I'm watching my teammate getting murdered in front of me. Yeah." I kiss a freckle on her shoulder. "Thought I was going mental for a long time. At the beginning, it was… awful."

"You're not mental," she says softly. "Unless being really goddamn *annoying* is a new diagnosis."

I snort, reaching out to touch her hair. "You should go sleep with the others."

"Are you trying to get rid of me?" She pinches my hip. "You can't delegate post-coital cuddling."

"I don't want to," I admit, "but at the rate I'm going, I'll probably wake you up screaming."

She takes my free hand, pressing our palms together. "How do I help? When you do?"

It's the last thing I expect her to say. For a moment, I'm speechless, struggling to find an answer. She stays quiet, breathing softly against me. "I don't know," I say eventually. "I don't think you can."

"I'll find ways," she decides, and a soft noise falls out of my throat. I tug her closer to me, but something's wrong. She's not relaxed.

I frown. "What is it?"

"What's what?"

"You're all tense." I squeeze her butt. "Go soft."

"I can't believe you don't think you're bossy," she mumbles, obediently letting her body relax against me. Happiness rumbles through me, and she laughs, petting my chest. "You're purring."

I bury my lips in her hair. "What's wrong?"

She winces. "Do you think X will respond to what I said at the press event?"

"Honestly?"

"No. Please present me with your most elaborate lie."

"Yes." I press a kiss to her ear. "I do."

She swears under her breath. "Badly?"

"I don't know. But we'll deal with it tomorrow. We'll keep you safe, princess. 'S'long as you let us."

She sighs, sitting up and leaning over the edge of the bed. I watch through hooded eyes as she pats around the pile of discarded clothes on the floor, eventually pulling out her phone. She settles back down next to me, bringing up her twitter account, and starts writing a new tweet. I look over her shoulder. It's just three words.

I'm sorry X

She publishes the tweet and drops her phone, grimacing with disgust.

"Let no one say I didn't try," she mumbles, curling up against me, her eyes falling closed. "It's his move, now."

CHAPTER 32

X

I t's very easy to make a petrol bomb. Almost worryingly easy, really; any old criminal could do it.

After Briar left the press event, I was upset for a very long time. For hours, I paced up and down my cabin, crying, screaming, breaking things. Trying to decide what I should do.

It's the middle of the night by the time I make my decision.

I drive myself to the nearest gas station to buy petrol, some cloth, and a glass bottle of pop.

I am very, very, very angry.

I admit, I'm not thinking clearly. My head is in a haze. I'm just so mad at Briar. I have worked so hard, building her a home. I have spent years sending her gifts and messages. And she's thrown it all in my face.

Well. I'll show her. I know where she's staying. I think I might just pay her a visit.

As I'm checking out my shopping, I see a couple of young teenagers loitering in the candy aisle, holding hands. I stand and watch in disgust as the guy bends and kisses the girl on the lips. They start making out, right in the middle of the store.

Fury lashes through me, so strong I almost drop my shopping. Why the Hell should a fifteen-year-old *boy* be able to get a girl, when I can't? Things like this make me feel so angry I want to kill someone.

I take all of my materials home and set about making the bomb. I've just finished when my phone buzzes. I look and see that Briar's sent another tweet. Not the bullshit one her PR people published earlier this evening. A tweet just for me.

I'm sorry X

Oh.

Heat rolls down my whole body as I read it again, and again. I moan. Oh, God. She's talking to me. She's talking right to me.

I feel light-headed. My breathing gets fast. I lean back against the sofa, blushing furiously, and force myself to take some time to calm down and really rationalise.

I've gotten it all wrong.

Briar is a sweet girl. I know she wouldn't say those nasty things about me if she didn't have to. Celebrities are like puppets on strings. They have managers, and PR people, and agents. Every-body is always telling them what to do and what to say. My angel is being manipulated. That's why, as soon as she could, she tweeted out that apology to me. I imagine her lying in bed right now, typing out the tweet before her people can notice.

God, my poor girl. I remember her face as that security guard carried her away from the event. He's the same guard who keeps making her kiss him in front of the cameras. She's being controlled!

But soon, she'll be free. In two days, she'll be here with me. I'll give her a new life.

I look down at the petrol bomb. I guess I may as well use it. Ideally, I would blow up that awful guard, but he's staying at the same hotel as her. She could get hurt.

I glance at the clock. It's past midnight. Technically her birthday. An idea forms in my brain. I'll use the bomb as a birthday present.

There's one man my angel has always hated. One man who hurt her more than anybody else. Who turned the world against her, and spread vicious, awful lies about her. I'm sure she wants him dead.

So I'll make that happen. To prove to her that I'm not mad at her. And as an extra-special birthday present.

I stand up and grab my car keys. She's going to love it.

CHAPTER 33
MATT

I'm woken by an insistent buzzing under my pillow. Twisting my head, I blink around the unfamiliar room. Something warm shifts against me, and I turn to see Briar curled up under my arm. Her pink lips are slightly parted, and her eyelashes flutter as she dreams. She's unbelievably sweet when she's asleep.

Hell. She's kind of unbelievably sweet in general. I hazily remember her holding my hand in the car yesterday evening. Even through all of her anger and frustration, she was still so gentle.

I must have looked like a goddamn idiot.

My phone vibrates again. I hook it out from under my pillow and frown at the contact, recognising the FBI number. Settling against the headboard, I swipe to accept the call, stroking my fingers down Briar's arm.

"Hello?" I ask, keeping my voice low.

"Matvey. I hear you're back in the States."

"Anfisa. Nice to hear from you again." I first met Anfisa fifteen years ago. Her husband worked on the FBI hostage rescue team, and they trained with the British SAS back in the day. Kenta, Glen, Damon and I actually attended their wedding. And his funeral.

Anfisa's one of the best FBI employees I've ever met. Whip-smart, and almost scarily analytical. We've worked together a few times on US jobs, and every time, she's blown us away.

"I wish the circumstances were more pleasant," she says crisply. *"Colette called and informed me of your client's issue a few days ago; I looked through it briefly, just as a matter of interest."*

"And? You have any idea who it is?"

"No. But we had agents investigating a separate case a few hours ago, and I think it may be related to Miss Saint's stalker."

"What do you mean?" I rub my eyes. "Is the guy branching out? Finding new girls?"

She hesitates. *"Would you be able to meet at my office? I want to ask your opinion on some of the evidence we've collected."*

"Sure. When do you want me?"

"Now, if you can."

I look down at Briar. She's shifted slightly, and a piece of her blonde hair is curling silkily against my chest, fluttering as she breathes in and out. "Send me the address."

I get washed and dressed quickly. When I step into the suite's living room, Kenta is sitting awake at the breakfast bar, his gun by his elbow, reading a book. He glances up at me as I grab my jacket and wallet.

"Going somewhere?"

"Anfisa called. Thinks they've got a lead."

He nods, turning a page. "Bring coffee on your way back."

I've worked with the FBI plenty of times before, mostly when we were protecting US political figures. All of their offices look pretty much the same: grey walls, grey carpets, and desks jammed too close to each other. People in cheap shirts and suits hunched over their computer screens. Even though it's early morning, the LA office is pretty full. No one pays me any notice, lost in their work.

"Matvey."

I turn to see Anfisa, holding two takeaway cups of coffee. She looks exactly the same as when I last saw her—tired-looking, black hair scraped back in a bun, dressed in a dark trouser suit. "Anfisa," I greet. "Do you only own one set of clothes?"

"I don't think you are in any place to judge my fashion sense," she says briskly, breezing past me and opening the door to her office with her hip. "Inside. I think you're going to be very interested in what we found."

I glance around her office as I step inside. It's bare. A desk covered in papers, empty shelves, blank walls. The only decoration I can see is a picture of her late husband tacked over the door. I sit down.

Anfisa smiles at me tightly as she slides a paper cup of coffee over the desk. "It's swill," she warns.

"Used to it. What did you find?"

She settles in her desk chair. "You know Thomas Petty?"

I nod. "I've already assessed him, I'm pretty sure he's not a suspect."

She purses her lips. "I'd say we can definitely cross him off the list. He had a petrol bomb thrown into the first floor of his LA residence at two AM this morning."

"Shit." I rub the back of my head. "He okay?"

"His property is heavily damaged, but he's fine." She opens a file and pulls out a glossy A4 photograph, sliding it across the table to me. "The assailant got away before we arrived, but left this pinned on the windshield of Mr Petty's car."

I examine the photo. It's the cover of a gossip magazine. The headline emblazoned across the top of the page reads:

> THE FEUD CONTINUES?? Sources claim that Briar Saint and Thom Petty are still unfriendly thirteen years after cheating scandal.

Underneath is a blown-up paparazzi shot of Briar and Thom awkwardly talking at the charity gala.

Thom's eyes have both been crossed out in felt-tip.

"Christ."

She pushes another photograph across the table, this time of the back of the magazine page. Scrawled in black marker are the words, *You hurt her.*

"That's his handwriting," I say immediately.

"Almost a definite match," she agrees. "A bit sloppier, which suggests he was in a rush, or maybe under the influence. But it's distinctly him." She sits back. "I contacted Angel Security and spoke to one of your cyber intelligence workers. Two minutes before the attack, Briar's Facebook page received another message from an anonymous account." Her eyes flick down to the file. "'*This is for you. Happy birthday, angel. X*' It's her birthday today?"

"As of midnight."

She nods. "Thomas and Briar have a history of animosity, don't they?"

"I don't know the full story. They dated as teenagers. He says that she cheated on him. She says she didn't."

"We've seen it before: stalkers injuring or attacking perceived enemies of celebrities, in the hope of winning the celebrity's favour. You're familiar with the Jodie Foster case?"

"When her stalker tried to assassinate Ronald Reagan for her? Yeah."

Her face is grim. "This may be something similar. But there is some good news. This time around, he was a lot less careful about hiding his identity. We caught him on Mr Petty's CCTV cameras, and we were able to get fingerprints off the magazine page. We're still processing the results, but we'll let you know if we catch a match with any of your X suspects."

"Thank you, Anfisa."

She shrugs. "Thank Colette for sending the info on your case. If we find out that these incidents are linked, you can expect full cooperation from the FBI. It should speed up your search a bit."

Thank God for that. I stand, shake her hand, and leave the office.

When I step back into the hotel suite, my arms laden down with shopping, it's pushing 9AM. Briar is sprawled on the sofa, draped in a silky pink robe, kissing Glen deeply. Her feet are in Kenta's lap, and she moans as he presses his thumbs into her heel. I pause in the doorway to watch for a second.

She looks happy. Really happy. Like a carefree young woman celebrating on her birthday morning. I feel almost dirty, carrying around a secret that I know will burst all of this happiness.

She pulls away from Glen's mouth and looks at me from under heavy eyelids. "It's rude to run away the morning after." Her voice is hushed and husky. "I was very offended."

"I had some errands to run." I pull a huge doughnut box out of one of the shopping bags, setting it on the coffee table. "Happy Birthday, princess. Don't worry, they're vegan."

She groans, leaning forward to open the box. Her eyes widen as she looks at all the pastries inside. "Yeah, okay, you're forgiven."

I push down a smile, rooting through the bag for the pack of birthday candles I picked up. "I wasn't sure if you'd like them. Thought you might complain about fitting into your dress."

"I'm supposed to be on liquids all day, but I've given up." She pulls a face as I toss the candles onto the table. "Men are apparently going to sexually harass me whatever I do. I don't see why I should starve myself to look hotter for them. I'd turn up to the premiere in a space suit if I could. See how easy it is to wank over me then."

Her words are lighthearted, but I can hear the edge of bitterness running through them. Kenta squeezes her shoulder, reaching into the box and picking out a strawberry, heart-shaped doughnut. He sticks a candle in it and passes it to her. Glen pulls a lighter out of his pocket and leans over, lighting the wick. She smiles between them.

"Thank you guys," she says softly. "This is perfect." Kenta kisses her cheek, and she blows out the candle, taking a massive bite of the doughnut. "Help yourself," she mumbles, waving at the box. "I'll die if I eat all of these."

As everyone is distracted by the food, I pull out my phone and quickly summarise my meeting with Anfisa, sending the message off to Kenta, Glen, and Colette. Both men frown as they read the text. Kenta's eyes flash up to mine, and he jerks his head slightly towards Briar, a question in his face.

I glance at Briar. She's lolling against Glen's side, stroking up and down his arm. He doesn't seem to notice her petting him, fully focussed on his phone. He's holding his chocolate doughnut in his other hand. As I watch, she tosses him a mischievous look, then pops her head up and steals a tiny bite. When he doesn't react, she takes another bite, then pokes her little pink tongue out and licks chocolate cream out of the centre like a cat. It's adorable, and it hits me that this is probably the most relaxed I've ever seen her.

I give Kenta a minute head-shake. No. I don't want to tell her, yet. We'll wait for the FBI to confirm X's identity, first. She'll find out sooner or later, and it's her birthday, for God's sake. She may as well enjoy the day before she finds out that her stalker has progressed to incendiary weapons.

Kenta's lips press together unhappily, but he nods.

Glen starts tapping a reply to me, absentmindedly bringing his doughnut to his mouth. He starts when he realises it's almost all gone. He narrows his eyes at Briar.

"What?" She blinks up at him innocently, then picks up her phone as it buzzes. "*Ugh.*"

"News?" Kenta asks, putting his chin on her shoulder.

She shakes her head, scrolling down the screen. "Thom keeps texting me."

I freeze. "Petty? What is he saying?"

"Not much." She frowns at her phone, her plump lips pursing slightly. "He wants to meet up. He's being very insistent." She snorts. "As if. I wouldn't sit down and have coffee with him if he was the last man on planet Earth. Little skeeze." She taps out a firm reply, then switches her phone on silent, tossing it across the couch.

I hesitate, then stride over, picking it up. "You mind?"

"I thought you decided that he's not X?" She studies the ends of her hair, picking out a split end.

"I'd like to re-assess. Better safe than sorry."

"He's really not. He's too… mild. Meek. And he definitely doesn't fancy me."

"Even so."

She waves me off, arching to lick icing off Glen's lips. I key in her passcode, opening the text thread.

Jesus. Thom must be desperate. He's sent her twenty messages in the last ten minutes.

I have something I want to tell you.

It's nothing bad.

Please, B. It's important.

I just want to apologise.

Briar's response is just: *No thanks, shithead xo*

I frown, remembering the message on the back of the magazine cover. *You hurt her.*

There's two options here. Either Thom's mad, and wants to confront her about her crazy fan; or he's *scared,* and he wants to get back into her good books so he won't get targeted again.

Either way, I don't like it. I tap the call button and bring the phone to my ear.

Thom picks up on the second ring. "*B, thank God. Thanks so much for calling. I was thinking we could go out and grab a coffee, or something—*"

"This is Matthew Carter," I interrupt him. "You might remember me. We met at the charity event for homeless children, back in London."

He stutters into silence. *"Th-the weapons guy?"*

"Good memory. Stop trying to contact my client. She doesn't want to talk to you."

"But—"

I end the call and pass Briar's phone back to her.

She looks vaguely amused. "Okay, then." She sits up, rolling out her shoulders. "We're doing something tonight, right? Please tell me I'm not spending my birthday trapped inside a hotel room."

I tense. "It's an unnecessary risk."

She sighs. "I can't stay cooped up here all day, just because one man *might* send another inappropriate picture. It's not like I want to go clubbing. Just a walk would be fine."

"What about dinner?" Kenta offers. "I'm sure we can find a secure restaurant. Glen's off-duty this evening, so Matt and I could cover the two of you while you have a meal."

I glare at him. Briar sighs, fiddling with the bottom of her robe. "I guess there's no chance of all of you joining me, is there?"

Kenta shakes his head apologetically. "We'll be there, just sitting at a nearby table. You can still talk to us."

She considers, then twists to look up at Glen. "What do you think, big boy? You ready to take me on a date?"

Glen turns bright red, alarm flashing across his face.

CHAPTER 34
GLEN

When we step into the restaurant that evening, Briar's mouth drops open. She spins a full circle, taking in the room with sparkly eyes. "Oh my God," she whispers, turning to me. "You picked this out?"

I nod awkwardly.

It took most of the day to find a restaurant secure enough to bring her to. Eventually, hotel security recommended this little gem tucked into a street corner in West Hollywood. Apparently, it's the number one spot for celebrities who want to eat without being hassled by fans or paparazzi. It's perfect. The restaurant floor is just one spacious room, without any nooks or crannies for people to hide in. The staff is small and discreet, and the building has its own security and plenty of CCTV cameras.

Although I doubt it's the video surveillance that has Briar so excited.

The place is beautiful. It's themed like a Grecian garden. The walls are white stone, decorated with turquoise mosaic tiles and covered in clinging ivy. Lush green ferns and miniature lemon trees surround each table, and the entire place is strewn with fresh flowers, drifting in long garlands from the ceiling and draping over the chairs and floor. The whole place is illuminated by flickering candles in glass lanterns, giving the room a dreamy, soft feel. Tables usually book half a year in advance, but when I mentioned Briar's name on the phone, a few spots magically became vacated.

Briar slips her hand into mine as the *maitre d'* leads us to a couple of tables right in the corner of the restaurant, facing the door. Briar and I sit down at one, and Matt and Kenta take the other, just a few feet away. The position gives us a good outlook over the whole room.

A sommelier appears out of thin air, and Briar smiles up at him. "What are your best sweet wines?"

The man considers. "If madam likes Sauternes, we have some *Château d'Yquem* from Graves, Bordeaux. *Sauvignon blanc, Semillon,* and slightly raisined Muscadelle grapes. Incredibly high quality."

She looks at me, and I shrug. "I'll have whatever," I say. I don't know shit about wine. Briar orders the bottle, and the man drifts off. She leans against my side and looks around the restaurant, smiling.

"You like it?" I check.

I'm kind of worried. I haven't really dated since I left the force. Every now and then, Kenta and Matt bully me into meeting a girl for drinks, but the poor woman always spends half of the time trying not to stare at my face. I generally call it quits after one beer and just head home. I don't even remember the last time I took a girl out to dinner.

She looks at me incredulously. "Are you kidding me? This is the nicest place a guy has ever taken me. And you're not even angling for money."

"Actually, we all want a raise," I tell her, and she laughs, picking up my hand to kiss my knuckles.

"As if. You should be paying *me* to wear this dress."

I run my eyes over her body. She's wearing a slinky, glittery number covered in pale pink sequins. The fabric clings to her figure, and the sequins reflect little iridescent specks of light all over her arms and bare neck. I think she's wearing some kind of body glitter, too, because her skin is shimmering softly under the golden lamps. She looks like the world's sexiest fairy.

"You look gorgeous," I tell her, and her smile widens.

God, I love seeing her smile. The first week or so, I don't think I saw her smile *once.* It was always the same tight, sardonic smirk. Now she's beaming at me, eyes sparkling, and it's tying my stomach into knots.

"You look pretty nice yourself." She lifts a glittery fingernail and trails it down my Adam's apple, laughing when I swallow reflexively. "I like you in grey."

The waiter returns with our wine. As I readjust my chair to give him room, I catch a sudden glimpse of my reflection in the dark window. My good mood dissolves immediately.

You'd think, after five years, I'd get used to seeing my face. But I don't. Every single time, I get a shock. Tonight, it looks even more horrific than usual. The soft overhead lighting that makes Briar glow like an angel casts shadows over the bumps of my scar, so my whole cheek looks mangled.

I hate this shit.

I don't think I'm vain. That's why I never bothered to get it fixed. I don't usually mind being ugly; I don't exist in the world to be pretty. I'm not a bloody model.

The issue isn't the way my face looks. It's the memories that come with it. People turn and stare at me in the street. They look at the scar when they talk to me. Every day, I see the tiny flicker of revulsion in the eyes of strangers. And I *remember.*

I scan the room, and my stomach sinks as I see guests from other tables staring. Of course they are. This whole industry is based on looks. I stick out like a sore thumb. I watch an actress I vaguely recognise look me over, her eyes flicking between me and Briar. She picks up her phone and starts texting rapidly.

Crap.

I didn't even think about this when I picked out the restaurant. Of course, as a celebrity hotspot, it will be full of really important industry people. Who will gossip. A sense of panic rises up in me. I screwed up. Tomorrow, the magazines will probably be splashed with pictures of Briar on a date with some scarred, grizzled giant, and rumours will start flying.

I shift my weight, trying to block the woman's line of vision with some of the foliage hanging around the table. She leans forwards. From the angle her phone is at, I'm pretty sure she just took a photo of us.

"Why are you trying to hide behind that fern?" Briar's voice cuts through my thoughts. "It won't work, you're much bigger than it."

I feel heat rushing to my cheeks. "I wasn't," I mumble.

"You were."

I shake my head, looking down at the menu. "Why do they have entrées and appetisers? What's the difference? Is it a rich people thing?"

"Americans call main dishes entrées. Why are you hiding?"

I frown, thumbing through the gilt-edged pages. "That makes no sense."

"*Glen.*"

I sigh, putting down the menu and waving a hand around the restaurant. "You know some of these people?"

She nods. "They're all pretty big fish. So?"

"So," I shrug awkwardly. "People talk, right? You might not want to be seen in public with me."

She laughs. "What, because of the pictures of me kissing Matt? Everyone already thinks I'm a slag. I may as well take advantage of it and snog who I want."

"It's not that," I bluster, "I just—"

Her eyes widen. Emotions cross her face, too quick to count. Anger. Sadness. Sympathy. *Hurt.* "You just *what*?" She snaps. "You think that I'm happy to shag you in private, but that I'm too bloody shallow to be seen with you in public? Fuck you, Glen. You think I'm that disgusting?"

I run a hand through my hair. This is going all wrong. "It's not like that. I just... I know I don't go with your brand, exactly."

It's the wrong thing to say. She straightens, rage flashing in her eyes. "For fuck's sake, I'm not a damn *brand.* Jesus, I thought you guys were actually starting to look at me like a person!"

I put my hands up. "That's not what I mean! I just don't want to do anything that will harm your public image. That's all." God, this is so embarrassing.

She narrows her eyes. "You think you're so hideous that *sitting next to you* will harm my public image? Who the Hell do you think you are, the Phantom of the fucking Opera?"

I open my mouth to respond, but before I can, she curls a mani-cured hand in my tie and *tugs,* yanking me down for a kiss.

My body pretty much collapses into hers. She doesn't bother with any closed-mouth pecking, plunging her tongue straight into me. I feel a groan rising in my chest as I kiss her back, hard and desperate. She arches against me, pressing her body against mine.

This isn't a socially acceptable kiss. It's not the kind of kiss you share in an incredibly upmarket restaurant, where they lay the table with six different sizes of fork and the bottles of wine run into five figures.

But Briar doesn't care. She twists her hands in my collar, pulling me closer, delving deeper. It feels like she's trying to pour weeks' worth of desire and frustration and sexual tension into one kiss.

Eventually, we gasp apart. My ears are ringing. I can feel the stares of scandalised diners piercing into me from all directions, but I can't bring myself to look away from Briar. She tightens her grip on my collar, her blue eyes angry.

"You see," she pants, "how *hideous* I find you?"

Before I can respond, she pushes forward for a series of smaller kisses, like gentle bites. Her hand comes to stroke through my hair, and my heart literally flutters. I don't think I've ever liked a girl so much she gave me damn heart palpitations; but there's something about the soft, tiny kisses, peppered all over my top and bottom lip, that hits me right in the stomach.

Finally, she stops, her lips still pressed to mine, breathing in my air. Her face is flushed, and her eyes are shiny with unshed tears. She blinks them back fiercely.

Shit. Did I make her *cry?* "Briar—" I start.

She glares up at me, then takes my face in her little hands. "*Glen.*" She leans forward and presses another tiny kiss to my lips. "You *seriously* worry about this stuff?"

"You're so beautiful," I rough out. "I don't think you understand how beautiful."

"Of course I understand, I own a mirror. I'm hot as shit." Matt snorts softly in the background. "*I'm* not the deluded one, here." Her thumb strokes my cheekbone, skating over the glossy, damaged scar tissue. I close my eyes, forcing myself not to flinch away. "You're beautiful, too."

I laugh humourlessly. "I'm hideous. You don't have to lie to me."

"Says *who?*" She demands. "Jesus Christ, I practically popped a boner when you came out of the room in your suit tonight."

"I think you're stunning, mate," Kenta offers. I give him the finger.

Briar ignores us both. "For God's sake, you're not some hulking Quasimodo. You're a very attractive man with an impressive scar. That's *it*. Okay?"

I lick my lips. "But—"

"Just say okay."

"Okay," I mutter.

She nods crossly, sitting back in her seat just as a waiter steps forward with our starters. She waits for him to put our plates down, then grabs my chair, trying to tug it closer to her. Bemused, I stand up, letting her drag the chair to sit right by hers. She glares at me until I sit back down. "Good. Now put your arm around me and feed me pasta, like a good date."

When I don't move, she huffs, picking up my hand and wrapping my arm around her. "Jesus," she complains, snuggling aggressively against my chest. "Do I have to do everything around here?"

I thread my fingers through her soft, honey-coloured curls. "I've never been so violently hugged," I say mildly.

She sniffs. "Get used to it."

We settle down, focussing on the food. It's great, but not even the three-starred Michelin chef could distract me from the feel of Briar tucked up against me. She leans her head on my arm as she eats, occasionally glaring at people that turn and stare at us. Matt and Kenta eat too, although they're taking turns, one of them taking a few bites while the other scans the room. Briar finishes her wine, so I lean forward to grab the bottle. I've just pulled out the cork when she casually drops a hand below the table, running her fingers over my crotch.

CHAPTER 35
GLEN

jolt, looking down at her. She smiles at me, her eyes twinkling. Before I can say anything, our waiter reappears, holding an oversized pepper grinder.

"Pepper, sir?"

"I—" Briar squeezes the growing bulge in my trousers, and heat rolls through me. I grit my teeth and force myself to smile at the man. "Sure."

"Tell me when," he says, and starts grinding pepper onto my plate. I try to focus, but Briar tightens her grip, stroking me firmly, and all thoughts fly out of my head. Her palm rubs over my stiffening hard-on, and my thighs clench with the effort of sitting still.

When I don't say anything, the waiter stops. "This is enough, sir?" He prompts.

"That's good," I get out, my voice cracking.

"Are you alright, sir?" He asks mildly.

"Peachy."

"Hm. Perhaps some more water for the table?"

"That would be great," Briar says, smiling. The waiter nods and turns on his heel, and I slump in my seat, running a hand over my face.

"Briar—"

"What?" She stabs her ravioli one-handed, taking a casual bite. "You want me to stop?"

"No," falls out of my mouth before I can stop it, and she laughs, tracing down my shaft with her fingernail. I feel blood rush to my face, my hips rising as I grip the tablecloth. "Christ, Briar, I can't—"

"Don't worry," she pats my cheek, dropping her voice to a husky whisper. "I won't make you come."

An agonised sound falls out of my throat as she withdraws her hand and reaches for her wine glass.

The rest of the meal is like some perverted form of torture. We eat slowly, consuming course after course of ridiculously fancy food. I can barely taste any of it. Briar keeps her hand still in my lap, cupped gently over my throbbing erection, and every time I relax, she starts to stroke me. She pushes me right to the edge, squeezing and palming and rubbing at me until I'm white-knuckling the table and twitching in my underwear. Just as I'm certain I'm about to explode, she pulls away, leaving me a panting wreck.

She's making a mess out of me. And judging by Matt and Kenta's smirks, they know exactly what's happening under the table.

I get a little break when pudding arrives, and Briar gets distracted by her lava cake. We're just finishing up when her little hand slips back between my legs.

I swallow a groan. "Briar—"

"What?" She picks out a strawberry, licking the chocolate sauce off it. "Problem?"

I glare at her. She has a smudge of chocolate on her bottom lip, and I lean in to lick it off.

A few feet away, Kenta clears his throat. "You have a visitor, Briar," he says, his voice icy.

Startled, I pull back, glancing over Briar's head. Thom Petty is standing a few feet away, eyeing Matt and Kenta. He doesn't look good; there are dark circles under his eyes, and his face is pale.

Briar's hand stops moving as she twists to look at him, and I take the chance to grab my water glass and glug half of it down. It doesn't do much to quench the heat under my skin.

"Hey, B," Petty says, flashing her a weak smile.

Briar sighs, reluctantly sliding her palm off my lap. "You know, I've already got one stalker. I don't really want a full collection."

Petty shifts. "Yeah, I, uh… heard about that. Sorry."

"How did you know she was here?" Matt barks.

Petty startles and looks at him. "I just asked the paps, man," he says, jabbing a thumb in the direction of the door. "We have a few pap contacts, they hook us up with info."

Matt's eyes blaze. "There's paparazzi outside?"

"Yeah," Petty looks confused. "Like, fifty of them. She wasn't hard to find."

Kenta rubs his temples. "This makes no *sense*," he mumbles. "We checked the car for tracking. No one followed us."

Briar apparently doesn't care about the paparazzi. "What do you *want*, Petty?" She snaps. "I'm kind of on a date, here."

My face reddens.

Petty's eyes widen. "Uh." He turns and points at Matt, who stares back at him, his face stony. "Weren't you dating that one, last time?"

"I like to keep a few guys on retainer. I'm a massive slag, remember? Have been since I was *sixteen years old*." Her voice is bitter.

He winces. "That's what I wanted to talk to you about." He looks around again, like he's expecting someone to jump out of the shadows. His nervousness is making me edgy. I slip my hand under my jacket, curling my fingers around the butt of my gun.

"You wanted to talk about my childhood sexual reputation?" Briar asks flatly.

He sighs, shifting uncomfortably. "Look, can I sit?"

"No," Matt and I say immediately.

Briar rolls her eyes. "Get him a chair."

Kenta stands and pushes his own seat up to our table, waving for Thom to sit down. He does, with a nervous nod of thanks. Kenta waits for him to get settled, then braces his hands on the back of the chair, leaning casually over the smaller man.

Thom licks his lips, studying the white tablecloth. "I just want to apologise," he mutters. "For what happened when we were sixteen. I'm—" He takes a deep breath, fixing his brown eyes on Briar. "I'm really, really sorry."

For a second, Briar doesn't say anything. Then she leans back in her chair. "You mean what you *did*."

He blinks. "What?"

"Not what *happened*. That implies it wasn't your fault." She picks up a cherry and bites it off its stem, watching him thoughtfully. "You want to apologise for what you *did*."

"Yes," Petty says, his voice low. "I do. I really screwed up. I want to make it right."

"Why?" Briar demands.

He blinks. "I… I hurt you."

"You ruined my life," she agrees. "You were my *best friend*, Thom. And you hurt me so bad, I spent years on meds and in therapy, fighting the urge to lay down in traffic. I'm surprised I got out of that shit alive." I feel the blood drain out of my face. I've never heard about this. "But that apparently hasn't bothered you for the last thirteen years. So why now?"

Petty's cheeks flush. He looks down at his hands. Behind him, I can see Kenta gripping the back of his chair, anger pouring off him in silent waves.

"What is this about?" Briar presses. "Are your PR people trying to clean up your past? You need me to invest in your new cologne brand? Is *Hollywood House* doing a reunion season, or something?"

"I don't want anything from you," he says quietly. "Just for you to forgive me. Yeah, it took me a while, but after seeing you at the charity gala, I realised just how much I hurt you."

For an actor, he really is a remarkably bad liar.

Briar considers him. "Will you make a statement? Tell the world that you were lying?"

He hesitates for a long time. "Yeah," he says eventually. "Yeah. If you want me to."

Briar holds his gaze for a few beats. Long enough to make him squirm in his seat. Then she snorts, picking up her wine glass. "I'm kidding. I'm not going to mess with your career. Fine. I accept your apology."

He looks at her with wide, earnest eyes. "You always were a better person than me."

She rolls her eyes. "What you did was shitty. But you were a kid, too. We were just children. I don't think we'll ever be friends again, but I appreciate the apology."

He nods, relief crossing his face. A few seconds pass.

"Can you go now?" She prompts. "I was trying to give my boyfriend *du jour* a handjob under the table."

My mouth drops open, but Thom just laughs, clearly not believing her. He stands, pushing back his chair. "Alright, I'll leave you to it." He gives me, Kenta and Matt an awkward smile that none of us return. "Uh. Have a good one."

We all watch silently as he turns and disappears back through the foliage and tables.

"Well, that was weird," Briar notes.

Matt stands. "We have to get out of here. I'll bring the car around."

Kenta nods. "I'm sorry, Briar. But if the paparazzi have found you, we need to get you away before they attract any unwanted attention. We don't want anyone following you back to the hotel."

Briar looks unbothered. "That's okay. We were finished eating, anyway." She presses a quick kiss to my lips, stroking a hand down my chest. "I think I'm ready to go back to the room."

"You're going to kill me," I mutter, and she laughs brightly, tossing back the rest of her wine and grabbing her clutch.

"Let's go."

As soon as we step onto the street, everything erupts into white light. Hundreds of flashes spark through the night. I swear. The crowd of paparazzi is huge and heaving. I wrap my arm around Briar's shoulder, and Kenta takes her other side as we hurtle her towards the road. The men's shouts come in thick and fast.

"HAPPY BIRTHDAY, BRIAR!"

"BRIAR! WE JUST SAW THOM COMING OUT, ARE THE TWO OF YOU GETTING BACK TOGETHER? ARE YOU GETTING BACK TOGETHER, BRIAR?"

"ANY NEWS FROM THE STALKER? HAVE THEY CAUGHT HIM YET?"

I shove a couple guys back as they reach for her, trying to grab her attention. "Get back. Get the fuck *back*," I repeat, over and over, scanning the men, checking all of their hands. This is damn near impossible. Anyone could be holding a gun, and I wouldn't even be able to *see* with the flashes blinding me. People jostle us on all sides, pressing close as we try to plough through the hot, sweaty bodies. Through it all, Briar's face stays in the same frozen, cold look that I recognise from the magazines. The one that tabloids always slap the words 'bitchy' or 'stuck-up' on. As if she can be expected to *smile* when people mob her in the street.

Ahead of me, a photographer lunges forward and grabs Briar's arm. "Tell me, Briar. Has Thom finally forgiven you for cheating on him?"

"Don't *touch* her," I growl, pushing the guy back. He staggers, tripping over his own feet and falling onto the pavement. Instead of getting up, he rolls onto his stomach and stretches out the arm holding his camera. Rage floods through me as I realise he's trying to take a shot up Briar's skirt. I start to bend down to grab him, but before I can, Briar kicks the guy's camera out of his hands and stamps on it, the lens cracking under her stiletto.

"You can't do that!" He yells at her. "You can't destroy my property! This is assault! I'll sue you!"

"Try it," she says flatly. "See what happens."

The man looks up at her, slack-jawed. I tighten my grip on her arm and hurry her along. "Bitch!" He hollers after her, and she tosses him the finger over her shoulder.

Matt pulls the car up to the curb, and Kenta yanks the door open, standing in front of it to ward off the press of photographers as I slide inside, tugging Briar along with me. Kenta climbs into the seat on her other side, slamming the door shut behind him. The clamour outside is instantly muffled, and Matt pulls out into the road.

"Are you okay?" I ask Briar, running my hands down her body. She's dishevelled and out of breath. "Shit, I should've gotten that guy further away from you—"

"Shut up," she says, grabbing my collar and pulling me in for a kiss. I wrap my arm around her waist and pull her into me.

"You almost killed me tonight," I breathe in her ear.

She shrugs, blasé. "What are you gonna do about it?"

I turn to Kenta. "Give me a hand?"

He grins. "Gladly." As Matt turns into a line of traffic, we both reach under the hem of her dress. She gasps as we each slide a hand up the inside of one thigh.

"*Finally*," she murmurs. "I've been waiting for my birthday sex all day."

I slip my hand up higher, until my fingers brush soft, damp curls. My eyes widen. "You're not wearing…"

She shrugs. "I didn't want panty lines."

I think back to the photographer lying on the ground, and my whole body tenses. "That guy—"

"Is on film attempting to commit a crime," she finishes. "And you'd better believe I'm gonna report him. So stop worrying about him and *get inside me.*"

"You heard the lady," Kenta murmurs, tugging down the strap of her dress with his teeth. I dip my head to kiss her ear, trailing my fingers lightly between her legs. She's dripping and throbbing. As I press my thumb against her hood, swirling her wetness across her skin, she turns, pressing her hot cheek to mine and mouthing at my throat. I can feel all of her muscles tightening as her breath speeds up. Kenta tugs down the neckline of her dress and licks a line down her cleavage. Briar jerks and arches against me, moaning urgently.

"We're being followed," Matt says suddenly.

We all freeze. "What?" I say.

He doesn't answer, staring at the rearview mirror. Kenta twists and looks out of the windshield. "Blue Sedan," Matt says.

"Slow down," Kenta orders, and Matt lifts his foot. "Okay. Switch lanes." Matt does. Kenta swears, and I fight the urge to twist and see what's happening behind us. We don't want this guy seeing we've noticed him. Briar shivers again, and I gently reach over her body and clip on her seat belt. She clutches at my shirt.

"License?" Matt barks.

"Can't see it," Kenta replies, "he's got his brights on."

"Could just be paparazzi," Briar pipes up.

I cup the back of her head, tugging it down against my chest, and reach for my gun. "Either way, we don't want anyone following you back to the hotel."

"Everyone buckled in?" Matt asks. "I can lose him, but it'll take some fancy driving."

"Yeah," we chorus.

"Hang on, then, princess," he mutters, and hits the gas.

CHAPTER 36
BRIAR

The mood when we finally get back to the hotel is subdued. Matt lost the car pretty quickly—the driver stopped tailing us when he realised that we'd noticed him. Which is worrying. If it were just a paparazzo, he wouldn't have cared whether or not we saw him. No one mentions it, but we all know what it means.

X was there tonight. He knew exactly where I was. He followed me.

As soon as we step inside the suite, I kick off my heels and flop down on the sofa, fiddling with the clasp on my clutch. My mind is going at a hundred miles a minute.

"Wine?" Glen offers.

I nod. "Thanks."

Kenta pulls off his suit jacket and drapes it over the back of the sofa, coming to sit by me. "Sorry if the drama ruined your evening."

I flash him a smile. "It didn't. This is the best birthday I've had since I was a kid."

He looks surprised. "Really?"

I loll my head back against the sofa cushions, watching as he unbuttons his collar and loosens his tie. "Is that so shocking?" I murmur, dropping my eyes to his forearms as he rolls up his sleeves. Do guys know how hot it is when they do that? I swear to God, there is nothing sexier than a guy in a half-undone suit.

He gives me a little smile. "I thought no one parties better than a rich woman in her twenties."

I shrug. I don't exactly feel like telling him that I haven't had any real friends since I got back into the industry. It's an unfortunate side-effect of being a notorious bitch; the only people who want to be friends with me are also massive bitches. I spend most birthdays either working or watching movies with a takeaway on my lap.

I budge closer to Kenta and grab his hand, winding his arm around my shoulders. "Like this, please."

He smiles, dipping to press his lips to my head. "Can I ask you a question?" He murmurs into my hair.

"Absolutely not," I reply haughtily, fiddling with his fingers. "I do not permit my employees to address me."

Glen passes me a glass of white and hands Kenta a beer, sitting down next to me. Matt slumps down on his other side. I stretch between the men, smiling contentedly. Snuggled between three big muscly bodyguards, the impromptu car chase suddenly doesn't seem like such a big deal.

"Fine," I allow. "You may ask your question. Since I'm in such a good mood."

"You said Petty ruined your life," Kenta says. "The two of you worked on the same show, right?" I nod, taking a sip of wine. "What did he actually do?"

I open my mouth to give him my automatic response—some derisory comment about how I cheated on Thom because of his tiny fungus-ridden dick—but for some reason, the words die in my throat. A few seconds of silence go by as I try to work out what to say.

"You don't have to tell me," Kenta says quickly.

"No, it's just…." I trail off, fiddling with the stem of my glass. "I don't talk about this. Ever."

I've kept all the memories of my teenage years locked up inside me for over a decade, now. I figure, if I don't talk about them, gossip rags can't sell them.

But I know the guys won't sell my secrets to the press. The idea is laughable. They just want to keep me safe. They've trusted me with their secrets, and I trust them back.

Suddenly, I really, *really* want to tell them.

I study my wine, pursing my lips, then take a long swig. "When you start in the industry," I start, "you're given a brand by your PR people. You know what my brand was, when I was signed onto my first contract at thirteen?"

They all shrug.

"'The Teenage Sweetheart'," I pronounce the words carefully.

Matt snorts.

I nod. "I know, right? It's hard to imagine now, but when I was thirteen, fourteen, fifteen years old, I was the good girl. The 'innocent one'. I was really shy, back then. *Painfully* polite. All I wanted was for everybody to like me. My PR people decided to play off that, and they branded me as this sweet, gentle angel. Think early-era Taylor Swift."

The guys exchange a blank look.

"Okay. Think Princess Di. My PR manager decided I always had to be dressed in white or pink dresses. Minimal makeup. I wasn't allowed to go to parties, or post on social media. I was completely banned from taking selfies, under any circumstances. I was encouraged to do a lot of charity work. That, at least, stuck with me." I stare down at my drink. "For years, that's how everyone knew me. The good girl. And people *liked* me. I was one of the most popular child actors in the industry. I had a great career set up for when I turned eighteen. And then Thom Petty ruined everything, by telling the whole world I cheated on him."

"You didn't?" Glen asks.

"We were never even dating. He was my friend. My only friend, really. We met on the set of *Hollywood House*, and he was just like me. A British kid plucked out of secondary school and flung into Hollywood. We kind of clung to each other, I guess, and the press theorised that we were together. But we never dated." I examine my fingernails. "When I was sixteen, I went on a date with this guy. The paps stalked us around the city and got a shot of us kissing. It was my first real, off-camera kiss, and I was so excited to see Thom the next day, to tell him about it."

Nausea starts swimming in my stomach, and I put my wine glass down. I haven't thought about this in such a long time. I almost forgot how much it hurt. "The next morning, I woke up to all of these headlines. *Thomas Petty Heartbroken after Briar Saint Cheating Scandal.* Thom had made a statement that we'd been dating for the last two years, and I kissed this other guy behind his back. I was getting *eviscerated* in the press. I went round to his house and begged him to just tell everyone the truth, but he refused to see me."

"Shit," Glen mutters.

I purse my lips. "It was a great PR move on his part. He went from being a regular kid actor to the poor, spurned lover. He went around for months, looking all dejected and teary-eyed in front of the paps. Which of course just meant people hated me even more."

"It was bad?" Matt asks.

I take a deep breath. "Awful. The fans were so outraged, they started boycotting the show. The directors kicked me off the project because I was affecting numbers so badly. *Hollywood House* was my life. I knew the actors better than my own family. But none of that mattered." I shrug. "And that's how The Wicked Bitch of the West was born. It didn't matter how much I told the truth. Everyone hated me."

"It must have been terrifying," Kenta says quietly.

I laugh humourlessly. "I've never been so scared in my life. I was a child, and it felt like the whole world had turned against me. The people who used to be my fans were now sending me death threats. I couldn't do anything right: If I was photographed standing next to a man, I was being a hoe. If I looked upset in public, I was trying to get sympathy. If I was ignoring the paps, I was a stuck-up bitch who thought she was better than everyone else. I wanted to disappear off the face of the planet."

"What did you do?" Matt asks, his voice low.

I sigh, taking another swig of wine. "I disappeared. I bought a house in Devon and lived there alone for years. Ordered all of my shopping online, ate takeaway, and refused to see anyone."

I pick at a loose sequin on my dress. "For a few years, I was really depressed. I just didn't see the point of existing. I couldn't leave my house without being verbally abused by strangers and harassed in the press. I figured I'd never have real friends, or a partner, or a family. Everyone hated me too much. My life was already over, so what was the point?"

I'm surprised when a tear rolls down my face and lands on the pale fabric of my dress. I pull my hand free from Kenta's and cross my arms over my chest, curling back into myself. Someone passes me a tissue.

"Thanks." I dab at my face. "Yeah. Those were a few really dark years. Then, when I was twenty, I was watching a movie, and Thom came on screen. I looked him up, and I was shocked at how successful he was. He was doing *so* well. Movies, brand deals, music. He had his own line of cologne, for God's sake. And it was like a switch flipped in my brain. I wasn't sad anymore, I was just really, *really* angry." I grit my teeth. "*He* was the one who lied. *He* was the one who should be being punished, not me. I missed acting so much. So I figured, I'd moped around enough. I'd try to get back into the industry."

Glen shifts, but no one says anything.

"I decided, instead of trying to fix my reputation, I'd lean into it. If people wanted me to be a bitch, fine. I'd be a bitch. I moved back to LA. Started taking jobs again." I smirk. "For my very first audition, I actually tried for a movie at my old studio. They were expecting the same wounded little deer I was before I left. A mouse who just wanted to be liked and accepted by them. And instead they got me." I jab a thumb at my chest. "I didn't get the job, obviously. But I left that audition room feeling like... like a lion."

I take another sip of wine, swirling the golden liquid around the glass. "It's funny. I used to be so scared of people thinking I was mean, or stuck up, or rude. Now, if anything, I'm scared of people thinking I'm *nice*. I'm strongest when no one likes me. I'm safest when I'm being a bitch."

"You're not, though." Kenta says quietly.

I glance up at him. "Hm?"

"You're not rude, or stuck up, or any of it. On the inside, you're still that sweet kid." He takes my hand again. "You do so much charity work. You care about people. You care about us. That sweetness is still inside you."

"I know," I say. "That's kind of the point. If I go out in public, and be my authentic self, and then everyone decides that they hate me —what am I supposed to do with that? There's only so much therapy can do. But *now?*" I wave a hand over my face. "I'm playing a role. The bitchy diva. They're not criticising the real *me*, just my actions. And that's a Hell of a lot easier to handle."

"You did all of this to protect yourself," he realises. "You didn't want to make yourself hard. You just wanted to keep the soft parts of you safe from everyone else."

"I guess you could say that, yeah." I lean forward, fire suddenly sparking inside my belly. "And you know what else? Now people listen to me. They know I'm not a doormat. They know if they screw me over, I won't keep my mouth shut." I glance at Matt. "You asked a while ago why I would try to ruin that creep Mario Vasquez' life, just because I didn't like him. The truth is, I have people contacting me every day, saying that someone powerful in the industry abused them, or cheated them out of money, or sexually harassed them, and they can't say anything without becoming a target. But I can blow as many whistles as I want without consequence. I live outside these power games the rest of Hollywood has to play. People are scared of me, and they fucking should be."

"I think you're the strongest woman I've ever met," Glen says quietly.

I look at him, then nod. "Thank you." I clear my throat, grabbing my wine and downing the rest of it in one long swallow. I slam the glass down on the coffee table and look between the three men. "Right. That's enough of my tragic backstory. Do you guys want a birthday foursome?"

Glen's laugh bursts out of him. "I thought you'd never ask."

Matt stands slowly, heading for his bedroom. "I actually have something for you," he calls over his shoulder. "I picked it up this morning."

I raise an eyebrow. There's a plastic rustling sound from the bedroom, then Matt returns, chucking something into my lap. I pick it up, examining the plastic packaging. My face flushes as I realise what my gift is.

A pink bullet vibrator.

"You didn't," I say, my eyes flashing up to him.

He smirks. "Princess, I've been dreaming of you coming around that thing for the past week. You'd better believe I did."

I pull open the packaging and roll the toy into my palm. My whole body suddenly feels too hot.

Matt squats in front of me, holding out his hand. I pass it to him, and he presses the tiny button. All four of us watch it buzz between his fingers.

"Thank you for telling us," Matt says quietly, meeting my eyes.

"I said I'd try to trust you. There you go." I tilt my head. "Do I get a reward, now?"

"Yes," he says simply. "Li, pull down the top of her dress."

Kenta obediently slides the strap of my dress off my left shoulder. I let my eyes fall closed as Matt reaches up, pressing the tip of the bullet against the curve of my throat.

CHAPTER 37
MATT

Briar exhales slowly as I trace the trembling vibe down the delicate line of her throat. I graze over her cleavage, circling the soft white mound of her left breast. When I finally touch the tip to her hardening pink bud, she twitches towards me, her hands clutching at my shoulders.

Kenta starts massaging her neck as I pull away the bullet and slide it under the skirt of her dress, stroking it slowly up her quivering thighs. Wetness is already pooling between her folds, and I have to fight the urge to press forward and lick up every drop. There'll be time for that later. Her eyes fall closed as I circle around her core, getting the toy wet and slick with her juices.

"Feel good?" I ask, my voice coming out lower than I expect.

"More," she mumbles. Glen slides closer to her across the sofa, and she puts her hot cheek on his shoulder. I obediently turn the bullet up a few notches, dipping it teasingly into her entrance. She shivers. A flush rolls down her body, and she murmurs under her breath as the vibrations rock through her. I play with the settings, flicking them up and down, and she starts to rock back and forth, twitching her hips for more stimulation.

"More," she orders again.

I grin. "You sure you can handle it?"

She nods breathlessly, gyrating down on my hand. "*More*, Matt."

"*Alright.*" I press the tiny button again, turning up the bullet to its highest setting. It buzzes furiously in my hand as I slip it inside her, pushing it in as deep as I can. I know I've hit the right spot when her whole body jerks forward violently. I make sure it's positioned right, then remove my hand, sucking off my fingers.

Briar's eyes widen. "What are you doing?" She whispers, her hips giving a little, uncontrollable buck.

"What?"

"I—" her hips buck again, as the frantic vibration pounds against her sweet spot. Her fingers claw at my shoulders. "Are you just going to *leave it in me*?"

I shrug. "Seems like the best place for it."

She gapes, lost for words. "But. But—" Her pelvis jerks again, and she makes a pained noise.

I rub my lips over her thigh, then pull back. "I think we should relocate," I tell Kenta. "Bedroom?"

He nods, kissing a freckle on her collarbone.

"Thank *God*." Briar lifts her arms. "Carry me."

I smirk. "I don't think so, princess. You've got legs. Use 'em."

She frowns. "Y-you can't expect me to walk with this inside me."

"You've done much harder things."

She looks shocked. "Are you serious?"

"As a heart attack."

Her face flushes crossly. She scowls at me and stands, taking a few stubborn steps towards our bedroom door. She stumbles as she steps into the doorway. "*Oh.*" Her eyes flutter. She leans heavily against the wall, pressing a hand to her belly. Her chest is rising and falling in pants. Her cheeks are flushing bright red. "Jesus." She mumbles, tipping her head back against the wall. "Wh-what setting did you put this thing on?"

"Is it uncomfortable?" Glen asks.

"Yes," she moans. "No. I… I can't fucking walk with it inside me. I can't—" We all watch, open-mouthed, as she slips a hand between her legs and starts to touch herself desperately.

"Fuck this," Kenta mutters, crossing the room and dropping to his knees next to her. She reaches down and tugs at his hair, gasping as he gently parts her legs and buries his face between her thighs. She starts to jerk over him, riding his face as he clutches at her thighs, groaning. It's barely twenty seconds before she throws out her hands, bracing herself in the door frame as her body tenses and starts to shake. She half-collapses on Kenta's face, her knees buckling as she chokes and comes.

"Oh my God," she murmurs over and over as he licks her through it. "Oh, God." She presses a hand over her stomach again, her blue eyes wide. "I still need—"

Kenta straightens, kisses her hard on her open mouth, then slides an arm under her knees and sweeps her right off her feet, carrying her into our bedroom.

Glen and I both follow, watching as Kenta sits at the head of his bed, setting our shivering client between his legs. He strips her methodically, kissing slowly down her neck as he carefully pulls off her clothes, until all that's left is the jewellery dangling delicately from her earlobes. She looks up at him, her blonde hair mussed. "Please," she says hoarsely. She's rocking slightly against the quilt.

"Lay down," he says, leading her head into his lap. She does, twisting to mouth at the bulge tenting his dress pants.

He gently turns her face away. "No, don't worry about that."

"About what? Your dick?" She reaches up and strokes it. "*Worried* isn't the word I'd use."

Kenta's jaw flexes. "Smith," he barks, "get in position."

I snort. Briar wriggles. "I'm a beautiful woman," she reminds us, "not a tactical war ground."

Glen kneels on the mattress between her legs. "I'm very aware of that, lass," he says quietly, spreading her thighs.

"Well then, maybe refer to me as one, instead of—"

Kenta reaches forward and clasps her face, holding it in place as Glen lowers his head and starts to eat her out like a starving man. Her eyes fly wide open. She gasps, arching right off the bed. I sit back on the edge of the mattress, slowly unbuttoning my shirt as I enjoy the show. Between the toy, Glen's mouth, and Kenta's hands slowly sliding down to cup her breasts, Briar is going crazy. She tightens her thighs around the Scottish man's neck, squirming over his lips as she desperately tries to soothe the ache of the bullet inside her. I can hear the tinny buzz of the vibrations between her breathy gasps.

"Oh," she keens, reaching down and grabbing his head. Her spine is bending, her feet scrabbling for purchase on the silky sheets. She's about to come. "Oh *God*—"

Glen suddenly pulls back, wiping off his wet face. His cheeks are pink as he meets my eye and politely waves a hand between her legs, like he's inviting me to take his spot.

Briar pops her head up, eyes burning. "Why did you stop?!" She squawks. "I was just about to—"

I brace myself with a hand on each knee and bury my face between her legs, lapping up the hot beads of her arousal. She tastes hot and sweet and a little sharp. I can feel the tiny bullet vibrating deep inside of her as I lick into her entrance.

Glen went hard on her, setting a punishing pace as he ravaged her with his tongue. I'm not surprised, given how much she teased him at dinner. I go slower, taking my time, nuzzling into her damp curls until Glen taps my shoulder and I pull back.

We take turns going down on her, each of us spending a minute or so between her thighs, lavishing her with attention, before switching out again. When she finally loses it, I'm tongue-deep in her, and she's gyrating over my face, choking.

Suddenly, she freezes, flinging an arm over her eyes. Her centre pulses and floods as she explodes against my face. She twists her head and bites Kenta's thigh, muffling her cries into his trousers as she comes wrenchingly. Her climax seems to last forever, and I greedily suck up the wetness dripping from her fluttering, aching core. When she finally quiets down, she flops back against the mattress, exhausted and shivering.

"Feel better?" I ask, giving her one last little lick.

She shakes her head. "Still f-feel like I n-need to come," she mumbles, shifting and moaning softly. It takes me a second to realise that with the bullet still lodged inside her, she can't get any real relief. Smiling, I reach up and slide my fingers into her, curling them inside her entrance. Her body jerks again, a smaller climax rocking through her almost immediately. I see a tear streak down her cheek as she grips the sheets weakly, gasping and sobbing. I run my free hand soothingly over her quivering stomach, and keep touching her until she finally goes quiet, still rocking slightly in the growing damp patch on the bed. She looks at us through eyelashes spiked with tears.

"I'm going to die," Kenta mutters, stroking back her hair.

"Enough," she squeaks, squirming upright. "I need someone." She narrows her eyes at Glen. "You. I'm gonna fuck some body positivity into you."

He immediately starts to strip.

"I have really low self-esteem," I say, trying to look pathetic. "It's hard, being this hideous."

She snorts. "Carter, if I left you in a room with a mirror, I'd come back to find you sucking your own dick."

"Maybe we should just leave that vibe in there," Glen muses, shucking off his boxers and rolling on a condom. "See how deep we can get it inside you."

Her eyes widen. "No, *God*, take it out first, I'll actually die!"

He huffs a laugh. "Just kidding, sweetheart." He rubs his lips against hers, sliding his fingers into her and slipping out the bullet. We all stare at it, pinched between his fingers. It's soaking wet and slippery with her juices. For a moment, no one says anything.

Then Briar launches herself at Glen, practically attacking him as she throws herself into his lap, sheathing herself over him in one fast stroke. He barely has enough time to grab a hold of her hips before she starts riding him, fast and desperate. Their sweaty skin slaps together. I watch her breasts bounce, her teeth gritting as she grinds her hips down.

She glances at me sideways. "You. Here," she commands.

I scooch forward. "Yes, princess?"

She reaches for my belt, fumbling at the clasp. I watch amusedly as her fingers slip over the buckle.

"Can I help you?" I ask politely.

She growls under her breath. "Take it out. Get in my mouth. Now."

I ignore the desperate throbbing in my balls. "Tonight is about you, princess. Not us."

She snorts. "So, what? You're all going to get me off in ten different positions, and then whack off together in the showers? Where's the fun in that?" Still frantically riding Glen, she reaches out and rubs over the bulge in my pants, squeezing with her manicured fingers. "I *like* making you come," she says huskily. "Just as much as you like the reverse. So, for the love of God, please give me the birthday gift of your dick in my mouth."

CHAPTER 38
MATT

I don't need telling twice. I have my trousers and underwear dropped before she can even blink. Her blue eyes darken hungrily as she wraps her hand around my length and *tugs*, pulling me closer towards her.

"Jesus, woman! It's not a fucking leash!"

She flutters her eyelashes at me, then takes me halfway down her throat.

I shout, half in surprise, half in pleasure. Her mouth is burning hot and wet as she slides her lips slowly towards my base, millimetre by torturous millimetre.

"You know, she just learned to do that," Kenta says, kneeling on the sheets next to us. "Very steep learning curve."

She gives him the finger, curling her tongue under my shaft. I want to say something, but I can't. I don't think I can form human language. Her head bobs, her pink cheeks hollowing as she sucks me down. Noises I swear I've never made before fall out of my chest as she effortlessly rides Glen and sucks at me, her small body sandwiched between us both.

She suddenly yelps. I look down. Kenta has dropped to his knees by the bed, spread her cheeks, and just about buried his face in her ass.

"No?" he murmurs, trailing his lips over her cheek.

"Y-yes? I—" She gasps in a breath. "I don't know."

He nuzzles into her, running his lips lightly down her crack. She shivers.

"What about this?" He reaches across the bed, patting around until he finds the glossy pink bullet. Licking the end of it, he taps the button on the base, starting up a faint vibration. Not taking his eyes off Briar's, he gently touches the softly pointed tip against her puckered entrance.

She jolts in Glen's arms, and the movement thrusts me even further down her throat. I grip my hand in her hair and take a deep breath.

"I think she likes it," I say.

She groans affirmatively, then pulls away from me, her lips making a little popping sound.

"Come here," she orders Kenta, grabbing his hand and tugging him to take my place. He steps forward, and she immediately slides him into her mouth. He cups her cheeks, gently stroking her cheekbones as she bobs up and down his length. I sit back and enjoy the view. Briar brings Kenta right to the edge, waiting until my friend is panting and fisting his hands in her hair, then pulls away again and reaches for me.

She keeps doing this, blowing us until we're right at the point of exploding, then switching between us. The whole time, she's screwing her hips over Glen, gasping slightly as he thumps into her.

I try to hold back, but eventually, while she's going down hard on me, I can't take it anymore. I'm covered in sweat and struggling to breathe as she rolls my balls in her hands. If I could, I'd make this last forever, but I can't stop my dick thickening and throbbing in her mouth.

"Briar," I murmur. "I'm going to come."

Instead of pulling out, she tightens her grip on me, taking me even deeper.

I frown, wiping a hand over my face. "Are you sure?" I ask, remembering her freakout when Nin spilt lotion all over her bed.

She says something unintelligible.

"What?"

"She says she likes swallowing," Kenta says helpfully, stroking his cheek against Briar's back.

"Fuck," I say, losing it. Her throat relaxes around me, and I roar as I blast into her, filling her with a hot burst of come. She drinks down everything I give her, arching against Glen as she rocks over his hips. She's making soft noises now, shuddering against me. A warm, sleepy haze falls over my brain. I thread my fingers through her hair, tugging slightly at the silky blonde strands.

"Baby," I mumble.

She pulls back, licking her swollen lips. "*Baby,* huh?"

I'm too blissed out to be embarrassed. "Slipped out."

"Hm." She leans forward, pressing a kiss to my stomach. "I prefer *princess,*" she whispers, kissing my tip, before waving forward Kenta. The man looks a mess, his long hair falling loose around his face.

"I won't be long," he warns, and she nods, taking him in her mouth again, her pretty lips stretching around him. She was definitely wearing lipstick at the beginning of the night, but it's long gone now, kissed and sucked away. I watch unabashedly as she blows Kenta, her sex-flushed body bouncing between him and Glen until he throws back his head and shouts his release, spilling into her mouth.

I think the sight of her gulping down his seed is what sends Glen over the edge.

"Briar," he starts, and she nods, turning shakily toward him. The two of them start riding each other faster and faster, setting an almost inhuman pace. Sweat is dripping down Glen's face. As I watch, Briar leans forward and licks a line down the side of his cheek, brushing her lips over Glen's scar. He looks up at her through his lashes, his throat contracting in a swallow as she nuzzles the bumpy skin, kissing it.

"God," she murmurs, pressing her face against his. Her thighs are flexing and shivering as her back arches. "Fuck. You're so hot."

He blushes. Briar throws out her arms and grasps the headboard, bracing herself to come. All of her muscles strain. Kenta finds the bullet again, switching it on and bringing it back to Briar's breast right as she reaches her peak.

The headboard rattles alarmingly against the wall. Briar tips her head back, lips parting, and I can't stop myself from pressing my mouth to hers as she screams her climax. I kiss her the whole way through, drinking up her cries and gasps as she claws at the headboard, her fingernails gouging marks in the expensive wood. Below us, I vaguely register Glen tensing and shouting, gripping her thighs as he blows his load inside of her. I ignore him. All I can think of is the girl coming against me. I clasp her close to me, running my hands over her shivery skin as she trembles and sighs.

Eventually, they both stop moving. Briar's mouth goes slack against mine. She nuzzles into my neck, sagging against me.

"I'm dead," she mumbles. "You all killed me. I'm a ghost. You guys need to run. The tabloids will be here in an hour."

"Fuck," Kenta murmurs, burying his face in her hip. "We can't get charged with murdering a celeb. It'd ruin us."

Groaning, Briar lifts herself carefully off Glen, pressing a kiss to his hair before flopping, exhausted, onto the sheets. I can see the insides of her thighs shining with her arousal, and lean forward, swiping a finger between her folds and bringing it up to my mouth to lick. She shudders and glares at me.

"Here," she orders. "All of you. Now."

I crash into the bed next to her as Glen hobbles off to the bathroom to clean up. He and Kenta both lay down on Briar's other side, sandwiching her between us.

"Move your *leg*," Kenta mumbles to Glen. "I don't want to bloody spoon you, mate."

Glen blows him a very audible kiss. "Love you too, Kenny."

Briar sighs happily.

On the bedside table, my phone buzzes. I check my messages. Glen's sent us both a link to a jewellery website.

G: *We should get her a real present*

"Sure," I say out loud. "Tomorrow."

"Something silver," Kenta murmurs.

"What are you guys talking about?" Briar asks, rolling to see over my shoulder.

I hide my phone. "Security arrangements."

"Silver?"

"It's code."

"For what?"

"If I told you, it wouldn't be a code."

She yawns. "Whatever. You're shit liars." She nudges her head back. "Play with my hair, please."

Kenta obediently starts brushing through her blonde waves.

"Diva," I mumble.

She just bats her eyelashes at me and pulls me closer.

We stay like that for a while. I can feel Briar slowly falling asleep on top of me, her breaths evening out and her body getting heavier. I stroke a hand slowly over her chest, feeling her heart beating under my fingers. There's a kernel of emotion burning behind my rib cage.

"Shouldn't someone be working?" Kenta mutters. "Smith. You got to eat dinner with her. Get up."

Glen groans, heaving himself out of bed.

"*No*—" Briar rouses and reaches after him, but he presses a hand to the centre of her chest, pushing her gently back down onto the mattress.

"I've got patrol, lass."

She tilts her head up for a kiss. He slips his hand under her chin, kissing her deeply, then pulls away, pressing his lips to her forehead. "Call me if you need me." He steps to the door.

"Wait!" She cries out as he reaches for the handle. He pauses. "I need you. I'm horny again."

He snorts. "Nice try. Carter, give her a kiss from me."

I pull her into me, brushing my lips across hers. She sighs, snuggling up against me, and falls asleep again in seconds.

"Matt."

I wake up in a hot, bright room, panting. My body is slick with sweat, my heart is pounding like I just ran ten miles, and my muscles are cramping.

"*Matt*," someone calls.

I blink blearily around me. The reading lamp is on. Briar is sitting up next to me, watching me closely. Her blonde hair is falling around her face.

"Matt?" She says again, and I realise she's squeezing my shoulder. "Are you awake? Or just creepily dream-staring at me?"

I blink hard. My eyes are wet.

Jesus.

I sit up and run my hands over my face. "Princess."

"Hey." She strokes through my sweaty hair. "You had a nightmare. I'm glad to inform you that nothing you just dreamt of is real, and you're actually in bed with a beautiful naked woman. What an upgrade."

My shoulders slump. "Shit," I mutter. "I woke you up."

She shrugs. "Not a big deal."

"You've got a big day tomorrow. I should…" I start to roll out of the bed. Embarrassment is thumping through me. This is exactly what I was afraid of.

She rolls her eyes. "Oh, come back to bed, you little dipshit," she mutters, trying to tug me back into her. "I'm not done hugging you yet. Here." She takes my hand and slides it up to her breasts. "Touch my tits, that will make you feel loads better."

I'm too tired to argue, so I just let her roll me closer, pressing my face into her cleavage. On the other side of the bed, Kenta shifts, reaching over and groggily patting my head. "You're fine, mate," he slurs, and Briar smothers a giggle.

The door cracks open. Glen glances in, taking in the scene, gun in hand.

"He's fine," Briar whispers.

"Aye, I can see that," he mutters, glaring at me buried in her chest. "He's in bloody heaven, far as I'm concerned. If I have a nightmare, will you let me sleep like that? I'll start watching horror movies before bed."

I flip him off lazily, pressing closer into Briar.

She wriggles, threading her fingers through my hair. "Don't be jealous, you can motorboat me tomorrow," she promises Glen. I can't even see the man, but I can practically *hear* his cheeks go pink. The door closes with a click, and Kenta reaches up to flip off the light.

It usually takes me hours to get back to sleep after a nightmare, but with Briar's heartbeat pressed against my cheek, I'm out in minutes.

CHAPTER 39
MATT

Briar sighs softly, leaning her slick, naked body across my front as I massage soap into her breasts. "God," she whimpers, tipping her head back onto my shoulder. "Oh, *shit*, Matt—" she bites her lip as I roll her nipples, tugging them away from her body. I swallow, feeling her writhe against me.

It's been a good morning. Briar doesn't have to be at the premiere until five, so we slept in and ate breakfast in bed. Kenta and I left her cuddled up with Glen to hit the gym, and when I came back up to shower, Briar slunk into the bathroom behind me and dropped to her knees. Now, it's just past midday, and Briar's working through a long, complex beauty routine. It involves hair masks and exfoliators and waxing, and God knows what else. She dragged me in here for her pamper-session bubble bath, and we've been soaking in the tub for the past half an hour. She's already come three times, but she's showing no signs of slowing down.

She starts grinding her ass back into me. "Come on," she mumbles. "*Matt—*"

"You're insatiable," I mutter, slipping a finger inside her. Even under the water, I can feel how hot and wet she is inside. She clenches and flutters against me as I start to pump in and out of her.

"I never used to like sex before," she pants, reaching back to run her fingers through my hair.

"Yeah? What changed?" I twitch my finger inside of her, making her hum happily. "You seem to like it plenty now."

"I trust you, I guess. I have…" I add another finger, and she gasps, rocking back into me. "A bad track record with men. They like to take advantage." I freeze, going still in the water, and she frowns. "Wait, not like that. Men like to use me for connections, or money, or status. Just being seen in public with a man can boost his popularity overnight."

"Like Thom Petty?"

"Exactly like Thom Petty."

"Hm." I reach over the edge of the bath and pick up her drink of ice water, rolling the cold glass over her chest. She shudders, crying out. A bead of sweat rolls down her neck.

"B-but I trust you guys. It makes the sex a lot more enjoyable."

"I'm honoured."

She nods, shivering as I hook an ice cube out of the glass and trace it down her stomach. "P-plus, I'm at the horny part of my cycle."

I laugh. "Is that a thing? I don't remember that from my Biology classes."

She wriggles against my front. "Sure is. Total nuisance, too. I get turned on at the drop of a hat." She looks up at me through her lashes. "And then I just have to walk around all day wet."

Even though I've already gotten off once this morning, I feel my balls start to ache, and shift uncomfortably in the hard tub. "You're a menace."

She smiles at me, really smiles, big and bright and white, and for a second, I'm dazzled.

I still can't believe that this girl exists. That under the spoiled princess act, and the money, and the clothes, there's a sweet, gentle, *normal* young woman.

I slip a third finger into her, rubbing the bumpy patch of nerves on her inner wall. She starts to moan desperately, rocking against me faster and faster. She's close. So close. I keep thrusting inside of her, fluttering my fingers, and she buries her face in my shoulder, biting down. Just as I feel her starting to clench around me, my phone rings.

I sigh, gently removing my fingers and standing up, stepping out of the bath.

Briar clutches at me, her eyes wide. "What? But!"

"It's probably important, princess." I check the number. Anfisa.

She tugs at my hand. "So? You can take the call here."

"You're far too loud for that." I pat her shoulder. "I know you're used to getting whatever you want, but I'm sure you can handle waiting a bit. It'll be good for you."

She reaches down into the water, scoops up a handful of suds, and throws them in my face.

"As if. I've got three of you for a reason." She raises her voice. "Excuse me!" She calls through the suite. "I am the biggest celebrity diva of the year, and I am *demanding* that someone comes in here to finish me off!"

There's a few second's pause, then Kenta comes into the bathroom, smiling wider than I've seen in years. He leans in the doorway and looks at us. "Problem, Briar?"

"Your *useless* partner won't finish what he started," she complains loudly. "Get in here."

He's already started unbuttoning his shirt.

I step into the bedroom, listening to the bathwater splash as he joins her in the tub. There's a flurry of giggles, then a long groan. Trying not to smile, I accept the call. "Hey, I—"

"We've got him."

Shock flashes through me. "You've apprehended him?"

"No. But we know who X is. We found a fingerprint match for the magazine, and you're right; it is one of the suspects you picked up for online activity."

"Let me guess. Daniel F."

"Oh, yes." Anfisa sounds exhausted. *"You need to come and see this. It's not good."*

Thirty minutes later, I'm back at the FBI building, sitting opposite Anfisa in her eerily bare office. She looks like she's been up all night: her face is pale, and her dark suit is rumpled and wrinkled. She slides a photograph across the desk to me. "This is X," she says. "Real name, Daniel Filch. Forty-one years old, grew up in Anaheim, his mother was an unmarried British immigrant. She died when he turned twenty."

I study the man. He doesn't look like much of anything. Thinning brown hair, watery eyes, an insipid, weak smile. It's hard to believe that *this* is the man who's been running rings around us.

"He dropped out of high school at sixteen," Anfisa continues, "no further education. We're not sure what he does for a living right now, if he works, but he had a string of menial jobs when he was younger. They never lasted long. We called up a cafe he worked at when he was seventeen; apparently he was fired for sexual misconduct. Wouldn't stop groping the waitresses."

"Shocker."

"Mm. Another position as a janitor at a gas station; he got fired after CCTV caught him putting cameras into the women's bathroom."

"Jesus. You manage to get his location?"

She purses her lips unhappily. "Kind of. Our agents did some cold-calling around the city and managed to find a local motel which reported a man of his description checking into a room a few days ago. He used a fake name, but the physical appearance and handwriting all match. He only stayed for one night, paid in cash. We have no idea where he moved to after that."

I nod, studying her face. She looks worried. Far more worried than I'd like. "What aren't you telling me?"

She grimaces. "We swabbed down the motel room."

My stomach twists. "And?"

"Traces of black powder."

"Christ." I rub my face. "You think he's making bombs?"

"Well, he's not using it in a goddamn gun. It'd be like sending us up a smoke signal."

I close my eyes. "The premiere is tonight."

She nods solemnly. "We'll brief the officers at the event, give them his picture. If he does turn up, we can arrest him quietly."

I frown. It's not enough. "She's not going."

"That's your prerogative. We have no idea what he could be using the explosives for, so I'd advise you check your cars very thoroughly, and give your hotel security his picture. Briar might not even be the target. She wasn't last time."

"Not a risk I'm willing to take." I stand up, scraping the chair back. I don't like being this far from her. I need to get back to the hotel. "Thanks, Anfisa. For everything. Keep me updated."

She nods, and I turn to go.

"*Matvey*?"

I glance back at her. She smiles wryly. "Be careful. He attacked Petty because of their romantic history. You've been seen getting cosy with her, too."

"I'm not the person I'm worried about," I mutter, and she nods, waving me away.

My head is spinning as I head back to my car. I don't know what to do.

Realistically, I know I shouldn't tell Briar that we've identified X. That would be a terrible idea. If one dickpic prompted her to run her mouth in front of tens of thousands of live viewers, God knows how she'll react when she finds out he's been cooking up bombs in his motel room. I can practically see it unfolding in front of me: if I tell her everything we know about X, she'll insist on attending the premiere. She'll probably use herself as bait to lure him out. And then she'll try to confront him. She'll yell at him and humiliate him, and then he'll probably blow her up.

As a bodyguard, your job isn't only to protect the principal from external threats; you also have to protect them from themselves. And quite often, that means withholding information. If I suspect that Briar will put herself in danger if I tell her the news about X, it's in my *job description* not to tell her.

The only problem is, when she finds out that I lied to her, she's going to absolutely hate me.

It surprises me how much that thought terrifies me.

I grit my teeth, pulling open the car door and sliding inside. This is ridiculous. The only reason I'm even debating this is because I was stupid enough to get involved with Briar. I'm not letting my feelings for a client get in the way of her safety. Not ever. Even if it means destroying the fragile relationship we've started, I'm not putting her life in danger. Even if she ends up hating me, I'm not letting her die.

I care about her far too much for that.

CHAPTER 40
BRIAR

"What do you think?" I ask, twisting in the mirror to examine my dress from the back. "Too much?"

Julie looks up from her spot on my bed. She's been curled up in my bedroom for the last couple of hours, frantically answering emails and texts as I get ready for the premiere. As she glances me over, the straw of her iced coffee falls out of her lips.

"Ho. Ly. Shit." She says slowly.

I smile. "Yeah. I thought so, too."

I'd originally planned on wearing a trouser suit tonight. I didn't like the idea of parading around in revealing outfits, just so X can dream of me sucking him off. But when I tried the suit on, I felt flat. Weak. Like I was hiding. So I called my LA stylists, and they hooked me up with this little beauty. It's a blood-red bodycon made of a thick, stretchy scuba material. The fabric clings to my hips and waist, wrapping around me as tight as cling film. The really impressive part, though, is what it does to my boobs. The neckline is low and square, and the built-in support means that the amount of cleavage is astonishing.

I feel great in it. Hot. Strong. Powerful. I can't wait for the guys to see me in it.

Just as the thought crosses my mind, there's a knock at the door. Glen steps inside, holding a small boutique bag. He stops in the doorway, staring at me. His eyes run up and down my body, freezing on my chest.

"Jesus." He runs a hand over his face. "Seriously? You expect us to be able to concentrate on our jobs, with you wearing *that?*"

I can't hold back my smile. "You're a big boy. You can keep your hands out of your pants and your eyes on the crowd."

He swallows thickly and takes a step towards me. I feel goose-bumps raise over my skin as his eyes zero in on my boobs. When he reaches me, he trails his fingertip very lightly over the neckline.

I ignore the growing heat under my skin, and nod at the little bag he's holding. It's clearly from a fancy shop; the lettering is embossed in gold, and the handles are made from silky cream ribbons. "What's that?"

He clears his throat. "We all got you something. We picked it out online, and then Kenta collected it from the store this morning. It's a late birthday present."

My eyes widen. "Really?" He nods, handing it to me. I carefully pull apart the layers of sparkly tissue paper to reveal a small flat box.

I glance up at Glen. His face flushes.

I open up the box. Nestled on the velvet cushion inside is a neck-lace. I lift it out carefully. A rose-shaped pendant swings from the fine silver chain, glimmering softly under the bedroom light. The petals are made of pale pink crystals, surrounded by delicately twisting thorns.

"You don't have to wear it tonight. I don't know if it goes with your dress. And you probably already have jewellery that you're supposed to wear. But—"

"Glen, this is gorgeous." I turn the little rose charm around, watching it scatter spots of light over my skin. "A briar rose, right?"

I don't remember the last time someone bought me a present just because they thought I'd like it. Not because they wanted me to shout out their product, or they wanted to butter me up to sign a contract, or they wanted to get close to me. I have to blink hard to fight the tears pressing against the backs of my eyes.

I go up on my tiptoes and press my lips to his. "Thank you. Put it on me?"

Julie frowns, tapping at her phone. "Excalibur Jewellery sent you their new ruby collection. I think they were hoping you would—"

"Excalibur can wait until the next event," I interrupt. "I'm not a billboard for companies to stick signs all over."

"It's valued at over twenty-five thousand," she snips.

"You'd better send it back, then. I'd hate for all that money to go to waste."

"But—"

"Julie, I'm trying to have a romantic moment, here. Could you please work outside?"

She harrumphs and jumps to her feet. "Bet you're glad I found you new security now," she mumbles, sashaying out of the room and slamming the door.

"Yes, thank you!" I call after her, pressing the necklace into Glen's hand. "Please?" I ask him.

"Are you sure?" His lip quirks. "It's not worth twenty-five thousand."

"It's worth a Hell of a lot more, as far as I'm concerned."

He lets out a soft breath and carefully drapes the necklace around my throat. His big hands are almost unbearably gentle as he fastens the clasp, and I shiver as the cool chain slides over my skin.

Behind us, the door clicks open again. "Oh. Holy shit." I turn to face Kenta. He trails his eyes over me. "Holy *shit*." He repeats.

"Thank you," I say, flattered. "And thank you for the necklace. It's beautiful."

Kenta smiles. "He wanted us all to give it to you together, but I thought you'd enjoy watching him blush."

"Oh, I definitely did."

He steps forward, kissing me hard. "Happy Birthday, sweetheart." His hands slip down over my hips, then back to my waist. "Christ, it's going to be hard not to touch you tonight."

"You can touch me plenty as soon as the premiere is over," I promise. "Where's Matt? I want to thank him."

The guys exchange a look. "He left to speak with the FBI a few hours ago," Glen says. "He hasn't gotten back yet."

That's weird. "Is there a problem?"

They both shrug. "We wouldn't know until he gets back," Kenta says, dragging his hand up my waist, snagging the fabric on my skin. My eyelashes flutter, and my eyes flick over to the bed. Temptation tugs at me.

I sigh. "You should go, now. If I get distracted, I won't be ready in time."

Kenta laughs, planting one last kiss on my lips. "Yes, ma'am. We'd better suit up as well."

"See you soon," I whisper.

The guys leave, and I head back to my dresser, examining my face in the mirror. I usually have a hair and makeup team, but the guys didn't want to risk letting a bunch of people into the suite, so I pick up my curling wand and set it to warm up.

I spend the next hour and a half fixing my hair and makeup. I go for a modern pin-up look, with big cat eyes, a red lip, and bouncy pinned-back curls. When I'm finally done, it's almost time for us to leave. I touch up my lipstick, then drop the tube into my clutch, along with some tissues, a bobble, and some mints. After a moment's thought, I pull out the bottle of pepper spray Matt gave me, and toss that in, too. Better safe than sorry.

The excitement in my belly flares as there's a hard knock at the door.

"Come in," I call, and it flies open. Matt strides inside. "Hang on a sec," I say, sliding my feet into my heels. "I'm almost ready—"

"You're not going," he interrupts me, crossing his arms.

I look up at him, aghast. "What?"

He shrugs, like it's a minor demand. "The premiere tonight. You're not going." He nods to the dress. "Get out of that. I'll have Kenta pick up some takeaway."

My mouth falls open. "Are you out of your mind? I can't not go to the premiere of *my own movie*."

"It's too public. Anyone could find out the location and the time."

"So? That's why I have you, isn't it? Matt, the whole reason we came to America was for this one event!"

"I'm in charge of your security, and I've changed my mind. We're not taking you."

I throw up my hands. "Fine. I'll find someone else to do it. I'm not sure why you let me *hire* you if you don't actually want to *do your job,* but there are plenty of bodyguards in LA." I reach across the dressing table to unplug my phone.

His hand flies out, grasping my wrist. "No. You. Won't. You're not going. Please, just trust me on this."

I shake him off. "This isn't my choice! I've signed contracts, the studio needs me to be there—"

"So break the contracts!" He shouts, heat rising in his cheeks. "You don't need the money! You're richer than God, for fuck's sake!"

"That's not what this is about! If I piss off the studio, they're not going to want to work with me anymore. I have a bad enough reputation without all of Hollywood's directors deciding I'm too difficult to work with." I grab a bottle of perfume and dab some on my wrists. "I really don't see the issue. There's going to be security at the premiere. It's no more dangerous than any other event I've been to. And really, all X has done so far is leave messages and send me photos of his junk." I strap on my other heel and stand, heading for the doorway. "I'm going, whether you want to come with me or not." My hand closes on the doorknob.

"You're being unbelievably selfish." Matt says quietly behind me.

I sputter, spinning on him. "*Excuse me?*"

"This isn't just about you. Kenta and Glen will be at that carpet. You want to put them in danger? Those are my men, I'm not putting them at risk because you want to go to a bloody party!"

My mouth falls open. "Why are you trying to *guilt trip me?* You all signed up for this! And we said from the beginning: your job is not to stop me from doing my work, it's to *protect* me while I do it."

"Your work doesn't matter!" He snaps, his face white with anger. "None of this fucking matters!"

I take a step back. I feel like he's smacked me in the chest. "Right," I say slowly. "Of course it doesn't. That's what this is about, isn't it? You don't think my work has any value."

He runs a hand through his hair. "I didn't mean it like that," he mutters. "Of course it has value. But not as much value as your *life*. A few hours of you prancing around in front of a camera is not worth more than your *safety*. No contract is worth more than that, princess."

Rage rises up in me. "Look, I might not be an SAS soldier. I might not be saving lives. But I am *good* at my job. I take pride in my work, and I do it properly. If nothing else, my movies give people a couple hours' reprieve from this shitty planet. That means *something*."

He shakes his head slowly. "In the grand scheme of things, Briar, it means absolutely nothing at all."

I swallow. There are tears shimmering in my eyes. "None of the shit that I told you last night matters, does it?" I ask, my voice breaking. "I thought you understood me. But you don't. You don't want to. You'll always think that I'm a spoiled little child star, who's had everything in her life handed to her. You don't care how much it hurt me, growing up like this. You don't care."

For a few seconds, he doesn't say anything. His face is stony. His chest rises and falls with fast, shallow breaths.

"Please. Just take off the outfit," he mutters, then turns on his heel and leaves.

I press a hand to my chest. Suddenly, my tight dress feels constricting, not sexy. The hours I've spent on the makeup, and the hair, and the nails, all seem frivolous and vain. Because that's how he sees me.

Stupid. I've been so, so stupid.

I storm into the bathroom, locking the door behind me and sinking onto the closed toilet seat. The necklace burns against my throat. I reach back and unclasp it, letting it fall to the ground. It doesn't mean anything.

I've spent my whole life feeling completely alone. And for a second, I thought things had finally changed. I thought I'd found three men who saw past the fame, and the money, and my shitty reputation, and saw the real me. I thought they *liked* the real me. But of course not. That will never happen.

You make a deal with the devil when you become famous. You sign away your right to a normal life. To normal friendships and relationships. To walking down the street without being harassed. And that's fair enough, if you want money and notoriety that badly; but it wasn't even *me* who signed my life away. I think of my mother, studiously ignoring me as she sunbathes on the yacht I bought her, and sadness overwhelms me. I'm still completely alone.

There's a tap at the bathroom door.

"Go away," I say.

"I've called a security company," Julie calls, her voice muffled by the door. "Their driver is downstairs now."

I yank the door open. She stands there in the doorway, all five-foot-two of her, her arms crossed over her chest and her pretty red lips twisted in a look of fierce determination.

"What?"

"You're going to that premiere, babe. I don't care how many asshole soldiers we need to piss off to get you there." She passes me my red beaded clutch. "This is your night. They have no right to mess around with your career like this. That self-inflated knob-head might not think your job is worth his time, but it is. You know it is."

I take the clutch off her and follow her slowly back into the bedroom. I can hear the men walking around in the hallway outside, talking in low voices.

"How am I supposed to get downstairs? They'll never let me leave." In a matter of minutes, I've gone from client to prisoner.

"Actually," she smiles, turning her gaze to the fire escape, "they were kind enough to leave you an emergency exit."

I consider the door for a few seconds. Pain and anger and frustration all whirl inside me.

"Get my heels," I mutter, and she squeaks in excitement, clapping her hands.

CHAPTER 41
KENTA

I go down to reception to show hotel security X's picture, and then perform a quick sweep of the public areas. When I get back inside the suite, Matt is sitting at the dining table, a bottle of sparkling water in front of him, scowling at his phone.

"Hotel security agreed to have a night guard monitor the live CCTV tonight," I tell him, hanging up my jacket, "and they're checking the IDs of everyone that comes in and out." I look around the lounge. "Where's Briar?"

"Sulking in her room," Matt mutters.

I glance at her door. The light is on, and I can hear the low hum of her television playing. "I don't know what you expected. If you don't tell her *why* she can't go, of course she's going to be pissed. You're treating her like a kid."

His jaw clenches. "She hired us to protect her. What's the point of having security if she doesn't follow my advice?"

I snort. "You mean your orders?"

He looks up at me, his eyes icy. "Does it matter?"

"This is her *life*. Her *career*. You really think that she's going to let you come in and disrupt all of that for no apparent reason?" I shake my head and make for her door. "When we tell her, I'm sure she'll understand completely."

Matt grabs my wrist. "We can't tell her about the gunpowder."

"*What*?" I shake him off me. "She has to know! It's her life at stake!"

He's breathing hard. "We can't control her. She completely disobeyed us the last time this happened. If we tell her, she'll just get mad and make everything worse." He rubs his face. "*Bombs,* Kenta. Not ammo, bloody *bombs*."

I frown. "I think you're underestimating her. She lashed out last time, because that's how she's learnt to deal with harassment in the industry. Now that we've told her about the differences in stalker psychology, she won't make the same mistake twice. If anything, it was our fault for not briefing her properly."

Matt slams a hand onto the table. "How do you know that she won't do it again?"

I shrug. "I just do. I know her."

"And you're willing to bet her life on it?" He asks, his eyes wild. "You're willing to bet the lives of everybody at that premiere? Every fan, every celebrity, every worker and photographer and *kid*?"

I suddenly realise what's happening. He's not seeing what's in front of him. In his head, he's right back in that cave. The last time he took a chance on our lives, we ended up getting tortured for months. Now, it's hardly surprising that he wants to err on the side of caution.

It's not *surprising*, but it's still not right.

"I would happily leave their lives in her hands, yes. She's a gentle girl, Matt. She wouldn't knowingly do anything that would put someone innocent in danger."

"But—"

I throw up my hands, exasperated. "What are we supposed to do for the rest of the trip, keep her locked up in here, and not tell her why? Sooner or later, she'll just end up firing us and doing whatever the Hell she wants. It's not fair to keep her in the dark like this." I shake my head. "I'm telling her."

He stands, squaring off against me. "You are not."

I grit my teeth. "You're not my commander anymore. I'm. Telling. Her. She needs—"

I'm interrupted by a loud beep from my two-way. I unclip it, bringing it to my mouth.

"Hello?"

"Turn on the TV," Glen says without any preamble. He's breathing hard, like he's running. *"Channel 17."*

"What?" I'm confused. "Do you need backup? Why are you out of breath?"

"Coming up from the gym now. Channel 17."

Matt grabs the remote and starts flicking through channels.

"Why are we doing this?" I ask. "What's happening?"

"Coverage of the premiere just came up on the screens in the gym. She's—"

"She's there," Matt says, his voice full of horror. I glance up at the wide-screen plasma, and my stomach drops. It's a wide shot, showing thirty-odd celebrities walking down the red carpet, smiling and signing autographs. Hundreds of fans press against red velvet ropes cording them away from the stars. Briar is easy to pick out in her bright red dress and scarlet lipstick. She's beaming at a teenage girl holding a baby, leaning over the rope line to take a selfie with them. Behind her, a man in sunglasses and an earpiece is checking his phone and completely ignoring the crowd. I vaguely recognise him from a popular LA security company.

Shit.

The door to the suite opens, and Glen slams inside, gym bag over his shoulder and sweat staining the front of his shirt. He doesn't say anything, immediately grabbing his gun from the case by the door. "We're leaving. Now."

I go to pick up my pistol, but before I can, my phone rings. Anfisa's number flashes across the screen. I pick it up and slam it onto the table as I strap up.

"Kenta Li. You're on speaker, Matt and Glen are here."

"Good. You need to see this," Anfisa says, her voice clipped. *"It landed in her DMs a few minutes ago. Our research team just clocked it."*

My phone dings with an incoming image. It's a screenshot from one of Briar's social media accounts.

I can't wait to see you tonight, angel. I'll be there to pick you up and take you home.

If you don't come quietly, people will die. X

Underneath, there's a low-quality photograph of a pile of short silver pipes stacked in a pyramid. Closing my eyes, I pass my phone to the others, reaching for my gun again.

"Pipe bombs," Glen says quietly.

"We lost track of her," I tell Anfisa. "She's at the event now."

Anfisa's silent for a moment, then a stream of Russian swearing pours out of the phone. I catch a few words. *Idiotic. British. Moron.*

"We know," Matt snaps, heading to the door. I join him, stepping into my shoes. "What the Hell are you going to do?"

"I'm doubling police presence and calling in the LAPD bomb squad. We'll try and get the area evacuated ASAP, but it'll be tricky with all the media. The studio will probably kick in their heels. Not to mention all the celebs." She sounds exhausted.

"Do what you have to," Matt says. "We'll go in and extract her."

She sighs. *"I don't like this. We've been on the back foot almost this entire investigation. He's clearly smart enough to evade detection. The fact that he literally* told *you about the bomb threat means that he just doesn't give a shit anymore."*

I don't know how to respond to that. "See you there, Anfisa," I mutter, and she hangs up. I turn to Matt, irritation buzzing through me. "Nice job," I say flatly. "Now she's right where he wants her, and she doesn't even know that the bastard threatened to blow her up."

All the colour drains from Matt's face.

CHAPTER 42
BRIAR

The premiere is beautiful. The studio pulled out all the stops for the event. Going along with the 1920s murder mystery theme, they picked out an old-style cinema in the middle of LA for the screening, and cordoned off a square in front of the building with heavy velvet ropes. Bright lamps are erected throughout the square, illuminating massive hanging posters, each depicting one of the characters clutching a weapon and spattered in blood. There are ushers dressed in traditional red uniforms handing out goodie bags full of merch. The sweet, buttery smells of popcorn and candyfloss drift through the evening air from the complimentary concessions stand, and crackly, old-timey music plays through hidden speakers.

It's definitely one of the more tasteful premieres I've ever attended, but as I step away from the photography pit and start trailing down the press line, I feel like I'm in a haze. I answer journalists' questions robotically, barely taking in my surroundings.

I'm hurt. Really hurt.

Last night was a big deal for me. I don't ever open up to people. Ever. I hate talking about growing up in the industry. I hate talking about how much it broke me down. Last night, it felt like I was showing the men all the chinks in my armour. But I did it, because for a moment, I actually thought they cared. But of course, they don't. If they cared, they'd be here, doing their damn jobs.

As I say goodbye to one reporter and turn to the next, hands suddenly grab me from behind. I bite back the urge to scream, spinning to see a young man in a dark hoodie, clutching a crumpled t-shirt. For a moment, my heart drops to my stomach. It's *him*. He's found me.

"Let me go," I whisper, ice dripping down my throat. "Please."

The man grips me even harder, raking his fingernails down my arm. "Briar, oh my God, I'm your biggest fan," he chants, specks of spit flying through the air.

I force myself to take a deep breath, really looking at him. There's no way this is X. I remember the security footage; this guy is smaller and heavier than the man on the tapes.

He keeps babbling. "Please please please sign my merch oh my God I can't believe you're finally here I can't believe I'm *touching you*."

"Neither can I," I say flatly. "Let go of me." I try to shake him off. When he doesn't let go, I grab his fingers and yank them back, hard, until he howls in pain, dropping my arm. "Get back in line."

His bottom lip trembles. *"Please, Briar!"*

I shake my head. "Wait in line like everyone else. You don't get special treatment for assaulting me." I twist, looking in disgust at the red lines his fingernails left down my arm. "And clip your fucking nails. What is wrong with you?"

"B-but—"

I glance back at my temporary bodyguard, Chris. He's engrossed in his phone. "Excuse me," I say flatly. "So sorry to interrupt. Can you please get rid of this guy?"

He blinks up from his phone, looks around owlishly, then waves the fan back, reaching for his gun.

"Jesus, don't *shoot* him!" I snap. "Just get him off the damn carpet!"

God, he's useless. Julie said that he's from one of the best close protection services in LA, but as far as I can tell, he's spent the whole night trying to beat his high score on Candy Crush.

It makes me nervous, not having the men around me. I miss Kenta's calm eyes watching over me, Glen's silhouette shadowing me a few steps behind. Hell, I even miss Matt's hand on the small of my back as he leads me through the reporters.

Matt mentioned that they thought X might be here tonight. Since he refused to tell me any reasons *why* he thought that, I'm assuming he was just trying to scare me. If it is true, though, I might be screwed. Chris here wouldn't notice if someone leapt out of the crowd and held a gun to my head.

Shaking off the dread stroking down my spine, I screw my smile back on and turn to the next interviewer. The guy is gross-looking; greasy hair covered by a backwards baseball cap, and jeans hanging so low over his hips that I can see his underwear.

We exchange pleasantries, and he asks me the same, overused questions that everybody else asked. *What's it like working with a female director? You look great in all the promo shots, what was your diet plan? Did you have a personal trainer? Was your co-star a good kisser?*

Same old, same old.

The reporter shuffles his question cards and leans in. I can smell his onion breath. "You had an almost all-female cast—how did that work? Was there any cattiness in the group?"

I notice the cameraman focussing on my cleavage and fight the urge to slap him with my clutch. "Oh, you know, only when all of our periods synced up."

He gives me a bright smile, not sensing the sarcasm in my tone. "Yeah, wow. I imagine that was a bit of a bitchfest."

"A bloodbath," I agree. "Hey, do you have any not-sexist questions? Those are my favourite kind—"

A hand closes around my arm, and I jump, spinning to see Matt looming over me. He's dressed sloppily, his suit wrinkled and his tie crooked, but he still outshines pretty much every man on the carpet. For a split second, happiness sparks in my belly. *He changed his mind. He came.*

Then I register the anger hardening his sharp features. "You're leaving," he rumbles. "Now."

"Matt?" I squawk. "What are you doing here?"

He ignores me, pulling me away from the journalist and across the carpet to the exit. I try to shake him off me, but his grip is like iron. "Get off me! Don't pull me around!"

I see my co-stars look away from their interviews, concern crossing their faces. Liam, the movie's villain, actually steps away from his journalist and reaches for me.

"Briar? Are you alright?"

"Out of my way," Matt barks.

Liam frowns, putting his hands up. "Look, man, it doesn't look like she wants to go with you—"

Matt just tightens his fingers on my arm and drags me away.

"Ow!" I dig my heels in. "Stop! You'll leave marks on me! And then I'll be in a domestic abuse scandal! For God's sake, what is wrong with you? Let me *go*."

"You promised," he mutters, his eyes fixed straight ahead as we plough through the crowd. He's seething; anger is rolling off his body like physical heat. "You *promised* you would trust me."

"I promised I would *try,*" I hiss back. "How the Hell am I meant to trust you when you constantly belittle my work? You don't treat me like an equal, you keep me in the dark about my own safety—" I trip over my heels, and he grabs me, gently righting me. I shove him off. "You've done nothing to *earn* my trust. All you're doing is shit-talking my job and ordering me around! I'm sick of it! You might think my contract isn't important, but I'm going to do my *useless, meaningless* job whether you approve or not, so you might as well—"

He turns a corner and presses me up against the brick wall of the cinema.

"He's made bombs, Briar!" He snaps out. "He's here, and he's made bombs. This has nothing to do with your *job,* and if you say one more word about it—"

He keeps talking, but my ears are full of static. Everything in me freezes. For a second, I can't breathe. "What?" I whisper, interrupting his tirade.

His blue eyes burn into mine. "He's threatened to blow up the whole event if he can't get his hands on you. We have to get you out of here, now."

I stagger a step back, almost tripping in my heels. Horror is flooding through me. "D-did you know?"

"The FBI found traces of explosives in his motel room this morning," he says stiffly.

"This *morning?!*"

He reaches for me again, but I push away from him. My head is spinning.

"Why? Why wouldn't you tell me?" I look around the red carpet. Fans scream and press up against the barriers, waving phones and posters to sign. There must be three hundred people invited to watch the screening tonight. Nausea rises up in my throat as I see a handful of tween girls huddled together. "There are… children here," I gasp. Matt says something, but I can't hear it. Panic is sweeping through me in a strong, sickly wave. "Get me out," I whisper. When he doesn't move, I throw myself at him, shoving my body into his chest. "Get me the Hell *out. Now!*"

Matt puts his arm around my shoulder and keeps leading me along the edges of the carpet towards one of the exits. We pass the wide-eyed studio director, who hurries to follow us. "Briar, sweetheart, you're not leaving, are you? The screening is in fifteen minutes, we need you ready to make your speech!"

We both ignore him, swanning right past.

"I hate you," I whisper. "How dare you do this to me? How dare you put me in a position where I could get all these people hurt without even *realising* it?!"

"You can fire us when we're out of here," he grinds out, looking around. His radio crackles, and I hear a woman's voice rattle off a string of numbers that I don't understand. Some kind of code.

"Oh, trust me, I will. What the Hell is wrong with you?" I shake my head. "When we get home, I never want to see you again."

His hand tightens on my wrist. "Fine."

I don't even realise I'm crying until tears start rolling down my cheeks. We reach the edge of the carpet, and Matt tugs me to a stop, pulling me behind a hanging sign. "Here." He grabs his radio. "I have Princess. Bring the car to exit point two," he barks. "*Now.*"

I yank my wrist out of his grip, crossing my arms over my chest. "Why the Hell wouldn't you tell me?" I demand.

He takes a deep breath. "Because you have a shitty track record. You care more about your pride than your own safety." He glares at his radio, like it will make the car get here faster.

Tears catch in my throat. "Fuck you! I stand up for myself, but I would never, *ever* put someone in danger just to protect my pride. Why the Hell would you—"

Something snaps. He whirls on me. "Because I'd die for you!" He bellows.

My whole body jerks. *"Excuse* me?"

"I'd die for you," he repeats, his chest heaving. The streetlights light him up from behind, drenching him in bright highlights and sharp shadows. "I'd do anything to keep you safe. Anything. I'm sorry if you don't like the way I did it, but every decision I make, I make to keep you safe! Because the idea of losing you *fucking terrifies me!"*

"That doesn't give you an excuse to *lie* to me!" I shout back. "This is inexcusable, Matt! You can't hide this shit from someone! You can't let someone accidentally endanger hundreds of people, just because you don't trust them with the truth!"

He opens his mouth to respond—then his eyes travel over my shoulder, widening. He wraps his arms around my waist, yanking me into him.

I try to struggle away. "No, no, I don't forgive you, don't *touch me—"*

And then all of the air leaves my lungs as he throws me to the ground and slams his body on top of mine, right as an explosion rips through the square.

CHAPTER 43
BRIAR

For a few seconds, everything is complete chaos.

Fans scream behind the barriers, some ducking down, others staggering backwards. I hear shrieks as people get trampled. Out of the corner of my eye, I see my costars dropping to their knees, choking. Most of the videographers stay standing, panning their cameras over the panic.

A thick, foul-smelling smoke is spreading through the square, grey and heavy. It tickles my throat, and I cough as it fills my mouth and lungs. I can't *breathe*. Panic stabs me, and a terrified whimper falls out of my mouth as I claw at the asphalt under my hands.

I feel Matt touching my face, and I realise he's talking into his radio. "I've got her." He strokes my cheek. "Shh. Shh. Shallow breaths, princess. You're okay. Try not to panic, I've got you."

I squint through the smoke, but it's just getting thicker, and I can barely see a metre in front of me. "Where's Kenta and Glen?" I squeak, but I don't think he hears me over the screaming.

His radio hisses. *"Suspect spotted,"* a female voice says, then sputters off into choking. *"Qu-quadrant f-five, by the entrance."*

Matt swears. "Stay down," he says in my ear, then pulls himself off me.

"No!" I shout, reaching for him. My fingers brush the hem of his jacket.

Another explosion rocks through the crowd.

This one feels even worse than the first. There's an awful tearing sound, and then a crash. I look up and realise the rigging that's been holding up the giant movie posters has fallen, smashing heavy iron bars into the crowd.

"Matt!" I scream, but there's no response. He's gone. He's *gone.*

Suddenly, a hand grabs me around the throat, yanking me backwards and upright. I'm pulled into a man's chest.

"NO!" I shout, jabbing my elbow hard into his stomach. There's a low grunt, but no other reaction. He starts to tug me away from the carpet, through the chaos. Struggling, I manage to wriggle a hand free, fumbling at my clutch and yanking out the tube of pepper spray. Fiddling with the cap, I twist and spray it where I'm guessing X's face is. "GET OFF ME!"

The guy swears, letting me go, and I stagger away.

The smoke is so thick I can't see anything. It's completely opaque. I don't even know what direction I'm going. There's another explosion, this one further away, and I double over as I run, hacking coughs wracking my body. I slam into someone. They reach out to grab at me, but I just shake them off, plunging forward. Out. I need to get out. I kick off my heels as I run, but barely make it three more steps before I trip, falling face-first onto something warm and soft. I feel silky hair under my fingers and pull away like I've been burned.

A body. Oh my God.

"BRIAR!" I hear someone bellow through the smoke, and warmth erupts in my chest as I recognise Glen's throaty Scottish accent. I scrabble to stand upright, turning towards the voice—

Something slams onto my mouth and nose. A damp cloth. A sour, chemical smell fills my nostrils, and I cough, trying to shove it away. The hand on my face just clamps the cloth down harder, forcing me to breathe in. A thick arm snakes around my waist, holding me in place. Tears fill my eyes as I feel my head start to get fuzzy.

God. I'm being *chloroformed*. How cliché is that? It's *embarrassing*. The man starts to drag me away, and I kick aimlessly at him, trying to trip him up. When that doesn't work, I turn my head, trying to bite his hand, but I just get a mouthful of the damp cloth.

A flurry of gunshots suddenly crack through the smoke. I scream as I feel a bullet whiz over my head.

"Don't shoot!" I hear Kenta shout from far away, and some of the tension around my chest loosens. He's okay. He didn't get hurt. "You'll hit her!"

I open my mouth to shout to him, to scream, but I can't make my voice work. Nausea rolls up in my chest, and I feel my legs bending under me. I blink hard as the shapes in the smoke start to swirl and distort. The hand on my waist tightens.

"There we are. You're okay, angel," a voice coos in my ear. "Just relax. I've got something to show you."

"I'll gouge out your balls and stuff them down your throat until you choke, you ugly little *piece of shit!*" I spit out. Or at least, I try to spit out. My mouth feels numb, and the words aren't coming. Instead, I just moan. My vision is going in and out. My heart is pounding painfully. This is it. I'm going to die.

Lips brush against my ear. "Aw, it's okay. I know you're scared, but we'll get you out of here. Come on, I've got you."

I moan again and try to push away, but my arms just twitch. My eyes widen. I can't move. I'm completely paralysed. X swings me up into his arms and starts to carry me away. The smoke is shifting and dissipating, and for a second, I see Kenta. He's holding his gun and scanning the crowd, his face frantic.

As I watch him, our eyes lock. His mouth drops open in horror as he sees me getting carried away.

"BRIAR!" He shouts, running forward. I try to scream for him, but the world finally blinks out into nothing.

CHAPTER 44

X

I almost forgot how beautiful Briar looks when she's sleeping.

Right now, she's asleep on the sofa in my living room, breathing softly. Her hair is loose, and it's all spread out over my couch cushions. It's a really nice golden colour. And soft, too. I know how soft it is. When I was putting her in the car, I gagged her, and then I got to run my fingers through it. It was cheating, I suppose; I made a promise to myself that I wouldn't touch her until she'd woken up and I'd fed her dinner and kissed her. That's the proper order to do it in. But I couldn't help touching her hair when I was gagging her.

She was very quiet on the drive down here. I wasn't sure how long the chloroform would last, so I put some on her gag, too, and tied it over her mouth. Just in case she did wake up, I used zip ties for her wrists. When I bought them in the supply store (along with some craft blades, duct tape, and more insulation for my walls) the sales lady laughed and said that I was all set for my career as a serial killer. I scarpered quick. I didn't want her to remember my face. Maybe I was being paranoid, but I've been so worried the past few weeks. I've had nightmares that the police will find me and catch me before I can bring Briar home.

It turns out, all of that worry was for nothing. Tonight went off without a hitch. The bombs worked perfectly. When I threw them into the crowd, the explosions sent all the security and police running towards the blast. It was simple enough to knock Briar out and slip away.

Briar twitches in her sleep, and a massive smile spreads across my face. She's waking up. I'm *so* excited to finally talk to her. I've been dreaming of this exact moment for years.

She twitches again, harder this time, and then groans. I stand slowly. "Angel? Are you waking up?"

She groans again, then starts to choke horribly.

I rush over to help her as she doubles over, heaving over the edge of the couch. Nothing comes up, but she looks awful. Her face is chalky white and sweaty.

My chest aches. "Oh, angel. I'm sorry. It's the anaesthetic, isn't it?" I sit down on the couch next to her, putting a hand on her back. Her bare back. She shudders and coughs. "I'm sorry," I say again. "I tried the drugs on myself, to make sure they wouldn't make you feel too bad. But I guess you're reacting differently to them."

She heaves a breath, then reaches out to grab my hand weakly. My heart stops. Trying to breathe, I squeeze her fingers.

"I'm so dizzy," she mumbles. "Kent…"

I frown. Kent? Is that a name? Or is she just talking gibberish?

She leans into me, whimpering. "I don't feel… I'm… help me—"

"I'm here, love," I murmur, smoothing my hand down her back. Her skin is like satin, but warm and alive under my fingertips. "I'm here. You're safe, now."

She shakes her head and gags again. I let her go and rush to find a bin, kicking it in front of her right as she starts to get sick. It goes on for a long time. I think maybe putting the chloroform on her gag was a bad idea.

"I'm so sorry," I murmur over and over. "So, so sorry. Poor darling. You'll feel better soon." I feel terrible. This isn't how I wanted us to meet at all. I never wanted to hurt her. But really, how was I supposed to know she'd have a bad reaction to chloroform?

Eventually, she sits up, leaning heavily against the back of the couch. Her face is very white and her eyes are hazy. She blinks heavily a few times, trying to focus on me.

"X?" She says slowly.

I smile. "Hello, baby. Please, call me Daniel."

She doesn't say anything. Worry pinches me. Maybe she prefers 'X'? I suppose it is more sexy and mysterious than *Daniel*. "Or 'X' is fine," I tell her quickly. "Whatever you want, love."

Her eyes flick around the room. Then she looks down at her hands.

"Untie me," she rasps.

I pat her hand. "Not yet, love. I want to make sure you've got all your faculties back, first. You're still a bit under the influence. You might do something rash."

She stares at me, breathing heavily. I wonder if she understood everything that I just said.

"Can I brush my teeth," she whispers eventually.

I perk up. "Of course!" I run into the bathroom, picking out the sparkly pink toothbrush I propped next to my blue one, loading it up with toothpaste. I usually just get store-brand, but I got extra-special whitening stuff for her, the most expensive they had. I grab a cup for her to spit, then bring them back to her. She's sitting slumped against the sofa arm, her eyes glassy.

"It's your favourite colour." I show her. "Pink!" I kneel back down next to her. "Come on, now, angel. Let me help you."

She tries to flinch away, but I grip her head to hold her in place, and brush her teeth for her. I've never brushed somebody else's teeth before. She glares at me the whole time. When I finish up, I give her the cup to spit into. "There. You must feel better now, right?"

She's still for a moment, her eyes fixed on my face, every muscle in her body quivering.

Then she bolts, staggering upright and flying for the front door. I swear, lunging after her as she pounds at the thick metal pane, her hands patting all over to look for a handle. It's no use. She wouldn't be able to get out of this room if she had a sledgehammer. I wrap my arms around her and start to tug her away. She's fit, but she's still weak from the drugs. I lift her right off the ground and carry her back to the sofa. She squirms in my arms, trying to kick me, and I blush as her body rubs against mine.

Soon.

"Okay, okay, none of that." I prop her back against the sofa cushions. "Listen up," I say firmly. "I am a very nice person, but you have to play fair with me, okay? You have to play by the rules."

"Play *fair?*" She breathes incredulously. "What about this is *fair?*"

I squat down next to the couch so I can look right into her beautiful face. "Fair means no more trying to get away, okay? You won't be able to do it; I've arranged the house so you won't be able to get out. And the insulation means that nobody can hear you." I push some hair gently behind her ear, and she flicks her head away, trying to throw me off. This makes me mad. I grab a handful of her hair and hold it very, very tight.

"I am going to be very kind to you," I tell her, pulling on her hair hard. "You don't need to worry about that. I'll get you anything you need. But you must remember that I am in charge. Okay?"

"If you let me out, I won't call the police," she says, her voice shaking. "No one ever needs to know this happened. I'll go back to my hotel. We can pretend that I ran and hid when the bombs went off, then I snuck off home."

I smile. "Angel, you know that's not going to work. That's not what I want at all."

She leans forward. "What do you want? Money? I'll give you all the money I have, I don't care about it."

"I know you don't. It's one of the things I love about you." I stand up, brushing off my trousers. "I don't want your money. I just want you to be my guest."

"Your… guest?" She repeats slowly.

"I want you to live here with me. I want to eat meals with you. And watch TV with you. And just…" I shrug, my face going red. "Be with you."

"You want to trap me here," she says flatly.

"I know it must seem like that," I say gently. "But really, you'll be very comfortable. I have plenty of money. Not as much as you're used to," I frown. "I'm sorry about that. I'll earn more. But I can get you anything you want. And it's not forever."

She raises an eyebrow. "Really? When will you let me go?"

"When you fall in love with me," I say simply. "When you agree to marry me, then we can leave the cabin and do whatever you want. Shopping, cinema. You can… can…" I try to think of things girls like. "Have your nails painted. You won't be able to work, of course. If I could, I'd delete every copy of every video and movie you've ever been in. I'd burn every magazine and poster. I don't like other people looking at you."

She doesn't say anything.

I shake my head. "No. No more working. But I know you like to act." I lick my lips. "If you want to put on little shows for me, sometimes, I'd be very happy to watch them. But first, you have to agree to marry me. And I have to believe that you mean it. So that will probably take a few months, at least."

She's silent for a long time, her eyes cold as she studies me. Eventually, she flicks her hair back and shakes her head. "I'll never love you."

This really annoys me. She's just decided that she won't love me without ever giving me a chance. All my life, women have done this. I want to love them, but they just decide I'm not worthy of them. It's cruel.

"You need to understand," I snap. "That I don't have anybody else."

"Why does that mean you should have *me*?!" She argues.

"Don't you think that everybody deserves someone?"

"Sure. But no one's *entitled* to love. You have to earn it."

"I have earned you!" I shout, losing my temper. "I've worked so hard for you. Look at everything I've done for you." I wave around the room. She doesn't look away from me. She's breathing hard, her breasts heaving and trembling in her low-cut dress. I want to look so badly, but I know that will just make her more angry. "You'll never understand," I tell her. "Right now, I bet there are so many people looking for you. Your agent, and your bodyguards, and your fans—they all want you back. If I disappeared, no one would care. No one would notice. So." I take a deep breath. "I think I deserve to be happy with the woman I love."

"You don't love me," she whispers. "You don't even know me."

I frown. What a stupid thing to say. "Of course I love you. You're all I think about. Everything I do, I do for you." She stares up at me impassively. "I love the way you walk," I continue. "I love your voice. Your smile. Your hair. I love everything about you." I swallow. "I... I think I've gone mad over you. You've made me mad."

But that's what love is, right? It makes you mad. I clear my throat. "So, yes, I do love you. And I do know you. Ever since the day we met, I've studied up on you. I know the clothes you like, where you work out, your favourite snacks. Loads of things."

She blinks. "We've met before?"

"You might not recognise me that easily," I smile. "You were sixteen years old. I went to a convention you spoke at. You dropped your handbag, and I picked it up for you, and you smiled at me." I take a deep breath, remembering. "You smiled right at me, and I could feel how much you cared about me. I felt the connection between us."

Her face twists. "Whatever *connection* you felt was completely one-sided," she spits. "You made it up in your head."

She may as well have kicked me in the chest. I stagger a step back. "You're lying."

She glares up at me. "I'm not. I smile at thousands of people a day at those events."

"You *are*. You *have* to be. I..." I trail off, running a hand through my hair. I'm very stressed and upset. "You're really starting to hurt my feelings," I warn her.

"Really?" Her eyes widen. "I'm so sorry! I'd hate to hurt your *feelings*."

She's being sarcastic. I scowl. I don't like this side of her. This isn't how this was supposed to go. "I think you need a time out," I decide. "I don't know what's wrong with you, but you're really upsetting me."

I pick up the gag on the table and stomp into the bathroom, bending under the sink and pulling out the sealed bucket of chloroform I made earlier today. I dip the gag in it, then head back into the lounge, waving it to dry it out.

Her eyes widen when she sees what I'm holding. She tries to get up again, but I grab her by the shoulder and push her back onto the couch. I don't mean to push her hard, but her head cracks against the wall, and she cries out, trying to tug away.

"X, please, no—"

I slap the cloth onto her face. "No, no, I think you should have some more of this. I don't want to talk to you right now." I hold the gag tightly to her mouth until she groans and goes still again.

I'm not really sure what to do next, so I go and make myself a cup of tea, trying not to cry.

CHAPTER 45
MATT

I look around me. The brightly lit glamour of the premiere has been completely destroyed. Ten minutes ago, the square was full of beautiful men and women waving to adoring fans. Now, it looks like the aftermath of a horror movie. Cameras lie on the red carpet, their lenses shattered. Women are hunched together, crying. Nearby, a man lies unconscious on the floor, blood trickling out of his ears.

Nervous-looking paramedics pick through the crowd, bending to talk to people or roll them onto stretchers. The LAPD bomb squad is trawling the area, ushering guests away from whatever's left of the explosives. Red and blue lights flash over the whole scene, and every minute, more police cars are drawing up in the road.

I watch a kid—a *child,* probably ten or eleven—get unearthed from a pile of rubble, sobbing. I feel completely empty inside.

This is my fault. I'm the reason this happened. Me. I was the one who hid X's threat from Briar. I let her slip away in the hotel room.

And now she could be dead. Because of me.

A few feet away, a woman in a diamond-studded dress gets helped onto a stretcher. I'm pretty sure she's the director of the movie. She's crying, her makeup running down her cheeks.

Is this all I do? Hurt people?

A hand clamps down on my shoulder. "Stop it," Kenta snaps. I look up at him. His face is hard. "Stop beating yourself up and focus. You're not helping anyone like this."

I nod. He's right. There's no time to reflect right now. We have to act.

"Carter." I turn and see Anfisa waving us over. There's a whole group of FBI agents here. They've set up a quasi-booth on one of the agents' cars, balancing laptops and equipment on the car boot. "We've got CCTV footage," she says as we approach, stepping back so we can see the laptops. Each screen is split into quarters, showing camera footage the agents are scrolling through. I stoop down to watch over the screens.

Glen, who's been talking with a member of the bomb squad, comes to join us. "Looked like a mixture of flashbangs and pipe bombs. The pipes were definitely homemade."

"Any deaths?" Kenta asks.

He shakes his head. "None so far. A couple broken bones, a few injuries from shrapnel, but nothing too severe. Paramedics can't reach everyone yet, though. They're only treating people at the edges of the blast zone."

I tune them out, focussing on the CCTV tapes. So far, I haven't seen anything useful. Just the odd worker walking around behind the scenes, holding camera equipment or trays of drinks. I zero in on one screen, watching as the explosion starts and a waitress drops her tray, falling to her knees and covering her ears.

There's a tap on my shoulder. "Excuse me, sir," a man says politely. I glance across. Paramedic. He smiles at me. "Were you caught in the bombing?"

"Obviously," I mutter, scrolling through the cameras. I didn't just roll around in the shrapnel for fun.

"Well, then, if you'd allow me to examine—"

"I'm fine."

"You may *feel* fine, sir, but bombs like this can cause internal bleeding from the wave of pressure they emit, rather than the physical—"

"I know how a bloody bomb works," I snap, "I've thrown plenty of them."

The paramedic looks vaguely concerned.

"We're former SAS soldiers," Kenta explains quickly. "We're currently working, so we really don't have much time."

"Th-thank you for your service," the guy stutters. Anfisa snorts. I ignore them all, leaning in closer to study the footage. There's a flash of red in one of the cameras, and I stab the space bar, pausing the recording. "This one. Camera six." I check the tag. "Employee entrance B."

"I'll go check it out," a policeman says, jogging away. I expand the video and watch, my stomach twisting, as a man in a dark grey hoodie strolls to a blue car, carrying a limp blonde woman in his arms. The area is dark, lit by a single streetlamp, but as he turns to check behind him, his face is perfectly illuminated.

It's him. No doubt about it. Daniel Filch. He looks exactly like his photo; weak-jawed and puffy, his small eyes pale and beady behind his wire-frame glasses.

My throat tightens as he turns back around and opens the car door. Briar comes into view. Her body is as lifeless as a doll's, and her hair is falling over her face in wild curls. I close my eyes. "Check the license plate," I mutter.

Kenta's already tapping at his phone. "It's a rental. Blue Lotus Car Dispensary."

"Get them on the phone. Check if they have lojack or GPS tracking."

"On it." He puts his phone to his ear and walks away from us.

I keep watching the video. X caresses Briar's cheeks as he pulls out a rag and ties it around her mouth, then zip-ties her wrists. Fear rolls through me as he reaches into his pocket, pulling something out. The sharp edge of a knife flashes under the streetlamp.

Wetness on me. Wetness down my back. A knife, shining under the light. Kenta's eyes are terrified.
"Just give us the information. Nothing needs to happen to your friends."

"Matt."

The words are on the tip of my tongue, but I can't say them. I know I can't say them.

"Matt. Look at me."

I can't say them I can't say them I can't say them

"Matt, I'm squeezing your arm. You can feel it. C'mon, man, we need you."

I squeeze my eyes shut. It's not real, I know it's not real. I manage to pull myself out of the memory, with a sensation like I'm dragging myself up out of a deep pool of water. Kenta's dark eyes burn into mine. "It's good news," he says. "They do have lojack. Apparently, they were approached today and offered a large amount of money to switch it off."

I blink hard. "We'll give them twice as much to turn it back on."

"Already done," Anfisa says. She's looking at me with a soft expression I don't think I've ever seen on her face before. "They're linking us up to the GPS signal now." She nods to an agent typing furiously at one of the laptops. As I watch, a map appears on the screen, with a red blinking light to show the car's position.

I frown. That can't be right. It's off any roads, there aren't any houses nearby.

Glen swears. "Is that—"

"It looks like the middle of the forest." I can't breathe. He's taken her to the middle of a forest. Not his house. A forest. What would he do to her in a forest? Images flash in my mind. Of him cutting her. Stripping her. Killing her.

Kenta clasps my shoulder. "*Breathe,*" he mutters in my ear. And then, louder, "Are there any properties there?"

Anfisa leans over my shoulder. "The house."

My head swings around. "What?"

"We went through his mother's will. It was filed with the probate court, it's public access. He inherited a small property that looks to be around that area." She barks some commands into her radio, then rattles off a zip code. Kenta checks it against the GPS coordinates. The two red blips on the map are almost perfectly aligned.

I straighten, relief flooding through me. "Got it. We'll take our car. Dispatch an ambulance to meet us there."

Anfisa shakes her head. "You come with us in one of our cars. Yours might have been tampered with, and we don't want you entering the scene if you get there first."

I nod impatiently, watching as Kenta sets up his phone GPS.

"It's a good sign, right?" A nearby policeman asks, his voice nervous. "He's using his own property, as opposed to some old abandoned barn. Maybe he really does want to just… take her in."

We all stare at him like he's an idiot.

He shrugs defensively. "You saw the messages. They say he loves her. He wants her to be his wife, or whatever."

"He doesn't love her." Kenta snaps. "He drugged and kidnapped her. He's obsessed with her. When she doesn't play out his fantasies, his entire fake reality will come crashing down around him. And then…" He trails off.

We can all fill in the blank. This is a man who is happy to bomb an event full of strangers. He's clearly violent.

"She's an actress, right?" Anfisa asks.

I nod.

She purses her lips. "Well, let's hope she manages to keep up the act until we get there."

CHAPTER 46
BRIAR

When I open my eyes, the first thing I register is the smell of cooking meat. I lie still, staring up at the ceiling. My head is pounding and my mouth is dry. I feel like I've got the worst hangover of my life. Despite the fogginess in my brain, I know immediately where I am.

X's house.

I have no clue how I got here. The last thing I remember was the premiere filling up with smoke, and this asshole choking me with a chloroform-soaked gag. Fear rolls over me as I remember the explosions. The screaming. Matt disappearing in the crowd. I have to press my lips together to force back a sob. Oh my God. Is he okay? Did he get hurt? Did people *die* at the premiere, because of *me*?

I force myself to take a deep breath. I can't break down right now. It could kill me. I have to stay calm. Squeezing my eyes shut again, I try to steady my breathing. I need to come up with a plan.

"I know you're awake," X says, his voice hard with irritation. "There's no point pretending."

Grimacing, I push myself upright. I'm still on the sofa where he left me. Thankfully, he's removed the bucket I threw up into, and he's cut the zip ties on my wrists. Something about that fact sends fear rushing down my spine. If he's decided to untie me, he must know there's no way for me to escape.

I look blearily around the room, taking in my surroundings. I'm in what looks like a cabin. This room is an open-plan lounge-slash-kitchen; I'm sitting on a stained pink sofa. In front of me is a small kitchen nook with an oven, a fridge-freezer, and a dining room table covered in a red-checked cloth. There are layers of thick foam stuck to the walls, which I guess must act as sound insulation.

I turn my head. There aren't any windows, but I note the corridor running off to the right, lined with doors. I know one of them leads to a bathroom, but I'm not sure about the others. There must be an exit somewhere.

There's a clatter, and I look back at X. He's standing in the kitchen in a pink apron, pulling a roast chicken out of the oven.

He doesn't look anything like I expected. I'd been picturing him as some terrifying, muscle-bound behemoth. A movie villain. Instead, he just looks like a regular middle-aged man. His pale brown hair is thinning, and his eyes are small and watery under a pair of wire-frame glasses. He's not tall or short. Not attractive or ugly. His accent sounds like a mix of English and American. He's just… average. It seems ridiculous that someone so average could do something so terrible.

"I hope you're hungry," he drones. "I cooked dinner for us both." He sets down the tray of chicken with an angry clatter, slamming the oven door shut with his thigh. "It's going to be lovely."

I need to buy myself time. The last time I woke up, he was pretty gentle with me in the beginning. I shudder as I remember him stroking my back as I threw up. His hands felt horrible—

sweaty and soft, the pads too fleshy. But I prefer gross to dangerous.

"X," I say softly. He doesn't respond, lifting the lid off a saucepan and checking inside. "X."

"What?" He snaps.

"I'm sorry," I whisper. "I'm sorry for being rude. I didn't mean to upset you."

He turns on me, his pale eyes flashing. "*Are* you? Or are you just saying that so I'll let you go?"

I hunch up. "I'm sorry. I think it was the drugs. My head wasn't clear, I didn't realise what was happening."

He grunts, turning back to the stove.

I lick my lips. "I was… disorientated. But I do remember you."

He snorts. "Yeah? Where did we meet?"

"I don't remember the venue. I just remember—" I fight the violent urge to gag, "a, ah, handsome man with kind eyes, picking up my handbag."

He doesn't say anything, stabbing a carving fork into the chicken.

I try a different tack. "When I woke up here, I thought you wanted to hurt me. I'm used to men trying to take advantage of me."

He twitches with interest, but doesn't look up, pulling the meat off the bone.

"But… " I swallow thickly. "But I can see now, you're not like the other guys. You want to take care of me."

"And what about that man?" He asks, loading a plate with chicken. "The bodyguard?"

"Who?"

"I saw you kissing him. It was all over the magazines. I wanted to give you the benefit of the doubt. I thought maybe he was going undercover as your date. Maybe the studio was making you take those pictures. I know that happens in the industry all the time. But now—" His lips press together. "I don't know if I believe that anymore."

He must be talking about Matt. I swallow, my mind running so fast I can barely catch my thoughts. *What does this man want to hear?*

"He made me," I whisper, my voice breaking. "He's... so much bigger than me."

It's the right thing to say. His shoulders relax. He drops the knife with a clang into the sink and rushes over to me, dropping to his knees at my side. "I *knew* it. Oh, sweetheart," he croons. I close my eyes, letting real tears slip down my cheeks, and he makes a soft noise. "Oh, it's okay, darling. You're safe, now. He can't touch you anymore. I promise. I'll keep you safe." He wipes tears off my skin. "You perfect, perfect girl. Of course he forced you. I'm so sorry for ever thinking otherwise. God, I'm such an *idiot.*" He slaps himself in the forehead.

"Thank you," I whisper. "For believing me."

He takes a deep breath. "I'm going to kill him."

I shake my head. "No. Don't hurt him. C-could you call the police? I've been too scared to do it myself. I want to report him."

He cups my cheek, his hot, sour breath fanning over my face. "I wish I could, angel. But then the police would ask to come and see you. And I don't trust you enough for that, yet." He taps his finger on the tip of my nose like I'm a little girl. My stomach churns. "Anyway, they'll probably be looking for me. Because of the bombs. I'll need to lie low for a while." He smiles. "We'll get to spend some time together, just us. That's what you want, right?"

I can't speak, so I just nod. He beams.

"Come now, angel." He stands and wraps an arm around my waist, helping me up. I try not to shudder under his hands as he leads me to the small dining table. He pulls out my chair with a flourish, and I sit down slowly, looking over the table. It's like something out of a cheesy romance; checked tablecloth, napkins folded into swans, a long-stem rose in a vase. A battery-operated tea-light flickers light over the cutlery.

X goes back to the counter, returning with two steaming plates. He sets one down in front of me. "Here we are, angel. Eat up."

I stare at the plate. He's cooked a full roast dinner: chicken, potatoes, sprouts, and carrots, all drenched in gravy. Maybe it's the lighting, or the drugs lingering in my system, but the food looks fake and plasticky, like the inedible prop food we sometimes have on set.

"I don't eat meat."

He sighs. "I thought you might complain about this. I don't want you doing any of those LA fad diets anymore, they're unhealthy and dumb. Human beings were made to eat meat. It's just biology." He strokes my hand. I close my eyes, forcing myself to keep still. "I think the celebrity lifestyle has gotten to your head, darling."

I lick my lips. "I'm not really hungry."

"You need to eat."

"I'm still nauseous. From the drugs."

"I'm sorry about that," he says, his face softening again. "I'm very sorry about that. But you have to eat the food, I'm afraid. It's part of the plan."

"What plan?"

"It's how my mother taught me," he says, proudly. "You always have to take a girl to dinner first."

"First?" Ice slides down my spine. "What comes next?"

His eyes narrow. "Don't tease me. You know what comes next. Here." He shuffles his chair closer to mine. "I always imagined us eating like this." He cuts a few bites of food and stacks them up on his fork, then holds the mouthful to my lips. "Open up!" He says brightly. It takes everything in me not to spit in his face. Slowly, I open my mouth, letting him push the fork inside. I chew and chew and chew, hyper-aware of his face just millimetres from mine, and eventually manage to swallow.

"Very nice," I croak out, and his smile spreads to a beam.

"I thought you'd like it. My mother taught me to cook, when I was younger. I didn't want to learn, I didn't think it was really a man's place," he sloshes some wine into our glasses. "But she insisted that a good man should be able to feed his woman. And I guess she was right, huh?"

I nod, looking down at the plate. "Can I lie down? My head hurts."

He shakes his head. "Not until you eat everything. There's pudding, too. I'm doing this *right*."

"Right."

X reaches out and squeezes my hand. "I am so happy that you're here," he says quietly. "I love you, Briar. I know you might not believe that yet. But just give me a chance to prove it to you."

I force myself to smile, turning back to my plate of meat.

And I eat it. I eat every last bite. When I lay my cutlery back down, my stomach is churning.

"Pudding time!" X announces brightly. "It's a little late, but I made you a birthday cake! Chocolate, your favourite!" He goes to the fridge and pulls out a covered plate. He places it in front of me and pulls off the lid with a flourish, revealing a thickly frosted chocolate cake with my name piped on top in shaky calligraphy. "Do you like it?" He asks, looking anxious. "It took me four tries to get it perfect."

I think of Kenta handing me the heart-shaped doughnut, Glen sparking up the candle with his lighter, and tears press behind my eyes. "Thank you," I whisper. "I'm really full, though."

X considers for a moment, then smiles. "Well, that's okay," he decides. "We can have dessert after, I suppose." He takes my hand, helping me out of the chair.

I press a hand to my stomach. "What now?"

He giggles—actually *giggles*—and the sound is so creepy that goosebumps brush down my spine. "Come. Sit on the sofa here with me."

I sit stiffly next to him. X slides closer, wrapping an awkward arm around my shoulder. His fingertips skim my back, left bare in my dress, and I can't hold back my full-body flinch as he reaches for the zip.

X sighs. "That security guard really hurt you, didn't he?" He coos. "You poor baby. Don't worry. I'm not like him. I'll never make you do anything you don't want to." He lets go of the zip and cups my face. I close my eyes. "Don't be nervous," he whispers. "We'll go slow."

"What's the time?" I ask.

He pauses, then checks his watch. "Quarter to nine. Why?"

"No reason," I whisper.

Three hours. I got to the premiere at four thirty, and I was probably only there for an hour before the bombs went off. Which means that I've been kidnapped for over *three hours.* And no one has come.

How is that possible? Can the Angels not find me? Isn't this their job?

If they haven't been able to track me down by now, something must have gone wrong. My heart sinks. God. They must be hurt. Or dead. I don't know what happened after we left. Maybe more bombs went off. For all I know, the entire premiere got blown up.

Whatever's happened, I've bought myself as much time as I can afford. X's free hand slides up my thigh, and I bite the inside of my cheek.

I can't do it. This sweet, submissive act seems to be working, but there's only so far I'm willing to go. I'd rather die than let X rape me.

I can't wait for the men anymore. I'm going to have to find my own way out of here.

X shifts even closer, touching his thumb to my lips. "I've been waiting for this moment for years," he whispers. "I've imagined it so many times. In bed, late at night." His breath touches the side of my cheek. It smells like sour wine and meat. His hand slides higher under my dress, caressing my thigh.

I grab his wrist, holding it in place. "Touch me," I say clearly, "and I'll gouge out your motherfucking eyes."

CHAPTER 47
KENTA

The drive to the location is a nightmare.

Matt is losing it. I haven't seen him get so lost in his flash-backs in a long, long time. It's like they're rolling over him in waves. Every few minutes, he's clenching up, panting, trying to wrestle out of his seatbelt or slamming a fist against the inside of the car door. I try to talk him through them, but it's getting harder and harder to reach him. I can tell he feels trapped in here, so I have Glen open the skylight in the car's roof—then shut it again almost immediately, as Matt grabs onto it like he's going to climb right out of the car and jump onto the road.

The officer in the driver's seat looks downright terrified. He keeps twisting in his seat to stare at Matt, as if he's about to pull out his gun and start shooting us all.

"Is he going to…" he starts, as Matt slams a hand against the car door, panting.

"Stop looking at him," I snap, and the man's eyes widen. He turns to face forward. I check the GPS. We're twelve minutes out. Just twelve minutes. I swear to God, every second feels like an hour. The road ahead of us is dark and empty; it's really more of a dirt trail, and the trees are so dense here that the headlights only light the path a few metres ahead. We're forced to drive slower so we don't crash. I grit my teeth. It's taking too long. We need to be there *now*.

Matt jerks in his seat. I sigh. "Matt. C'mon, man. You're good."

I put a hand on his shoulder, and he wheels, throwing his fist at me sloppily. I shift out of the way, catch his wrist, and force my fingers between his, holding his hand. Holding his *hand*. If any of the guys back at Angel HQ ever saw this, they'd probably take a photo and distribute it to all the staff in a high priority email. Frame it and hang it in everyone's offices. Get an artist to turn it into the company Christmas card. But I don't know what else to do. It worked when Briar did it.

"C'mon," I mutter. "You're good. I'm squeezing your hand. You can feel that, right? Squeeze back."

He looks down at our joined hands. His throat jumps. "I love her," he says suddenly.

"I noticed."

His fingers tighten on mine, gripping me hard, and my heart just about breaks.

CHAPTER 48
BRIAR

"What?" X smiles widely, shaking his head like he has water in his ears. "Sorry, angel. I must have misheard. What did you say?"

"I don't think you misheard," I say, finally dropping the sickly sweet tone. "Get off me, before I rip out your intestine, blow it up, and knot it into a fucking balloon animal while you watch. How's that for a *private, personal show,* you sexist, psychopathic little freak?"

X's eyes widen. "W-what?"

"Get off me." When he doesn't move, I flatten my hands on his chest and shove him so hard he lands sprawled on the floor. He looks up at me, his glasses sitting lopsided on his nose, his pale eyes wide and wounded.

"No," he mutters. "No, no, no. I—" he runs a trembling hand through his dirty hair. "I don't understand."

"I'm sure you very rarely do," I bite out. "Don't worry, I'll use nice, small words." I stand up, advancing on him slowly. "I. Don't. Want. To. Fuck. You." I jab my finger at the door. "I'm done playing your games. Let me out. Now."

He slaps a palm on the ground. "Why do you have to keep ruining things?" He cries out. "I have imagined this so many times in my head. But you keep doing the wrong thing. Why? I know how this is supposed to go." He glares up at me. "I've been sending you presents for *months*—"

If that's true, I need to deep-clean my mail room. "Aw, shit, I forgot I could be bought. I guess you own me, then. I'll have my agent write you up a receipt." I shake my head. "What the Hell is wrong with you? Are you really so desperate for action that you have to make up a whole relationship in your head? Are you so goddamn annoying that you don't have any friends to give you an intervention?"

He glances sideways to the chloroform-soaked gag, and I scowl at him. "Try it. I'll snap off your skull and vomit down your throat, you ugly piece of shit."

He jumps to his feet. I step backwards into the dining table. Keeping my face turned towards him, I pat around behind me for the bread knife.

"Screw you!" He snarls. "I did everything right!"

I snort. "Says who? Where did you get these dating tips? You know *You* is supposed to be a thriller, not a how-to guide, right?" My hand skims over my cold, gravy-filled plate, and I fight the urge to wince. "Listen to me. I will never want you. If you were the last man on Earth, I'd cross the ocean to get away from you. And so would any woman, you little mop-haired, musty-breathed *freak*." Shit, where's the goddamn knife?

His eyes blaze. "You know what? They were right! You *are a* bitch! The *biggest bitch in the world!*" He shakes his head. "Why do you have to be so cruel? How could you hurt me like this?"

My fingers skim over cutlery, plates, glasses. No knife. "*I* hurt *you?*" I ask, my voice rising. "You're the one who bombed me, drugged me, kidnapped me and tied me up!"

"So we could be together!" He insists. "I have dedicated my whole life to loving you, and you don't even care, do you? You don't care about me at all."

My hand finally closes on the cool, thick handle of the knife.

X is still raving. "God, how could I have been so stupid? You lied to me, all this time. You *pretended* like you *loved me!*"

"I never pretended anything, you demented idiot! You made all of this up in your head!" I carefully lift the knife up, trying to keep the movement subtle.

X steps forward. He's panting like a dog. "Stop. Lying."

"I'm not *lying*. You're the one who's deluded."

I flip the knife behind my back, turning it blade-up. There's a soft *clink*. To my horror, I hear a glass fall over, rolling across the table-top. I shut my eyes as it falls and shatters on the ground.

Shit.

X glances behind me. His face hardens. He grabs my wrist and twists it hard, yanking the knife from my grip. "You little *bitch*. What, you were going to stab me? After everything I've done for you?" His eyes are on fire. He looks terrifying. "Years and years, I've loved you. And now you're just rejecting me. You've *wasted* all those years of my life." He steps closer, dropping his voice. Fear wells up in my throat. "I don't understand why all women want to hurt me." He lifts the knife, and we both watch it gleam under the cabin lights. "You need to pay for hurting me." He decides. "I want you to hurt, too."

Shit. I stumble a step back, my eyes on the knife tip. "X—"

"Fuck *you*," he snarls, and stabs me.

I scream as I feel the knife slice into my hip. Oh my God. Oh my God. I didn't think he'd actually do it. X yanks the knife out, and I shout as the serrated edge cuts into my skin. Blood gushes up from the wound, soaking into my red dress. Before I can respond, he lifts his hand and stabs at me again, aiming for my face. I jerk away at the last moment, and the blade slashes right across my cheek. He pulls back his arm a third time, and my old combat training finally kicks in. I twist automatically, slamming my shoulder *hard* into his neck. It's a good trick to take people off-guard; everyone expects you to fight with your hands. It works on X. He staggers backwards, grabbing his throat.

I nod to myself. Okay. That's good. This isn't a totally unfair fight. I'm rusty, but I can still remember plenty from all of my martial arts training. He's untrained, but he's much stronger than me. We're on a somewhat even playing field.

I'll just have to get creative.

Lunging for the table, I grab the carving fork stuck inside the chicken and rip it out, aiming straight for X's eyes. It's a wild, uncontrolled swing, but I'm not actually trying to stab him—just distract him. As his gaze follows the fork, I slam my knee into his crotch.

"Bitch!" he screeches, dropping to his knees as I dodge past him towards the front door. I throw myself at the pane of metal, but it's locked solid. I can't even jiggle the handle. I try ramming my shoulder into it, and cry out at the impact. Behind me, I hear X scramble to his feet, so I change tactics, turning on my heel and flying down the hallway. I fall through the first open door I come to, spinning and slamming it shut behind me, then look around wildly for something to barricade myself in with. There's a ratty-looking wooden chair in one corner of the room, and I grab it, wedging it under the door handle. Does that actually work? I don't know, but I've seen it in movies, and my options are pretty limited right now.

The room is dark. I pat around the wall for a light switch. When the ceiling lights flicker on, I lean heavily against the door to examine my stab wound. The fabric on my left hip is soaked through with blood. Wincing, I lift the hem of my dress to check out the cut. The slash is wide, but I can't tell how deep it is through all of the blood. I look around the room for something to stem the bleeding—and almost throw up.

Oh my God.

It's like a shrine.

There are pictures of me everywhere. *Everywhere.* Posters, magazine covers, printouts of movie stills. Several candid pictures of me, which I'm pretty sure X took himself. They're pasted all over the wall, overlapping two or three images deep. In one corner of the room is a door leading to a dirty-looking ensuite; in the other, there's a stained mattress shoved against the walls. A grimy white body pillow is poking out from under the sheets, with a crude naked woman scribbled on it in Sharpie. Judging by the bright yellow hair, I think I can safely assume it's me. I smother a sob.

There's a knock on the door behind my head. "Angel," X calls, and another sob rises up in my chest. "Angel, love, open the door, or I'll shoot you through it."

I keep my mouth shut, closing my eyes.

And that's when I hear it. Sirens.

They're far, far away in the distance, but they must be for me, right? They have to be. Some of the tension in my chest eases. I take what feels like my first breath in minutes.

My tiny second of rest is interrupted when the door suddenly buckles inwards, breaking the wooden chair into pieces. I scream, scrambling back as X appears in the doorway.

He looks nothing like the mild-mannered, awkward guy I first met. Now, his chest is heaving, his face is flushed red, and my blood is staining the side of his shirt. He looks like a monster. And he really is holding a gun.

I'm so fucked.

I shake off the rising panic. I need a weapon. I look around the room, but there's nothing. Lunging for the broken chair on the ground, I yank off one of the legs and straighten, wielding the piece of wood like a club as I back up against the wall.

The sirens are louder now. They're coming for me. I just need to distract X long enough for them to get inside.

"I lied," I spit. "I am sleeping with Matt."

He blinks. "What?"

"My bodyguard." I force myself to smirk. "He didn't force me at all. In fact, I'm sleeping with *all three* of my bodyguards. They're great in bed. Massive dicks."

Maybe it's not the smartest move to antagonise him, but right now, I just want to keep him talking.

X's face twists into a snarl. "You Goddamn *whore!*" He shouts.

"Yeah, yeah. I'm sure it looks that way to someone who can't get any action."

"Why? Why? What the Hell do they have that I don't?" He runs a hand through his hair, tugging hard. "You'll open your legs for any goddamn idiot, just because he's *handsome,* but not for me? I worked for this! I'm *smart!* I'm a nice guy!"

"Yeah?" I pant. "Well, I guess I'm not a very nice girl, then."

He points the gun at me and pulls the trigger. I scream and duck as a bullet shoots towards me, smashing into the wall over my head. "You *coward,*" I scream. "You want to fight me, fight me *fair!*"

"I don't want to fight you, you stupid woman." He lunges at me, pressing me up against the wall. I struggle against his heavy weight, then freeze when I feel the barrel of the gun pressing into my thigh.

"Wh-what do you want, then?" I choke.

He grabs my face and forces it closer to his. We're practically nose to nose. His muddy eyes blaze. "To *have* you." He hisses. "I want you to be *mine*. And if you're not going to play nice, that's okay." I try to shove out of his arms, but he's too strong. He tugs me back. His hot breath strokes the side of my face. "We can die together," he whispers. "We'll live together forever in Hell."

I close my eyes. The sound of the sirens is much louder now. Maybe I'm hallucinating, but I swear I can hear shouts coming from outside the house. Whatever sound insulation X is using, it's pretty shit quality.

"They'll come for me," I say, gasping. "You hear that? They're coming now."

He throws his head back and laughs. "Yeah. I figured. Don't worry, I'll take care of them."

I frown, but before I can ask what he means, an explosion shakes through the ground, trembling the floor under my feet. Dust rains down from the ceiling, and I twist, looking for the source of the blast. Ice slides down my spine when I realise the sound came from outside. "What was that?"

"What? You really think I left this place unprotected?" He tightens his grip on my jaw, his dirty fingernails digging into my throat. "I knew people would come looking for you. I couldn't let that happen."

My eyes widen. "What do you mean?" I whisper.

"I planted explosives around the house. Sounds like one of your friends just stepped in one."

CHAPTER 49
BRIAR

I squeeze my eyes shut as another explosion rips through the earth. There's a loud yell, then a cry of pain. Oh my God. Oh my God. He's going to kill them. My heart speeds up, beating so fast that my head spins.

I try to rationalise. Glen is a demolitions expert. He'll know that they're walking into a trap, right? He'll be able to tell?

Another explosion. Another shout. The sirens are getting louder. Blood rushes through my brain. I can't breathe. My hand tightens on the chair leg, gripping the splintered wood. I have to get away from X before he shoots me. The only other door in this room leads to the ensuite bathroom. I could lock myself in there and try to regroup. There might be something in the cupboards that I can use as a weapon.

I don't have time to think. I gather my strength and stab the chair leg backwards, aiming right for X's crotch. X howls, his grip on me loosening, and I pull free, stumbling towards the ensuite. He's hot on my heels, but I just about manage to slip inside the bathroom. I spin, trying to slam the door shut, but he shoves it from the other side, thrusting his whole weight into it. It starts to gradually eek open.

"Angel, please. You're being ridiculous," he purrs through the crack. The door opens one inch, and then another. My arms are burning. I look frantically around the bathroom. There's a bucket of something foul-smelling in here, and I recognise the scent from the inside of my gag.

The door pushes open another inch, and my weakened arms scream. I can't hold it closed anymore. I let go of the door suddenly, stepping aside so X comes flying into the room, almost falling. While he's trying to catch his balance, I grab at the rim of the bucket and toss it over his head, dousing his face in whatever vile concoction he mixed up for me. His scream half-deafens me. He drops to his knees and claws at his face. I start to cough, feeling nausea spiral back up through my throat. My eyes water so hard I can't even see what's in front of me. I cough again, and again, bending double as I stagger back out of the bathroom and down the hallway, heading for the main room. Behind me, I hear X retching painfully.

Good. Give him a taste of what it feels like.

My head spinning viciously, I stumble over to the front door, throwing myself at it. It doesn't budge. My palms pound against the thick metal pane. Shit. Shit. Shit.

I whip around, fighting the growing weakness in my muscles, looking for somewhere, *anywhere*, I can escape. There are no windows, no other doors. Not even a chimney I can wiggle up.

I can definitely hear voices now, from outside the cabin. There's a loud clanging sound, and I realise someone is trying to shove the door open. I step back, giving them room, and double over with a burst of hacking coughs that tear at my throat. My legs finally give in, and I sink to the ground.

"Briar," X rasps behind me. I turn. He's *crawling* out of the corridor towards me, like something out of a horror movie. His eyes are weeping and red. His shirt is ripped open and bloody. He's still clutching the gun in one hand.

I scrabble for my chair leg, but the mixture of drugs and panic and blood loss is too much, and I can't even feel my fingers anymore. I shuffle backwards across the floor, away from him.

There's a thump on the outside of the door. X looks up at it hazily, then lifts his gun and fires, shooting clean through the metal. I hear a yell from the other side.

"Get away from the door!" I try to shout, but my voice is thin and reedy. "He's—" I break off coughing. "He's got a gun!"

There's a pause, and then I hear Kenta's voice. "Briar?"

Relief floods me. Thank *God*.

"Briar," Kenta's voice is frantic. "Are you okay?"

I open my mouth to answer, but X shoots again, and I scream as the bullet whizzes past my ear.

"They can't have you," he mutters, still army-crawling towards me. "If I can't have you, no one can." He flings out an arm and grabs my ankle. "I'M GOING TO KILL HER!" He roars to the men outside. "IT'S ALREADY TOO LATE!"

"Cutter, get the cutter," someone says outside. X yanks on my leg, pulling me towards him. I cry out, twisting and slamming the heel of my foot into his nose. He shrieks, letting me go, and I scoot away from him. Up. I need to get up. Shuffling back to the kitchen table, I grab the leg and lever myself upright. My vision goes dark as all the blood falls out of my head, but I cling to the table and wait for it to pass.

A loud buzzing rips through the room as a blade starts to saw around the edges of the front door. Sparks fly off the metal. "POLICE!" A voice calls. "STEP AWAY FROM THE DOOR!"

I watch, almost in slow motion, as X twists on the floor, pointing the gun at me. I stare down the black hole of the barrel. My legs buckle under me. I can't run away anymore. I can't make myself move. I squeeze my eyes shut, waiting for the bullet to rip through me.

Nothing.

I open my eyes and watch as X squeezes the trigger again and again, staring stupidly at the pistol. Nothing. He's out of bullets.

It's the biggest fight scene movie cliché imaginable. And it just saved my life.

"Ha!" Relief floods through me, giving me one last surge of power. X's eyes widen as I force myself to straighten, coming to stand over him. I'm still clutching the chair leg in one shaking hand.

"You're done," I tell him, hardly believing it myself. "You're *done*. You lost!"

Then I lift the chair leg and slam it down into his side. He howls. "You're going to rot in a cell—" I hit him again, "for the rest of your *goddamn life.*" I sneer down at him. "I doubt you'll make any friends in prison. You haven't made any out here, have you? They'll hate you just as much as everybody else."

He grabs at my ankle and yanks, trying to tug me down, but I kick him off me. I feel feral. Like a wild animal. My throat is full up of thorns, my heart is beating out of my chest. This man has had power over me for so long, and now, finally, I'm standing over him holding a weapon. It feels good. I want to hurt him. I want to hurt him so badly he can never hurt another woman again.

"You're pathetic," I spit. "Everything about you is pathetic. This whole seduction routine was pathetic. You kidnapping me like you're a bloody Bond villain is pathetic." I shake my head.

"What, you can't get a girl to like you the normal way, so you decide to just *take* her? Is that it? You think you have the *right* to women?"

He sputters. "I deserve—"

I lift the chair leg and drive it down like a stake into his crotch. He screams, but I barely hear it. "You deserve nothing! You are not entitled to have sex with me!" I scream at him. "You're a *joke*. You're a disgusting human being. You're a goddamn roach." I drop my makeshift club and grab the bloody, serrated knife on the dining table, pointing it at him. He goes still.

My head swims, and my fingers shake on the knife handle. I could do it. I could end this, right now.

He looks up at me. He looks battered. One of his eyes is swollen, his glasses are shattered, and there's blood coming out of his mouth. Matching blood trickles down my slashed cheek and onto my neck, soaking into my dress.

"Angel," he says softly, his eyes imploring.

I drop the knife with a clatter, then bend and spit in his face.

There's a deafening bang, and the huge metal door falls inward. Light flares through the doorway, and I see silhouettes stepping forward. Shouts fill the room. All of the adrenaline fades out of me, and I drop to my knees.

I did it. I did it. I stayed alive long enough for them to come.

I did it.

I watch through hazy eyes as the men charge into the room. It's almost like watching a dream. I see X rolling over, grasping for the gun. I see a group of officers, led by Kenta, diving onto him, holding him down.

I see Matt and Glen standing in the doorway, frantically scanning the room. Matt turns to me, his eyes on fire. His gaze trails over my front, and I suddenly realise what I look like. There's blood on me. All over me. On my dress, my skin, in my hair.

For a second, everything seems still. Then Matt lunges at me.

I flinch hard. If I had any energy left, I'd get up and run, but all I can do is go still as he throws himself onto his knees next to me, grabbing me.

"You're bleeding," he whispers. "Bleeding—" He starts frantically running his hands over me, trying to cover my wounds.

"No," I choke. "Get off." He doesn't respond. The look in his eyes is terrifying me.

It's Matt. A voice in the back of my head reminds me. *Just Matt. Just Matt.* I try to remember that, but looking at the wild man in front of me, I don't see Matt at all. Just another violent man trying to maul me. "No!" I shout, trying to shove him off me. "No, no, no, no, *no*—"

"MATT," Kenta barks. "You're scaring her! Stop, man!"

Behind him, there's a sudden volley of gunshots. X screams. I freeze at the sound, and Matt goes still on top of me, jerking back to reality. I lay under him, my heart thudding in my chest. He's panting, breathing too hard.

"Matt." I flap my hand out and hold his hand, lacing our fingers together. "I'm okay."

His eyes shine suddenly. "Briar," he whispers, lifting a hand to my cheek. He swallows thickly, then drops his hand and stands jerkily. I want to reach after him, but warm arms wrap around me from behind, and I slump back onto a hard chest. "I'm here, lass, it's okay," Glen whispers in my ear. I could cry. "It's okay. God, you're bleeding. Oh, God, your poor *face*." He tugs me closer into his arms. "Is this okay, baby? Am I hurting you?"

I shake my head, burying my face in his shoulder.

He keeps talking, rocking me back and forth. "That was incredible. I think we should invite you to join the team. You'd make a very convincing Angel." He presses a kiss to the top of my head. "Look at you. You didn't even need us, you took him out all by yourself. God, let me look at your face, sweetheart. What the Hell did he do to you?" He tries to pull my face out of the crook of his neck, and I shake my head.

"No."

"You don't want me to look at you?" He cups my cheek, and his fingers come back wet with blood. "It won't be as bad as mine, love, nowhere near that bad. I... we'll find you the best surgeon, sweetheart. The best in the whole country, I promise, there won't even be a mark."

"Shut. Up." I groan. Everything is spinning. I can feel my heart rate getting faster and faster. I cling to him, huffing in his dark earthy scent. I just want to hide away where no one can see me. I try to gasp in a breath, but I can't. I start to shake.

"Briar." His hand cups the back of my head. "Briar. Breathe."

I can't. I can't breathe. I try to take in a breath, but my lungs are too tight. I try harder and harder, my breathing turning to noisy, frantic gasps, but nothing is getting in.

"God." He starts sliding his hands over my body, checking my waist and rib cage. "You didn't get stabbed in the chest, did you?"

I shake my head.

"Panic attack?"

I nod, and he wraps his big arms gently around me. "Then it's okay, love. It's okay to panic. Don't fight it. Just let yourself feel it. You're safe, now. You're safe."

I start sobbing, grabbing at him. I can feel my nails scratching at his skin, but I can't stop. I'm shaking apart, just a ball of frantic energy. I'm probably hurting him, thrashing around and clawing at him like this, but if I am, he doesn't say anything. Just sits calmly with me in his arms, breathing steadily and exuding the comforting smell of grass and trees. Around me, I hear radios chattering and sirens approaching and the low voices of detectives and police.

Footsteps tread closer to us. "Excuse me," a woman says, "we'd like to talk to Miss Saint about—"

"Not now," Glen orders, his voice deep. The woman slinks off again. I sob, clutching his shirt.

"It's okay," he says in my ear. "He's gone now. He's gone. I'm here." He keeps stroking my back, my hair, my face, murmuring soothing things to me, until the panic finally drains away, and I go limp against his chest.

CHAPTER 50
GLEN

Even though the ambulance crew arrives almost immediately, the police don't let them into the building until they've secured the scene. Which means Briar just lays in my arms, slowly bleeding out into my shirt, and I can't do shit about it.

She's not okay. At all. After that first wave of panic died down, it's like it took all of her energy with it. Now she's just slumped against me, her eyes glassy and cold, her fingers twitching in my shirt. I'm hoping it's just shock; as far as I can tell, she's been stabbed once in the side, and slashed across the face. The abdominal wound is worrying me. It doesn't look deep, but she's definitely lost a pint or so of blood, and there's no way of knowing without a proper examination exactly how much damage has been done. For all I know, X could've nicked a vital organ.

I keep pressure on her side and try to keep her talking. "Baby. Are you okay? Can you say something for me, honey? Did you hit your head?"

She doesn't respond.

"Briar. Please." I give her the tiniest little shake. "Don't fall asleep yet, love, you need to get looked at first, okay? Ambulance will be here in a few minutes. Just stay with me until then, lass."

She looks up at me. She doesn't look sleepy at all, but her lips stay firmly sealed.

I stroke her cheek. "Please?"

"How is she?" Kenta asks over my shoulder, stepping away from the detective he was talking to. As per usual, he was the most responsible out of all three of us. He somehow managed to stop himself from running straight to Briar as soon as we got the door open, instead helping the agents to get X into a pair of handcuffs.

"Conscious," I murmur. "Pretty unresponsive."

He kneels down next to us. "Briar, sweetheart? Can you look at me?"

She doesn't even twitch. He sighs and dips to kiss her on the cheek, but she flinches away hard, burying her face in my front.

"Okay, sweetheart," he says softly. "Sorry. Someone will come and help you soon, okay?"

He straightens, dropping a hand on my shoulder. "I'm going to talk to Matt."

"He okay?" I ask.

Kenta's face is pinched. "He's fucking falling apart. Almost lunged at one of the officers. Luckily, she was understanding."

I swear, tugging Briar closer to me. "Go to him." I know exactly what's going on in Matt's head. He blames himself. Briar getting kidnapped and slashed up with a knife is hitting him far too close to home.

I just wish he could get over this. Kenta, Damon and I knew what we were getting into when we signed onto our last mission. We knew there was a decent chance we'd be captured. It wasn't his fault, any more than it was ours. But he can't get over it. Sooner or later, the guilt is going to rip him into shreds.

When Kenta's gone, Briar starts to shake, hard, and I wrap my jacket carefully around her, trying not to jog her too much. I can't think of anything to say, so we just listen to the sirens and wait.

When the ambulances are finally cleared to enter, most of the paramedics immediately crowd around X. Only one, a smiling woman with a blonde ponytail, comes to kneel down next to Briar. Her nametag reads AMANDA.

"Seriously?" I snap. "He's getting all of the attention? None of this would've happened if he wasn't a damn pervert!"

Amanda smiles sympathetically. "Triage. It's not our job to judge the patients, sir. Just keep them alive." She gives Briar a bright smile. "Hey, honey. We're gonna take care of you, okay?"

Briar doesn't say anything, looking over my shoulder. I turn and see the other medics pulling X's unconscious body onto a stretcher. His hands and ankles are cuffed, and his head lolls to one side.

"Don't," I whisper in her ear, cupping her chin and pulling her to face me. "Just look at me."

Her eyes meet mine, then trail over my scarred cheek. She winces.

Shit. With that cut across her cheek, my mangled face is probably the last thing she wants to see right now.

"Yeah, I suppose the view's not really much nicer," I try to joke. "We can get Kenta in for you to stare at, if you want." She frowns, tightening her hands on me.

Amanda starts prepping Briar for the ambulance. Kenta walks back into the cabin, talking to an officer, and I wave him over, lowering my voice.

"Maybe you should go with her to the hospital."

He frowns. "What? Why?"

"I think it's upsetting her." I wave at my cheek. "To see this. It's probably why she got so panicky."

Kenta looks at me like I'm stupid. "Well, yes," he says slowly. "I suppose it *could* be your face that scared her. Or it could be the fact that she just got drugged, kidnapped, stabbed and shot at. Either's possible, really. Who knows?"

I grit my teeth. "I just think she'd be more relaxed with you."

He gives Briar a longing look, then steps back. "No."

"What do you mean, no?"

"*I'm* not the one she sleeps with every night like a goddamn teddy bear, Smith. You're what she needs, right now."

"You're a psychologist! You can help her!"

His face hardens. "She doesn't need a shrink, she needs *comfort*. So get over your issues and look after her. We'll meet you there after we speak to the police."

And then he goes. I look down at the girl in my lap.

You're what she needs.

I'll never be what Briar needs. The idea is unfeasible. But as I sift through her hair, she pushes into me, and love bursts in my chest.

I gave up on love a long time ago. When we got off our last tour, I was traumatised. I was scarred. I'd been so broken down, I couldn't imagine ever recovering enough to open myself up to someone. I figured, I'd never get the wife, and the kids, and the picket fence. That's why I joined Angel Security. I was never going to be happy, but I could still protect the happiness of other people. Normal people.

I touch Briar's cheek. I'll never be what Briar needs. Never. But God, I love her so desperately that I ache.

Briar doesn't say anything on the ambulance ride to the hospital. She's conscious, nodding or shaking her head when the paramedics ask her questions, but her lips stay firmly sealed. They cut off her clothes, slicing her red dress right off her, and gently remove all of her jewellery, putting it in paper bags as evidence. I notice she's taken off the necklace we gave her. It's probably for the best, but it still stings.

An oxygen mask gets strapped over her nose and mouth, but she yanks it off after a few minutes to throw up in a little cardboard bowl.

"Oh, baby." I pull her hair back as her slim shoulders shudder. "Shit." I turn to Amanda. "Do you think she has internal damage?"

Briar makes a panicky noise, and I stroke her back.

Amanda shakes her head. "Can't say for sure, of course, but the wound on her side looks superficial. Probably whatever he drugged her with. Looked like chloroform. I saw a bleach bottle in the bathroom."

"*Jesus.*" I run a hand over my face. "Long term effects?"

"Well, she's not seizing or in a coma, so I would guess she'll get through it fine. It takes a lot to do significant damage. The nausea is probably a combination of the drugs, pain, shock, and anxiety."

Briar straightens, and I pass down a paper towel for her to wipe her face. She grabs my hand and squeezes it tight.

The rest of the journey is torturous. Even with the sirens blaring, LA traffic keeps us moving at a snail's pace. My phone is blowing up with messages from Matt and Kenta. Briar throws up every few minutes. When she's not getting sick, she sits propped up against me, leaning her head against my chest and breathing slowly. Even though she's staying quiet, I can feel the panic simmering underneath the surface. I run my hand through her matted hair, trying to help keep her calm.

Right before we pull into the hospital, Amanda crouches down in front of the cot, looking Briar directly in the eyes. "Okay, hon. When we get inside, the police are going to take your clothes as evidence, and the doctors are going to look at you properly. Can you tell me now if we need to examine for sexual assault?"

My throat closes. I grip Briar's arm tighter. The thought of that man touching her makes me want to vomit, too. Or stop the ambulance, track him down, and finish him.

Briar shakes her head.

"I'd like a verbal response, please," Amanda says, her voice gentle.

Briar shakes her head again. I stroke through her hair. "Are you sure?" I murmur into her skin. She nods.

Amanda smiles. "Okay. Good, that's good. If you change your mind, you can tell any one of us, okay? We've called ahead for a VIP admission, so when we get to the hospital, you'll be given a private room, to stop you getting bothered by fans. I can't guarantee there won't be paparazzi in the parking lot, but our guys will do their best to keep them from getting shots of you."

Briar starts to cry again, silently. It must be so humiliating for her, I realise suddenly. Everybody here knows who she is. Every single person. She has no privacy, even in her lowest moments. At least when I was stuck in hospital, recovering from our last tour, no one gave a shit about a random bandaged-up soldier. But to the public, her being injured is *gossip*.

I gently pull her face away from me and check the cut on her cheek. It's stopped bleeding badly, but it still looks shocking, curving down from below her eyes to her chin. If she doesn't get it seen by a proper plastic surgeon, she'll be scarred for life. Her career will be over. The thought makes my insides cold.

As I watch, she covers her slashed cheek with her hand and glares up at me. I force myself not to stare. I know better than anyone else just how bad that feels.

"You're gonna be okay," I tell her. She closes her eyes and nods.

At the hospital, everything speeds up. As soon as the doctors lay eyes on her, she's transferred onto a bed and wheeled into a private room for examination. They hook her up with an IV, switch out her clothes for a hospital gown, and take a blood sample for a tox screen in a matter of seconds. Briar floats silently through it all, letting people move her around and stick needles in her, all without complaining. It's so far from her usual bolshy bossiness that it terrifies me. She's like a doll, empty and unre-sisting as her body gets manipulated. The doctors assess her wound and decide the cut on her hip is superficial; the knife sliced through the skin, but missed any major nerves or blood vessels. They clean the cut and stitch her back up so quickly I barely process it happening.

She doesn't regain the ability to speak until all of the tests are done, and a surgeon is standing in front of her with some thread and a needle. "Last of all," he says cheerfully, "we just need to patch up your cheek, Miss Saint."

She eyes the needle in his hands. "I want to go home," she orders, her voice thin but firm.

I'm so relieved to hear her talk that I could cry. "You're almost done, love." I press a kiss to her hair. A nurse in the back of the room raises an eyebrow, and I quickly pull back again, biting my tongue. Even now, after a near-death experience, any PDA is dangerous for Briar. Hell, that little kiss could end up in the magazines tomorrow. I slide across the bed, putting a professional distance between me and her. She stares at me blankly.

The surgeon nods. "Just let me stitch up your cuts, and you'll be good to go." He snaps on a pair of rubber gloves, but Briar shakes her head.

"I don't care about the cuts." She tries to slip off the bed. "I want to go home, now."

"You will," I soothe, stroking her arm, "You will. We'll all go back to the hotel, and you can get some sleep. You just need to sit still for a bit longer." I lift her gently back onto the bed.

The doctor smiles, reaching out to prod at the cut.

Briar flinches back. "No! I don't want the stitches!"

"You've already had more in your side, ma'am," he points out. "I'm not talking about major surgery. You'll likely have to come in for a few revisions, but we'll get your face looking completely healed in no time."

"I'll hold your hand," I tell her. "They'll numb you up, it won't hurt bad."

Briar looks at me with wide eyes. I have absolutely no idea what's going through her head.

A nurse steps forward with a syringe, and the surgeon accepts it. "Exactly. A bit of this, and you'll barely feel a thing." He puts his gloved hand on her cheek, and lines up the needle. Briar jerks away, and the surgeon bites back a curse as he almost stabs her in the eye. "No. No."

"Ma'am—"

"I do not consent to these stitches," she slurs, trying to bat the man away from her. "Stop. No. *No.*"

The surgeon sighs. "Ma'am, you're not in your right mind. I would strongly advise you to listen to your boyfriend. He can tell you himself; living with facial scarring can be difficult."

"I'm not her boyfriend," I correct, trying to stay calm. "But yeah, it's very fucking difficult." I have no idea why she's digging her heels in now. I can't stand the thought of her having to live with this scar forever. With a reminder of what happened tonight stuck to her face for the rest of her life.

Briar scowls at us both. "So? I can do things that are difficult."

I try a different angle. "This isn't just about how you look. It's about your career, lass. You might struggle to find acting and modelling jobs with a great big scar over your face."

Her face twists. "I don't care about *modelling*," she spits.

"Then what is it?" I demand, suddenly losing my shit. "Why are you being so stubborn about this? Why?!"

She glares at me. "Because maybe if I have the scars, you'll finally get it through your thick head that I'm in love with you!"

Everything goes quiet. For a second, I think it's just in my head; but I realise that the low chatter from the doctors and nurses passing in the hallway has died down. People are listening in. Right now, I don't think I care. Her voice keeps echoing around and around my head.

I'm in love with you.

Christ.

I shift awkwardly on the bed. "Briar, you've had a bad shock—"

"I love you," she repeats stubbornly, then raises her voice, "and he is my boyfriend!"

"I'm not," I say, panic building. God, this *hurts*. "Briar, please," I beg, "please, you're not thinking straight."

"Why do you think I'm lying?" She demands, her eyes burning.

"I don't think you're *lying*, I think you're tired and in pain and confused—"

"*Why*?" She repeats, cutting me off.

I sputter. "Because—"

Because the idea of her loving me is ludicrous. This isn't Beauty and the bloody Beast, this is real life. Briar's not my girlfriend; she's a completely unattainable famous actress who likes shagging her bodyguards. That's *it*.

"Because of your face," she finishes for me. "I'm sick of it, Glen, I'm *done* with you acting like you're not worthy of me just because of some goddamn collagen! I'm sick of you hiding from photographers *to save my image*. I'm sick of you hiding your face from *me*. I adore your face! I love it so much! I want to see it every day for the rest of my life!" Her chest hitches with a sob. I can barely breathe. "I thought you might be *dead* when that bomb went off. Do you think it would have hurt me less, because of your *scars*?"

"It's not like that—" I protest.

She's having none of it. "It's *exactly* like that. You think you're worth less than me." She reaches up and brushes my cheek, and I have to fight the urge to pull away. Her lips purse. "These don't make you worth less than any other man. If anything, they show how much *better* you are than most people. You're one of the *best people* I've ever met. And maybe I'm selfish, but that's why I want you, all for myself."

I take a deep breath, trying to slow down my brain. "It's not just the scars. It's…" I lick my lips. I'm not good with words. I don't know how to say this right. "You're so good. And pretty. And delicate." Her eyes narrow. Shit. "That's not an insult," I backtrack. "I just mean—when you've served, all civilians seem delicate. And soft. The things I remember, the places I've been… they've made me hard. The shit I've seen feels too dark and dirty for someone so *normal*. I'm not as bad as Matt, but I still have nightmares. I still have the memories. It feels like there's this part of me that I have to keep away from you. It's too *dark*. And you don't need that in your life."

"Oh, Glen," she says softly. A warm hand touches my face. I close my eyes. She understands. "You know everything you just said is complete bullshit, right?"

I choke on my own spit.

She shakes her head. "I mean, I get it. I do. I don't mean to demean your feelings, or whatever. But… your thoughts are bullshit. They're wrong. They're lying to you." She strokes a finger down my cheekbone. "I'm not good, or pure, or delicate, and you're not damaged, or dirty, or hard. You've been through Hell. And you're right; I will never truly understand all the places that you've been." She runs her hand down the side of my face. "But that doesn't mean we can't be together. It doesn't mean I can't love you."

A throat clears behind us. "Ma'am?" The surgeon prompts. "If you don't want my services, they're needed elsewhere."

Briar doesn't look away from me, her blue eyes imploring. "Okay," I tell her. "Okay. I believe you. I—love you, too."

She shivers, a full-body shiver, and presses her mouth to mine. "Okay," she mumbles over my shoulder. "Sorry. You can do it."

The surgeon numbs her face, and I hold her hand as he methodically stitches her back up. She squeezes my hand so hard she almost crushes it, but when I look into her eyes, I know it's not because of the pain at all.

CHAPTER 51
BRIAR

The other Angels join us as I'm being questioned by police officers in a private room. It's excruciating. Nurses keep interrupting to stab me with needles or check my vitals, and Matt and Glen won't stop growling at the officers for 'pushing me too hard'. It's driving me up the wall. I have to talk to the police, and the sooner I finish, the sooner I can leave, but they're both acting like I might break down at any moment.

I eventually send them both out before they get tazed or stabbed with a scalpel, and stay with Kenta. He sits in the chair opposite me, watching me with dark eyes. Letting me do what I need to do. Trusting that I'm strong enough to do it. When I hold out my hand, he comes and takes it, massaging my fingers as I dully recount everything that happened to the police. I feel odd and distant, like someone else is operating my body, and I'm just watching it happen.

Eventually, I'm let loose from the hospital with some painkillers, antibiotic cream, and a diagnosis of 'two superficial lacerations, and symptoms of psychological shock'. The doctors try to keep me in overnight for observation, which is dumb, since they've basically admitted that the only thing wrong with me is a couple of cuts and a case of anxiety. I have to put my foot down, but eventually they let me go.

We drive back to the hotel in silence. I sit in the back seat with Glen's arm wrapped tightly around my shoulders. Matt is sitting in the front passenger seat as Kenta drives. He's frozen in place, staring straight ahead at the road. He hasn't said one word to me since he tackled me back at the cabin. He hasn't even made eye contact. He's ignoring me completely. Because apparently, my day hasn't been bad enough.

We get a lot of odd looks when we traipse into the hotel foyer. I'm not surprised. We're all dirty and stained. I'm wearing a hospital gown under Glen's jacket. Matt's white shirt is covered in so much blood, he looks like he murdered someone.

We make it back to the suite, and I shuffle like a zombie into the bathroom. I pee, wash my hands, then stand and stare at myself in the mirror over the sink. Under the harsh fluorescent lighting, my reflection looks hard. Sharp. My face is all shadows and high-lights, like a mask. I study my expression for any kind of life, any spark of emotion, but there's nothing at all.

I don't know how I feel, and it's scaring me. I should be crying. Or panicking. Or relieved. Or angry. I should be feeling some kind of emotion, but I'm not. I'm just numb and tired. Too tired to even stand.

Slowly, I sink down onto the bathmat. The soft blue fabric feels fluffy and comforting under my skin, so I lay myself carefully down and close my eyes. It feels like gravity is pulling me down. I know I should get up and wash, but I can't.

I can't.

I don't think I can do anything, right now. I'm empty.

I'm just starting to sink into sleep when I hear a knock at the door. "Briar?" Glen calls, in his low, rolling burr. "Are you okay in there?"

I open my mouth, but I'm too heavy to move. I hear the door shove open, then Glen's sharp intake of breath.

"Briar?" He sounds horrified. Guilt squeezes me. He steps closer, dropping to his knees next to me. "Shit, did you fall? Do you feel dizzy? Oh, God, baby, we need to drive you back to the ER—"

"No. 'M okay," I mumble.

"Yeah?" He brushes some hair away from my face, his expression soft. "Did you have another panic attack, love?"

I shake my head. "I just—" I try to think of the reason I'm lying on the ground. "I can't do it?"

"Can't do what?"

"Anything. I'm really tired."

He makes a low noise. "Okay. That's okay. You don't have to do anything. Here." Big hands lift me up, hooking under my armpits to avoid touching my hip. Glen sets me gently on the rim of the bath, then gets to work stripping off the hospital gown. I watch him uncover my bloody skin.

"I'm sorry," I say, as he picks a flannel out of the basket of complimentary bathroom products, running it under the tap.

"For what, sweetheart?" He kneels at my feet, carefully taking my foot in his hand and swiping it clean.

"Not being able to do it myself." I'm just sitting here like a sad, naked lump.

He looks up at me. "It's normal, love. I've seen it with plenty of guys after they've been fighting."

I watch as he rubs the flannel up my calf. "Mm?"

"Yeah. Hell, after we got brought back to hospital after our last tour, I don't think Kenny spoke for a week. Just sat in his bed all day, staring at the wall. Sometimes your brain needs to recover." He kisses my knee. "It'll pass. I promise."

I nod.

Glen cleans my entire body in soft, soothing strokes, then wrings the flannel out and tosses it into the trash. "You want me to wash your hair, sweetheart?"

I think, then nod. My hair is full of sweat and dirt and blood. I let him tip my head back in the sink, carefully shampooing my scalp under the warm running water. His fingers are rough, but almost unbearably tender as he rinses away the grime. We don't say much. I close my eyes, basking in his touch. One tiny thread of emotion tugs inside me, shining through the big cavernous emptiness in my brain.

"I love you," I whisper, and he sighs and bends over me, pressing his mouth very gently to mine.

"The feeling's mutual, lass."

When I'm as clean as I'm going to get, Glen dries off my hair, then brings me one of his shirts and a pair of joggers. As we head back into the lounge, Kenta is setting out foil takeaway containers on the coffee table.

"I'm not hungry," I tell him, wavering. I think of the plate of roast chicken and almost run back to the bathroom to hurl.

Glen squeezes my shoulder, leading me to the sofa. "Just try it. We've got a bit of everything. Just grab whatever takes your fancy."

Matt, who hasn't changed out of his stained suit, swoops in and grabs a box at random, heading for the balcony. "I'll keep guard," he mutters.

"For what?" I snap, my voice cold. "He's gone."

He pauses in the doorway, then slides open the glass pane and steps outside.

"You want the black bean noodles?" Kenta offers me a box. "Spring rolls?"

I shake my head, pressing my face into Glen's neck and sucking up his scent.

Kenta sits down next to me. I might be imagining it, but he looks shockingly pale. "You lost blood, sweetheart. And you threw up everything in your stomach. You should eat something."

"I still feel sick."

"Just some plain rice, then." He leans over to scoop some onto a plate. "It might make you feel better."

Glen rubs his scratchy cheek against mine, and I feel something tightening in my throat. My lip starts to wobble. Kenta hands me the small portion of rice. I take it, lift the fork to my mouth—then immediately burst into tears.

Glen holds me tighter. "Oh, Briar."

"It's not fair!" I shout. It's like a dam has collapsed inside of me, and I'm suddenly being swamped with emotion. With *anger*. "I didn't do anything wrong!"

"You didn't," they both soothe.

I wave my hand at the balcony door. "Then why the Hell is he hiding from me?! Why is he acting like I *messed up?* Why am I getting the silent treatment?!"

Kenta pauses. "Wait. You mean Matt?"

"I got *stabbed* and he won't *hold me*." I grit my teeth, wiping my cheeks angrily.

The men share a look. "He's scared," Kenta says.

"He's *scared*." I stand up, dropping my plate onto the table with a loud clatter. "This man was in the SAS, but he's too much of a coward to give me a hug? *I'm* scared, too, for God's sake. I thought he cared about that!"

"I think he understands guns a lot more than his own feelings," Kenta says ruefully.

"I don't care!" Flicking back my damp hair, I stomp over to the terrace and shove open the sliding door. Matt is sitting in a garden chair, staring out over the skyline. LA glitters below us, full of brightly coloured lights.

"You're keeping watch on the balcony?" I bite out. "Isn't that a sniper risk, or something?"

He turns and looks at me. A jolt runs through me as his cool eyes meet mine. For a few seconds, we just stare at each other. I try to sort through the emotions blowing through my mind. Hurt, that he isn't talking to me. Anger, that he lied to me. Relief, that he's okay.

Love, drawing me into him like I'm a shell caught in a tide.

I scowl, shoving the feeling down. "I'm really cold," I mutter.

"It's an anxiety response," he says slowly. "Adrenaline forces blood to your internal organs so you can defend yourself more efficiently. The loss of circulation can make you feel cold."

I snort. "Yeah, thanks, WebMD." I cross my arms over my chest. "I'm *cold*," I repeat.

"Do you want to go back inside?"

"No."

He shifts, tugging at his rumpled, dirty tux. "Want my jacket?"

I wrinkle my nose. "No."

He waits. A couple beats pass. "Then… what are you waiting for?"

"For you to offer to warm me up, dumbass."

"Oh." He pauses, then tentatively opens his arms. I climb into them, nestling against his chest. I can hear his heart thumping against my ear. "I thought—"

"I'm still mad at you," I warn him. "But I can be mad and hug you at the same time."

"Okay." He sounds kind of dazed. I burrow my face in him, trying to breathe evenly. We're quiet for a while. Car engines hum in the streets below, and I hear some drunken shouts spiralling through the night. A light breeze touches my hair. Police sirens wail past, and I start to cry again. He tugs me closer.

"I'm sorry," he roughs out. "Briar, I'm so sorry. None of this would've happened if I'd just been honest with you."

I clutch my fist in his shirt. "What hurt me most was that you thought so little of me. That you thought I was spoiled and selfish and *stupid* enough to put other people's lives in danger, j-just to get back at this guy. I really thought you knew me. That you respected me."

He frowns. "I don't think little of you. I was just so scared. So, so scared of losing you. When you're leading a team, you're responsible for their lives. And sometimes—you pick wrong." I hear him swallow. "I tried to play it safe, but it backfired, and I'm sorry. I needed you alive, and in my head, keeping you in the dark was the best possible way of doing that." He sighs. "I underestimated you."

"You did. And bombs went off because of it. *I* put people in danger, because *you* didn't give me the full picture. People were injured because of *me*, Matt. I know you know how that feels. Why the Hell would you make me do that?"

He flinches. "I... I've lost people before. Friends. Brothers. I've seen them die in front of me. And every goddamn time, I feel a bit of myself die with them. I take their wedding rings home to their wives and look at their babies who don't have a dad anymore, and I feel a piece more dead than I did before. But I've never..." He shakes his head. "A *bit* of me wouldn't have died, if you went. I just wouldn't exist anymore. I'd—I'd be done. It would all just go dark. I wouldn't come back from it."

"Mm." I run a finger up the front of his shirt. "I love you, too."

His breath hitches in his chest. He goes very still around me, apart from the one hand stroking soothingly up and down my back. I nuzzle into him, feeling the choking knot of strong emotions in my chest slowly loosen and unravel. I'm almost asleep when I feel something warm drip into my hair. "I—are you *crying*?"

I try to look up and peer at his face, but he just clasps me tighter to him. His chest shudders against me. Another tear splashes onto my cheek.

Behind us, the door to the balcony cracks open, and the others step out.

"Is she sleeping?" Kenta asks. I shake my head, but before I can speak, Matt starts to talk.

"I'm sorry," he chokes out. "I'm sorry. I'm so sorry I messed up. I'm so *fucking sorry*."

I know from the tone of his voice that he's not talking about what happened tonight. I try to wiggle away, to give the men better access to each other, but Matt grabs at me like a comfort blanket, dragging me back onto his lap.

"There's nothing to forgive," Kenta says, his face calm. "You know that."

"Never blamed ye," Glen mutters thickly, coming to stand by my side. "We'd both have done the same. You were just following orders." His hand drops to my face, and he cups my cheek with calloused fingers. I tip into the touch.

"I know you don't blame me," Matt protests, "but—"

Kenta puts a hand on his shoulder. "Let it go," he says gently. "It's time."

Matt nods jerkily.

I smile up at him. "Does this mean you'll finally go to therapy?"

He laughs shakily, nodding. "I didn't want…" The words catch in his throat. I suddenly understand.

"You didn't want to forget what happened. You wanted to punish yourself with the nightmares and the flashbacks."

His throat bobs as he swallows. Glen gives him an awkward slap on the back, and I roll my eyes. These men have gone through Hell together, and they're slapping each other on the back like fraternity dudebros. I grab Glen's wrist and yank him down to my level. "Hug him," I order. He does, wrapping his arms around us both. After a moment, Kenta does the same, crouching next to us and joining the huddle. For a while, we all just sit there, pressed together. I curl up between them, breathing them all in. It feels amazing.

Eventually, though, someone shifts, and I hiss as an elbow knocks into my side.

Like clockwork, the men stand. Matt picks me up and carries me back inside, and the others follow, shutting the balcony door behind them. Someone's made a sort of nest on the giant sofa, dragged in all of the quilts, blankets, and squishy pillows in the suite.

"We won't all fit comfortably in one bed," Kenta explains. "You can sleep in your room if you prefer, but we'd like to all be with you, tonight."

I nod and burrow down in the quilts, shivering. The guys crowd around me. I fall asleep fast, with my head tucked into someone's shoulder, and somebody else gently stroking through my hair.

CHAPTER 52
BRIAR

I wake up in a tangle of arms and legs. Glen is sleeping with his chest against my back, his lips brushing the inside of my neck. Matt is on my other side, his heavy arm slung over my waist. Something stings in my chest when I realise Kenta isn't here, but I guess it makes sense. He must be on the morning shift.

I wonder what's going to happen now the threat has been eliminated. Will the guys loosen up? Will they move onto another job? Of course, I'm still going to need some kind of security, but as long as I'm not being stalked, three ex-SAS soldiers probably won't be necessary. I could hire a regular close protection officer.

The idea makes my stomach turn. If the guys take on other jobs, they'll be in danger again. They almost died yesterday, and I know this is far from the most dangerous assignment they've ever had.

But I know I can't keep them here with me, either. They'd get bored, chaperoning me on shopping trips and keeping the paps at bay while I head to brunch. The last thing I want is for any of them to get bored.

So I don't really know where that leaves me.

Matt grunts as I carefully extricate myself from his grasp, slipping out of the sofa bed and padding across the thick carpet to the kitchenette. I'm pouring myself a coffee when I see movement on the balcony. Kenta's sitting in the sun, a book in his lap. I pour a second cup, then go out to join him.

It's a shockingly beautiful day in LA. The sky is burning blue, completely cloudless, and the city sprawls out beneath us like a movie backdrop. I can already see the morning gridlock starting, tiny coloured cars backing up in long lines filling the roads. It's hard to believe that the rest of the world is still trundling along, as if the most horrific event of my life didn't happen last night. It's kind of comforting. Life goes on.

I touch the top of Kenta's head. "Morning," I say, setting his coffee on the table by his elbow.

He puts down his book. "Morning. How do you feel today, sweetheart?"

I roll out my shoulders, considering. Every muscle in my body is sore, and my stitches are painful and itchy. The sticky nausea from last night is finally gone, though, and my headache isn't too bad, even under the glaring sunlight. "Hungry," I decide, and he laughs, pulling out his phone.

"I can get a full English here in twenty minutes."

"Wow," I drawl. "you really *are* an angel. Budge." I gently push aside his hands and climb into his lap. He looks surprised for a second, then wraps his arms around me, letting me curl up against him like a cat. I turn my face into the soft fabric of his linen shirt, breathing in the scent of spice. "How are *you*?" I mumble.

He looks out over the view. "I'm doing well," he says lightly. "Just glad that everybody's okay."

I glance up at him. There's something different about him today. Kenta is always reserved, but he seems more distant than usual, like he doesn't want to look me in the eye. I catch his face and bring his lips to mine for a quick kiss, but he pulls away too soon. It's like there's a wall between us.

I snuggle into his chest, reaching for my coffee, and decide not to push it. I'm not the only one who has a terrible event to recover from; he almost got blown up twice, yesterday. He's probably trying to process that.

We're silent for a while, watching the city move beneath us. I feel his heart beating steadily under my ear, and fiddle with the buttons on his cuffs.

"What happens now?" I ask eventually. "Will you guys move on to another job?"

"Well, we'll all have to discuss it together. We would usually stay with the client for a cooling-off period. You're going to be at the centre of a media frenzy, and events like this can encourage copycats."

"Copycats?"

He nods. "Unstable people who see how much attention the stalker has attracted, or how close he got to actually killing you, and are inspired to do the same."

My heart sinks a bit. "Great," I mutter. "I thought I was finally done with this."

He strokes a hand tentatively down my back. "Trust me, the threat is much, much lower than actually having a confirmed stalker. It's all just a precaution, really."

"Mm." I take his hand, and he looks down at his rough fingers tangled with mine. His sigh tickles my hair against my cheek.

"After that—I don't know. I feel ready for a break. I could do with a holiday."

I frown. "You don't have to do that for me. If you want to move on to protecting someone else… well, I'm not going to lie, I'll be a bit jealous, but I'll get over it."

He shakes his head. "It wouldn't be for you. We're all tired. And if Matt is finally going to do some trauma processing, it would be smart for him to not be holding a gun while he does it. These things often get worse before they get better."

My insides ache. "What does that mean for him? More flashbacks? More nightmares?"

"Probably."

"We'll help him through it."

"Yes."

I let my mind wander. "Maybe we could go somewhere, for a bit. I think I need a break, too, from everyone staring at me. I'm sure I could find a private island to rent." God, just the thought of it is lush. Maybe we could go to the tropics. White sand and fruity drinks and endless days just eating good food, snorkelling, shagging under the sun—

I realise Kenta hasn't said anything, and check his face. "What do you think?" Maybe the boys' idea of a holiday is more action-packed. Jet skis, or snowboarding, or whatever. I could do that, too. I think I'd enjoy doing anything with them.

"I think Glen and Matt would like that a lot," he says carefully.

I frown. That seems like a strange way of putting it. Would *he* not like that a lot? I'm about to ask him when my phone rings. I've been getting notifications all night, but I have it set to only ring for priority numbers. I check the screen and sigh. "Julie." I swipe to answer the call. "Hello?"

"Briar, darling! Are you okay? Why haven't you been answering my texts?"

"I was sleeping. The painkillers were doing a number on me."

"But you're okay, now? Kenta called last night and said you got stabbed, is that true?"

Wow. She actually sounds concerned. "Yeah. I got some stitches, but I'm fine."

"Where are the cuts?"

"Uh... my hip and my face?"

"Your face?" She squeals. *"Oh God. Oh God. Oh God. Where on your face? Send me a picture. Go on video chat right now."*

"Yeah, no. It's on my cheek."

She heaves out a relieved breath. *"Cheek. Okay. Cheek, I can work with. We'll play it off as a warrior-princess, Lara Croft sort of look. Thank God he didn't get your nose. You have the best nose in the business."*

Ah. I see. She doesn't actually care at all. She's just checking her product isn't too damaged to be sold. I rub my eyes. "What did you want, Julie?"

"To discuss how we're going to handle the news of the kidnapping, of course! I've been just flooded *with requests to interview. Not just magazines, but real news stations. I can't keep them on hold much longer, the story will get stale."*

I sigh. I really don't want to, but I'm going to have to face this eventually. I guess I should get it over with. "Fine. Come to the suite."

She hums. *"Oh, I'm out shopping, babe. You should come join me. Ambrose, eleven o'clock? We can work all of this out over mimosas."*

"Not Ambrose. That place is a fishbowl. All the walls are made of glass. And I can't have mimosas, I'm on pain medication."

I can practically hear her frown down the line. *"Well, it's a little early for Nobu —"*

"I don't want expensive sushi. I want something cheap and fatty." She's shocked into silence. I turn to Kenta. "I'm sure you've done shady business in LA before, haven't you? D'you know any private spots we can meet? And I can get actual food with carbs in?"

His lips curl up. "I'll send you a postcode, Julie," he says, raising his voice so she can hear him.

"Perfect." I press a kiss to his cheek, then say goodbye to Julie and hang up. "I should shower," I mumble, slipping off Kenta's lap. "And make myself look semi-presentable."

He nods. "I'll wake the others up."

I frown. "Why? X is gone. Do I really need more than one guard taking me to breakfast?"

He blinks. "One of us should be fine, yes."

"Then… why do we need to wake them up?"

He looks confused. "You want to take me? Alone?"

"Yes, you weirdo. Even if they were awake, I'd pick you to come with me."

I really would. I get different things from each man. Comfort and gentleness from Glen. Fight and strength from Matt.

But from Kenta—

I get steadiness. Calm. Support. Both Glen and Matt like to shield me from things that are painful, and I understand why. They've seen so much pain. And right down to their cores, they're protectors.

But Kenta wants to see me work through obstacles. He really believes I can do anything. He makes *me* believe I can do anything. So, yeah. I need Kenta, right now.

CHAPTER 53
KENTA

Briar insists on driving us to the cafe. Normally, I would never let a client drive; if something goes wrong, Matt, Glen and I have all been trained in escape and evasion driving, so we can make a quick getaway. But the danger has technically been eliminated. And if I'm honest, I think she needs it. She needs some sense of control, after everything that happened last night. So I key the zip code of a veteran's cafe into the sat nav and let her have at it.

We're quiet as she navigates the sunbaked LA roads. It's a beautiful day. The sky is bright blue, and the California palm trees ruffle their long green leaves like streamers in the gentle morning breeze.

I look across at Briar, taking in her unstyled blonde hair and bare face. The necklace that we bought her sparkles on her collarbone. My chest clenches with a sudden wave of pain, which I quickly stamp down.

I shouldn't be sad. I should be over the damn moon that she's here. And safe. And whole.

The few minutes it took us to bust down the door to X's cabin last night were the worst of my entire life. I shudder as I remember standing outside the thick metal door, hearing Briar screaming and sobbing as gunshots fired. X's deranged shouts echo in my ears. *I'm going to kill her. You're too late.*

In that moment, I thought for sure that we'd open the door to find her dead, bloody corpse. And I knew that when that happened, my life would never be the same again. Never. I've never loved a girl so much. Losing her might just break me.

But now she's sitting next to me, relatively unscathed, and I can barely look at her.

Last night, when I went to pay the delivery guy, I passed Briar's open bedroom door. I heard her whispering to Glen in the bathroom. Telling him that she loved him. He didn't sound shocked; it clearly wasn't the first time she'd said it. Then, when I walked out onto the balcony half an hour later, she was telling Matt the exact same thing. She's in love with both of them.

Which is fine. I'm used to it. I've always been the one who fades into the background. Matt is such a loudmouth no one could ever ignore him, and Glen has a kind of gentle-giant sweetness which gets him a lot of attention, even if he doesn't realise it. I've always been the boring one. The sensible one. And I like that, most of the time. God knows we need a bit of sense in our team.

Right now, though, I wish I could be anybody else.

Briar leans forward and fiddles with a button on the dash, turning on the radio. Her long hair drapes over my bare arm, and I close my eyes as 'Hotel California' starts blaring through the sound system. She lingers there for a moment, her soft body pressed against mine, before slowly pulling back. I let out a quiet sigh of relief.

In a few days this will all be over.

While I was out on the terrace this morning, I made a plan. I'll stay here in LA for the next day or two, until Angel Security can find another guard to replace me. Then I'll fly back to London and ask Colette to find me a solo job. Preferably a very difficult, dangerous one that will distract me for a few months. I don't like the idea of leaving Matt and Glen; we've worked as a unit for so long. But I just can't be around them if they're both going to be dating her. I'll get over it in time. I always do. But right now, I can't sit around watching her fall more and more in love with them. I can't do it.

A small hand touches my arm. Briar scans my face carefully, then nods out of the windshield. "We're here."

I blink, suddenly realising that the car has stopped. Looking around us, I can't help but swear.

The street she's driven us to barely looks like LA at all. It could be London, with its grubby shops and brightly coloured signs. There are bins huddled on the pavement and graffiti tags sprayed on the walls. I thought this place would be safe, but there's already a handful of photographers hanging around Cricket's Café. They're huddled together, smoking cigarettes and chatting in the late-morning sunshine.

"This makes no sense," I mutter. "How does this keep happening? How did they know we'd be meeting here? We haven't put it on any of your socials." I pull out my phone. "I know another location. I'll text it to Julie."

Briar stares at the men clutching their cameras. "Kenta," she says slowly, "only three people knew we were going to be here. You, me, and Julie."

I close my eyes as everything falls into place. "Shit."

It all makes sense. How the paparazzi kept finding her, no matter how secure the location was. No wonder X managed to follow our car back from the restaurant; he was probably paying off the paparazzi for her location. The paparazzi, who had been tipped off by her fame-hungry, cash-grabbing PR manager.

I shake my head, pushing open my car door. "I'll talk to her—"

Briar reaches out to grab my arm. "Don't. Let me handle it."

I grit my teeth, but back down, giving her a reluctant nod. I wait for her to step out of the car, but she doesn't move to grab the door handle. Instead, she leans forward, brushing a tiny kiss to my cheek. My heart stutters in my chest. I feel blood rushing through my body.

"Thank you," she whispers, nudging her nose against mine.

"For what?" I croak.

"For being you." I stare at her. She shrugs. "If you were Glen, you would've argued with me. If you were Matt, you would've ignored me. But you just—trust that I can take care of myself."

"I know you can, sweetheart."

She gives me another very gentle kiss, then pulls back, grabbing my hand. "Me, too."

We both slide out of the car. Instantly, the photographers swarm around us, snapping shots and shouting at her.

"How are you feeling, Briar?"

"Will you make a statement about what happened last night? Were you injured in the bombing?"

"Is your stalker dead, Miss Saint?"

She flinches at that last one. I wrap my arm around her, tugging her into my side as I steer her through the crowd and across the road towards Cricket's Café. My head is spinning. Holding her so close to me is jumbling up my thoughts. Why did she kiss me? What is she thinking?

I shake my head hard. I need to pull myself together. It doesn't mean anything. Not really. A kiss on the cheek is hardly the same as her confessing her *love* to me. Maybe she still has a casual interest in me. Maybe she wants to keep me around because she enjoys foursomes. If that's the case, I have to get out of here ASAP. I'd rather be alone than be her last resort.

Briar reaches for my hand, and I gently pull it away, scanning the throng of paparazzi. She glances up at me. "Are you okay?" She asks slowly.

I nod, leading her onto the pavement and towards the diner. A bell over the glass door jangles as we step inside. It's an adorable place: black-and-white checked tiles on the floors, vintage photos on the walls, worn red leather booths. Dolly Parton is crackling quietly from a radio in the kitchen, and the whole place smells of cooking waffles.

There's a burly man sitting at a table by the door, swilling a coffee. He gives me a wolfish grin. "Li."

"Cricket," I greet. "How's business?"

He shrugs. "We get by." His eyes flick to Briar. He obviously recognises her, but he doesn't mention it. "Mornin', darlin'. You Li's new client?"

She smiles and nods. I jerk my head at the windows. "Keep the scum out, will you? She's attracted a lot of attention."

Cricket's grin just gets wider. "Gladly."

"You know each other?" Briar asks as I lead her inside.

"We trained together for a while. He's ex-special forces."

"And he retired and—"

"Bought a diner, yes. A lot of vets hang out here."

She smiles. "That's cute."

Julie is sitting, predictably, in a booth by the window, where the photographers can see right through to her. She stands up and gives Briar an air-hug as we come over. "This place is disgusting," she announces.

"I think it's perfect," Briar says quietly.

I scan the room, then go to take a nearby table, but Briar catches my hand, tugging me close. "No, sit with us."

"I need to sit here," I nod to the table by the kitchen, "so I can see the full room."

"We'll sit there too, then."

I blink in surprise, but nod, and we move over to the corner table. Briar slides into the window seat next to me, handing me a menu. A smiling waitress bustles over with a notebook in hand, and we both order orange juice, tea, and an inordinate amount of hash browns. Julie orders a club soda and a melon plate, then sits back in her booth and examines Briar critically.

"God, your face looks *awful*," she drawls. "Please tell me that it'll heal better than it looks."

Briar shrugs. "The doctors said scarring would be minimal. If there is a mark, makeup can cover it whenever I'm on set."

"Hm." Julie winces as the waitress sets two plates of golden, crispy fried food in front of us. "You're eating like a pig."

I hand Briar some cutlery and keep my mouth carefully shut. But, Jesus. The girl almost died last night, and she's still being expected to *diet?* My annoyance fades away as I watch Briar take her first bite, her eyes practically rolling back into her head. She hums happily, leaning against my side. "I love you for bringing me here," she whispers.

My stomach contracts. I smile tightly and turn back to my plate.

"Ugh," Julie mutters. "I guess you can't do a video interview until they take your stitches out anyway, you look disgusting like this. So it's not the end of the world if you're bloated for a bit. But you'll have to get back to working out tomorrow." She pulls a notebook out of her designer purse and licks a finger, flipping to the right page. "The first few interviews will have to be radio or print," she sighs, scribbling a note. "That knocks about half of these offers off the list."

"I'm not doing any interviews," Briar says. "I don't want to talk about what happened."

Julie waves her off. "Oh, babe, don't worry, we'll have private interviews. No talk shows, nothing like that until you're ready."

Briar frowns. "There's no such thing as a *private interview.* What does that even mean?" She shakes her head. "Julie, I'm serious. This isn't something I want to share with people. I don't want people flipping through magazines in a hair salon, casually reading about the most horrific night of my life. This isn't *entertainment,* and I'm not going to let the media treat it like that."

Julie sighs deeply, reaching across the table to take her hand. "Darling," she says, her voice low and confidential. "I know it's difficult. I know it's painful. But you've been suffering in silence for so long. It will feel good to open up about what's happened to you. Like a catharsis."

"There is absolutely nothing good about gossip rags *profiting* off me getting drugged, kidnapped and almost killed."

"Darling, where have you been the last five years? This is what the Me Too movement is all about!"

I choke on my food. Briar's mouth falls open. "The Me Too movement is about people choosing to fight back against an entire industry which wants to silence them, not their PR managers *forcing* them to sensationalise traumatic events as part of a publicity campaign!" She straightens her spine, obviously trying to compose herself. "Julie, have you been tipping off the paparazzi?"

CHAPTER 54
KENTA

J ulie sputters, leaning back in her booth. "Of course not! Why would you even say that, babe?"

Briar sighs and holds out her hand. "Give me your phone."

"What? No—"

"Fine." Briar leans over and knocks on the glass window. The paps outside all jump. She points at one, a short guy wearing a baseball cap, and waves for him to come inside. I stiffen slightly, priming for action, but mostly I'm just amused. This should be fun to watch.

The bell rings as the guy enters the café, looking nervously at Cricket, but I wave him over to our table. He stands awkwardly next to us, shifting on his feet.

"Hello." Briar smiles up at him. "I'm Briar."

He looks at her like she's an idiot. "Uh. Yeah. I know."

"What's your name?"

"Roger."

"Well, Roger, I was just wondering how you knew I was going to be here, today."

He blinks. "We got a tip-off. Like, ninety-nine percent of our photos, of any celebrity, are from tip-offs."

"Who from?"

"Just some lady that works for you. She calls us, sometimes." He eyes me nervously. I raise an eyebrow, and he drops his gaze, flushing.

"What was her name?" Briar presses.

"Don't remember."

"And how did this woman contact you?"

He lifts up his phone.

"Do me a favour," Briar turns to face Julie, who is shrinking back into her seat like a cornered animal. "Call her back."

"Right. Yeah." He fumbles with his phone. A high-pitched jangle starts blaring from Julie's bag. I take a massive gulp of coffee, sitting back to enjoy the show.

"Don't you want to pick that up?" Briar asks mildly.

Colour flushes Julie's face. "Fine," she snaps. "Fine. Yes. I've been giving paparazzi tip-offs. It's like the kid says; everyone does it. Any good PR manager would."

Briar glances up at Roger. "Thank you. Could you wait outside?"

"Um… Could I…" He lifts his camera hopefully.

"When we get outside, I'll give you some really good ones," she promises. He looks a bit disappointed, but Cricket is already cracking his knuckles, so he makes a hasty exit.

Briar turns back to her PR manager, her expression cold. "You know that's how X was finding me, right? He was just following the paparazzi. Because of you, he knew what restaurants I was going to. What hotel I was staying at. It's how he recognised and followed our car. God, I bet it wasn't even Rodriguez who leaked the break-in story, was it? It was you."

She looks a bit chastised, but mostly defensive. "I didn't know he was going to try and kidnap you, did I? Look, babe—you have to understand. It's really hard to stay relevant in this industry. You just turned twenty-nine. That's almost *thirty*."

"I know. Practically an old crone."

"You may as well be," she snaps. "We all know women age like milk in Hollywood. You're already losing traction."

"So?"

"*So*, the stalker angle was bringing you interest, keeping you relevant. I just wanted to make sure you made the most of that, by being seen."

Something in Briar snaps. She slams her juice glass on the table. "Cut the crap! This isn't about me! If it were about me, you would have, I don't know, tried to keep me *alive*? This is about you, and your percentage cut. I lose public favour, you lose money. That's it. We both know it, so don't bullshit me."

Julie leans back in her chair, chewing her gum hard. Her cheeks are red.

Briar sighs. "Look, I'm glad I met you. Because you—inadvertently, whilst trying to save your ass—introduced me to some people who really, truly care about me. But I don't want to surround myself with people who see me as a paycheck instead of a person."

Julie sneers, her glossy lips stretching. "You don't want your *hired* staff to see you as a paycheck? Good luck finding someone."

"I actually already have someone in mind." Briar gives me a little smile. "It's over, Julie. You're fired. I would say I'm sorry, but I'm really, *really* not."

Julie doesn't move.

"You can leave, now," Briar prompts.

Julie purses her lips, her eyes flicking between us, then to the paps outside. I can see her mind running at a mile a minute, trying to find a way to convince Briar to let her stay.

"Babe—" she starts.

"No. Go."

"Would you like me to escort her out?" I ask mildly. Heat flushes Julie's face. She stands and shoves her notebook into her bag.

"You'll be sorry for this," she mutters. "Just wait and see. Without me, you'll fall out of the public eye faster than you can bloody blink." She tosses the bag over her shoulder and marches to the café door.

"Bye, babe," Briar calls after her. Julie gives us one last glare, then slams the door shut, the little welcome bell tinkling.

There's a few beats of silence, then I pull her untouched bowl towards us and divvy up the melon slices onto both our plates. "Nicely done," I murmur approvingly. Briar looks down, a wide smile spreading across her face.

When we step back out onto the sunny street, our stomachs full to bursting, the photographers are ready and waiting. Before I've even shut the café door, they start snapping away, coming to our left side to get a good shot of Briar's stitched-up cheek. I tighten my grip on her, trying to block the lenses as I hurry her along, but she digs in her heels.

"No," she says. I watch as she catches Roger's eye and points to a spot on her other side. I'm not sure what she's doing, but now isn't the time.

"Come on," I scowl at the clamouring photographers. "Christ, they're all bloody vultures." I pull her gently away, trying to ignore the sweet scent of her shampoo as her hair tickles my face. This is probably the last time I'll ever be this close to her.

She tugs at my arm. "Stop. Kenta, *stop*."

I still, and she reaches up to cup my cheek, turning me to face her.

I frown. "Briar, what—"

Before I can protest, she goes up on her tiptoes and brushes her lips against mine. My heart practically stops in my chest.

This isn't like any of our other kisses. It's soft and sweet and gentle, so quick I barely feel it. When she pulls away, I stare at her, breathing hard. The paps are shouting and running around us, trying to get a better angle, but I ignore them. My hand unconsciously clenches on Briar's waist, like I'm trying to keep her close to me. "What... was that for, sweetheart?"

She shrugs. "I just remembered. I've only been photographed kissing Glen and Matt. I don't want the magazines to get the wrong impression and think I'm only in love with two of you."

I'm not even walking, but I still almost trip over my own feet. "In *love*?" I manage eventually.

"Madly, I'm afraid," she says, tilting her head. "Are you going to pass out?"

I stammer. "But... Matt and Glen..."

She sighs dramatically. "I guess *Goss* magazine was right all along. I'm a massive hoe-bag. But I don't just whore out my body, I whore out my *heart*." She shakes her head sorrowfully. "It's embarrassing. I spend so long keeping men at a distance, then three of you seduce me at once. It's kind of ruining my ice-queen reputation." I don't say anything. I don't think I can. I think I've temporarily forgotten English.

She sighs, stroking my cheek. "*Kenta*. You are one of the smartest, kindest, most loving men I've ever met. No one has ever believed in me like you do." She steps even closer, so our bodies are pressed together. I vaguely register a wolf-whistle from one of the paps, but it sounds like it comes from a thousand miles away. "You're *stunning*," she continues, "and gentle. Empathic. Intelligent. You care about other people. How the Hell could I not fall for you?"

My voice gets stuck in my throat. "I love you, too," I choke out. She smiles, big and bright and beautiful, and I can't help myself. I wrap a hand around the back of her neck and bring her lips to mine.

It's the kind of kiss that ends a movie. Everything else fades away. Our tongues dance together slowly as we hold each other under the baking-hot LA sunshine. Briar hums underneath me, shivering as I trace my hand down the small of her back, pressing her closer. I can taste strawberry chapstick and orange juice on her soft lips.

Seconds, or minutes, or hours later, we pull apart slightly, shifting to a series of long, open-mouthed pecks. Our foreheads rest together as we breathe each other's air.

"Mmm," Briar hums under her breath, slowly licking my bottom lip. "I could kiss you forever."

My fingers curl into the soft fabric of her dress. I nuzzle down the side of her neck. Around us, cameras flash and shutters click. "We can kiss for as long as you want back in the hotel room," I murmur. "But we should get going."

She frowns slightly. "Why? I don't care about the paps."

"I know." I give her another lingering kiss, then finally straighten, pushing a strand of wavy hair behind her ear. "And I also know Matt. I know that as soon as he wakes up and sees you're gone, he's going to freak out. He's probably climbing the walls by now."

She sighs happily, leaning against my front. "I'm so excited to have you love me."

I laugh. It's such an odd thing to say. "What?"

"You're so wonderful to people you love," she says, catching my hand. "You're the best. Okay. Let's go."

CHAPTER 55
MATT

When I wake up, I hold myself still for a few seconds, tuning into my surroundings. It's a habit I got into when I was serving. Stopped me rolling over and groaning awake when we were in the middle of a stealth mission.

I'm lying in an unfamiliar room, under a heavy pile of quilts. My muscles are tight and sore, my throat is burning, and my head hurts like a bitch. As I try to piece all of this information together, memories from last night wash over me.

Briar lying on the cabin floor, covered in blood, her cheek and side slashed open. Briar standing over X's body, clutching a blood-covered knife. Briar lying under me, scrabbling to get away. The images are so vivid, they almost seem real. For a moment, I just lie there, shaking.

Then I stand up.

The lounge is empty. The nest-bed Kenta and Glen made on the couch is just a rumpled pile of quilts and pillows. I look around the room, peering into the kitchenette, then through the window onto the balcony, but there's no sign of life.

"Briar!" I call. My voice is rough and hoarse from inhaling all the goddamn smoke last night. I clear my throat, trying again. "Briar!" There's no response. The hotel suite is completely still. Outside, a bird lands on the terrace railing, twittering.

I push out of the living room and towards her bedroom, but when I let myself inside, everything is untouched. There are still hair products and bits of makeup scattered around on the dresser from when she was getting ready last night. My chest tightens. I head into the ensuite. It's empty. Her toothbrush is wet, and the sweet scent of her body wash hangs in the air. Where the Hell is she?

There's no way anyone could've got in here without us noticing, right? X is in custody. And I doubt he'll be able to walk anytime soon, let alone sneak into a guarded hotel room.

Still. This is freaking me out.

I slam out of her bedroom and stride down the suite to the guys' shared room, yanking open the door. Again, it's empty. I feel panic rise up in me. She's gone. She's disappeared. Something's happened to her. I'm about to run and raise the alarm when I hear running water coming from the ensuite bathroom.

"Briar!" I cross the room and slam my fist against the door. "Briar. Are you in there?"

The door opens, and Glen steps out in a t-shirt and jeans, a towel around his neck.

"Hey, man." He runs his eyes over me. "You good?"

"Where is she?" I rasp. "Where the Hell is she?"

"Kenta took her to meet Julie. They needed to decide how much they were going to tell the media."

Fear slams into me. "Alone? He took her out *alone*?!"

Glen sighs, swiping the towel through his hair as he pushes past me into the bedroom. "The threat is gone, Matt. He took her to a private spot, she's only going to need one guard."

"You don't know that!" I grab a pair of jeans out of my open suitcase and yank them on. "Tell me where they are."

"I don't know," Glen says slowly, lowering the towel to watch me. "Matt—"

"Well, I'll just ask him." I cast around for my phone. It's on the bedside table, charging. I lunge for it.

Glen steps in front of me. "Matt." I try to push past him, but he grabs my neck in both hands, forcing me to look at him. "Matt, listen." His voice is steady. "You need to calm down. She's been through Hell. You'll just scare her again, if she comes back to you freaking out like this. She's *okay*."

I don't say anything. My fists clench by my sides. I'm breathing too hard.

Glen claps a hand on my back. "C'mon. It's okay. Sit down."

He shoves me into the lounge and pushes me toward the sofa. I sit down, running my hands through my hair. "She's okay?" I ask, my voice hoarse.

"She's okay."

I close my eyes, shaking my head. I can't breathe right. "She's not okay." I know she's in danger. I can feel it. My hands are shaking violently. "She's not okay."

"She is okay. You need to call her?"

"No." Sweat drips down my back. I fist my hands in my hair. I don't want her to see me like this.

I think this is the worst part of the PTSD. It's not the flashbacks or the night terrors. It's the slow, seeping fear that permeates everything.

During my time serving, I saw people get blown up. Stabbed. Shot. I saw entire villages get bombed. I saw kids step in landmines, and innocent civilians caught in crossfire. Five years ago, I made a split-second decision that plunged three of the people I loved most into a waking nightmare for months.

And then, out of nowhere, I got pulled out of it all, patched up, and sent home. People suddenly expected me to get a nine-to-five job, working in an office and saving up for a mortgage. I was surrounded by people who cared about getting promotions, and going on diets, and seeing the new Marvel movie.

To function in society, you need to believe that you're safe. We all know it's a lie, but it's a lie you need to believe to survive. Realistically, everybody knows that they'll die one day. Everybody knows that, every second, around the world, people are getting killed, and assaulted, and robbed, and hurt. At this very moment, people are losing their kids, being run over, getting diagnosed with terminal illnesses. We're living in a motherfucking horror movie, but most people can convince themselves that they're safe. And they go about their lives, thinking about money, and their annoying neighbours, and celebrity gossip, like any of that fucking matters.

My brain won't let me do that, anymore. It won't let me pretend that I'm safe. Or that Kenta and Glen are safe. Or that Briar's safe. No one is safe. No one is going to be okay. Sooner or later, terrible things are going to happen to everyone I love. The veil has been pulled back, and now I'll only ever see the world as one giant war zone.

The truth is, I am scared. All the fucking time. Every waking second. When I'm taking a piss, or eating cereal, or walking down the street, I'm terrified. Some part of me has never left the room where I watched my best friends get tortured. Some part of me is still watching it on repeat. And I'm so *fucking* scared. *That's* why I didn't tell Briar about X's threats. It wasn't the nightmares or the flashbacks; it was the deep, gnawing fear that lives inside me. I can't get rid of it.

That's the worst part of PTSD. The disconnect. I live in the same physical world as everyone else, but I don't see it the same. I just see danger. And blood. And death.

"Fuck," I gasp, rubbing my chest. My shirt is sticking to me with sweat. "Jesus. It never stops."

Glen sits in front of me. "It'll get better, man. When you see a therapist."

I rub my eyes with the heels of my hands. I'm choked up. "It won't ever go away." I can't unsee what I've seen. It happened. It was real.

"No," he agrees. "But it will get better." He reaches over and puts a hand on my shoulder, squeezing.

Almost two hours pass before I hear the buzz of a keycard in the front door. I've spent the entire time pacing up and down the suite like a caged animal. I wheel on Briar as she pushes inside the suite, Kenta stepping in quietly behind her. The man is beaming.

"What the Hell," I bite out. Briar looks up at me. She looks much better than yesterday; sparkly-eyed and pink-cheeked. She's dressed in a little yellow sundress, and her loose hair is falling in waves around her face. The rose necklace we all picked out for her glitters around her neck. I have to fight the urge to just grab at her. "Where the Hell have you been? We've been worried sick."

"Why?" She kicks off her shoes. "Kenta texted, didn't he?"

I scowl. "Because the last time you disappeared, you got kidnapped."

"Well, this time, I just got hash browns."

"What happened to you?" Glen asks Kenta. "You win the damn lottery?"

Kenta shrugs, still smiling. "Pretty much."

I ignore them both, striding towards Briar. She steps right into my open arms, letting me pull her close and burrow my face into her hair. My breathing is embarrassingly ragged as she reaches up and squeezes the back of my neck.

"That bad?" She says quietly.

I grunt, winding my hands in her soft hair. "Don't *leave* me like that."

She stiffens in surprise. I clear my throat. "I mean. Just. Please don't leave the *building* without me."

Glen snorts. Briar studies me for a moment, then goes up on her tiptoes. "I might leave the building without you," she whispers, her lips brushing my cheek. "But I have no current plans of leaving you." She presses a kiss to my mouth. "I love you. Please make me coffee."

I straighten. My chest is aching worse than the time I punctured my lung in training. I give the rose charm on her necklace a little tug. "Diva."

"So I've been told." She tosses me a smile, and I head to the breakfast bar to get the coffee started, trying to ignore my heart battering in my chest.

Glen comes up behind her, gently touching her cheek to check out her stitches. "How are you feeling, lass? Sore? Still sick?"

She shakes her head, cuddling into his chest. "I feel much better."

"We figured out how X was tracking her," Kenta says, dropping onto the sofa. "It was Julie." He gives us a quick rundown of everything that happened during their breakfast meeting.

When he finishes, I swear. "That greedy, money-hungry, self-serving little piece of shit. She almost got Briar killed, for what? A bigger paycheck?"

"Do you think Nin will want the job?" Briar asks, plopping down next to Kenta and picking up the TV remote. "I promise I won't shout at her again."

"I think she'd love it. She's definitely qualified."

"Great." She starts flipping through TV channels. "Maybe I can have a positive impact on *one* person's life. I got a lot of people hurt last night."

Kenta frowns. "Briar, none of what happened was your fault. It was X who rigged the bombs. You didn't even know what he was planning before it was too late."

She sighs. "Yeah, yeah. I know. Doesn't stop me feeling like shit." She stops on a news channel playing a piece on the premiere bombing. I'm not surprised she found one so easily. It's by far the biggest news story in LA. It's probably being shown on repeat.

I carry over her coffee, sitting on the sofa next to her. "Are you sure you want to watch that?"

She turns up the volume. "I want to see what happened. I missed so much."

I grimace, but stay quiet as the newsreader starts to speak.

'Last night, at the premiere for the upcoming Unity Productions film 'Players', fifteen bombs were set off on the red carpet and in the crowd, causing chaos among celebrities and fans alike.'

Footage from one of the press cameras comes up on the screen. I watch, jaw clenched, as the elegant, luxurious red carpet scene erupts into screams and explosions. Kenta winces, and even Glen flinches. I glance across at Briar. She watches silently, worrying at her lip. A shot of a woman being lifted into an ambulance flashes across the screen, and she reaches out and grabs my hand, squeezing.

'Over thirty attendees were injured in the blast, but no fatalities have been reported.'

"Oh, thank God." Briar sags against Kenta's chest, and he wraps his arms around her, pressing a kiss into her hair. "Thank *God*."

The reporter keeps droning on.

'Whilst police have yet to make a statement on the night's events, many believe that the bombing is linked to celebrity actress Briar Saint's widely publicised stalking incident. The starlet has spoken openly about her recent struggles with an obsessive fan, who has previously sent her lewd images, broken into her house, and stalked her across the globe. Miss Saint was present at the premiere last night, and several eye-witnesses report seeing the actress being captured, gagged, and dragged from the event by a man in dark clothing.'

I rub my thumb over the back of Briar's hand. The shot changes to one of her with Kenta this morning, his arm wrapped around her shoulders as they walk down a sunny LA street.

'Briar Saint was seen, sporting several injuries, at a local café this morning. She made no comment addressing the kidnapping rumours, but seemed unfazed by the event.'

The camera zooms in on Briar and Kenta kissing deeply in the middle of the street. When they pull apart, they're both pink-cheeked and beaming. She pops up and nuzzles his cheek.

Lucky bastard.

The news channel moves on to the next story, and Glen reaches for the remote to switch it off. Briar stares at the screen blankly, chewing on her bottom lip. "How come they didn't mention X yet?"

I shrug. "The police must have decided to hold on to the information."

Her face is pale. "Do… you know what happened to him?"

I turn to Glen. I've been too busy losing my shit for the last couple of hours to keep up to date on news.

"He still hasn't woken up," Glen says shortly.

She frowns. "I only smacked him with a chair leg. And poured chloroform on him."

"The police shot him a couple times, while Matt was busy tackling you to the floor. He kept waving his gun at them, the idiot."

"Do you think he'll be a problem, if he recovers?"

Glen softens. "No, honey. Between the first-degree attempted murder and bombing a public place, I'd be very surprised if he doesn't receive a life sentence."

Kenta kisses her cheek. "He's done for good, sweetheart. He can't hurt you, now. He's never getting anywhere near you again."

She nods, looking down into her mug, and swallows hard. "I wanted to kill him," she says. "For a second. When I was standing over him with the knife."

"If you had, no one would have blamed you," Kenta says. "It would have been self-defence. But I'm glad you didn't."

"And it's okay?" She asks. "That I wanted to?" Her voice is unbearably quiet. I don't think I've ever seen Briar like this. Uncertain. Looking for assurance.

My throat feels thick. "Of course it's okay, baby. However you feel is okay. You did perfect."

She takes a deep breath, nodding to herself. "Okay. Okay." She sets her coffee mug on the table. "Can we talk about something else, then? Like, anything non-X-related?"

"Sure," Kenta says. "Want to watch a movie, or something?"

"I have the new *Superspy* film," she offers.

"Really?" Glen looks up, his eyes widening, and I snort. He loves the big-budget action crap. "It's not out for release for months."

Briar smiles. "Perks. One of my old co-stars was in it, he sent me the final cut. If you tell anyone about the ending before it comes out, though, I think the Hollywood mafia will kill you."

Glen nods seriously. "I'm willing to take that risk, lass."

"Great." She connects the TV to her laptop and loads up the movie, then drags one of last night's blankets over our laps. The opening credits start to play.

I'm not really focussing on what's in front of me. My head is back in the cabin last night. I can't stop thinking about the moment I saw Briar, collapsed on the floor, covered in blood and sweat and dirt. I'd lunged at her like a rabid tiger, even when she froze up and tried to push me off.

I must have scared the ever-living shit out of her.

Next to me, Briar shuffles a bit on the couch cushions. I glance down at her, but she seems completely engrossed in the car chase unfolding on the screen. I run my hand gently down her spine, wanting her closer, and she snuggles into my side.

We're quiet for a bit, watching the movie. I try to pay attention, but I can't. Briar keeps fidgeting. At first, she's just shifting around a little, but it just gets worse and worse, until after ten minutes, she's full-on wriggling under the blanket. I clear my throat. Every time she moves, her soft body presses up against mine. It's starting to become a problem.

"Okay?" I ask. She nods, letting out a soft, annoyed sound. I wince as the noise goes straight between my legs. "You sure, princess? Kind of looks like something is bothering you."

"'M fine," she breathes. "Just fidgety, I guess. Stitches are itchy."

I press a kiss to her head. "Sorry."

She turns her face into my shoulder and breathes hotly against my neck. I grit my teeth as her lips brush my Adam's apple, and the thudding ache in my balls flares. This is messed up. The poor girl is injured and uncomfortable, and I'm hard as a goddamn rod. I force myself to stare at the TV screen, but I don't see anything at all.

Briar suddenly gasps, her whole body jerking against mine. I look down, alarmed. She's flushed and feverish-looking, sweat sticking her blonde hair to her temples. I'm about to ask her what's wrong when Kenta starts laughing. I glance up—and see his hand moving subtly in Briar's lap, hidden under the blanket.

"You piece of shit," I mutter as Briar arches into me, biting the collar of my shirt. "I thought she was in *pain*."

He just laughs harder.

Briar's hand flies out, twisting in my shirt. "Oh," she says, "Oh God I need to—" Her breath catches as she wriggles and squirms around Kenta's fingers.

"Briar," I breathe, sliding off the couch and coming to kneel in front of her. My hands are shaking as I push back her hair and put my mouth on her neck. She leans into me, shivering. "What do you want?" I mumble against her skin.

She curves her back, pressing her chest into my face. I reach up for the buttons on the front of her sundress. They're tiny and ridiculously fiddly, but I slowly get each one undone, in a series of long, slow presses that have her arching up into me, biting her lip. Underneath, she's wearing a bra—pretty, pale yellow with lace up the cups. I tug the straps down and push my face between her tits. She's unbelievably soft. I can feel her heart hammering against my cheek as I press rough, open-mouth kisses down her cleavage.

"God. Matt," she whispers.

"I'm here, baby." I squeeze one of her pert pink nipples, then bend and suckle on it hard. She cries out, shuddering, digging her nails into my back.

"Oh, God." She twists under me, fisting a hand in Kenta's shirt. "Ken—"

He dips and starts kissing her neck as he fucks her with his fingers. I can't see what he's doing under the blanket, but she jerks forward with every movement, letting out a soft moan. I tilt my head up to catch her lips, and she gasps into my mouth, greedily inhaling my breaths. We keep this up for a few minutes, arousal slowly building, skin sliding over skin. Then Kenta twists his hand, changing his angle slightly, and Briar suddenly goes crazy, writhing under me.

"Kenta!" She pants. "Please!"

He blinks innocently. "What?"

She rocks her hips, her face flushing. "It's not enough," she whines. "For God's sake. *Touch* me, dumbass."

He just laughs, and she scowls at him, kicking off the blanket and grabbing my wrist, shoving it up her dress. I fight the urge to groan. Her thighs are hot and soft and slippery, and they rub over my palm as she crosses her legs, writhing to get the pressure she needs. I roll the pad of my thumb over her sweet spot, and her head tips back against the sofa, her red lips parting.

Kenta leans in next to me, still touching her deep inside, and she starts making noises, little gasps that get higher and higher. Her hips are jerking in little helpless circles as she grinds herself against our hands. "Shit," she whispers, over and over. "Oh, shit, Matt. Kenta. Shit."

She's almost there. I can feel her fluttering urgently under my fingers, and I'm ninety percent sure my balls are about to explode. I've never been this turned on in my life. She leans forward suddenly, gripping at my shoulders, bracing herself to come.

Kenta and I move in at the same moment. He leans in to lock lips with her, and I dip to catch her earlobe in my mouth, biting down. Briar makes a squeaking sound and falls apart, gasping, her whole body trembling under me. We wring the orgasm right out of her, until she eventually flops down against the couch cushions, her body limp. Kenta and I both carefully retract our hands as she pants, her eyes lidded. For a few moments, the room is silent. I glance up and see Glen has paused the film and is watching us, a hand pressed over the bulge in his jeans. Briar curls up next to me, not saying anything.

"Are you okay?" I ask, pushing back her hair. "We didn't hurt you, did we?"

"Are you guys clean?" She whispers.

I freeze.

"The company runs bloodwork on us before every new job," Kenta explains, "to check we're healthy enough to take it on."

"Well. So am I." She says.

Kenta nods. "We know."

"What?"

"We have access to your health records."

"That's creepy." She gives a little shrug. "Guess you know that I'm on birth control as well, then."

There's a pause. "Yes," I say, my voice coming out ridiculously husky.

She rolls over in Kenta's arms. "Can we? Please?"

He closes his eyes. "Are you sure you want that?" He asks carefully. "You don't think it might freak you out?"

She shrugs. "I guess it might. There's only one way to find out, right? I'm not letting X control my sex life forever."

"You're so much braver than me," I say, completely seriously. A blush blooms on her cheeks.

She lifts her arms to me. "Carry me," she orders. "I'm too horny to walk."

I can't hold back my snort as I stand, picking her up gently. "Diva."

"You love it."

CHAPTER 56
BRIAR

Matt drops me in the middle of my giant bed, and the boys immediately start stripping like it's some kind of race. I watch, entranced, as a gorgeous array of abs, biceps, and thighs get unveiled right in front of my eyes. Kenta gets undressed first, and climbs on top of me, wrapping a hand around my throat and slanting his mouth over mine. His whole body is practically thrumming against me; he still hasn't lost that thrilled golden glow he's been sporting ever since I kissed him in front of the paparazzi.

I gasp as he starts rocking his hips over me, his stiff hard-on rubbing against me as our tongues stroke together. He slides one hand under my thigh, tugging me even closer, and my eyes practically roll back as the base of his shaft crushes against my core. I twist, watching through lowered lids as Glen peels off his undershirt, pulling it over his head and leaving it crumpled on the floor. I reach for him, stretching out to run my fingers down his muscled chest—

Kenta lines up and slides into me in one firm stroke. I gasp as he pushes in deep.

"Jesus! Kenta!"

He starts thrusting into me, fast and shallow, quicker than I'd usually like. Today, though, the overstimulation feels perfect, sending electricity fizzling through all my nerve endings. I shudder, my fingers clawing at his back, rubbing against the rough scar tissue. He freezes on top of me, and I lift my hands. "Shit. Sorry. Does that hurt?"

"Not at all," he rolls his shoulders, then presses down on me, kissing the side of my throat. "Never thought that someone touching my back would make me feel *good*," he murmurs. "Kinda used to the opposite."

"I'm gonna give you so many massages," I promise. "It's going to become your number one erogenous zone."

He laughs into my mouth and kisses me again, rolling his hips much deeper this time. I cry out as he hits the sensitive spot deep inside of me. And then keeps hitting it.

"Roll her over," Glen says behind us. "I want her on top."

"Careful," Matt adds. "Don't hurt her side."

Kenta obediently hooks a leg under mine and rolls gracefully, landing flat on his back with me sprawled on top of him. Glen kneels behind me, and I feel his strong, calloused hands slowly stroke over my ass cheeks. "You're so soft," he murmurs, trailing a finger down my crack. "Yes?"

"*Yes*," I breathe.

There's the pop of a plastic cap, and I feel cool wetness stroking between my cheeks. "This should feel really good," Glen says quietly. "Tell me if you don't like anything. Ken—"

Kenta sighs, slowing his thrusts until he's just gently rocking his hips in me. I squirm, but he refuses to move any faster. Glen rubs his lube-slick finger gently around my hole, massaging the ring of tight muscle. A gasp falls out of my mouth as his thick finger burrows inside my ass. I wriggle at the odd pressure. It's not like anything I've ever really felt before, but it's a delicious feeling of fullness.

"More," I demand, bucking back against him, and he laughs, obediently sawing into me with his finger. Suddenly, Kenta starts moving again. The two start drilling into me in rhythm: each of them pulls out and pushes back into me at the same time. My whole body jerks as I feel two sensitive spots, deep inside me, getting hammered from both sides. "*God,*" I whisper, writhing. "Oh. Oh, *fuck ME.*"

They both laugh. My head lolls as I shudder forwards and back, trying to work myself against both men at once. It's overwhelming, this feeling of fullness. It's short-circuiting something in my brain. I feel like a primal animal, scrabbling and wriggling, desperate to find some release. Glen strokes a hand over my butt, smoothing over the skin. "Love this position," he mutters. "Every time he pushes into you, your whole arse jiggles."

I sputter. "*Jiggles.*"

"Aye." He gives one of my cheeks a slap, and I keen. "Very pretty. Another?"

I nod, and he slowly adds another finger. He starts to pump into me, fluttering his fingers, and I automatically clench around Kenta. The man underneath me groans, his hands coming up to pluck at my breasts. My mouth falls slack. I close my eyes, trying to process the sensation overload.

A low voice comes from over my head. "Princess."

I open my eyes again and look up at Matt. He's completely nude, and I let my gaze travel up his front, taking in the thick thighs covered in dark hair, the sculpted abs, the hard biceps. When my eyes finally reach his handsome face, though, he still looks concerned. Aroused as Hell—but concerned. He leans forward to kiss me, and I sigh, melting under the press of his perfectly shaped lips. Our tongues slide against each other in time with Glen and Kenta's rolling thrusts. When we finally pull apart, Matt's eyes look hazy and drugged, and his lips are swollen.

"You're so hot," I gasp, trembling. "Get in my mouth."

Matt's eyes twinkle. "I want that on a keychain." He steps forward, and I reach greedily for him, wanting to touch him. He catches my hand. "Briar. If you want us to stop halfway through and put on a rubber, that's fine."

"I really, really want to. But yes. Of course, I'll ask to stop if I need to."

"Okay," he says softly. "Okay."

I smile, then wrap my fingers around his length. He's perfect, thick and hard. I run my hand down his shaft a couple of times, twisting slightly near the base, and he shudders, a hand curling in my hair.

"Ready for another, love?" Glen asks. I nod, and he presses a third thick finger inside me. I keen at the stretching sensation, then dip forward and take Matt in my mouth, swirling my tongue.

"God," he murmurs, running his fingertips through my hair. "God. You're so beautiful."

I don't say anything, licking along the underside of his shaft. Underneath me, Kenta grinds upwards, and I moan, making Matt hiss.

God, I love this. I love being with all three of them at the same time, feeling the way we all affect each other.

Glen presses a tickly kiss to the curve of my neck and slowly pulls out his fingers, leaving me aching with emptiness. "Ready for me, lass?"

"Please," I breathe, closing my eyes as I feel his smooth tip rub between my cheeks. He thrusts in slowly, in one long, firm press.

At first I think he won't fit; but after the initial push of resistance, my muscles loosen, and I feel him bottom out inside of me.

For a second, it's almost too much. I freeze, trying to get used to the sensation. I feel pinned down on both sides. I can barely move. There's the tiniest little flash of fear as X pops into my mind. For half a second, I'm back in his horrid little cabin, tied up and unable to move.

Then the image melts away as Matt starts stroking down my arms. "So beautiful," he mutters. "You good, princess?"

I take a deep breath and nod, pulling my mouth off him to speak. "Move, please," I say. They do, Kenta and Glen starting a slow, see-sawing motion, thrusting in tandem. I squeeze my eyes shut. Sparks rush over my skin, and I claw at Kenta's shoulders, feeling pressure building up from deep in me. A sob bursts out of my chest.

Glen strokes my hip, thudding deep into my ass. "Okay, lass?"

I nod fiercely, turning my attention back to Matt. I can't do anything fancy now; I suck him hard and sloppy, licking and kissing, finding all the spots that make his breathing hitch or his hands clench in my hair. My body rocks between Glen and Kenta, and another sob chokes up my chest. Matt twitches in my mouth, and I tug him in deeper, daring to press the tiniest hint of my teeth against his shaft.

He *bellows,* grasping at my hair and shouting at the ceiling, so I do it again and again, alternating the rough licks with gentle scrapes of teeth, rocking back into Kenta as he slams repeatedly into me. Sweat rolls down my neck and thighs. I've been on the edge so long, I'm getting desperate.

Suddenly, Matt's pulling out of my mouth. "No," he mutters. "No. Not yet." He snakes a hand over my hip, grazing a circle against the small of my back. "I want to be inside you. Hurry up, Li."

Kenta laughs breathily and immediately slows down his thrusts to a glacial, torturous roll. Matt and I make identical annoyed noises. I grip Kenta's shoulders as the tingle of my climax starts to fade. "Faster," I growl. "Harder."

"Jesus," Glen mutters, dropping his face into the crook of my neck. "You're so tight, sweetheart. Christ."

I clench, squeezing around him and Kenta simultaneously, and both men yell in surprise. Kenta speeds back up, slamming into my G-spot, his thrusts almost frantic.

"Christ." He wraps a hand around my throat, stroking the nape of my neck. "I'm so close, gorgeous."

"Me too," I moan, as Matt kneels next to me and starts biting and sucking on my neck. "Come with me."

Kenta doesn't respond. Sliding a hand down between our bouncing hips, I cup my palm under his tight, swollen balls and *squeeze.*

CHAPTER 57
BRIAR

Kenta cries out, his hand tightening on my neck as he explodes. The sudden, powerful rush of his come inside of me shocks me, tipping me over the edge. I shudder and clutch at him as we ride the wave, our sweaty skin slapping together. Glen shouts and falls apart a few moments later, and my eyes fly open as he floods my ass. I didn't think I'd be able to feel it, but I can; I can feel a deep pressure and seeping heat. I clench my muscles around him as he fills me up deep, and he groans, his hands kneading my ass cheeks as he keeps shakily hammering into me. I writhe between the two men, my whole body trembling and aching and burning as they pound me to completion.

Eventually, the pleasure fades, replaced by overwhelming sensitivity. I flinch at Glen's next thrust, trying to pull away.

"God," I choke, every nerve in my body fritzing and shuddering. "Stop, Ken—Glen—whoever, just—oh my God I'm gonna *die*—"

Glen kisses my back and pulls out of me, drawing an embarrassingly loud moan from my mouth as I feel his hardness slicking against my walls. Kenta wraps his arms around my neck, tugging my mouth to his. I start making out with him, deep and hot and heavy, our sweaty bodies rubbing against each other.

Matt reaches over, putting a heavy hand on Kenta's shoulder. "Move," he orders, and Kenta chuckles, sitting up and pulling out slowly. My lashes flutter, and I rub my legs together, feeling the hot, sticky gush of his come against my skin.

Kenta touches my cheek, turning my face towards him. He's flushed and mussed and panting. His dark eyes scan mine, then he smiles brightly. "You're good," he says. It's not a question.

I nod anyway, then laugh, relief relaxing my chest. I'm good. No freakout. Happiness bursts inside of me. "I'm very very very good."

He pushes forward and gives me one last kiss. "You're amazing," he says in my ear, then finally slides off the bed.

I sit back on my haunches and look up at Matt. He looks debauched. His dark hair is mussed and ruffled, his eyes are practically black, and his chest is heaving.

"On your back," he says roughly. "I want to see your face."

I sigh heavily. "Matt. How many times do I have to tell you?" I reach forward and wrap my hand around his thick erection. I give him a couple of quick pumps, and he grunts, his hips thrusting forward and his head falling back. "Don't. Tell. Me. What. To. Do."

He sighs, meeting my eyes. "Please," he says quietly. "Please, baby. Roll over for me."

I smile. "*Good boy.*"

His eyes flash—and then drop straight between my legs as I obediently flip over onto my back, parting my thighs. He licks his lips, crawling up onto the bed and pressing his body over me. He takes my face in his hands. "Briar." His voice is a low rasp.

I tilt my lips up to him. "Matt."

"I'm so glad you're okay."

"Me too," I whisper.

He dips his head and kisses me deeply as he lines himself up and pushes into me. I'm already so wet that he slides right in. There's no stretch, no pain or tightness. Just pleasure. He kisses me again, taking a long pull from my lips as he rolls his hips into me.

It's different from the other times I've slept with him. This time, it's not just sex. We're making love. As he thrusts deeply into me, his cheek pressed against mine, I feel Glen kneel down by the edge of the bed, taking my foot in his hand. He presses his thumb into the arch, and I gasp as he starts massaging me. On my other side, Kenta starts kneading the muscles in my hand. I shudder at the sensation.

When I imagined a foursome, I certainly didn't picture having slow, luxurious sex with one hot guy while two other gorgeous men *massage me,* but it is a *delicious* experience. I feel so warm and wanted and cared-for, I can feel tears thrumming in the back of my throat.

Keeping up his steady thrusts, Matt switches from his deep French kisses to smaller, soft little bites. I hum softly, leaning my head back against the pillow. My thighs start to twitch around his hips. "I—I'm close."

"Me too, love." I know he is. I can see his biceps trembling on either side of my head. He takes my face in his big hand. "Open your eyes. I want to see."

I do, looking straight into his crystal-blue irises.

"Smile," I whisper. His whole face lights up with a megawatt smile, and I fall apart in his arms, a scream tearing from my chest. I can feel him shaking on top of me; I can hear Glen's low groan at my feet, and Kenta's sudden intake of breath against my chest. But all of that is just background noise. In my head, I'm flying, shooting like a comet through the bright blue sky and burning through rings of stars. Pleasure batters me, surging through all of my veins like light. I feel like I'm barely inside my body as I ride out the waves, floating far, far above the rest of the world.

When I finally come back down, I find myself being gently rolled over. Glen and Kenta have climbed back onto the bed, and all three of my men are covering every inch of me with soft, reverent little kisses. I feel like I'm being cocooned, wrapped up in blankets and cuddled up in layers and layers of love. Matt slides slowly out of me, and I moan weakly at the sensation of thick, hot wetness seeping down my thighs. Someone asks me a question, and I mumble something nonsensical in response. I'm kind of out of it; I'm still exhausted from last night, and the endorphins have fried my brain. Now everything is soft and hazy. I just lay there, limp and satisfied, as hands pat over me, stroking and caressing. There's a cool sensation down my legs as someone gently wipes off my skin. Low voices murmur over my head.

I'm soon cleaned up and settled down in fresh sheets, tucked between three hot, muscled bodies. Sunshine pours into the room, and I snuggle up against Glen's chest, stroking the fine sprinkling of hair curling over his pecs. We're quiet for a long time, just holding each other as we settle back down.

"Do you guys wanna be my boyfriends?" I whisper, turning to brush a kiss to Kenta's wrist.

Three laughs rumble around me. "If you'll take us," Matt says. "We know you can be quite picky."

"You'll do in a pinch." I pat his shoulder. He pinches my arm, making me yelp. We lie in silence for a few more minutes, listening to the birds tweeting outside. Our breathing slowly matches up, our chests rising and falling in sync.

"Are you sure, though?" I prod. "My life is... well. You've seen how hectic it is. There will be paparazzi, and journalists and photographers. You'll probably be put into magazines." I turn to look at Glen. He watches me, his grey eyes serious. I tilt my head to nuzzle down his scarred jaw, then press a kiss to his lips. "I understand if that puts you off."

"We'll work with it," he says, lifting a big hand to cup my stitched-up cheek. "We'll do anything. Anything to be with you."

I shiver. "Really?"

"Yes," Matt and Kenta both say immediately. I close my eyes. How the Hell did I get this lucky? I swallow down the tears before they start to fall.

"Then I want to go on a date. All four of us. Together. Somewhere nice. Maybe a picnic in a park, or on the beach."

Kenta picks up my hand and starts massaging it. "You sure about that? The tabloids are going to have a field day."

I snort. "I'm counting on it."

"It might make you a target for hate, lass," Glen points out. "We've seen your social media comments. Those people are cruel. I doubt the public will enjoy seeing you with three men."

I shrug. "Haven't you heard? I'm Britain's Biggest Bitch." I look out of the window, at the LA skyline glittering and shimmering under the midday sun, and smile. "I can do whatever the fuck I want."

EPILOGUE

TWO YEARS LATER

Hands slide down my body, cupping the curve of my bare hip. I gasp and tilt my neck back as warm lips press gently against my throat. "God," I whisper, rocking my hips slightly. "Baby… please."

"Please what?" A low voice grumbles. The light sea breeze drifts between our joined bodies, ruffling my hair and trailing goose-bumps over my skin. In the corners of my vision, camera lenses flash, but I ignore them, focussing on the man in front of me.

"I need you," I murmur, grabbing ahold of his jaw and yanking his mouth to mine. I close my eyes and part my lips, waiting for a kiss.

Nothing happens.

My eyes flutter open.

"CUT!" Our director calls.

I frown at Thom Petty, who's gone stiff underneath me. "You're supposed to kiss me, you knob. Is it really that hard?"

He doesn't respond. He's looking over my shoulder, wide-eyed. I sigh, slipping off his lap and brushing my thighs clean as I look around.

We've been filming this beach sex scene since dawn this morning. I've still not gotten over how pretty the location is. The sea is churning in and out just a few metres away, and the morning sky is marbled pale pink and baby blue. A white pavilion is pitched in the sand nearby, where various crew members are sitting in folding chairs, watching the action unfold through the screens.

As I watch, our director Gina storms out of the tent towards us. She looks haggard and tired, her hair falling out of its sloppy ponytail and her glasses slipping down her nose. The last few days of filming are always gruelling, as we reshoot all of the scenes that we somehow messed up. None of us have slept much this week.

"Briar," she practically begs. "*Please.*"

"Please what?" I blink up at her. "Am *I* doing something wrong?" I thought Petty was the problem.

"*You're* not," Gina mutters. "But we want the audience to root for you and Thom to be together. And I doubt they're going to be able to do that when he looks like he's about to wet himself."

I look down at Thom, sprawled under me. "*Are* you about to wet yourself?" I ask. "I'll sue you."

He blinks up at me stupidly. "F-for what?"

"Being gross." We're both almost completely naked. I'm wearing a flesh-coloured thong and no bra, and he's just wearing a very strategically placed sock. I look at it suspiciously for signs of pee. He covers it with his hand. I flick his cheek, making him yelp.

I didn't know when I booked this role that Thom would be playing my love interest. When I found out, I considered dropping out of the movie, but the role was too good to pass up on. During the three-month shoot, Thom and I have, weirdly enough, become friends again. I felt pretty bad when I found out that his house had been blown up because of me. We've had a lot of time to hash out our issues. It's nice, having my very first showbiz friend back.

Still. If he pees on me, I will be calling my lawyer.

Gina rubs the bridge of her nose. "This is the last day of filming. We all want to get this wrapped so we can go home. So for the love of *God,* just tell your boyfriends to leave, so we can get this shot done and catch our flights."

Oh.

I turn, looking over my shoulder. The Angels are all standing in one corner of the pavilion, staring Thom down like they're a gang about to beat him up. I try not to laugh.

We've been filming my movie *Sunstruck* for over three months now. We did most of it in London studios, using sets built specially for the film, but some of the shots required a beach setting, so the cast and crew have spent the last two weeks shooting on-location on a little private island just off Sardinia. It's a beautiful place: icy-white beaches, palm trees, tropical blue oceans. When I told the guys that I'd be travelling abroad, they offered to come with me as my security detail.

I was thrilled. They only recently got back from a stint in America, protecting a politician in a very tumultuous swing state. What with my busy filming schedule, and their back-to-back assignments, it's been hard to get any time with them recently. That's why it's so perfect that they came with me to Italy.

Still. If they keep pulling stunts like this, it's unlikely that they'll ever be invited on another shoot again. I narrow my eyes at the three men. I only need one security guard on set with me at a time, but it's funny; whenever I'm shooting an intimate scene, they all suddenly seem to have nothing better to do than come and observe.

As I watch, Kenta's cold eyes flick from Thom to me. His expression relaxes, and he smiles, waving.

I turn back to Thom. "Pull yourself together," I tell him. "They won't do anything to you."

He bites his lip. "You won't let them, right, B?"

Jesus. "I'll have a word with them," I tell Gina.

She nods. "Take ten, everyone!" She calls.

An assistant runs up and offers me a robe, and I stand, draping it over my body. None of the boys look even remotely embarrassed as I march up to them.

"Briar," Kenta smiles, running his eyes down the gap in my silk robe. "You're doing great, sweetheart."

"Unlike *him*," Glen mutters. "Any man sleeping with you should look a Hell of a lot more enthusiastic."

I bat away his hand as he reaches for me. "The director has politely asked that you all leave the premises."

They have the audacity to look surprised.

"Why?" Glen demands.

"Because you're scaring my co-star so much he can't remember his lines."

"He can't be a very good actor, then," Kenta says peaceably.

"He can't be expected to perform well under the threat of castration."

"I don't know what you're talking about. We're just watching, love." He tilts his head, taking in my wig. "You look so pretty with brown hair."

"You need security," Glen adds, tossing a scowl over my shoulder.

"From *what?*" I cast my arm around the beach. "Literally everything is getting recorded!"

"He has your naked breasts in his face," Kenta murmurs, reaching out to carefully re-adjust my robe. The movement looks innocent enough, but as the soft fabric slides over my skin, tingles skitter over my nerve endings. I fight the urge to shiver in pleasure. "We just want to make sure he doesn't step out of line. It would kill us if he got handsy with you."

I snort. "Trust me, he knows better than that. With the fuss I'd kick up, he'd never work again. Or regain the use of his fingers."

"Better safe than sorry, love."

I roll my eyes, turning to Matt. He hasn't said anything yet. He's still looking over at Thom, his expression troubled. "Matt?"

He swallows and reaches for me. I usually have a no-PDA rule on set. It's unprofessional, and the men are *supposed* to be here as my guards, not my boyfriends. But I can tell when Matt's being a grumpy git who just needs a cup of coffee, and when he's genuinely unsettled, and this time, it's the latter. So I let him press me close.

"You okay?" I ask quietly.

He nods into my hair.

"Neanderthal instincts kicking in?" He pulls back and scowls at me.

"They're changing the scene. This isn't what you rehearsed."

I shrug. "So?" Gina delivered me the revised script last night, after she decided that the sex on the beach scene wasn't raunchy enough.

Matt sighs, cupping my cheek. "I know you've signed contracts, but if you ever change your mind, you know you can back out, right? I don't give a shit if they sue you. No amount of money is worth you getting hurt."

Oh. My insides warm.

It's been two years since X kidnapped me. He got a full life sentence, as predicted. Even so, it took me a long time to feel safe again. This is the first role I've taken since the attack which shows any kind of skin. I've been so scared of somebody else 'falling in love with me' that I've flat-out refused to play love interests at all.

But I'm over it now. I'm ready to face the world again. What happened wasn't my fault, and I'm not going to hide myself away just because some creep got hung up on a fantasy years ago.

"I really am okay." I stroke my thumb over Matt's cheekbone. "I love you."

Matt surges forward and presses his mouth to mine. I think I hear the makeup artist groan a few metres away, but I don't care. I kiss him back. His hand curves down over my waist, sliding over the silky fabric of the robe and finally landing on my ass. He gives it a little possessive pat, and I snort against his lips.

"Okay. I think Thom gets the message." He nips my top lip then steps back.

"Go," I tell the other two. "We'll be able to finish a lot quicker without you scaring the shit out of my hero. And then I'm all yours."

Glen and Kenta both nod, dropping to press a kiss to either side of my neck—*they*, at least, care about my poor makeup artist—then the three men finally turn to leave.

When I walk back to my spot in the sand, Gina is watching them with red cheeks. "How the Hell did you land that deal?" She mutters.

I shrug, dropping my robe. "I must have done something good in a past life, I guess."

"You must have been a damn *angel*."

I laugh, tilting my head back so the continuity supervisor can rearrange my hair. "I guess I must."

Hair and makeup flutter over me, fixing me back up, then I sit down again, resettling my weight on Thom's hips.

"Better?" I ask him.

"Uh." He glances over my shoulder. I turn to see Glen loitering behind one of the cameras, giving him one last cold look.

I sigh. "*Glen.*"

He flashes me a bright grin and turns to leave. I look down, feeling warmth bloom in my chest.

"Hurry up," Gina calls to the cameraman. "Let's get the shot, before she stops blushing."

Shooting ends at about five in the evening, and after a quick glass of champagne, everyone scatters, grabbing their bags and heading for the pier. The last boat to mainland Italy leaves at six PM, but most of the cast and crew left earlier in the day. I'm the only one staying behind; now that shooting is over, me and the guys have arranged to stay on the island for the next two weeks, taking advantage of the sun and the sea.

Thom catches up with me as I'm grabbing my stuff. He's now changed out of his penis sock, and is dressed much more appropriately in jeans and a t-shirt.

"Hey, B. Walk me to the pier?" He asks.

I shrug, falling into step with him as he drags his suitcase across the white sand. I look out over the view, taking in the slopes of the sand dunes and the brilliant turquoise sea.

"You know," he says, "when you told me you were seeing all three of them, I really didn't believe you."

I laugh. "You're not the only one. I think half the tabloids are convinced they're just hookers I've hired."

"It's brave," he says earnestly. "Having a relationship that society doesn't approve of."

I think about it. I suppose it is. We've certainly taken Hollywood by storm. Every time I leave the house with the guys, it's front page news. The tabloids are always full of made-up stories about our love life: stuff like 'MATTHEW VS KENTA—THE BOYFRIENDS' SECRET FEUD' or 'BRIAR REVEALS HER FAVOURITE BEAU'. It's all BS, but I actually don't mind that so many people are invested in the relationship. I think bringing awareness to different kinds of love can only ever be a good thing.

"Society hasn't approved of me since I was sixteen. I've had to get brave." I tilt my head, looking at him sideways. "Maybe I should thank you for that. It was unbelievably shitty, but I guess it worked out alright in the end." I can't even imagine the kind of person I would be if the cheating scandal had never happened. Would I still be that anxious, polite girl, always terrified of offending anybody, completely unable to assert herself? Perhaps this is the best thing that ever could have happened to me.

He nods, rubbing the back of his head. The big white ferry pulls up to the pier, and people start climbing aboard. Thom turns to look at me. "I'm happy for you," he says. "Honestly."

I roll my eyes. "Don't get sappy. Call me when you get in."

He gives me a quick hug and grabs his suitcase, climbing onto the boat. The director, Gina, is next, and she tugs me in for a hug before I know what's happening.

"Lock them down," she hisses in my ear, tossing me a wink. I laugh, waving as the ferry unmoors and starts cutting through the water, back to Italy. I wait until it's completely faded into the distance, then turn and head back to find the guys.

"You are all terrible," I announce, as I open the door to our beach hut. During filming, the studio put the cast and crew up in small chalets on one side of the island. Naturally, me and the guys are all sharing one. It's adorable. Nautical-themed, with sea-foam coloured linen and furniture made of driftwood and shells. The cabin is pretty small, just big enough for us all to fit in. Then again, we don't need much room. Just one very, very big bed.

Excitement hums in my stomach as I kick off my flip-flops. My schedule has been pretty unpredictable since we came to the island: some days, I'm working from five AM to the middle of the night. Others, I'm not needed at all. Me and the guys have squeezed in as many activities as we can, snorkelling and wake-boarding and windsurfing. On my evenings off, we stay in and cook together, eating fresh food and wine under the sunset. And then at night—

We keep ourselves busy. I think we've shagged in every room of this house. I'm *so excited* to finally be able to fully relax, instead of worrying about call times or last-minute script changes. The next two weeks are going to be amazing.

As I step into the lounge, I'm expecting all three guys to be there. Weirdly, the only one I see right away is Kenta, standing in the little kitchen by the stove. He looks up and smiles at me. He looks incredible; tanned and relaxed, wearing just a pair of swimming trunks and a white linen shirt that he's left open. His hair has been pulled back into a loose plait, tendrils falling out around his face.

"Finally wrapped?" He asks. I nod, crossing the room to him. He's got the wok going, and is tossing chunks of sweet potato into a creamy-looking coconut curry sauce. I lean against his arm, watching as he gives the pan a stir, then bends to check something in the oven. The mouth-watering scent of chocolate and nuts pours out of the oven door.

"What's this? You're making dinner?"

He nods, straightening to give me a lingering kiss. "Thought we'd celebrate."

"The end of the shoot?"

His eyes flash down to mine. He hums noncommittally, slicing a tomato in half and popping it into my mouth. "Among other things," he says, tapping under my chin to make me chew. "Maybe. Or maybe I just want to feed you back up again."

I had to lose ten pounds for this role. The men are convinced that if I don't gain the weight back immediately, I'll just collapse and spontaneously die.

I smile, licking his fingers. "I think I'll like that a lot."

There's a sudden crash from outside. I turn. The doors to the patio are open, and Glen is in the little garden area out back, dragging all of the kitchen furniture onto the sand. I watch as he swears, picking up the chair that's fallen over.

"Don't break anything," Kenta calls. The wok spits, and he lunges to turn down the knob on the stove. I give his cheek one last kiss, then go to join Glen outside, squinting against the bright sun. I think he must have just come in from swimming; his hair is still darkened by sea water, and he's only wearing a pair of damp trunks.

"Hey, hottie," I call, leaning in the doorway. It's my new favourite nickname for him. Has been, ever since *Hello* listed him as one of this year's 'Top Ten Red Carpet Hotties'. It makes him blush every time.

He glances up, and a smile swipes across his face. "Hey, love. All done shooting?"

I nod. "It went a lot quicker when Thom wasn't afraid of getting disembowelled." I look across the table settings. He's gone all out, filling glasses of wine and folding napkins onto each plate. A bouquet of expensive-looking tropical flowers is sitting in a glass vase in the middle of the table, tied up in a pink ribbon.

I point. "For me?"

"I picked them up at the market after you kicked us off set."

I smile. "They're beautiful."

He picks out a hot pink lily, tucking it behind my ear. "Not as much as you, lass."

I roll my eyes, letting him pull me in for a kiss, then look around. There's only one thing missing from this perfect scene. "Where's Matt?"

"He had a call with his therapist about an hour ago," Kenta says, coming out of the kitchen and pressing a fruity-looking mixed drink into my hand. The rim of the glass is decorated with chunks of pineapple and a pink paper umbrella. "We thought he'd be back by now."

I take a sip of the drink, my insides warming at the taste of coconuts and rum. "He's not due an appointment, is he?" I lick sugar off my lips. "I thought that was Saturdays."

Kenta shakes his head. "It was... impromptu."

I frown. Matt's doing much better now. *Much* better. He still has nightmares sometimes, but I don't remember the last time I saw him have a flashback. I guess this must mean he broke his streak. "Is he okay?"

"Shaken."

I put my drink down. "I should go find him before we eat."

He nods. "Be quick. Food's almost done. We're having bruschetta for starters."

"Have I mentioned I love you?"

He laughs. "I'm not sure." He curls a knuckle under my chin, tilting my mouth to his. "You could always tell me again."

I find Matt about a minute's walk away, sitting near the sea. He's slumped down in the shade of a couple of palm trees, staring out at the ocean. He's holding something small in his hand, flipping it over and over between his fingers.

"Hey." I approach him slowly. "You okay?"

He nods jerkily.

"Can I sit with you?"

Another nod. I slide down next to him, curling my legs under me. He dips his head, not meeting my eyes. I put my hand in his lap, and after a moment, he takes it, lacing our fingers together.

"Freak out?" I guess.

He nods.

"Why? Did something happen?" I rub my thumb into his palm. "You seem stressed."

He huffs a laugh. "Not stressed. Nervous." He looks at me sideways. The ocean air breezes over us, ruffling his thick black curls. "I love you so much."

A smile spreads over my face. "I love you, too."

He swallows thickly. *"So* much," he repeats.

"And… that makes you nervous? Have I told you recently that you're the most emotionally constipated man I've ever met?"

"Yes," he says. "I just…" he looks down at our joined hands. "I don't want to screw this up."

"Screw what up?"

He hesitates, then shows me the object in his other hand. My mouth drops open. It's a ring box covered in black velvet. As I watch, he flips it open with his thumb, revealing a silver ring, inset with a square-shaped white stone that glitters in the sunlight.

It's beautiful. Absolutely stunning. I swallow. "Matt…"

"The guys are going to kill me for giving this to you now," he mutters. "We said we'd all do it together."

I stare at him. "We?"

"All three of us. We all wanted to propose together." He frowns, rubbing his thumb against the hinge of the ring box. "But of course, I fucked it up."

I study his face. He still looks hesitant, like he's not sure he actually wants to give me the ring.

"What is it?" I whisper.

"What?"

"There's something holding you back from giving that to me." I curl up against his side. "I really want it," I tell him. "So please get over it fast."

He laughs, but the sound is hollow. "I just—" The words die in his mouth. A few agonising seconds pass, as he visibly struggles to find the words.

"Was it the flashback?" I guess. "Was it really bad?"

His shoulders slump. "Worst one I've had in a while. I honestly couldn't tell what was happening."

I put my chin in the crook of his neck, my heart hurting.

If there's one thing I've learned about Matt's PTSD, it's that the flashbacks don't end as soon as he gets out of them. The effects linger. Even though he tries to hide it, every single one scares the absolute shit out of him. He's usually a bit weird and snappy and shaky the whole rest of the day. I've found that cuddles work wonders to make him feel better, though, so I climb into his lap, plopping myself down between his knees. "I'm sorry."

He grunts, his strong arms banding around my waist. "I don't know why," he mumbles into my hair. "It came out of nowhere."

"Is that what's upsetting you?" I run my fingers across his tanned forearms, scratching his skin lightly with my nails.

"I've spent all this bloody time trying to work through my shit. I thought I was ready." He looks down at the ring in his hand.

"Ready for what?"

"For *you*. I don't want you to tie yourself to a man who wakes you up screaming every other night." A frustrated grumble shakes his chest. "How the Hell can I ask you to devote the rest of your life to me—to start a family with me, to one day have *kids* with me—when I can't even control my own damn brain?" He takes a deep breath, shaking his head. "I can't ask that of you. It's completely unfair."

"Are you done?" I ask. He cuts me a glare. I sigh. "Matt, I don't want to demean your emotions, or anything. But the soldier denying himself relationships because of his PTSD is, like, *so* overdone."

He snorts. "Yeah?"

"Yeah. Like, if I saw it in a script, I'd toss the whole thing into the trash. It's a cliché. And not even a good one. It always annoys the audience."

"Why?"

"'Cause it's dumb. Dummy." I twist in his lap so we're face to face. "Me loving you is not dependent on you 'getting better'. It never was. I didn't want you to go to therapy for *me*, dipshit. I wanted it for *you*." I lift my hand, running my fingers over his stubbly cheek. "Because I want you to be happy. You deserve happiness. You deserve love. And," I press my lips to his neck, feeling his pulse thrum under his skin, "you deserve a really hot, talented, smart wife. So gimme the ring, please."

He takes a deep breath, letting it gust out of him. "You're sure you want me?"

"Jesus, Matt. Yes. Forever."

The last syllable hasn't even left my lips before he pulls me into a kiss. I sigh, melting under him as he holds me close, his hot tongue swirling against mine.

I hear footsteps crunching through the sand towards us, and look up to see Glen and Kenta. Glen scowls when he sees the ring box in Matt's hand.

"I knew it. I bloody *knew* it," he mutters, throwing himself down onto one knee next to us and fumbling for a ring box in his own pocket. Without ceremony, he flips it open, showing me a silver ring with a pink heart-shaped stone set in the centre. I press a hand to my chest as my own heart flutters.

"Glen…"

"Figured it would go with all of your outfits," he mumbles, his entire face flushing red.

I laugh. He's right. Pink and sparkly. It matches my style to a tee.

I reach out and touch the stone lightly with the pad of my finger. "It's beautiful." I glance up to meet his eyes. "You're beautiful."

He blinks hard, reaching up to trace the thin scar on my cheek. It's barely noticeable—I had a couple of surgeries to fix it, and now it's just a faint white line down the side of my face, easily hidden by makeup when I'm on set. He leans forward and kisses it very gently. "Not as beautiful as you, lass."

I know he's not talking about the way I look. I lean forward, still in Matt's lap, and touch my mouth to his. His lips part, and I inhale his soft, pleased sigh.

There's another crunching footstep, and then Kenta kneels down next to me, offering me his own ring; a delicate silver band with a sparkling pink rose, matching the rose necklace currently hanging around my neck. I close my eyes as he cups my face gently.

"You're the most incredible person I've ever met," he says quietly.

"You're in my top three," I whisper back. He laughs and pulls me in for a kiss. When I re-emerge, my head is spinning. He offers me a hand, helping me upright. I stand there in the sand, with the sea glimmering to my right and palm leaves ruffling over my head.

And then they all propose.

I feel like I'm in a dream as they take turns to clasp me to them. They all have their own little speeches, but I can't keep up with them. I get the gist of the words. *We need you. We love you. We never want to have to live without you.*

It's too much. My heart is beating out of my chest. I can't get a full breath in. I lean my cheek against the trunk of the palm tree, overwhelmed.

Kenta frowns. "Briar—"

"I'm fine." I blink, tears pooling in my eyes. "You're all sure? You'll never live a normal life again."

"The only life we want is a life with you in it, lass," Glen says quietly.

I take a shaky breath, nodding. "Me, too."

"Nin is dying to work on the wedding," Kenta adds. "We can do it however you want. Private or public, we don't care."

"That would be perfect." It's more than I ever even dreamed. "I love you. All. *So* much."

"Then say yes," Matt says.

"*Yes.*" I hold out my hand, and each of them slides on their ring. They've sized them so they all fit on different fingers; my pinkie, my ring finger, and my index finger. The men huddle around me, and I close my eyes, savouring the moment. The scene is so perfect, it almost feels like the end of a movie. Except, out here, with nothing around us except the sand and the sky and the waves, I'm not an actress anymore. I'm not playing a part. I'm just being me.

Roll credits.

A tear slides down my cheek. Then another, and another. "I really thought I would always be alone," I whisper, watching the three stones catch the light and scatter rainbows all over my skin. "It's all I ever planned for."

Kenta smiles softly. "You're not alone anymore."

"You never will be," Glen adds.

"We promise," Matt finishes, pressing a kiss to each of my rings. I fist a hand in his collar and pull him in for a real kiss, delving my tongue deep into his mouth. I feel a hand on my back and turn to Glen, pressing my lips to his, before pulling away to kiss Kenta as well. I share myself between them, kissing them all in turn as six hands stroke over my skin, squeezing and caressing. And as we sit there, kissing, curled up on the sand as the evening sun streaks the sky, I feel the very last wall I once built around my heart crumble away to nothing.

And I don't die. I don't get weak. I don't fall apart.

I feel stronger than ever.

THANKS FOR READING!

Want to know what's next for Briar and her husbands? Sign up to my newsletter at https://www.lilygoldauthor.com/ to receive a FREE flash-forward short story! Already subscribed? Check the latest newsletter email for a link!

Want more Lily Gold content? Check out my readers group at:

www.facebook.com/groups/lilygoldreaders

for sneak previews, cut scenes, contests, and behind-the-scenes action!

ABOUT THE AUTHOR

Lily Gold is an Amazon-bestselling contemporary romance author living in London, England. As a big supporter of unconventional relationships, she believes that *love is better shared*.

She has a soft spot for strong guys with big hearts, and thinks the only thing better than one book boyfriend is TWO book boyfriends... or maybe three. When she's not writing, she's usually reading, accidentally killing her potted plants, or playing with whatever pet she can get her hands on.

You can connect with her at https://www.lilygoldauthor.com/

 instagram.com/authorlilygold

ALSO BY LILY GOLD

Three Swedish Mountain Men: An RH Romance

Three ripped, gorgeous men. One secluded Swedish mountain cabin. It looks like my vacation is about to heat up…

Nanny for the Neighbors: A Surprise Baby RH Romance

'To the boys in apartment 5A. Congratulations. You have a kid.'

That's what the note attached to the abandoned baby carrier says. And now my three gorgeous neighbors are in deep trouble.

Lucky for them, there's a nanny in the building.

Faking with Benefits: A Friends-to-Lovers RH Romance

WANTED: Three fake boyfriends. Must be tall, ripped — and willing to teach me how to kiss.

Made in United States
North Haven, CT
28 January 2023

31757183R00267